Jill Mansell loves nothing more  salad and telling lies. She is a n slim figure and some very delusional ideas. The upside of this, she has discovered, is that when she tells lies about fictional characters rather than real people, it becomes a novel and is allowed. Which is great, because otherwise by now Jill would probably be in prison.

OK, apparently some boring facts are also required in an author biography. Jill lives in Bristol with her noisy family and used to work in the field of clinical neurophysiology back in the day when she had a proper job. Her top secret affair with an A-list Hollywood actor has never become public knowledge because she is so utterly discreet. (Oh, but the stories she could tell. . .)

By Jill Mansell

Don't Want To Miss A Thing
A Walk In The Park
To The Moon And Back
Take A Chance On Me
Rumour Has It
An Offer You Can't Refuse
Thinking Of You
Making Your Mind Up
The One You Really Want
Falling For You
Nadia Knows Best
Staying At Daisy's
Millie's Fling
Good At Games
Miranda's Big Mistake
Head Over Heels
Mixed Doubles
Perfect Timing
Fast Friends
Solo
Kiss
Sheer Mischief
Open House
Two's Company

Jill Mansell

Don't Want to Miss a Thing

headline
review

Typeset in Bembo by Palimpsest Book Production Limited, Falkirk, Stirlingshire
Printed and bound in Great Britain by
CPI Group (UK) Ltd, Croydon CR0 4YY

Headline's policy is to use papers that are natural, renewable and recyclable
products and made from wood grown in sustainable forests. The logging and
manufacturing processes are expected to conform to the environmental
regulations of the country of origin.

HEADLINE PUBLISHING GROUP
An Hachette UK Company
338 Euston Road
London NW1 3BH

www.headline.co.uk
www.hachette.co.uk

For Dad, Paul and Judi, with my love.

Massive thanks are due to Helen Roberts, a Twitter friend and brilliant social worker who generously volunteered to advise me on the subjects of guardianship and adoption for this book. The information she gave me was wonderfully helpful, and I'm so grateful for her expertise and enthusiasm. Needless to say, any errors are mine alone.

Chapter 1

It was almost midnight and Dexter Yates was in bed with his girlfriend when his phone burst into life. Possessed of lightning reflexes, she grabbed it off the bedside table before he could reach it himself.

Honestly, some people were *so* mistrustful.

'It says Laura.' Her eyes narrowed at the sight of the name flashing up on the screen. 'Who's Laura?'

Jealousy was never a good look. 'Can I have my phone please?'

'Who *is* she?'

Heroically, Dexter didn't say, 'Someone an awful lot nicer than you.' He held out his hand and waited for her to pass the phone to him, which she did with the kind of huffy annoyance that meant he definitely wouldn't be seeing her again after tonight.

'Laura, hey.'

'Oh Dex, I'm sorry, I know it's late. Did I wake you up?'

He smiled; only Laura could think he might be asleep before midnight. 'Of course not. How's everything with you?'

'Everything . . . is perfect.' The joy was there in her voice, shimmering down the phone line, and in that moment he knew what had happened. 'It's a girl, Dex. She's here! And so beautiful, you won't believe it. Seven pounds twelve ounces. It's just the most amazing thing *ever*.'

His smile broadened. 'A girl! Fantastic. And why wouldn't she be beautiful? When can I come and see her?'

'Well, not tonight, obviously. Visiting hours are ten till twelve in the morning or seven till nine in the evening. Will you be able to make it tomorrow, d'you think? After work?'

'I'll make sure I can,' Dex promised. 'I'll be there. Does she look like me?'

'Don't be ridiculous, she's only an hour old. You're twenty-eight. You have stubble.'

'You know, you should really think about becoming a stand-up comedian.'

'After all the gas and air I've had tonight, I'm pretty sure I couldn't be a stand-up anything. OK, I'm getting low on battery here. I'd better go. Do you want me to email a photo or would you rather wait until you see her tomorrow?'

'Don't worry, I'll wait. And hey,' Dex's voice softened, 'well done, you.'

He ended the call, then lay back against the pillows and gazed up at the ceiling. *Wow*.

'At the risk of sounding repetitive, who's Laura?' The atmosphere in the bedroom had by this stage turned distinctly frosty. 'And why would you want to know if her baby looks like you?'

'Come on.' Dexter swung his legs out of bed and reached for his jeans and T-shirt. 'It's getting late. I'll give you a lift home.'

'Dex—'

'Seriously? OK,' said Dexter. 'Laura's my sister. And she's just given birth to my niece.'

★　★　★

Laura was dozing when the nurse tapped on the door and eased it open.

'Hello? Are you awake?'

Laura opened her eyes; now that she was a mother, she was going to have to get used to having her sleep interrupted. 'Kind of, yes. What is it?'

'You've got a visitor,' whispered the nurse.

'What, *now*?'

'I know, and it's not really allowed but when he explained the situation . . . well, what else could I do? I couldn't send him away.'

The way the girl's eyes were sparkling and her tone of voice told Laura all she needed to know. She hauled herself into a sitting position – *ooch, pain* – as the door opened wider and the nurse led their nocturnal visitor into the side ward. 'And the situation is?'

'I have to be at Heathrow in three hours to catch my flight to New York.' Dex turned to the nurse and said, 'Darling, thank you so much. You're an absolute star.'

Laura waited until the besotted girl had left the room before rolling her eyes. 'And on a scale of one to ten, exactly how true is *that* story?'

'Ah, but it got me in here, didn't it?' Dex's legendary charm was a long-standing joke between them. 'I couldn't wait. Too excited to sleep. These are for you, by the way. Sorry they're a bit crap.'

He'd dropped into the twenty-four-hour supermarket in West Kensington and bought up masses of luridly bright orange roses, a giant Toblerone, a toy octopus and many, many bags of jelly worms. As you do.

'They're lovely,' said Laura as he dumped everything on to the bed.

'Well, if you will go around having babies in the middle of the night, the choices are limited. Anyway, come here.' He gave her a hug and a noisy kiss on the cheek. 'You clever thing. Well done. So, where is it?'

'*It?*'

'Sorry, *she*.' Dex shrugged unrepentantly. 'But we've been calling it "it" for months. Where are you keeping her then? In a cage under the bed?'

'If you're going to be like this, I won't show her to you.' But Laura didn't mean it; from where he was standing, the cot was out of his line of vision. Tilting her head to the left, she indicated that Dex should come round to the other side of the bed.

That was when she sat back and watched as Dex – possibly for the first time in his life – fell in love.

It was unbelievable. You could actually see it happening. One minute he was interested, the next he was completely and utterly entranced. Before long, as if the momentousness of the occasion had made its presence felt, the newest addition to the family stirred and opened her eyes.

'Her name's Delphi,' said Laura.

'Oh my God.' Dex exhaled slowly. '*Look* at her.'

Laura smiled. 'She's looking at you.'

'She's beautiful. I mean, *really* beautiful.' He was transfixed.

Was it possible to burst with pride? Laura said, 'Told you she was.'

'Can I pick her up?'

'So long as you don't drop her.'

Dex's dark hair fell forward as he bent down and began to slide his hands beneath Delphi's tiny shoulders. He stopped and looked over at Laura. 'I don't know how.'

Dex spent his life being laid-back and supremely confident; it was endearing to see him admit to a weakness. Laura said encouragingly, 'You can do it. Just remember to support her head. Like this.' She demonstrated with her own hands and watched from the bed as Dex copied her. 'There you go, that's it.'

He lifted her up, exclaiming, 'She's like a sunflower with a wobbly neck. Oh wow, Delphi Yates, look at you. Look at your hands.' He shook his head in wonder. 'What about those fingernails? And the eyelashes! Look, she's *blinking* . . .'

Laura's smile broadened. He really was in love. She watched him take Delphi on a tour of the tiny side ward, finishing up in front of the mirror. Having carefully settled her into the crook of his arm, Dex studied the reflection of the two of them together. 'Hello, Delphi. That's you, that is! Go on, give us a little wave. Oh no, don't pull that face, it's your birthday, you're not allowed to cry . . . nooo, look in the mirror, have a dance!'

'She might be hungry,' said Laura.

'No problem, we'll give her some Haribo. Hey, Delph, fancy a jelly worm? What's your favourite colour?'

'Dex, you can't give her Haribo!'

He gave her a look and she realised he'd been joking. 'No? Well, that's good, more for us. There, she's not going to cry now anyway. Relax, *Mum*.'

Mum. After all this time, against all the odds, it had finally happened. Just as she'd given up hope that it ever would. At the age of forty-one she had miraculously fallen pregnant and now Delphi was here.

'I'm a mum,' said Laura. 'Can you believe it?'

'And this one's strong.' Dex's index finger was being grasped by Delphi's tiny curled hand; he mimed agonising pain. 'I think she's going to be a wrestler when she grows up.'

'Here, let me take a photo.' Laura scooped up her phone and signalled for him to move his face closer to Delphi's.

'So did it hurt, giving birth?' He grimaced. 'Don't give me any gory details.'

'It was easy,' Laura assured him. 'Like shelling peas. No pain at all.'

'Good girl.' Happy with the lie, Dex nodded approvingly at Delphi. 'Wait till you're older. I'm going to teach you all the tricks of the trade. How to keep boys under control, how to break their hearts . . .' Delphi was gazing solemnly up at him with saucer eyes as he spoke. 'I'll have to check them out first, see if they're worthy of a date with Delphi Yates before letting you out of the house with them. And they'll have me to answer to if they mess you around.'

'Can you imagine? She'll be a teenager,' Laura marvelled. 'Wearing unsuitable outfits, drinking cider and moaning about us behind our backs. One more photo.'

He held Delphi up again, careful to cradle her head in the palm of his hand, and Laura felt her heart take a picture of its own. There was a connection between the two of them that was clear to see; as they gazed into each other's eyes, it was as if they were sharing the most amazing secret. The physical similarities were there too, in the shape of their eyes and the angle of their dark brows; you just knew Delphi would grow up looking like Dex. Laura pressed the button and captured the moment forever. Magically, their images were now enclosed within the phone.

'Send me a copy,' said Dex.

'I will. You'll have to be careful who you show it to, mind. Might cramp your style.'

'True.' He grinned at Delphi. 'Is that what you're going to do, hmm? That's the plan? Oh my, you are *dangerous*.'

'How's the new girlfriend?' Laura couldn't remember her name but it didn't matter, Dex no longer expected her to. He got through them at such a rate of knots.

'It's over.' Dex looked mournful. 'I'm all alone and single again. Poor me.'

As if. Laura said, 'I know, you'll probably be a sad and lonely bachelor for the rest of your life.'

The door creaked open a few inches and the nurse popped her head round to whisper, 'Sorry, but you're going to have to go now before I get into trouble.'

Dex said at once, 'And we can't have that. Thanks so much for letting me in. You've been an angel and I really appreciate it.'

'That's OK.' Her cheeks dimpled with pleasure. 'At least you got the chance to see Delphi.'

'Which makes two new people I'm really glad I met tonight. Oh God, that sounds pukey, forget I said it.' Having carefully placed Delphi back in Laura's outstretched arms, Dex kissed each of them in turn and said, 'Time for you to get some sleep. By the way, you don't happen to know if Alice has a boyfriend, do you?'

Behind him, Alice was still hovering half in and half out of the door. She blushed scarlet at the realisation he'd checked out her name badge earlier.

'Funnily enough,' said Laura, 'I didn't get round to asking her. I was kind of busy having a baby.'

'Well, she isn't wearing any rings,' said Dex. 'So that's a good start.'

'I don't have a boyfriend,' said Alice. 'Why?'

He turned to look at her. 'I was just wondering when you're next due an evening off. Because if you think you might like to come out for a drink with me, I'd definitely like to go out for a drink with you.'

Laura watched and waited; he was completely incorrigible. Flirting came as naturally to Dexter as breathing. Were his chat-up lines spontaneous or did he keep to a tried and tested rota?

The recipient of this one, meanwhile, was flushing with pleasure. 'Um, well, I'm actually off tomorrow night . . .'

'Fantastic!'

'But that wouldn't be any good, would it?' Alice was shaking her head. 'Because you'll be in New York!'

Dex tapped his temple. 'You're right. I've got jetlag already. Although it's only a flying visit. I'll be back the day after that.'

'I'm free next Thursday.' Alice looked expectant.

'I tell you what, give me a contact number and I'll call you. I'm not an axe murderer, I promise.' He took out his mobile and keyed in the number she gave him. 'And now I must go before you get told off. This place is such a maze, isn't it? I don't know how I'm going to find my way out.'

Visibly bowled over, Alice said, 'Come on, I'll show you where the lifts are.'

'Bye.' Waving from the bed as they left the room, Laura called out mischievously, 'Don't forget to bring us back something fabulous from New York!'

Chapter 2

At the precise moment Dexter Yates was leaving one hospital in the early hours of the morning, a hundred miles away Molly Hayes was pulling up outside another.

And wondering how she'd been blackmailed into doing so.

Except there was an answer to that, and it was niggling at her like a tiny sharp-edged stone in her shoe. Because there was a fine line between being a good sport and a soft touch.

And she was beginning to think she might have just crossed it.

On the upside, at least there was space to park at this time of night, although from the sound of it, there were some pretty inebriated patients too, determined not to let the unfortunate turn their evening out had taken spoil their fun. Hopping out of the car — no she jolly well *wasn't* going to Pay and Display — Molly made her way past the ticket machine and headed across to A&E. Approaching the entrance, she caught her own reflection in the glass, blond hair uncombed and all over the place. Oh well, too bad.

It soon became apparent that the inebriated patient making the most noise of all was the one she'd come to pick up.

Oh joy.

'Hey, here she is!' Spotting her, Graham abruptly broke off his rendition of 'Return to Sender' and launched into 'The Most Beautiful Girl in the World'. Which was even more embarrassing than usual, given that she was currently looking more like Wurzel Gummidge.

Soon realising this for himself, Graham peered in puzzlement at Molly and said, 'What's happened to your hair? And your . . . you know, *face*?' He made scrunched-up motions with his fingers. 'Why are you all . . . different?'

Molly said evenly, 'It's three o'clock in the morning. Believe it or not, I was asleep when you called. This is what I look like without make-up. Just like this is what *you* look like after a night out with your rugby friends. Shall we go?'

'Ah no, you can't leave yet,' protested a woman sitting opposite with a toddler on her lap. 'Timmy'll start crying again if you do.' She turned to Molly. 'He loves the singing. Your husband's been a complete lifesaver tonight, keeping him entertained.'

'He's not my husband,' said Molly as, on cue, the little boy began to whimper in a fractious manner.

'Well, he's been a godsend,' the woman reiterated. 'And we're due to be seen soon. You can stay for just a bit longer, can't you?'

Why? Why did these things always have to happen to her? Graham resumed his singing – Elvis tracks were his speciality – and Timmy stopped whimpering in order to gaze at him in rapt adoration. Everyone else in the waiting room, astoundingly, appeared to be enjoying the show too. Realising that to drag him away now would make her some kind of hateful frozen-hearted witch, Molly found herself sinking on to an empty plastic chair and picking up one of the mangled magazines from the table in front of her.

Three months, that was how long they'd been seeing each other. She'd first met Graham in a cinema queue and in so many ways he'd seemed like excellent boyfriend material. Intelligent, tick. Kind-hearted, tick. Not a ladies' man, *big* tick. By day he was a chartered accountant, which had impressed her no end. And he didn't have any irritating habits along the lines of eating noisily, sniffing non-stop or laughing like a donkey.

But no one's perfect and Graham's irritating habit turned out to be his passion for rugby. Or, more to the point, for going out with his rugby-playing mates *even when the rugby season was over*, and getting absolutely plastered on a regular basis.

Actually, she wouldn't even mind if it didn't affect her, but it was reaching the stage where it *was*. Last month, one of Graham's epic hangovers had resulted in them not going to a barbecue. And a couple of weeks ago he'd managed to shoot a champagne cork into his own eye at a wedding. The subsequent bruising, which had been spectacular, had only just gone down.

And now this, tonight. To add insult to injury, she'd been having a brilliant dream when the phone had rung, waking her up.

'Hey, Molly, I love you, it's me.' His voice had been blurred around the edges. 'You won't believe what's happened. I've only gone and broken my foot. I can't *walk* . . .'

'Oh God, where are you?' She'd got head-rush sitting bolt upright, instantly conjuring up a mental picture of Graham lying in agony at the bottom of a ravine. This was what happened when you were jolted out of a dream that involved skiing in the Swiss Alps with Robert Downey Junior, and loaves of bread strapped to your shoes.

'I'm at the hospital, A&E. They've sorted me out but now I can't get home. I had to spend my taxi money getting here. And

I can't walk,' Graham said sadly. 'Oh Molly, I *do* love you. Could you come and pick me up?'

'Oh God . . .'

'If I had my credit card,' he wheedled, 'I wouldn't have to ask.'

Molly sighed; she was the one who'd told him to leave his bank cards at home after the last time he'd lost them on a night out.

See? Soft touch. And now that she was here, they *still* couldn't leave.

Thankfully the child's mother had been right and within minutes they were called through for treatment. When they'd disappeared, Graham held out his hands to Molly and said, 'There, he'll be fine. Shall we go now?'

She had to help him up. His right shoe was sticking out of his jacket pocket, his right foot bare and spattered with dried blood. There was tape wrapped around his toes.

Molly frowned. 'If you've broken your foot, shouldn't it be in a plaster cast?'

'Well, I didn't actually break my *foot*. It was the toes. The little one and the one next to it. They don't put them in a cast,' Graham explained. 'Just strap them together. Bloody hurts, though. Ow.' Leaning heavily on her shoulder, he took a step and flinched. '*Ow*, OW.'

He weighed fourteen stone to her eight. At this rate she'd end up putting her back out. 'Couldn't they give you crutches?' said Molly.

'What? Oh yeah, they did. What happened to them? They were here earlier. I forgot!'

The crutches were located under someone else's chair. It was finally time to leave. As they headed outside, a lad approached them. In his late teens and with his arm in a sling, he said, 'Mate,

I can't get a taxi and my girlfriend's mad as hell 'cos I should've been home ages ago. Couldn't give me a lift to Horfield, could you?'

'Sorry, we can't.' Molly shook her head, avoiding eye contact.

'Oh, Moll, don't say that! Of course we can give him a lift.' Graham wasn't just a drunk, he was a generous drunk. 'No problem, mate, come along with us, Horfield's not far out of our way. We'll drop you home!'

Once everyone was folded into the car, Molly buzzed down the driver's window to dispel the alcohol fumes.

'So how did you manage to break your toes?' she asked Graham.

'Fell off a table.' He shrugged as if it was entirely the table's fault for not managing to keep him on there.

'And where did all the blood come from?'

'I dropped my pint when I fell. There was glass everywhere. You should see Steve's hands, cut to ribbons where he landed on it!'

'So all in all you had a pretty disastrous night.'

'Are you kidding me?' Graham gave a shout of incredulous laughter. 'It was brilliant, best time ever!'

Nodding slowly, Molly decided for all their sakes to concentrate on the road ahead. And to think she'd been so thrilled last month when he'd helped her fill out her tax form online.

But accountant or no accountant, Graham definitely wasn't destined to be the man of her dreams.

He was going to have to go.

Chapter 3

Dexter was enjoying Alice's company. She was a nice girl with a neat figure and pretty grey eyes. Rather sweetly, she had refused to sleep with him after their first date, proudly announcing that she wasn't that sort of girl.

It had happened after the second date instead.

And now it was a fortnight later and to his eternal shame Dex could already feel his enthusiasm start to wane. He didn't want it to be like this, it just always seemed to happen regardless. The thrill was in the chase, the process of seduction. As soon as that aspect of it was over, the excitement began to subside, the shine wear off. He still had fun, enjoyed their company, liked being with them, but never *quite* as much as before.

The morning after their first night in bed, Alice had said, 'Don't go thinking I make a habit of this, by the way. I've never done it before.'

They always said that too.

Poor Alice, she deserved better than a no-hoper like him.

Dex made coffee as she wandered into the kitchen now, wearing his too-big towelling robe. While he'd been out of the bedroom she'd done her usual thing of hastily brushing her hair and teeth and dabbing on a bit of lip gloss.

'Here you go.' He passed her a cup. 'What time do you have to be at work?'

Her eyes danced. 'Trying to get rid of me?'

'Of course not. It's just that I've got a couple of appointments later.'

'I know.' Alice's tone was playful as she perched on one of the stainless steel stools and reached for the leaflets next to the coffee maker. She tapped the times and dates he'd scrawled across the top of each one. 'I saw them last night. Are these for *you*?'

'Well, not all of them. But one. Possibly.' It had started off, pretty much, as an idle whim. A friend at work had happened to mention how much he looked forward to heading out of London on Friday afternoons and spending lazy weekends at his cottage in the country. The idea had piqued Dex's interest and he'd registered his details on a couple of estate agents' websites. Then the glossy brochures had started arriving and the level of interest had grown. A refuge, somewhere to get away from it all, began to sound like something he might really enjoy. It wouldn't be a stretch to buy a smallish property. And whether he ended up liking it or not, choose wisely and it wasn't as if he'd be throwing money away. It would be an investment.

'They're gorgeous. So . . . *cottagey*.' Alice was lining the details up in a row on the steel countertop. 'Especially compared with this place.'

Dex took a gulp of coffee. *This place* was a sixth-floor apartment in an ultra-modern development overlooking the Thames and Canary Wharf. He'd bought it a couple of years ago, aware that it was the ultimate single guy's cliché. The views impressed everyone who came here. The living room had a spectacular mirrored wall to reflect the light, and opened on to a steel and glass balcony. Every technological gadget was top of the range. He had no idea how the oven worked, but that didn't matter; he generally ate out. And thanks to his cleaner, every inch of the flat was kept immaculate.

'I thought I'd go for something different.' He shrugged.

'Which one do you like best?'

'No idea, I haven't seen them yet.'

'Moreton-in-Marsh.' As she read out the names of the locations, Alice's robe gaped open a bit. 'Stow-on-the-Wold. Briarwood.' She mimed a swoon. 'They sound like something out of a Sunday-night costume drama. Maybe everyone'll be wearing long skirts and bonnets.'

'Bonnets don't suit me,' said Dex.

'I could come with you, if you like. Help you choose. I'm not working until this evening.'

Dex hesitated. When he'd told Laura about the viewings, she'd offered to go along with him. Which was a great idea in theory, but not quite so practical now that Delphi was part of the package. For a start, the baby seat wouldn't fit into the Porsche. When he'd pointed this out, Laura had said easily, 'Well, that's not problem, we can go in my car instead!'

But seriously, given the choice, who *would* prefer to drive down to the Cotswolds in a ratty old Ford Escort? Plus, much as he loved Delphi, she didn't have a handy volume button. Once she took it into her head to start bellowing at the top of her lungs, it wasn't easy to persuade her to stop.

Worse still, there was the ever-present risk of NNS – Nightmare Nappy Situation – an example of which he'd been subjected to last week when Laura had asked him to look after Delphi for twenty minutes while she had a bath. That had turned out to be twenty minutes he wouldn't forget in a hurry. Imagine if *that* were to happen while you were trundling down the motorway, trapped in an ancient Ford Escort . . .

OK, that was enough deliberation; he already knew the answer.

'Great, we'll set off in an hour.'

'Yay,' Alice said happily. Dex quelled a spasm of guilt. It was a sunny day; they'd have fun together. And, unlike Delphi, Alice hopefully wouldn't wail like a banshee all the way to Gloucestershire.

He'd give Laura a call and let her know. She'd understand.

With London behind them, traffic thinned out and the scenery grew steadily more attractive. By the time they reached Stow-on-the-Wold, Alice was in raptures. They found the estate agency and followed the agent to the cottage they'd arranged to view. The owner greeted them eagerly with tea and a homemade lemon drizzle sponge, and insisted on wrapping up the rest of the cake for them to take away when they left.

The cottage itself was nicely decorated and well cared for. Sadly the agency details had neglected to mention that it was situated next to a lorry depot. The more or less non-stop soundtrack of pantechnicons arriving, loading up then beeping as they reversed back out of the yard made it hard to hold a conversation.

'What time does this start up in the morning?' Dexter had to raise his voice to be heard.

'Oh, not until seven o'clock.' The agent's tone was soothing.

'And it's all stopped by nine at night,' the owner chimed in over-brightly.

So this was what estate agents meant when they said a house was 'close to local amenities'.

Dex felt sorry for the woman who was clearly desperate to

sell, but her cottage was so close you could feel the engine-rumblings in your bones. All the lemon drizzle cake in the world couldn't make up for that racket.

The next property was in Moreton-in-Marsh. It was perfectly positioned with wonderful views and there wasn't a depot in sight. There were even baby-pink roses growing up around the front door.

'Oh my God.' Alice clasped her hands together at the sight of it. 'This one is *perfect*.'

It certainly looked that way. Until the moment the estate agent opened the door and they stepped over the threshold.

Dex knew at once he couldn't live here. The actual atmosphere inside the house was completely at odds with the feel of it from the photos he'd seen in the brochure. It was like meeting a complete stranger and taking an instant dislike to them. The books in the oak bookshelf weren't real books at all, just plastic covers with the names of the classics written on their fake spines. There was a strong smell of cheap air freshener in the air. The walls were painted in cloying shades of pink and the art on the walls was anodyne.

None of this mattered a jot, of course; he knew that. The whole point of buying somewhere meant not having to put up with other people's choice of décor; the place was yours and you could do whatever you liked with it. But when the sense of revulsion was this extreme, it was impossible to overcome. Dex knew he just couldn't bear to live in a property that had previously been chosen by someone whose sense of style was so wrong.

'Shall we take a look around upstairs?' The bearded estate agent gestured for them to follow him and said jovially to Alice, 'The third bedroom's currently being used for storage but it would make a wonderful nursery.'

Oh good grief . . .

Dex shook his head. 'Sorry, there's no point, I don't like this place.'

'Why not?' Alice looked stunned. 'It's amazing. I love everything about it!'

Dex couldn't help himself; the fact that Alice was actually capable of loving this property caused his enthusiasm for her to bump down another couple of notches.

It shouldn't matter, but it did.

Then again, that was the story of his life, wasn't it?

Something *always* did.

Chapter 4

It was always awkward, finishing with someone who didn't want to be finished with. Molly didn't enjoy being the one causing the upset.

And in his own macho, blustering, rugbyish way, Graham *had* been upset when she'd broken the news to him that their relationship was over. Nor had the broken toes helped; the fact that he was only able to walk on the ball of his right foot and was limping around dramatically only served to increase her guilt. Even if he had been the one to bring the situation upon himself.

So she had finished with him, but he was currently still doing his level best to persuade her to change her mind.

Hence the fish.

'It's . . . lovely.'

'I know.' Graham was like a Labrador eagerly presenting his owner with a tennis ball covered in saliva. *Although saliva would have been less revolting than this.* 'It's for you,' he added with pride.

'Me?' Oh God. 'Why?'

'Because I know you like fish. And I caught it myself. Came home with three, but this one's the biggest. Eight pounds three ounces. That's a really good size.'

'Wow.' Eight pounds three ounces . . . eurgh, that was as much as a baby. How could she turn it down, though, without hurting his feelings? Molly said tentatively, 'But I don't know what I'd do with it.'

'It's a carp. You cook it!' He was starting to look offended.

'Right, OK.' Gingerly she peeled back the edges of the carrier bag and took another peep. The carp's single visible eye was gazing balefully back at her. No it wasn't, the carp was dead. 'I'll do that. Thanks.'

'I remembered how much you like fish,' Graham repeated.

This was true, she did like fish. Deep fried in batter and eaten with lovely chips. But it would clearly be cruel to explain to him that this one was turning her stomach. He'd driven all the way from Bristol. It was a *gift*.

'I do.' Molly nodded.

'I can gut it for you if you like. Or stay and help you cook it.' He looked hopeful.

'No, that's fine, I'll do it myself. Let me just put it in the fridge . . .'

'Molly, I've told you I'm sorry. And I've *changed*.' Oh help, he was moving back into begging mode. 'I haven't had a drink in over a fortnight. I told you I'd do it and I have! Please let me stay and cook the carp with you . . .'

'Oh Graham, don't say it.' She shook her head and held out the heavy carrier bag. 'I'm not going to change my mind. Maybe you should take the fish home with you.'

He raised his hands in defeat and limped away from her towards the door. 'No, I'm not taking it, I caught that carp for you. It's *yours*.'

'A what? A *cup*?' At the other end of the line, Frankie sounded mystified. 'Why are you trying to give me a cup?'

'Not a cup, a carp. Graham went fishing this morning, he brought one over for me, but I don't want it.'

'God, I'm not surprised. Carp are disgusting! Why would he do that?'

Molly looked at the dead carp with those weird dangly things at either side of its mouth. Frankie was right, it was disgusting. The dangly things made her feel squeamish. 'It's his way of being nice. He's trying to win me back.'

'Honestly, hasn't he heard of diamonds? Much nicer. Hang on, I'm just Googling it now.' She heard the sound of computer keys tapping away in the background. 'Here we are. Eastern Europeans eat carp on Christmas Day . . . and the way to do it is: nail it to a plank and roast over an open fire . . . carp have a muddy taste . . . some regard them as inedible . . . oh yeurgh, even worse than I thought. Don't bother trying to cook the thing,' Frankie said bluntly. 'Just chuck it away.'

'So the first place was too noisy,' Alice announced as they drove into Briarwood. 'And the second one was too . . . ?'

'Wrong in every conceivable way.' Dex slowed down as they passed the ivy-clad pub on the left. That was something else he'd have to check out; no point moving into a village with a rubbish pub.

'So let's hope this one will be just right!'

Please don't explain, please don't explain . . .

'Like Goldilocks and the three bears,' Alice added, and his enthusiasm for her dropped yet another notch. She was a sweet girl, but it was never going to work out.

'Or if it's no good,' Alice went on cheerily, 'we'll just have to keep looking, maybe make a weekend of it next time.'

'Hmm,' Dex murmured vaguely, because she was waiting for him to say something.

'You have reached your destination,' intoned the satnav.

'In fact, I kind of don't want you to like this one now.' Becoming bolder by the second, Alice rested her hand on his knee. 'Coming down for a weekend sounds like a fantastic plan.'

Oh dear. He'd have to tell her tonight.

The estate agent was blonde, buxom and businesslike. The cottage had been empty for four months, she explained, hence the musty smell, but it didn't mean there were any problems with damp because there definitely *weren't*.

Dexter wasn't bothered with whether there was a damp problem or not. He liked the cottage. It had a good feel, there was just something about it. The rooms might be empty but you could picture them full. The kichen was large with sun streaming in through the south-facing windows. There was an Aga, which was something he'd never seen in real life before but he knew people regarded them as a desirable feature. The living room had French windows opening out on to the over-grown back garden. And upstairs there were three good-sized bedrooms and an old-fashioned bathroom in serious need of a revamp.

Oh yes, he liked it. It felt right. This could definitely be the one.

'Why's it been empty for four months?' Dex decided he quite liked the musty smell.

'A previous sale fell through. The chain collapsed. It just came back on the market last week.' The estate agent nodded briskly. 'And let me tell you, it's going to be snapped up again in no time at all.'

Of course it would be. Standard estate agent spiel. Dex said, 'I bet there are other people already interested.'

'Absolutely. We've had a *lot* of interest.'

'So, what are the neighbours like?'

The woman didn't miss a beat. 'I hear they're *great*.'

'Well, that's lucky. They're the best kind to have.'

Her eyes gleamed. 'Does this mean you might be making an offer?'

'It's a possibility,' said Dex. 'I'll get back to you on that. I need to do some homework first.'

'Where are we going now?' said Alice as he pulled the car into the car park of the Saucy Swan. As if the answer might conceivably be, 'I thought we might climb Kilimanjaro.'

'To do our homework.' Dex regretted the 'our' as soon as he'd said it, implying as it did that she was included in his plans. 'Come on, let's see if the natives are friendly.'

He soon had his answer. Basically, they weren't. Attempting to strike up a conversation with the locals at the bar met with a crushing lack of success. The trio, of retirement age and grumpy demeanour, were evidently far more interested in their pints; it was like trying to gatecrash a private party filled with A-list celebs. Only the barmaid's saucy wink reassured him that not everyone was as spectacularly unwelcoming as the three stooges.

Giving up and taking their drinks outside, Dex and Alice sat down at a wooden table in front of the pub.

'Well, they were charming,' said Alice.

When the barmaid came out to collect the empties from the surrounding tables, Dex beckoned her over.

'Can I ask you a question?'

'Of course you can, my darling. And the answer is yes, I *am* single. So that's a bit of good news, isn't it?'

He grinned. She was in her thirties but wearing the clothes of a teenager and glittery earrings the size of saucers. 'Excellent news. But the other question is, what have I done to upset that crew in there?'

'The grumpy old farts? Oh, don't take it personally, darling. They hate pretty much everyone. But the ones they hate most of all are people like you.'

Alice was shocked. 'People like us? What's that supposed to mean?'

'Townies, pet. Whizzing down here in your fancy cars, on the lookout for a country pad you might bother to visit every couple of months, if the weather's good enough.'

'How do you know that's what we are?' said Alice.

'There's your fancy car.' The barmaid raised a pencilled eyebrow in the direction of the Porsche. 'You parked it outside Gin Cottage, got shown around the place for twenty minutes, now you've come to the pub to check us out, see if we're up to scratch. It's not rocket science, darling.'

Dex was liking this woman more and more. 'And they don't approve?'

'We're lucky here in Briarwood, haven't had too many week-enders. But some of the villages get it bad, you know? So many houses standing empty for weeks on end . . . it just sucks the life out of the community. We don't want that happening here if we can help it.'

'Fair enough,' said Dex. 'Why did you just call it Gin Cottage?'

'Oh, it was Dorothy's house. Did you notice the juniper trees growing in the garden? She used to make gin in her kitchen and sell it to the locals. Lethal stuff, it was. Sent a few people blind.'

'Really?' Alice's eyes widened in horror.

'Not really.' Amused, the barmaid said, 'But it was strong liquor, and that's why everyone called it Gin Cottage. So now you know.'

'Thanks.' Dex lowered his voice as the door opened and one of the disapproving pensioners left the pub. 'And could we not mention this conversation to the grumpy old farts?'

'No problem. Soul of discretion, me. Hey!' the barmaid bellowed across the car park. 'Guess what, Dad? This one just called you a grumpy old fart!'

'Thanks for that,' said Dex as the man paused and shook his head in disgust before heading off.

'My pleasure. You're not the first, you won't be the last. So what d'you think?' She shifted the tray of stacked-up dead glasses to her other hip. 'Are you two going to be buying Gin Cottage or not?'

You two.

'Might do.' Dex decided he liked her even more. 'Might not. What's your name, anyway?'

Her heavily outlined bright eyes sparkled with amusement. 'Me? I'm Lois.'

Chapter 5

'Lois fancies her chances with you.' Alice slipped a proprietorial hand into his as they strolled towards the car park.

'I think she was just being friendly.'

'Oh come on, she was totally obvious. *Now* where are we going?' She looked baffled as he walked straight past the car.

'I like the sound of the juniper trees,' said Dex. 'I want to see what they look like before we leave.'

Back at Gin Cottage, they followed the path round to the side of the house. The garden had probably once been well tended but was now overgrown, with a dandelion-strewn vegetable patch against the far wall, a pretty rose arbour in need of pruning, and colourful shrubs and flowers jostling with an explosion of weeds in the borders.

They had to Google juniper trees in order to identify them. And there they were, separating this garden from next door's, three evergreens with twisty trunks, sporting spiky needles and clumps of dark berries with a dusty blue bloom.

'I feel like Alan Titchmarsh.' Dex pulled down one of the branches, mindful of the sharp spikes. Some of the less ripe berries were smaller and still green. He picked one of the larger blue-black ones and squeezed it between his thumb and forefinger, inhaling the smell. It had a piney aromatic scent, like a mixture of Christmas trees and gin. Unable to resist, he bit the berry in half and experienced the flavour on his tongue.

Alice was watching him. 'What does it taste like?'

'Can't describe it. Like nothing I've ever tasted before. It's sharp and dry . . .' He tilted his head back in order to concentrate on the unfamiliar flavours. 'Kind of piney and weird.'

And that was when Dex saw the fish cartwheeling through the air towards him as it fell from the sky. He leapt back, yanking Alice with him, as the fish hit the paving slab with a wet FLHUPPPPP.

'Aarrgh!' Alice let out an ear-piercing shriek. 'WHAT'S THAT?'

'Oh no, oh *shit*,' exclaimed a female voice on the other side of the wall of trees.

'It's OK,' Dex told Alice. Because of course the fish hadn't fallen from the sky, it had been launched over the treetops by someone who was now seriously regretting it.

'How is it *possibly* OK? I could have been killed by that thing!'

'But you weren't. You're fine.'

'I'm definitely not fine. *Ugh*.' Alice was shuddering with revulsion and rubbing at her bare arms. 'Did you see the spray? I've got fish water all over my *skin*.'

'It was me. I'm so sorry, I didn't know you were there. I didn't know *anyone* was there.' Molly wanted to die; tempting though it had been to run back inside her house and hide in the airing cupboard, she'd known she had to stay and face the music.

And at least some of the music, she discovered as she made her way up the path, appeared to be pretty angry.

'So you just threw a fish into next door's garden? A bloody *enormous* fish, for crying out loud.' The girl's eyes blazed as she pointed at the creature on the ground before her. '*And* it splattered all over me when it landed. It's just gross!'

'I know, I'm sorry. The house has been empty for months. I saw you pulling up outside in your car earlier, and the estate agent turning up. Then you all left.' Molly's scalp prickled with mortification. 'I didn't know you'd come back.'

'Hey, don't worry, it was an accident. Could have happened to anyone.' The girl's husband or boyfriend appeared far less aggrieved.

'Fine for you to say,' the girl snapped.

Which was fair enough, Molly had to concede. He wasn't the one splattered in fish juice.

'Come over to my place and have a shower,' she begged. 'Please, you must.'

'I don't want a shower. But I'll come and have a wash, get it off my arms. Are you just planning to leave it there?' the girl demanded as they set off back down the path. 'It's going to reek to high heaven!'

Molly said simply, 'I know. That's why I threw it next door.'

Having shown her impromptu guest the bathroom, Molly headed downstairs and rejoined the husband outside.

'Look, I'm really, really sorry—'

'Shh, no need to keep apologising. And you don't have to worry about Alice. She's a nurse so she should be used to getting up close and personal with gross stuff.' He flashed a smile as he said it, his dark eyes creasing at the corners, and Molly realised with a thud how attractive he was. She'd been in too much of a fluster to take in the details before.

'Well, thanks. But maybe she thought she wouldn't have to put up with it on her day off.'

'True. I'm Dex, by the way.'

'Molly.'

'So can I ask you one thing? Was the fish already dead when you catapulted it over the trees?'

Molly liked his deadpan manner. 'It was, I promise. And I didn't use a catapult either.' She clasped her hands and held them out at arm's length. 'It was more of a shot-putt technique.'

'You're going to have to tell me why.' Dex pulled out one of the garden chairs. 'Otherwise I'll always wonder.'

It was a reasonable request.

'My ex-boyfriend caught the fish. He brought it over for me as a present. Basically, I'd rather cut off my own ears,' said Molly, 'than try and cook something like that. But I didn't know how to get rid of the thing. It's twelve days till the next bin collection. I thought this way, maybe foxes would eat it . . . well, anyway, it seemed like a good idea at the time.'

'What about all the people viewing the place?'

'There haven't been any viewings for four months.'

'Well, that's because they'd had an offer accepted and the sale was going ahead,' said Dex. 'Until it fell through last week.'

Molly shook her head at him. 'No offers made either. Did the estate agent tell you that?'

'Yes. To hear her, you'd think they were beating buyers off with a stick.' He frowned. 'But there's nothing wrong with the cottage. Why hasn't there been any interest?'

'Are you serious?' What kind of world did he live in? Although from the look of him and his car she could hazard a guess. 'It's massively overpriced. After Dorothy died, her daughter cleared the place out and put it on the market, but she wants far too much for it. Like, around fifty thousand too much.' She paused. 'Did it not seem like a lot to you?'

Dex was looking nonplussed. 'To be honest, no. Compared with London prices everything looks like a complete bargain.'

'Well, take it from me, it isn't. You'd be mad to pay that much. So are you thinking of buying it, then?'

'Maybe.' His eyes glinted with amusement. 'Would you hate it if I did?'

'Why would I hate it?'

'The old guys in the pub were grumbling about weekenders. That's what I'd be.'

Molly shrugged. 'Well, obviously you wouldn't be *living* here. But these things happen. If you're not going to be around for months on end, just promise me you won't have one of those burglar alarms that sets itself off every time a mouse squeaks.'

Dex said gravely, 'I promise. But other than that, you wouldn't mind too much?'

'I wouldn't mind. You seem OK. Would you be holding noisy parties that go on all night and disturb the peace?'

'It's a possibility.'

'Thank goodness for that,' said Molly. 'And you think your wife might forgive me for nearly killing her with a fish?'

'Don't worry about Alice. She isn't my wife.' The way he almost imperceptibly shook his head as he said it indicated that the relationship wasn't destined to be the lasting kind. Molly had already guessed what he was like; that laid-back manner, those sparkling brown eyes, the moneyed air . . . it all belonged to someone used to getting whatever he wanted and whoever happened to take his fancy.

Honestly, though, that car of his was a bit much. Wouldn't most girls find it off-putting to know that he was happy to drive around in something that was both canary yellow *and* a Porsche?

To change the subject, Molly said, 'What made you come back for a second look anyway?' Mischievously she added, 'Keen on gardening, are you?'

'I heard about it being called Gin Cottage. Wanted to see what juniper trees looked like.' He shook his head and grimaced. 'Those juniper berries taste weird.'

'Oh my God, you mean you *ate* some?' Molly let out a gasp of horror. 'Are you serious, you actually *swallowed* them?'

'Not some. Only one.' He looked alarmed. 'But . . . people use them in cooking.'

'Cooking, yes! Once they're *cooked* they're OK. But you can't eat them raw!'

'Shit, I didn't know they were poisonous.'

'It's OK.' Molly broke into a smile, putting him out of his misery. 'They're not.'

'What's going on?' Alice rejoined them, her arms bright pink from being scrubbed clean.

'First she almost killed us with a fish. Then she tried to give me a heart attack.' Dex clutched his chest. 'I guess it's all part of the master plan to keep the village safe from interlopers.'

'Oh, I love that word,' said Molly with enthusiasm. 'Interloper. It's so . . . *lollopy*.'

'Loopy,' Dex countered.

'Lollipoppy!'

Alice had been watching the two of them like a toddler not remotely keen on sharing her favourite toy. Tugging at Dex's shirtsleeve, she said, 'Anyway, we've seen the garden. All done now. Shall we go?'

Dex didn't say a word; he didn't need to. Molly could tell just by the look on his face that he was aware of Alice's possessiveness and found it less than enchanting. Put it this way, if her birthday happened to be a few weeks from now, she probably shouldn't hold her breath waiting for a present.

'I guess we should. Well,' he turned to Molly, 'thanks for letting Alice use your bathroom.'

Alice made a *tuh* noise of disbelief.

'No problem at all.' Molly kept a straight face.

His eyes glittering, Dex said, 'It's been . . . interesting to meet you.'

Man-wise, he fell into the category of Utterly Dangerous; anyone daft enough to get involved with someone like that would have to expect to get their heart broken as a matter of course. On the plus side, if you *weren't* romantically entangled with him, he'd undoubtedly be great fun.

'Same.' Molly wondered if he'd buy the cottage. 'And don't forget what I told you. If you offer them the full price, you're mad.'

Chapter 6

The party was being held at a house in Notting Hill that belonged to someone whose name Dex had forgotten, but never mind. The man was in his sixties and wore the permanently startled look of someone whose recent eye-lift has yet to bed in. But his home was spectacular and he'd had the foresight to invite along plenty of pretty girls.

Dex helped himself to another drink; the music was loud and people were dancing with abandon. He could have stayed in tonight, but Rob and Kenny from work had talked him into coming along.

'You can't stay at home!' Kenny had been incredulous. 'If you do that, you'll never know what you might have missed out on. It could be the party of the year.'

Rob had added, 'Could be the night your life changes *forever*.'

Which wasn't that likely, to be honest, but it had been easier to give in than to carry on saying no. As Kenny had concluded, at the very least he knew he could end up getting laid.

Anyway. Give it another hour and a couple more drinks, and maybe he'd start to feel in a bit more of a party mood.

And sure enough, an hour later the alcohol was working its

magic, blurring the edges of a long and stressful day at work and improving Dex's mood. His tolerance levels had risen; a startlingly pretty girl called Bibi had spent some time explaining how to spell her name and he'd actually listened with secret amusement rather than visible disbelief. 'It's not like ee ee, like bees.' Helpfully she'd flapped her arms as she said it. 'It's bee eye bee eye, with two *eyes*. Look,' she batted her lashes at him in a coquettish manner. 'See? These are my eyes! That's how you remember how to spell it!'

'Genius.' Dex nodded. 'You learn something new every day. And what do you do workwise?'

'Guess!'

'I can't guess. Surprise me.'

If she told him she was a neuroscientist he'd definitely be surprised. Or a maths teacher. Or a goatherd – that would be just *brilliant*.

'I work in promotion?' Bibi ended most of her sentences with upward inflections. 'And I do, like, loads of modelling jobs too? Do you think I've got a good figure?'

'Of course I do.' She was wearing a sky-blue satin dress that clung to every curve; only girls who knew they were truly gorgeous ever asked that question.

'How about my boobs?'

'Excuse me?'

'Do you like them?'

OK, these upward inflections were getting out of hand now. Dex said carefully, 'They seem . . . fine.'

'Not too big? I didn't want to go, like, massive.' Bibi mimed watermelons. 'I mean, that's just tarty, isn't it? So I went for these.' She stuck her chest out with pride. 'Thirty-six double D. Just right, don't you think? I had them done in November so they'd be ready for Christmas.'

Were they still actually having this conversation? 'Well,' said Dex, 'lucky old Christmas.'

'They're so much better than the last ones. They went all weird and, like, lumpy? But these are really soft.' Bibi mimed their softness with her thin bejewelled hands then said brightly, 'You can feel them if you like!'

Her perfume was cloying and the room was hot. Aware that people had been disappearing out on to the roof terrace to smoke, Dex said, 'Thanks, but I think I'm going to head outside, get myself some fresh air.' Holding his hands up before she could offer to go with him, he added, 'I'll see you later, OK?'

To be honest, the air outside on the terrace was a bit too fresh. It was February and the surrounding rooftops glittered with frost. Partygoers huddled together for warmth while they smoked their cigarettes at warp speed, getting their nicotine fixes before heading back inside again.

Dex, who didn't smoke, stood at the edge of the parapet and surveyed the view. The stars were out in force and a crescent moon hung in the sky. Uncurtained windows revealed glimpses of other people's lives. Across the street a woman in a pink dressing gown was rocking a toddler to sleep – had the music from their party woken it up? In another house, a family were sitting together ostensibly watching TV, although in reality they were each tapping away on their phones and laptops. Next door to the family, an overweight man was standing in front of his open fridge, eating spoonfuls of something from a bowl and glancing furtively over his shoulder. Further down the street, in a bedroom, a girl was blow-drying her hair and pulling faces at her reflection in the—

'Surprise!' Bracelets jangled and a pair of hands playfully covered his eyes. Dex knew it wasn't Bibi behind him; the perfume wasn't so noxious and the boobs pressing against his back were smaller.

'I know who that is,' Dex lied, smiling as he peeled away the hands and slowly turned to face . . .

Carla.

Hang on, is it Carla? Or Carina?

No, right first time. Carla.

Probably.

'Sweetheart, how are you? Haven't bumped into you for months.' He kissed her on both cheeks. 'Looking fantastic, as always.'

But even as the words were coming out of his mouth, he was slightly despising himself for saying them. It was what girls liked to hear, though. Every now and again Dex found himself feeling like an actor who'd been performing in the same stage play for far too long. The lines came out automatically, irrespective of whether or not they were true.

Although in this case they undoubtedly *were*. Carina-or-Carla was a stunning brunette with slanted eyes, exotic cheekbones and teeth like pearls.

If only she could have been wearing one of those necklaces with her name on it, she'd be perfect.

'Kisses on the cheek? What am I, your great-aunt? Come here.' Playfully drawing him towards her, she pressed her mouth against his for several seconds.

'It's so good to see you again,' said Dex.

'All you had to do was call me.'

'What can I say, sweetheart? Everything's been so crazy.'

'And I expect you lost my number.'

He nodded. 'I did. *Mea culpa.* Left my phone in a cab and never saw it again.'

'What's my name?'

'Sorry?'

'You've called me Sweetheart twice now. Is that to cover up the fact that you can't remember who I am?'

'As if anyone could forget you.' Dex broke into a smile; he'd always enjoyed a challenge.

'Except I'm pretty sure you have.'

'I haven't.' *This was more like it.*

'I'm going to count to three.' Her slanted eyes narrowed, signalling that he was in danger. 'One . . . two . . .'

'I'm insulted that you think I've forgotten.'

'Two and a half . . .'

'You need to learn to trust me more. Sweetheart.'

'Two and three-quarters . . .'

Once anyone counted to two and three-quarters you knew you'd won.

'And what happens if I get it wrong?'

'You'll be in big trouble.'

What the hell, here we go. 'Just so long as you don't throw me over the parapet . . . Carla.'

She held his gaze. For a moment he wondered if she might actually try it. The next moment she broke into a slow, relieved smile. 'You wicked man, such a tease. For a minute there I actually thought you couldn't remember.'

'Oh ye of little faith,' said Dex.

'So what are you doing out here in the cold? You don't even smoke.'

Dex shrugged. 'Escaping from someone. And admiring the view. Look.' He turned and showed her the lit-up rooms in the houses across the street. 'Other people's lives. Doesn't it make you want to know all about them?'

'Honest answer? No.' Carla slid her arm round his waist. 'Other people's lives are nearly always boring. I'm more interested in yours. What have you been up to lately?'

'Actually, he's with me.' Bibi had materialised behind them and there was a can-opener edge to her voice.

'*Really?*' Having turned round, Carla raised an eyebrow at the sight of Bibi's fake-tanned breasts bursting to escape over the top of her low-cut satin dress. But she took her hand away.

'Yes he is.' Bibi looked triumphant.

Choosing his words with care, Dex said reasonably, 'Well, I wouldn't say I was *with* you. We were just having a chat.'

At this, Carla's arm went back round his waist, which wasn't the most subtle move imaginable.

'You were with me when we were having a chat,' Bibi insisted. 'Back in the flat. You said you liked my boobs!'

'No.' Aware that both of Carla's eyebrows were now up, Dex said, 'You *asked* me if I liked them . . .'

'And you said yes!' Bibi's voice was getting shriller.

'I didn't know what else to do. I couldn't say no, could I?' *Ach*, he hadn't meant it to sound like that.

'So you were *lying*? Are you telling me you *don't* like them?' Cupping her enormous breasts in disbelief, Bibi wailed, 'They cost me six thousand pounds!'

OK, this wasn't going well. Everyone out on the terrace was turning to stare at them.

'Oh my God,' Carla drawled, 'listen to yourself. Do you have any idea how pathetic you sound? Why on earth would Dex be interested in someone like you?'

'Ooh, I don't know, maybe because I'm prettier than you are and my boobs are way bigger than yours.' Tossing her head, Bibi added spiritedly, 'Plus, unlike some people I could mention, I'm not a smug sarky bitch!'

The other guests were watching, enthralled. Several of them now burst out laughing. Dex wondered what he should do and why situations like this always seemed to happen to him; an elegant party in an upmarket house in Notting Hill was threatening to turn into Jerry Springer. When his mobile started ringing in his pocket he breathed a sigh of relief; whoever was on the other end of the line didn't know it yet, but they were about to come to his rescue. He would use their timely interruption as an excuse to leave.

'I'd rather be a smug sarky bitch,' Carla responded with disdain, 'than a slutty one in a cheap dress.'

'Whoa, what's going on here?' Bursting out on to the terrace with a giggling blonde tucked under one arm and a bottle of champagne in the other, Kenny surveyed the stand-off. 'Dex, you old dog! Causing trouble again?'

'Did you just say Dex?' The giggling blonde peered across the terrace then yelled, 'Oh my God, it *is* you! Dexter Yates, you're such a lying bastard, you promised you'd call me again and you never did!'

Oops. Time to get out of here, do a Tardis-style disappearing trick. Dex whisked out his still-ringing phone, pressed Answer and said cheerfully, 'Hello?'

Chapter 7

'I want to do what you do.' Alfie, Molly's newest pupil, was eager to explain. 'Because, like, it's a dead easy job, isn't it? Better than collecting trolleys at the supermarket. I've been doing that for six weeks now and it's, like, dead boring. I'd much rather sit and draw stuff.'

Molly was always encouraging and enthusiastic, but sixteen-year-old Alfie, bless him, didn't have the firmest grasp on reality. As the rest of the class gathered up their belongings and prepared to leave, she said, 'And you've done some great work tonight. You just need to keep practising,'

'I'm good at art. I nearly got a C in my exam.' He beamed at her. 'So, the people that own the newspaper, could you ask them to give me a job too? Because when it's weather like this, I really hate working in that car park.'

'The thing is, Alfie, the newspapers do get quite a lot of people wanting to work for them . . .'

'I know *that*.' He gave her a wounded I'm-not-stupid look. 'That's why I want you to say something to them about how I'm good at drawing and they should give me the job.'

'Come on, lad, time to go.' Celeste, who knew Alfie's parents, jangled her car keys at him. 'It's pouring down outside, so why don't I give you a lift home?'

Once everyone had left, Molly finished tidying up. The thing was, people *did* tend to think she had an easy job. Drawing a daily comic strip to appear in a newspaper? Quickly dashing off three or four simple line drawings that probably took, what, less than an hour in total? Talk about a cushy number! And when they learned that her little comic strip was syndicated to appear in dozens of newspapers around the world, well, what a goldmine. She must be raking it in. Best job in the world.

And it was lovely, but it wasn't always easy. For years she had practised and honed her self-taught craft, endlessly working on dozens of different ideas for strips that were never picked up. Finally, it had happened with Boogie and Boo, and seeing her work in print for the first time had been one of the very best moments of her life. The strip chronicled the adventures of Boo, a ditsy Californian It-girl, and Boogie, her adored but sardonic and world-weary pet chihuahua. The interaction between tiny plain-speaking dog and gullible owner had caught the readers' imagination, attracting positive feedback and wider interest. The number of syndications had taken off . . .

But this also meant people assumed you were making a jolly good living out of it. Whereas in reality it was more of an eke, all those small separate payments adding up to just about enough to survive on, which was why Molly supplemented her income by running evening classes in caricature and cartoonery. It didn't bring in a huge amount but every little helped. And it was fun; her pupils enjoyed coming to Briarwood, taking over the conservatory area of Frankie's café and catching up with each other's news while they worked. They were a chatty, sociable group who looked forward to their Monday nights, even when the weather was like this.

God, listen to that rain outside; it was really hammering down now. Molly finished collecting the empty cups and abandoned pencils and wished she'd thought to bring an umbrella. Last week's icy sub-zero temperatures had this morning given way to howling winds and a torrential storm – oh, look, someone had left their leather gloves behind. That must have been Celeste . . .

The outside door banged open and shut and Molly picked up the gloves, ready to return them to their rightful owner. But when she turned round, it wasn't Celeste after all. A man was standing in the doorway, soaked to the skin, with his hair plastered to his scalp and rain running down his face.

'Hi, you're open, are you? I'll have a coffee please.'

Was he serious? How likely was it that a small café in a village would be open at nine o'clock on a Monday night?

'Sorry,' said Molly. 'The café's closed.'

'Oh. I saw the lights were on. And people leaving.'

'That was my evening class.'

'Right. OK.'

'They serve coffee in the Swan.' He looked vaguely familiar but she couldn't place him.

'I don't want to go into the pub. Never mind,' said the man. 'Thanks anyway.'

It wasn't until he turned to leave and the light caught his face from a different angle that Molly realised who he was.

'Oh my God, it's *you*. I didn't recognise you with your hair all wet!' Embarrassed, she realised as she said it that he hadn't recognised her either. And she didn't have the excuse of dripping wet hair. But really, he wasn't *behaving* at all like he had the last time they'd met. Unless he was the unsmiling, unflirty, incredibly serious twin brother . . .

'I'm sorry?'

'Remember the fish?' Oh God, he was *still* looking blank. Already seriously regretting having started this, Molly went on in a rush, 'Flying through the air and splattering your girlfriend? I'm your next-door neighbour.'

He closed his eyes and shook his head as if to clear it. 'Of course. I remember now. Sorry.'

Whatever was *wrong* with him? Was he ill? On drugs? It had been eight months since the flying fish incident. A week after their first meeting on that sunny day at the end of June, the Sold sign had gone up outside Gin Cottage and she'd looked forward to seeing her new neighbour again.

But that hadn't happened. Instead, teams of workmen had turned up and the cottage had found itself on the receiving end of a comprehensive makeover. This had carried on until October, then the workmen had left and the place had sat there empty, pretty much ever since. Dexter had actually visited it twice in that time and on both weekends Molly had been away. Returning to Briarwood, she'd been informed on each occasion that he and his lady friend had graced the Swan with their presence. He'd been fun and friendly, by all accounts, and had charmed most of the female regulars before leaving after last orders. The following day, the Porsche would fire up and off they'd roar, back to London.

The first time he'd had a titian-haired beauty with him. For the second visit he had brought along a curvaceous brunette.

And that had been the sum total of Gin Cottage's occupation, apart from the single visit paid last week by a woman with a baby. On this occasion Molly *had* been around to see the visitor pull up in an old Ford Escort, unload some stuff from the boot of the car and enter the house. Several hours later she had re-emerged with the baby and jumped back into the car. Spotting Molly watching her, she'd wound down her window and call out cheerily, 'It's OK, I'm not a burglar,' before driving off.

Whatever had happened to put him into the state he was in now? Had the woman been a spurned ex? Had she completely trashed the cottage? Was the baby his?

Had he only just found out?

'Hang on, come back,' Molly called after him as he turned to leave. 'Are you all right?'

Which possibly counted as Stupidest Question of the Month, but it was short notice.

'I'm fine.'

'No you're not. Are you ill?'

He stood there, shaking his head.

'You can talk about it if you want. I won't tell anyone.' Would he think she was a hideously nosy neighbour? Molly said, 'Is it to do with the baby?'

'What?' He turned back to look at her, and there was a world of pain in his dark eyes.

'Sorry, I'm just trying to help. I saw them last week,' she explained. 'The woman in the red Escort. She had a baby with her. She was doing something in the cottage, but I don't know what. I just saw them from my window . . .' Her voice trailed off in dismay and she realised he was on the verge of tears. 'Look, it's OK, I'll do you a coffee.' Because that was why he'd come here, wasn't it?

'You don't have to. You're closed.'

'Don't be daft, look at the state of you.' He was drenched and shivering with cold; having decided he wasn't deranged, Molly held out her hands and said, 'Take off your jacket, for a start.'

The jacket was dripping water all over the floor. She peeled it off him and hung it over the back of the chair next to the radiator. 'Now wait there and I'll make that coffee. Milk, sugar?'

For a moment he looked as if he couldn't remember. Then he nodded and said, 'Milk and two sugars. Please.'

Chapter 8

What was he doing here? Dexter listened to the sounds of the coffee machine bubbling and hissing in the kitchen. God only knew what the girl must be thinking. But he'd needed to get away, to escape, and some instinct had propelled him down the M4 to Briarwood. No, not some instinct; he knew why he'd come here. Dammit, what was going on with his *eyes*? He hadn't cried since he was a kid, had forgotten how it felt.

Dexter sat down on the chair with his jacket hanging over the back of it and reached into the left-hand pocket. As he pulled out the handkerchief, something else came with it.

He turned the object over and held it in the icy palm of his hand. When had he bought it? Just before Christmas. An antique rose-gold frog on a shovel, roughly one centimetre in length, designed to be worn on a charm bracelet. After an extremely good lunch at the Savoy, he'd been on his way through the Burlington Arcade when it had somehow managed to catch his eye in a jeweller's window when he'd stopped to glance at the Patek Philippe watches on the next shelf up. Christmas was almost upon them and he hadn't done anything about presents yet. But the frog on the shovel charm was quirky, there was something

47

about the frog's expression that appealed to him, and Laura had a charm bracelet she liked to wear on special occasions. He'd gone into the shop and bought it for her. Not many girls would prefer a frog on a shovel to something flashy with diamonds but he'd known she would.

And he'd been right. When Laura had opened the jeweller's box on Christmas morning she'd been overjoyed . . . until he'd realised the charm bracelet she was wearing wasn't gold, it was silver.

'But it doesn't matter,' Laura had protested, laughing at the expression on his face. 'I still love it! Look, mix and match.' She'd held the gold frog charm up to the silver bracelet jangling on her wrist. 'He's fab!'

'You can't.' He couldn't believe he'd made the mistake. 'It'd look stupid. I'll get you a silver one instead.'

'Dex, you wouldn't be able to, this is Victorian or something. It's *old*.'

No one was more stubborn than Laura. There was only one way to stop her wearing a gold charm on a silver bracelet. 'Well, that's where you're wrong,' Dex lied, 'because they had an identical charm at the shop in silver. So I'll get that one for you instead.'

OK, maybe he was stubborn too.

'Really?' Delighted with this solution, Laura had promptly handed the gold charm over to him. 'In that case, fantastic. You can take this one back and do a swap.'

And Dex, equally delighted to have won, had made a mental note to find a silversmith or jewellery designer from somewhere. After all, how hard could it be to replicate something like that? It might not be Victorian but Laura wouldn't mind once she had it. In fact, if he didn't tell her, she'd never know.

Except he hadn't got around to organising it, had he, and now she never would. Because he'd been too occupied, it had slipped his mind, there had been too many other distractions in his busy, busy life . . .

OK, stop, don't think about it.

And now the girl was on her way back with the coffee, which no longer seemed like such a good idea. Shoving the charm back into his jacket pocket, Dex hurriedly wiped his eyes with the handkerchief. All very well trying not to think about it but his brain didn't have an Off switch.

'Thanks.' He took the coffee with trembling hands and instantly spilled some on the floor. Bending down to mop up the splashes with his handkerchief, he managed to spill some more.

'Leave it. Doesn't matter. Just drink your coffee,' said the girl. 'You look as if you need it.'

'You're Molly, right?' The name belatedly came back to him.

'I didn't think you'd remember.'

Well, that made a change. Dex said, 'We used to have a goldfish called Molly.'

'In many ways, I'm quite like a goldfish.'

'I drove down this evening. Forgot there wasn't anything in the house. Well, except the remains of a bottle of Scotch. So I finished that off. Then realised I couldn't drive anywhere to stock up on food and drink.' Dex shook his head. 'What this place needs is an all-night garage.'

'You're not in the big city now.'

'Clearly. How far would I have to go to find a shop that's open?'

Molly shrugged. 'A few miles.'

'Could you drive me there? I'd pay you. We can go in my car.'

'Don't worry, I've got stuff at home. I'll give you whatever you need for tonight, then tomorrow you can drive there yourself.' She paused. 'Or if you're not up to it, I can go.'

'I don't know. I can't think. My head's just . . . full.' She was being kind to him, he realised, without even knowing what was wrong.

'It's OK, not a problem. Decide tomorrow.'

Touched by her thoughtfulness, Dex heard himself blurt out, 'My sister died last night.'

'Oh no, that's awful.' Her hand flew to her mouth. 'I'm so sorry.'

Dex nodded, unable to speak. For the first time in his adult life, he wished she would wrap her arms around him and give him a non-sexual hug.

Laura had been twelve years older than him, and following the death of their parents she had become like a mother to him. This was like losing them all over again. And OK, he was twenty-eight and a proper adult now, but it almost felt worse.

Molly-the-neighbour wasn't going to give him a hug. He couldn't ask for one.

'Had she been ill for a long time?' Her question was delicately phrased. 'Or was it sudden?'

'Sudden. I spoke to her on the phone yesterday morning and she was fine. She collapsed in the street yesterday afternoon. Just outside her local bank. It was a brain haemorrhage, apparently. By the time the ambulance got her to the hospital she was gone.'

'I'm sorry.' The girl was gazing at him in horror. 'Such a terrible thing to happen. No wonder you're in shock. Hang on.' She disappeared, returning seconds later with a loo roll. Tearing off a metre of paper, she handed it to him. 'Here, you can cry as much as you want. Just let it all out. There's nothing worse than trying to hold it back.'

But his eyes were now aching and dry. Dex distractedly raked his fingers through his hair and took another gulp of coffee. If only he could stop *imagining* the scene outside the bank: Laura falling to the ground, concerned onlookers closing around her, unconcerned commuters hurrying past, the abandoned pushchair gathering momentum until it toppled off the pavement into the busy road—

'How old was she?' The girl's voice dragged him back to the present. 'Younger than you?'

She didn't know.

'Older,' said Dex. 'You saw her last week. Laura.'

Realisation dawned, and with it renewed dismay. 'That was her? With the baby? My *God* . . .'

'I know.'

'Any other children?'

'No.'

'Her poor husband . . . partner . . .'

'Neither, it was just the two of them. Her and Delphi.'

She closed her eyes at this fresh horror. 'Oh, poor darling, poor baby. I only saw her from a distance. How old is she . . . six months?'

'Eight.' His throat was tightening again at the thought of Delphi growing up without a mother; it looked like the balled-up length of loo roll was going to come in useful after all. 'Eight months old. She was in her pushchair when it happened. It rolled off the edge of the pavement and someone just managed to grab it in time before it went under a lorry. It's a miracle she didn't die too. I wasn't there,' Dex explained. 'Someone told the paramedics.'

'I don't know what to say.' The girl's expression was stricken. He'd forgotten her name again . . . goldfish . . . *Molly*.

'Me neither.'

51

'If it happened that fast, at least she didn't suffer.' She saw the look on Dex's face and said helplessly, 'I know, I'm sorry. Maybe one day it'll be a comfort.'

'Maybe. I suppose.' There was a sudden noise on the other side of the wall and he flinched. 'What's that?'

'It's my friend's living room. This is her café. If she knows I'm still here, she might come in.' Molly rose to her feet and took his almost empty mug from him. 'Shall we go?'

Dex lifted his jacket off the back of the chair and Molly reached for the unglamorous but deeply practical Barbour beneath it. She locked up the café and together they made their way through the village, past the Saucy Swan. The rain intensified as they crossed the elongated green; in no time at all he was drenched again, but it was so irrelevant, so unimportant, he barely noticed.

Laura was dead. How could Laura be dead? It wasn't possible. Head down, Dex carried on putting one foot in front of the other, scarcely aware of the girl alongside him.

What am I going to do?

Chapter 9

'Come on, let's get you some food.' Realising he was functioning on autopilot, Molly took out her keys and led Dexter up the path to her house.

In the kitchen she found him a packet of Kettle chips, half a tin of assorted biscuits, a jar of coffee and a carton of UHT milk perilously close to its use-by date. She poured sugar into a spare cup, chose a couple of the less wrinkly apples from the fruit bowl and said, 'How about bread and cereal? I've got white sliced or brown with seedy bits in, and some Crunchy Nut Cornflakes if you want them. Or there's sausages in the freezer.'

She was overcompensating horribly, she knew that, like the kind of awful bossy team leader no one wanted to have around.

Dexter briefly shook his head. 'Just stuff to make coffee, thanks.'

'Sorry, I'm trying to help and I don't know how.' Molly threw the pack of Porkinsons back into the freezer.

'Me neither. Actually I do. Got any wine?'

Molly pulled a face. Last week she'd won a bottle in the pub raffle, made by Lois's dad. But it was a murky brew and she couldn't inflict it on him.

'I don't think you'd like it. Homemade parsnip. But I've got some sherry left over from Christmas. Oh, and some dark rum too. Any good?'

Dexter nodded. 'It'll do.'

Basically, anything would do. Molly found a carrier bag and began loading everything into it, expecting Dex to take the bag and leave. Instead he unscrewed the top of the bottle of dark rum and said, 'What goes with this? I've never had it before.'

'Me neither. I just put it in stuff when I'm cooking. Rum and Coke, I suppose.'

'Got any Coke?'

Molly took two cans out of the fridge and handed them to him. When he carried on standing there she said, 'Do you want to go back to your place or stay here?'

'I think I'd rather stay here,' said Dex. 'For a bit, at least. Is that OK with you?'

She had a comic strip to finish but some things were more important. This counted as extenuating circumstances. It was shocking enough to think that the woman who had so cheerfully announced she wasn't a burglar was no longer alive. Her brother was here in the depths of grief. 'Of course it's OK.' She found two glasses for them to drink from. 'Come on, let's go and sit down.'

'I was just there, at this stupid party in Notting Hill with two girls hissing at each other like cats. Over *me*. I was drinking champagne.' Dexter shook his head at the memory. Now that he'd started, he was discovering he couldn't stop. 'Having a good time. It was just . . . you know, entertaining to see these girls getting so worked up. Ridiculous, but kind of amusing too. And it didn't even matter, because I didn't particularly like either of them anyway. When my phone started to ring I just thought it would be a brilliant excuse to get myself out of the situation. I was *glad* it had rung. So I answered it, all ready to use whoever it was as a reason to leave . . . and I'd tell them all about it later, turn it into a funny story, you know? Like I always do. But it wasn't a funny story.' He stopped abruptly, took another swallow of rum and Coke and shuddered at the memory. 'It was the police.'

Then he started talking about Laura when they'd been growing up. So many stories, some of which he hadn't even thought about in years. Like the time she'd tripped while giving him a piggyback and he'd gone sailing over her head like a jockey. The time she'd put him in a cardboard box and sent him tobogganing downstairs, resulting in him losing a tooth *well* before it had been ready to be lost. The time she'd been sunbathing on a rug in the garden and he'd ridden his bike over her outstretched hand, breaking two of her fingers.

'So it was a pretty violent relationship.' The way Molly said it made him smile.

'Not always. I drove her mad in other ways too. When I was about five I collected a jarful of dead insects from the garage and emptied them in her bed. And she hated mustard, so I used to secretly smear some in her sandwiches.'

'You were the naughty little brother. I bet you were a nightmare when she brought boyfriends home.'

Dexter laughed, taken by surprise by a memory he'd completely forgotten about. 'I was. There was one boy . . . the two of them were on the sofa watching TV and I was hiding behind the curtains. For *ages*. Then they started kissing. I waited and waited, and then I yelled out, "Laura Yates, WHAT ARE YOU DOING?" Ha, you should have seen them. I was so proud of myself. Funnily enough, we never did see that boyfriend again.' Ambushed by a fresh wave of grief, he stopped talking and finished his drink. 'Oh God, I can't believe she isn't here any more. I just don't know where she's gone.'

The next time he looked at his watch another hour had passed and the rum bottle was empty. They'd finished the rest of the sherry too. Molly, curled up in the armchair on the other side of the fireplace, was still apparently paying attention.

'Look at you, still listening. Good for you.' Dex held out his empty glass. 'Can't be much fun having to sit there and put up with me droning on.'

'Don't worry, this is what neighbours are for. What do you want me to do with that glass?'

'Fill it with something.'

'There isn't anything else. Apart from some weird Greek liqueur. We've drunk the house dry.'

Dex waggled the glass at her. 'Weird Greek liqueur it is then.'

'It smells like bonfires and paint-stripper. No one's ever been brave enough to drink it. Why don't I make you another coffee instead?'

'No. Just humour me.' He needed to sleep and he knew it wouldn't happen unless he knocked himself out. 'Don't worry, I'm not going to turn into a monster. But I'll buy it off you if you want. Take it next door.'

'You don't have to do that.' Unfolding her legs, she padded in her fluffy socks through to the kitchen and returned with the bottle.

'Thanks.' It definitely looked dodgy but Dex didn't care. Taking it from her, he poured himself half a glass.

'You should really eat something. I could do cheese on toast.'

He shook his head. 'Not hungry.'

'OK, you've talked a lot about Laura. But there's one thing you haven't mentioned.' The way Molly was looking at him made Dex not want to listen. He knew what she was going to say next.

'One time when I was about ten I left stink bombs in her shoes so they'd burst when she put her feet in them. That was just as she was heading off out on another date. It's actually a miracle I have any teeth left.' He stared distractedly into the fire and took a huge gulp of liqueur without thinking. *Jesus* . . .

Molly waited until he'd finished coughing. Then she said, 'What's going to happen to the baby?'

There it was. That was the question he'd been avoiding thinking about. Dex coughed some more.

'Where is she?' Her gaze was unwavering.

'Who?'

'You know who. Delphi.'

'She's safe. She isn't lying alone in an empty house, if that's what you mean. Someone's looking after her.'

'Good. Who?'

God, she was like an Exocet missile. 'Why are you asking that question?'

'Because you're looking so defensive.'

'Can we change the subject? I don't want to talk about this now.'

'I think you should. Look, I'm practically a stranger. We don't know each other. Where is Delphi?'

'With a foster family.' He hated even having to say the words. 'Someone arranged it at the hospital before I got there. They have emergency foster carers for . . . situations like this.'

Molly was nodding. 'Right. And who's going to be taking care of her after that?'

This was it, this was the question he didn't want to answer. But it wasn't going to go away.

'I don't know.' Dex briefly closed his eyes.

'What about the father?'

'Off the scene. It was just a fling. She never told him she was pregnant.'

'And your parents are both dead.' He'd mentioned it earlier when he'd been telling her about Laura. Molly said, 'But she must have thought about what she'd do if the worst happened. People make plans. Who are her friends, do you know them? Maybe she asked one of them to look after Delphi.'

Dexter shook his head. 'She didn't.'

'Well, did she make a will?'

'Yes.' He exhaled slowly. 'She made a will.'

'So it'll be in there.'

He nodded. 'Yes.'

'Do you know what it says?'

He avoided her gaze.

'Oh God,' said Molly. 'It's you, isn't it?'

'Yes.' He sank his head into his hands. 'She asked me to sign this document saying I'd be the guardian, but I only did it because I thought it wouldn't happen. You say you'll do these things but you never expect to actually have to.' There, he'd said it now. It was *out*.

'So you don't really want to do it.'

Her tone wasn't judgemental, but he felt judged anyway. Dexter said heavily, 'It's not a question of if I *want* to do it. I just can't.'

'No?'

'No! I mean, God, how *could* I?'

Molly looked at him and didn't answer. He knew what she was thinking: *In the normal way.*

'Look at me, look at my life.' How could he make her understand? 'I know nothing about babies. Before Delphi was born I'd never even *held* one. I work stupid hours, sometimes all night long. When I'm not at work, I'm . . . *out.* There isn't room for a baby. Plus, even if there was, I'm the last person in the world you'd want looking after another human being. It'd be a disaster. I can't even keep track of my car keys.'

'Right.'

'I know what you're thinking.'

She shook her head. 'No you don't.'

'Of course I do. You can't believe how anyone could be so selfish. That's it, isn't it? What a bastard, all he's thinking about is himself. But I'm just being honest, it's not something I can do. This isn't the kind of person I am.' He rubbed his eyes, which were prickling now with the effort of keeping them open; last night's sleeplessness and the combination of drinks was catching up with him now.

'Do you love her?' said Molly.

'Delphi? Of course I love her, but that's beside the point. I'm selfish, don't you see? She deserves better than to be stuck with someone like me. God, I've had to buy three new phones since Christmas – if I tried to take her anywhere I'd end up leaving her in the back of a cab.'

'You say that now.' Molly's voice softened. 'But she's a human being. It's different. You only lose car keys and phones because they *aren't* the most important things in the world. You don't love them with all your heart. Everyone panics when they first discover they're about to become a parent. It's completely normal to be terrified at the thought of being responsible for an actual baby. But that's the whole point of loving them unconditionally – it means you'll do everything it takes to keep them safe.'

'Do you really think that?'

'Yes,' she said simply. 'It's human nature. Look, if you don't want to bring up this baby, fine. If you *do* want to but you're just scared you aren't *able* to do it . . . well, I wouldn't worry about that. Because there's no reason at all why you can't.'

Wow, where had that little speech come from? And should she even be having this much faith in someone she barely knew? What if he took her at her word and *did* accidentally leave the baby on the back seat of a taxi?

Then again, was Dexter even listening to her anyway? He was currently peering into his glass and frowning.

'This is empty. Can I have some more?'

So much for the impassioned pep-talk.

'No problem. I'm just going to make myself a coffee. Wait there,' said Molly, getting up. 'I'll be back in a sec.'

In the kitchen, she put the kettle on and waited for it to come to the boil. She didn't bother making any coffee. After a few minutes she returned to the living room. Yes, he'd fallen asleep.

What a situation to find yourself in. You couldn't help feeling sorry for him. Having cleared away the glasses, Molly stood and watched him for a while. His breathing was deep and even. There were dark shadows beneath his eyes and with his head tilted back against the cushions, the curve of his visible cheekbone gleamed in the dim light. His dark hair had dried now. He looked beautiful but troubled, which he undoubtedly was.

He was also a virtual stranger, but this didn't worry her at all. She had a lock on her door and he wasn't likely to make off with her telly. It was safe to leave him here for tonight.

Molly spread his jacket over the radiator. Because there was only room for the one, she took her own Barbour upstairs, put it in the airing cupboard to dry out and brought the emergency duvet back down.

Dexter didn't move when she placed it over him. He'd be out for the count now, for the rest of the night.

Well, what a Monday evening this had been. Leaving two paracetamols next to a pint glass of water on the coffee table, Molly headed up to bed. After rum and sherry and burnt paint-stripper liqueur he was going to need them when he woke up.

When she came down the next morning he was gone. So were the paracetamols. The duvet, an oversized 10-tog version of Cinderella's glass slipper, had been left in a crumpled heap on the otherwise empty sofa. No note, no other sign that he'd been here.

Molly opened the front door and shivered as icy rain splattered her face. Urgh, February. And her Barbour was still upstairs. She ran barefoot down the path, saw that the lurid yellow Porsche was no longer parked outside Gin Cottage and raced inside again. Did this mean he'd gone out to buy food? Or that he was on his way up to London? In which case, she might never find out what he chose to do about Delphi.

Poor Dex, what a terrible situation to be in. Surely between them there was some way they could help him? Wiping the rain off her nose, Molly silently prayed he'd come back.

Chapter 10

It had never been part of Frankie Taylor's life plan to open and run a café. When she and Joe had moved to Briarwood almost twenty years ago, nothing could have been further from her mind and no one had ever heard of a sitcom called *Next to You*.

When they'd first viewed Ormond House, the previous occupiers had moved out several months earlier and the property had been rented out and used in the interim by a small independent TV production company as the location for a new show. With no money to spare and zero experience in the industry, operations were carried out on a shoestring and with no expectations of success. All was chaos for a while as six thirty-minute episodes were shot in and around the house in record time, then everyone left as suddenly as they'd arrived and village life returned to normal as if they'd never been there.

Frankie and Joe had bought the house and thought no more of it, until fourteen months later when the series finally aired on TV. *Next to You* featured a middle-aged Catholic priest, the lovely widowed lady next door, her batty-but-glamorous mother and a billy goat called Bert. It had touches of surrealism, gentle quirky humour in spades and the kind of can't-be-manufactured charisma between the lead characters that instantly captivated the nation. Against all the odds, everyone who watched the show fell under its magical spell; it was the ultimate *will-they, wont-they, but-they-CAN'T* scenario. Another series was immediately commissioned and this time Frankie and Joe, along with new arrival Amber, were moved out of the house for the duration of filming and put up in the nearby Colworth Manor Hotel. Which had been no hardship at all.

When it was shown on TV, the second series eclipsed the first. *Next to You* became a phenomenon, it was funnier than ever and the unacknowledged attraction between the two lead characters, Mags and Charles, tugged at the heartstrings like never before. Rumours began to circulate that the pair might be romantically involved in real life, but this was denied by the two actors themselves. Despite both being single and available, William Kingscott and Hope Johnson weren't publicity seekers and preferred to keep their private lives private.

But it was what everyone thought.

Then, less than a week before the final episode was due to be aired and at the height of the excitement surrounding the record-breaking second series, William Kingscott was hit by an out-of-control articulated lorry.

He was killed outright.

The country plunged into a state of shock; in the space of two years William had made the leap from unknown actor to national treasure. The last episode was shown on the evening of his funeral and viewing figures broke all records. The accident may have happened hundreds of miles away in Edinburgh but, in Briarwood, Frankie and Joe found their home turned into a shrine as weeping fans congregated and left flowers in front of the house.

The creator of the series announced that there would be no

replacement for William's character and no further episodes of *Next to You*. The show was over; Mags and Charles were no more. Hope Johnson never did speak publicly about her relationship with her co-star; she retired from acting and public view, becoming a recluse instead.

And the visitors to Briarwood stopped sobbing and leaving flowers, but their fascination with Ormond House remained. Over the years, *Next to You* became an acknowledged classic and embedded itself into the national consciousness. As cable channels multiplied, it continued to be shown, its popularity spreading worldwide. Visitors to England made pilgrimages to the village, took endless photographs of each other in front of the famous house and rang the doorbell to ask if they could come and look around inside.

They were always so sweet and polite, and Frankie was so soft-hearted she found it hard to refuse their requests. But it was a time-consuming business. Plus, in the show's second series, Mags had turned part of her home into a café as a money-making exercise; the visitors always wanted to know where the café was and were invariably disappointed to discover it didn't exist.

Frankie finally gave in and opened the café herself. It wasn't cashing in, it was fulfilling a need. By this time Amber was five and had started school, so it gave her something to do and meant she now actively welcomed the tourists rather than putting on a brave face and wishing they'd leave her alone.

And now, twelve years on, the visitors continued to come and here she was, still running the café. The décor was kept as it had been on TV and one wall was covered with photographs and memorabilia from the show. Opening hours were a nicely manageable eleven till four, sometimes later during the summer months if a coach party turned up. On the TV show, the sign outside said Mag's Café. Hers said Frankie's Café. It kept her busy. She enjoyed the chatter and the company, particularly with Joe working away as much as he did; as regional sales manager for a clothing firm he covered the whole of the south of England and spent a lot of time on the road.

'That bloody animal.' Coming into the café to say his goodbyes, Joe shook his head in mock despair. 'Just tried to eat my shirtsleeve.'

He had a long-running love-hate relationship with Young Bert, the family goat who spent his days tethered to a long rope in the garden and adored having his photo taken with tourists. When he wasn't trying to shred their clothes.

'That's because he loves you and doesn't want you to leave.' Frankie came out from behind the counter, smoothed down a wayward bit of brown hair at the crown of his head and gave him a hug. 'If I thought it would help, I'd do it too.'

'And that'd be a shame, seeing as you're the one who chose this shirt. Anyway,' Joe kissed her on the mouth. 'Won't be long. Back tomorrow evening. Behave yourself while I'm away.'

'You too.' It was a standing joke between them. Frankie told everyone the only reason they were still married was because Joe spent two or three nights a week away from home. *Absence makes the heart grow fonder* . . .

'Ew, *kissing*.' The café wasn't open yet but Molly had let herself in anyway. 'Hasn't anyone told you you're too old for all that smushy stuff?'

'You're right. It's disgusting. Shame on us.' Grinning, Joe kissed Frankie again. 'And all this canoodling means I'm going to be late. Better get going. See you tomorrow night.' One last hug and he was off. 'Bye, Moll, you two have fun without me.'

'Too right we will,' said Molly. 'There's male strippers at the Swan tonight.'

When Joe had left, Frankie said, 'Is there?'

'Sadly not. Unless hairy Phil has too much cider and gets his kit off.' They both paused and grimaced at this horrible thought. 'Anyway,' Molly was evidently keen to change the subject, 'I met my mystery neighbour again last night.'

'The one who bought Gin Cottage?' Ooh, this was interesting; Frankie hadn't seen him yet. 'What happened?'

'Well, he ended up staying the night. Not like *that*,' Molly added as Frankie's mouth fell open. 'Actually, it's really sad. His sister's just died and her baby's only eight months old. There isn't anyone else to look after her and Dex is the guardian but he says he can't do it. The thing is, he's in shock at the moment. I thought maybe you could have a chat with him about it.'

'How awful. Of course I will, if he wants to talk to me.' Just as running a café had never been one of Frankie's master plans, neither had becoming Briarwood's unofficial agony aunt. But somehow it had just happened; without ever meaning to, she'd become the kind of person other people felt the need to confide in. They told her their problems and she helped them find solutions. She was good at listening and apparently had a sympathetic face.

'He's not there at the moment,' said Molly. 'He fell asleep on my sofa last night. When I came down this morning he was gone. He's either driven to the supermarket to pick up food or disappeared back to London. But if he's still here, I'll tell him to come over and . . . aahh . . . aahh . . . *aah-choo*!' In the run-up to the sneeze Molly just had time to rummage in the pockets of her Barbour and whisk out a Kleenex. Something small and metallic flew out with it, skittering across the kitchen table. Frankie picked up the tiny charm and examined it.

'That's really pretty. Mind you don't lose it.'

'What is it? Let me see?' Molly frowned and held out her hand.

'It's a frog on a spade.'

'I've never seen it before! It's not mine!'

'Well, it definitely just came out of your pocket,' said Frankie.

'How weird. I don't know how it could have got there. Mystery.'

'Has someone else worn your coat?'

'No.' Molly studied the charm closely. 'And look, he's so cute. All I can think is that someone found it on the ground some-where and thought it was mine. I'll ask around. Except they wouldn't have just put it in my pocket, would they? Not without saying something.'

'You could mention it to Lois in the pub, see if anyone's lost it.' Frankie checked her watch. 'Oh crikey, look at the time, I'd better get a move on.'

'Me too. I've still got last night's work to catch up with.' Heading for the door, Molly said, 'If Dexter wants to talk to you, I'll give you a call.'

But by the evening there was still no sign of the garish yellow Porsche; Molly's next-door neighbour had evidently returned to London to sort out his problems himself. And when they asked around the village, no one knew anything about the little gold frog on the spade either; there were no clues as to where it had come from.

Chapter 11

Laura's house in Islington — the terraced house they'd both grown up in — might still be filled with her belongings but it felt indescribably empty. Dex felt as if he were trapped in a nightmare from which it was impossible to wake up. Each time the realisation hit him again, he just wanted to say, 'OK, enough now, please make it stop.'

It seemed unbelievable to try and take in the fact that it never would.

He made his way on autopilot through the familiar rooms. It was the social worker who had suggested he came here and collected up anything he thought Delphi would like to have with her while she was in the care of the foster family. Not that he had any idea what she might want or need. So far he'd thrown assorted baby clothes and soft toys into a holdall without knowing if she liked them or not. There was one small squishy yellow duckling that made plaintive quacking noises when you jiggled it — he'd seen her playing with that one over Christmas — but otherwise all he could do was guess.

Which was shameful. Poor Delphi, as if it wasn't tragic enough that she'd lost her mother, all she was left with now was some useless uncle who didn't even know which were her favourite toys.

Also, was she missing Laura? Of course she must be. But had she sensed that something this terrible had happened? According to the social worker, Delphi was fairly quiet and at times appeared to be bewilderedly searching for a face that wasn't there. There'd been a couple of bouts of crying but otherwise she seemed happy enough; surrounded by care and affection as she was, she seemed to be coping well with her new foster family. Dex didn't know how this made him feel; should he be reassured by her ability to adapt? He couldn't bear to think she might be feeling – in her helpless baby way – as bereft as he was.

Dex paused in the nursery to look out of the window. There was Laura's car parked outside, the red Escort she'd been so proud of, even though it was years old. Another fresh wave of grief hit him as he realised he would have to deal with sorting out all her belongings. *Oh God, Laura, I don't want to do this, it's time for you to come back and take charge again* . . .

The doorbell shrilled downstairs, jangling his nerves still further and making him think – just for a wild moment – that maybe this was Laura, ringing the bell because she'd forgotten her key.

Dex hurried down the staircase with the holdall and pulled open the front door.

'Oh hello, dear, haven't seen you for a *long* time!' It was Phyllis, who had lived in the house next door for the last fifty years. Her white hair was like dandelion fluff around her wizened face. 'Is Laura here, dear? Only I asked her to buy me some second-class stamps the other day, but she hasn't brought them round yet and I need to pay my electricity bill.'

He couldn't tell her on the doorstep. Dex found himself having to invite Phyllis into the house and make her a cup of tea before finally breaking the awful news. It was almost unbearable, being the one to make an eighty-year-old woman cry.

'Oh my word, oh no, I can't bear it. Such a lovely, lovely girl.' Phyllis's gnarled fingers trembled as she pulled a hanky out of the sleeve of her cardigan and wiped her faded eyes. 'And Delphi, that poor little angel. Whatever's going to happen to her now?'

'You OK?' Henry, in his habitually crumpled grey suit, was looking concerned.

'What do you think?' It was midday and Dexter wasn't dressed. He hadn't been asleep when the buzzer had gone but he'd still been in bed. Now, having dragged on a pair of jeans, he rubbed his hands over his bare chest and wearily indicated the kitchen. 'Help yourself if you want anything. What's up?'

They'd worked together for years and over that time had become friends of the odd-couple kind. At the age of thirty-seven, Henry Baron was a classic case of not judging a book by its cover. At six foot five and muscled to the hilt, he attracted attention wherever he went, chiefly from women enthralled by his resemblance to the actor Idris Elba, particularly if Idris Elba happened to be playing the part of a renegade boxer who had never been to school and had battled his way through life with his fists.

In fact, and it had taken Dexter some time to discover this, Henry had been bullied at his tough inner-London school for being highly intelligent and refusing to fight. He'd eventually graduated from university with a first in Maths, was terrified of predatory women and had battled to overcome a stammer all his life.

As a rule, he made a good job of it.

But, unlike the rest of the team at work, Henry was quiet, domesticated, conscientious and . . . well, kind. He was a gentle giant, a good bloke. Which, right now, was the very last thing Dex needed.

Dammit, he didn't want anyone else making him cry.

'You haven't been into work,' Henry was saying now. 'And your phone's been switched off. We were worried about you.'

Of course they were. 'Don't worry.' Dex shrugged. 'I'm still alive.'

'How did it go yesterday? Sorry,' said Henry with a grimace. 'Dumb question.'

Dexter exhaled slowly. The funeral had been every bit as horrific as expected. But it was over now. He and Laura's friends had said their final goodbyes to her and afterwards there had been a certain sense of closure. For the rest of them, if not for him.

'It was awful. Everyone was crying, saying what a tragedy it was for Delphi. Then they asked me what was going to happen to her and I said I hadn't decided yet but she was being looked after by a foster family. And they all told me it was the best place for her, she'd be fine, there were loads of families out there who'd love to adopt Delphi and give her a wonderful life, because obviously I couldn't do that myself.' Dex paused and massaged his aching temples. 'So then it started to get me mad and I asked them why I *obviously* couldn't do it, and they came out with all these reasons . . . *excuses* . . . and it was everything I'd been telling myself for the last week, plus it made sense, but there's one thing I can't stop thinking about.' He was on a roll now, all the thoughts that had been churning around in his brain tumbling out. 'She chose me, Henry. Laura chose *me* to be Delphi's guardian. If I don't do it, I'll be letting her down. So I said this to her friends after the funeral and you should have seen the looks on their faces. When I said maybe I could take Delphi on, they were just humouring me. It was like I was a kid announcing that I was going to play football for England when I grow up.'

'So basically they're right,' said Henry, 'and you know they're right. But you don't like hearing other people say it.'

And now Henry was joining in, taking their side. For fuck's sake. Dex said, 'If I want to do this thing, I can.'

'Hey, don't get mad with me. I'm just being honest.' Henry raised his hands. 'You wouldn't be able to cope.'

'I could if I had to.'

'It just isn't you.'

'So you're basically telling me I'm too selfish and shallow.'

'I'm not,' Henry said mildly. 'But as someone with a psychology A level, I can tell you that what you're actually doing there is describing the way you view yourself.'

'Henry, fuck off.' *It was exactly how he'd described himself last week when he'd been talking to that girl down in Briarwood.*

'I'm trying to help,' said Henry. 'The thing is, you don't have to feel guilty and beat yourself up about it. Some people are cut out for this sort of thing, and some aren't.'

'And I'm not.'

'Exactly. Apart from anything else, you work sixty hours a week.'

'I'd get a nanny.'

'You'd need two nannies. One for when you're working, one for when you're out on the town.'

'Fine, I'll do that.'

'And then you'd start sleeping with one of the nannies and the other one would get jealous. Then after a huge fight they'd both walk out and you'd have to turn up at work with Delphi strapped to your chest in one of those sling things . . .'

'They sent you over here to find out when I'd be back,' Dexter interrupted. 'Didn't they?'

Henry nodded. 'Yes.'

'They don't give a stuff about me, do they?'

'Well, they *do* . . .'

'Because they need me there to put deals together, schmooze the clients, work like fuck and make shedloads of money for them.'

'You make plenty for yourself too,' Henry pointed out reasonably.

Dexter, who wasn't in the mood for being reasonable, made up his mind in that split second. He took a bottle of Perrier out of the fridge and drank some. When he'd finished he said steadily, 'Tell them I'm not coming back. I quit. As of now.'

Henry sighed. 'You don't mean that.'

'Oh yes I do. There are more important things in life.' All the guilt and indecision slid away as he said the words. *This feels fantastic.*

'OK, now listen. This isn't like deciding to pick up a takeaway,' said Henry. 'You can't just turn up and announce to these fostering people that you're going to be taking Delphi home with you.'

'I know that.' Dex's neck prickled with panic. He hadn't known that.

'They don't give out other people's children to just anyone,' Henry went on. 'You have to prove you're up to the job.'

'Shit. How?' And why was Henry choosing today of all days to give him such a hard time?

A glimmer of a smile appeared around Henry's mouth. 'Well, probably by not swearing so bloody much for a start.'

'I think you've got yourself a fan,' said Molly.

'What?' Amber, who helped out in the café on Saturdays when it was busier, was energetically wiping down the next table.

'That boy over there. I've been watching him. He's keeping an eye on you.'

'Hm. Not my type.' At seventeen, Amber's interest was currently captured by skinny tattooed types with long hair and a taste for heavy rock. Evidently amused that Molly would think she might be remotely attracted to this one, she said, 'Too clean for me.'

He did look a bit as if he should be starring in a toothpaste ad. He was the kind of groomed, handsome lad any mother would want their daughter to bring home. Sadly, whenever Amber brought her boyfriends back to Ormond House, the only thing Frankie wanted to do was throw them fully clothed into a hot Dettol bath.

Amber headed through to the kitchen and Molly carried on working; for a change of scenery she liked coming over to the café to sketch out ideas for the next instalment of Boogie and Boo.

Ten minutes later the perfect punchline came to her and she broke into a smile of relief, looking up and startling the clean-cut boy who'd been watching her.

'Sorry!' Molly flapped her free hand by way of apology. 'It's OK, don't be scared, I'm not smiling at you.'

'That's all right. I wondered what you were doing.' He had a nice voice and an easy manner. 'You're drawing something, but I don't know what.'

'Comic strip.' She briefly held up the sketch pad.

'Really? Can I see?' When Molly nodded he came over to her table and had a look at what she'd done. 'Hey, that's Boogie and Boo. You're good.' He peered more closely at her sketches. 'That's almost as good as the real ones. You should let the artist know, so if he's ever off sick you could be his stand-in.'

'Thanks.' Molly, who always signed her work as M. Hayes, kept a straight face. 'Actually, the artist is me.'

'Oh God, I'm sorry.' His cheeks coloured up and he looked mortified.

'Hey, it's fine. You'd only have to be embarrassed if you'd just said I was rubbish. Everyone loves a bit of praise.'

'Well, I'm sorry anyway, but that's really brilliant. I love Boogie and Boo.' His brown hair flopped forward as he leaned down for another look. 'I wish I could draw like that.'

Molly didn't make a habit of touting for custom, but seeing as he'd mentioned it. 'If you're interested, I run evening classes.'

'You do? Cool. Where?'

'Right here.'

'Oh.' The boy looked torn.

'Monday evenings. It's good fun. Amber?' Twisting round in her seat, she called over, 'Are there any of my business cards behind the counter?'

The boy tensed up at the sound of Amber's name then pretended not to pay attention as she rummaged in the drawer next to the till.

'Yes, still a few left. Do you want one?'

'Please.' Molly nodded at the boy. 'There you are, she's found one for you. Why don't you go and get it from her?'

The boy headed over to the counter and mumbled, 'Thanks,' as he took the card from Amber.

So sweet.

'Whereabouts do you live?' said Molly helpfully.

'Um . . . not far from here.'

'Well, if you want to come along, you know where to find us. Mondays, seven till nine.'

'Right. OK. Well, I'd better be off now.' Still unable to look

Amber in the eye, he drained his black coffee and flashed a brief smile at Molly as he tucked the card into his jeans pocket. 'Thanks for this.'

'You're welcome. And Amber quite often joins us too. It's not all boring grown-ups. Maybe we'll see you next week,' said Molly. Well, a little matchmaking never went amiss, did it? Frankie would be overjoyed if Amber started seeing someone who didn't sport a dizzying selection of piercings and tattoos.

'Nice try,' said Amber, watching through the window as the boy headed off on foot down the high street. 'But I still don't fancy him.'

'He seems so charming.' OK, she *knew* that was the ultimate kiss-of-death thing to say.

Amber rolled her eyes. 'And that's why I never will.'

Chapter 12

Dex was shattered. Henry hadn't been kidding about social services; they didn't just hand out small children willy-nilly. Instead they asked hundreds of questions, made pages and pages of notes, filled in *many* complicated forms and drank the countless cups of tea he made for them in his gleaming, space-age kitchen.

Were they secretly marking him out of ten on his tea-making skills too?

Some of the social workers had been jolly pretty, but Dex sensed he should reign in his natural inclination to flirt. Taking responsibility for a nine-month-old baby was a serious matter and they needed to be convinced he was up to the task. Accordingly, he was giving an excellent impression of a serious and completely responsible adult.

Apart from when they'd asked how he'd cope with Delphi and a pushchair if all the lifts in the apartment building happened to be broken and he'd said, 'Maybe tie her to a bungee rope?'

But other than that he thought he was managing to acquit himself pretty well. And they were nice people, that was the thing; on his side and keen to do all they could to help. They even took it in their stride when they discovered the oven was full of crockery and Dex was forced to admit he didn't know how to switch it on.

When in doubt, eat out. That had always been his motto, and it had served him well.

'You won't be able to take Delphi out to the Ivy every night,' the younger social worker, Jen, had teased him.

Which was an alarming thought, although Dex thought he probably could. Children weren't actually banned from restaurants, were they? Train them up from a young age, surely, and they'd be OK.

He had to stretch the truth on a few occasions of course. It hadn't occurred to him that he'd be asked to provide character references from three different people who'd known him for at least five years. Luckily that excluded most of the girls he'd dated, who might have been less than complimentary about him if they'd been asked. He'd gone for Henry in the end, and a kind-hearted married friend who could always be relied upon to say nice things. The third reference had come from Phyllis, the dear old lady who had lived next door to Laura and liked to bake cakes for Dex, who in her mind was still the cheery helpful boy who had walked her dog for pocket money as a teenager. She'd got a bit flustered at the prospect of constructing a reference so he'd ended up having to dictate the words himself.

Well, didn't everyone like to portray themselves in a flattering light?

But, bit by bit, it was all beginning to come together. The requisite hoops had been jumped through, hurdles were steadily being overcome. As the weeks passed, what had initially seemed impossible was now actually starting to take shape. Having already walked out of his job, the days took on a holidayish glow. Delphi was still being cared for by the foster family in Islington and was palpably happy there; visiting her and being recognised made his heart expand every time. When her face lit up at the sight of him, Dex knew he was doing the right thing.

And when she drank too much milk too quickly and it made an untimely reappearance down the front of his shirt . . . well, he was still doing the right thing. It wasn't Delphi's fault the shirt was Ozwald Boateng.

It wasn't her fault her mother had died either. Thankfully, she was blissfully unaware of what had happened, at least for now.

Dex knew he'd made an impulsive decision that would change his life for good. One minute he was excited, the next minute terrified by the enormity of what he was taking on. But he couldn't back down now. This was what Laura had wanted.

Well, obviously it wasn't what she had *wanted*; she'd have far preferred to have carried on living and bringing her daughter up herself. But since that wasn't possible, he was just going to have to step up and learn how to be second best.

And no one could say he wasn't making sacrifices along the way. When eyebrows had been raised at the sight of him pulling up outside the foster family's house in the canary-yellow Porsche, Dex had said at once, 'Don't worry, I'm selling it.'

Mel, the social worker facilitating the initial meeting, had been visibly relieved. 'I think that's probably a sensible plan. Get yourself something a bit more appropriate.'

'I will.' Dex had nodded in agreement. 'I've always wanted a Ferrari Testarossa.'

But Mel, who was getting wise to him now, just said good-naturedly, 'How about a nice Fiat Panda?'

That had been a fortnight ago. He hadn't sold the Porsche yet but he would. Today his apartment was being checked over from a health and safety perspective. He was entering a world of fridge locks, electric-socket covers and unclimbable stair gates.

The intercom went and Dex pressed the button. 'Hi, is that Mel?'

'No it isn't, it's someone much nicer than that! Hey, babes, it's Bibi!'

Who? Oh God, the one with the boobs. From that fateful night.

'How did you know where I live?' He frowned.

'Just clever.' She giggled. 'Actually, I bumped into your friend Kenny from the party, said I needed to contact you again urgently, so he gave me your address. Can I come in?'

'Not really. I'm expecting a visitor. What's so urgent?'

'It'sh a shecret!'

OK, that was a definite slur. From the sound of it, Bibi had been enjoying a long and liquid lunch.

'Maybe some other time,' said Dex. *Like, never.*

'No no no, I need to see you now! Let me in,' Bibi wheedled. 'Pleeeeease?'

'Look, it's really not convenient.'

'Fine then, but I'm not going anywhere. I'll just wait here until you change your mind.'

Oh God. 'Hang on, I'm coming down.'

Stepping out of the lift on the ground floor, Dex's plan was to get rid of his unwelcome visitor as quickly as possible.

Unfortunately, Bibi had other ideas.

Even more unfortunately, Mel had arrived and had evidently just pressed the buzzer for his flat. As Dex made his way across the grey marble hallway he could see Bibi through the glass doors, talking to her. Whilst clutching a bottle of champagne . . .

'Hi, Dex! Oooh, it's so lovely to see you again!' Launching herself at him, Bibi kissed him noisily on the mouth sink-plunger style and clanked the bottle against the glass door as it tried to swing shut. 'It's OK, don't worry, I asked this one if she's your new girlfriend and she said she definitely isn't. So I did check. Mind you, she isn't your type at *all*.' Lowering her voice by one decibel, she added, 'Have you seen the shoes? Sooo frumpy.'

'Bibi, you can't come in. I have an important meeting with—'

'Hang on, hang on, just hear me out. The thing is, you don't know what you've done to me!' Shaking her head and exhaling alcohol fumes all over him, Bibi said, 'Since you left that night I haven't been able to forget you, Dex. You know how sometimes you meet someone and you just *know*? That's what it's like in here!' She clapped her hands dramatically to her chest. 'I just knew! And that other girl was being such a cow before, you didn't have the chance to appreciate me, so we need to start again, properly this time.'

'Mel, I'm sorry about this.' Dex grimaced apologetically at her.

'No problem at all.' Mel had her professional nothing-shocks-me face on.

'See?' Bibi clapped her on the shoulder. 'I knew you wouldn't mind! It's like one of those romantic movies, isn't it? Sometimes you just have to seize that moment and tell the man how you feel about him. Or you end up missing out! Can we go up to your flat now?'

'No,' Dex said firmly.

'Oh pleeease, just for a bit, I'm bursting for the loo!'

'Look, I really can't—'

'Dex, I'm desperate! I'm not going anywhere till you let me in. And if you leave me down here,' Bibi's voice rose and her eyes widened, 'I swear to God I'll wee on the *floor*.'

'I think we'd better let her in, Dex.' Mel's voice was calm. 'Don't you?'

Were the black marks stacking up against him? Behind that calm exterior, what was going through Mel's mind?

As they travelled up in the lift, Bibi said to Mel, 'You know what? If you did something with yourself you could be quite pretty.'

Mel replied gravely, 'Thanks.'

The moment Bibi had disappeared into the bathroom, Dex said, 'I'm so sorry. I only met her once. She's not my girlfriend. I can't believe she turned up like this.'

Needless to say, in answer to all the questions put to him by Mel and the rest of the fostering and adoption team he had passed himself off as altogether more sensible and sedate in his social life than the picture that was currently being painted. This was bad news. Plus, he was going to kill Kenny for giving Bibi his address.

'Don't worry,' said Mel. 'I'll put the kettle on.'

Never mind the kettle. Where was the Scotch?

'Ooh, that's better!' Bibi was back in record time, tottering into the kitchen adjusting her short skirt and putting away her lip gloss. *Seriously, how attractive was it to slather your mouth with a thick jammy coat of fluorescent pink gloop?*

'We do have an important meeting.' Dex indicated Mel. 'You'll have to go now.'

'He's a terror.' Blithely ignoring him, Bibi popped the cork off the champagne and beamed at Mel. 'He loves my boobs, you know. Just *loves* them.'

'No I don't,' Dex said quickly.

'Yes you do! And I knew he was a naughty boy. I mean, at the party, there were three of us fighting over him. It was crazy! But like I said, when you meet the right one, you don't let him get away. Even if he does have the naughtiest reputation on the planet!'

Dex's heart sank. 'I don't have a reputation.' He shook his head at Mel. 'She's making this up.'

'Your friend Kenny says you do. He told me you've slept with practically every girl in London. Hey, don't look so worried, that's not a bad thing!' Bibi rushed to reassure him. 'It means you've had loads of practice so now you're really good at it.'

He finally got rid of her, but not before she'd glugged half the Bollinger straight from the bottle and offered to come back later for a night of fun he'd never forget. Her parting shot to Mel was, 'Seriously, babe, a bit of Restylane injected into the soles of your feet and you'll be up on your Louboutins in no time! Give it a try and I promise you'll never look back!'

'Sorry,' said Dex when she'd gone.

'No worries.' Mel smiled briefly. Which would have been more reassuring if she weren't also scribbling something in her notebook. She closed it before he could see what she'd written.

'I had to say I'd give her a call. It was the only way to get rid of her. But I won't be doing it.'

'Right.' She nodded. 'Can I ask you something? The comment about you having slept with most of the girls in London . . . ?'

'I haven't. Of course I haven't. Just . . . you know, a few.' Dex paused; when Mel looked at you in that way it was kind of daunting, like being hypnotised into telling the truth.

And he definitely couldn't do *that*.

'A few?' Her tone was deceptively mild.

'Well, maybe a bit more than a few.' The back of his neck was starting to prickle with alarm; was she about to demand an actual number?

'Dex, relax. I'm not an ogre. I just hope you understand that certain aspects of your life will have to change if this placement goes ahead. I'm not here to lecture you, but I'm sure you appreciate what I'm trying to say.'

'I do.' He nodded and fiddled with the cuff of his shirt.

'As you know,' Mel continued patiently, 'when it comes to potential kinship carers, their marital status is irrelevant. We don't discriminate against single carers. But you have to consider the child, Dex. Delphi does need a stable home. Imagine how confusing it would be for her if there were an endless stream of ladies spending the night here at the flat.'

'There won't be. That isn't going to happen.' Dex knew he had to say it and mean it. 'There won't be anyone staying here, ever. I promise.'

And Mel didn't believe him, he could see that in her eyes.

'Well, I'm sure you understand the point I'm trying to put across.' She paused to make a couple of other entries in her notebook. 'Now, the other question I was going to ask today is about the kind of general support you'll be needing.'

Under the circumstances, he probably shouldn't make any truss jokes.

'You said if I was ever stuck I could always give you a call and ask you anything,' said Dex. The chances were that he'd be doing this a *lot*.

'Of course you can speak to us, but I'm thinking more of your situation here.' Mel made a circling gesture to indicate the apartment. 'How well do you get on with your neighbours, for example? In an emergency situation could you call on them for practical help?'

OK, this was definitely where he was meant to say yes. Whereas in all honesty the answer was no. The apartment to the left of him was occupied by a high-class hooker, the one on the right by a high court judge. Sometimes the judge paid late-night visits to the hooker, but Dex thought he was probably the only person aware of this. Anyway, neither of them would be ideal if he were to find himself in need of assistance with a baby-related crisis.

'Possibly.' He spoke with caution; the apartment building might be luxurious and expensive but it wasn't the kind of place that encouraged the occupants to become friendly – well, other than in your standard judge-and-hooker way. Maybe he should start knocking on doors and introducing himself to everyone, audition them as potential helper-outers.

'Because it makes a big difference, you know. Having people you can rely on. Good neighbours,' said Mel, 'are worth their weight in diamonds.' She looked over at Dex. 'What?'

It was like breathing in a scent that triggered a very particular memory. Dex stared out of the thirty-foot-wide window at the panoramic view spread before them; ultra-modern London, the steel-grey water of Canary Wharf, preoccupied city people scurrying along like insects, living anonymous busy lives.

Neighbours.

That's what neighbours are for.

You're welcome, no problem, anything I can do to help.

Aloud he said, 'Is a flat like this a good place to bring up a baby?'

I could do it, I could move to Briarwood.

'Dex, please don't worry. It's fine. There's absolutely no reason why you can't raise a child in this apartment.'

He nodded, still lost in thought. *I really could move. We don't have to stay here.*

'Are you OK, Dex? Everything all right?' Mel was starting to look concerned.

'Everything's fine.' Dex broke into a broad smile of relief. It was the answer, the absolute right thing to do. A fresh start, that was what he and Delphi needed; away from temptation, away from his old hedonistic life and disreputable ways.

The only mystery was why it hadn't occurred to him before.

Chapter 13

The thing about spending ages hunched on a stool over an angled drawing board was the havoc it played with your neck and shoulders. But when you were concentrating hard on getting your work perfect and it was all going well, you tended not to notice until it was too late.

Like now.

Molly put down her black pen, arched her back, stretched her arms and reached for her iPod. Time for a little dance to relax all those scrunched-up muscles. It had been a productive morning's work though. Two strips of Boogie and Boo completed in four hours and a new idea was already incubating for the next. Today was definitely a good day. Plugging in her earphones and turning the volume up far too loud, she hopped down from her stool and stepped away from the drawing board. Oh yes, brilliant song, perfect . . . *here we go* . . .

'So this is it,' said Dex. 'We're here, this is our new home. What do you think?'

Delphi, in his arms, took her fingers out of her mouth and said, 'Bbbbbrrrrrrrr.'

'Thank you.' He stuck his tongue out at her as she wiped her wet fingers messily down the side of his face. Who would have thought, before Delphi had come into his life, that this was something he would ever allow another living being to do? But somehow it wasn't as repulsive as you'd imagine. Or maybe when you loved the other person this much, it just didn't matter.

When she beamed gummily at him and made a grab for his left ear, Dex pretended to bite her hand. Delphi shrieked with delight and buried her face against his chest. Breathing in the baby smell of the top of her head, he kissed her downy dark hair. Six weeks ago, Laura had died. Yesterday he had attended the Regulation 38 Panel meeting and been granted kinship care of his niece Delphi Yates. After all the panic and worry that they would find him hopelessly unsuitable and laugh him off the premises, the waiting was over. Delphi had left her emergency foster family and was now in his care. It was terrifying and daunting, but at the same time kind of wonderful.

'Bbbbrrrrrrhhh.' She was now blowing raspberries against the front of his shirt. 'Bbbbbbbbbbbbbbrrrrrgh!'

Dex could feel the wet warmth sinking through the cotton; for such a small person, she certainly produced a lot of saliva. He checked his watch; it was one o'clock and their visitor was due at three.

'Come on then, you. First things first.' He lifted Delphi into the air and swooped her over his head, ducking in the nick of time as a ribbon of silver drool swung from her bottom lip. 'Favours to ask.'

'*Bah!*' shouted Delphi.

Aware that there were no florist's shops in Briarwood, Dex had picked up the bouquet from the fancy one close to his apartment building in Canary Wharf. In smart areas of London, you knew flowers had cost a fortune if they came tied up with a bit of old frayed string. As he made his way up the path with Delphi on his hip, Dex hoped that here in genuinely rustic Briarwood it didn't make you look like a cheapskate.

Molly's car was parked outside the cottage and the downstairs windows were open, so she must be in. This was good news. He rang the bell and waited.

Nothing.

Dexter rang the bell again.

More nothing.

Did people around here really leave their windows wide open when they went out? Surprised, he moved across and peered into the living room . . .

Ha, mystery solved.

There she was, with her streaky blond hair loosely pinned up, wearing a blue and white striped rugby shirt, knee-length white leggings and fluffy orange ankle socks. She had her back to the window and was dancing to music only she could hear.

Dex grinned. What was that expression: dance as if no one's watching? Molly was certainly doing that. Even better, when people were listening to music through their headphones, you generally couldn't tell what they were dancing to, but thanks to the arm gestures he knew exactly what was causing her to jig around like a hyperactive baboon.

Y . . . M . . . C . . . A . . .

Rather endearingly, she also kept getting her letters mixed up.

Y . . . C . . . M . . . A . . . As her arms this time made the correct shapes, Dex sang along in his head.

Enjoying the show, Delphi gazed intently at the exuberant display.

Y . . . M . . . C . . . *Whoops.* Having spun around in mid-star jump, Molly screeched to an emergency stop and did a cartoon squawk of horror. She ripped the wires from her ears and froze, clutching her throat and visibly hyperventilating.

'Klaaaaaah!' Delphi, who didn't like it one bit when entertainment ended prematurely, clapped her hands together like a maestro ordering the show to recommence.

'Sorry,' said Dex through the open window. 'I tried ringing the bell a few times but you didn't hear it.'

'That would be because I was too busy making an almighty prat of myself. OK, give me a moment to calm down.' Molly pressed her hands to her flaming cheeks; the next moment her attention was caught by the bundle in his arms and she broke into a slow smile. 'Is this her? Delphi?'

Dex nodded, touched she'd remembered the name. 'It is.'

'OK, wait there.' Molly disappeared from the living room. Moments later she flung open the front door. 'Come on in. I thought we'd never see you again. And look at *you*, you're so beautiful!' This last bit wasn't directed at him; she was stroking Delphi's face and tickling her under the chin to make her laugh. 'Hello, sweetie pie, aren't you gorgeous? Look at your eyes!' Turning to Dex, she said, 'They're just like yours. So what's this then, a day trip? How often are you allowed to see her?'

He followed her into the kitchen. 'First things first. These are for you.' Producing the flowers from their half-hidden position behind his back, Dex said, 'Sorry it's a bit late but thanks for everything.'

'Don't be daft.' He liked the way she batted away the gratitude. 'Anyone would have done the same.'

'But it was you. And you let me talk things through for hours. You were amazing and I just left the next morning without a word. Bloody rude.'

Molly took the bouquet from him. 'You were in shock. It's allowed.'

'Still, thank you again. I'm not usually that bad.' He watched her tickle Delphi's ear with one of the flowers, liking the way she concentrated all her attention on Delphi rather than him.

'You mean when you spend the night at a girl's place you usually say goodbye before racing out of their lives forever?'

'Something like that.' He liked her sense of humour too.

'The last few weeks must have been pretty horrific.' Her expression grew serious. 'How are you coping?'

Dex shrugged. 'Not so bad. The funeral was an ordeal but it's sunk in now. And I'm not crying any more, you'll be relieved to hear.'

'Don't worry about it. Crying's normal.'

'Not for me it isn't. I hadn't cried since I was seven when my hamster died.' Dex grimaced. 'And that was pretty embarrassing.'

'Oh, come on, how could it be? You were only seven!'

'My teacher at school told me my hamster had gone to heaven so I climbed a tree,' said Dex, 'to see if I could see it from up there. Then the teacher yelled at me and I fell out of the tree and broke my arm. It bloody hurt. I cried. Some of the other kids laughed.' Deadpan, he went on, 'I never cried again after that.'

'It's enough to mentally scar any seven year old for life.' Molly nodded in solemn agreement. 'And how's Delphi doing?'

'She's fine, just as happy as before. It sounds terrible, but it's better that she isn't old enough to understand.'

'That's good.' Another sympathetic nod. 'And how often do you get to see her?'

'It's been three or four visits a week up till now.' Dex shifted Delphi from one hip to the other, love and pride welling up in his chest. 'As of yesterday, it's going to be pretty much non-stop.'

'You mean . . . what does that mean?' As it slowly sank in, Molly's eyes widened. 'Are you going to be looking after her *yourself*?'

'I am.'

'Full time?'

'Twenty-four seven. I know, I can hardly believe it myself. The six-week assessment was yesterday. They've approved me as a Reg 38 carer.' *Listen to him, spouting technical jargon he hadn't even known existed two months ago.* 'I'm actually in sole charge of a helpless human being.'

'Oh my God,' Molly exclaimed, 'that is so brilliant! You said you couldn't do it!'

'And I meant it. But you made me think that maybe I could.' He smiled briefly. 'Something else I need to thank you for.'

'OK, now I'm the one feeling stupid. I'm welling up.' Quickly wiping her eyes with the backs of her hands, Molly said, 'This is crazy, but I just feel so proud of you. And Laura would be so . . . *happy*. Tell me everything that's been happening. What do you have to do to prove you're capable? Do they test you on stuff?'

'Like you wouldn't believe. I'm a kinship carer. Loads of questions, loads of checks. But the social workers are fantastic, I can't tell you how brilliant they've been.'

'So does that mean you seduced them? Sorry.' Molly grinned at his look of mock outrage. 'But you're the one who told me what you were like.'

'*Were* being the operative word. Past tense. I've made a promise to the fostering team.' Dexter could feel Delphi's head growing heavy against his shoulder as she nodded off. 'And to myself too. From now on I'm going to be a reformed character. No more sleeping around, no more high life. This is the new me. I've learned how to change nappies. I've had a CRB check. I've been on training courses in home safety and first aid.'

'Wow.'

'I know. I swear, I'm *this* far from learning how to put together a lentil bake.'

'You have no idea how impressed I am,' said Molly. 'Good for you. Are you having a nanny to help out while you're at work?'

He shook his head. 'No. I've given up work.'

'Crikey.'

'I've left London too. Meet your new neighbours.'

'Are you *serious*?' Her eyes widened. 'You're really moving here?'

'I'm not often serious,' said Dex. 'But yes, that's what we're doing. You did say the natives are friendly.'

'Even friendlier when you aren't just visiting once every few months.'

'Anyway, seems like a good place to bring up small children.'

Molly nodded. 'It really is.'

'And the neighbours don't seem too weird.'

'Apart from when they're dancing around like idiots to Vill—' she stopped abruptly.

'It's OK, I knew it was Village People.' With his free arm, Dex did the left hand half of the gestures. 'Call me psychic, but I could just tell.'

'Now I'm even more embarrassed,' said Molly.

'No need. Out and proud. If anyone thinks less of you for liking "YMCA" . . . well, they're not worth bothering about.'

She dropped a mini curtsy. 'Anyway, welcome to Briarwood. Both of you. Even though one of you's unconscious.'

'Thanks.' He could feel the tiny puffs of Delphi's warm breath against his neck. 'I need to put her in her cot. Actually, the flowers weren't just a thank you, they were a bribe too. Are you around later this afternoon?'

'I can be, no problem. What do you need a hand with?'

See? Just like that. No suspicion, no hesitation, just a straightforward offer of help.

Chapter 14

'So you two have known each other for almost a year.' The social worker from the local fostering team was making notes as she inspected Gin Cottage. 'Since Dexter first came to the village.'

'That's right.' Molly nodded; well, it was technically true, even if they'd only met twice. The woman just needed to be reassured that in moving down to Briarwood, Dexter would be among friends; if he needed help with Delphi she would be happy to chip in.

The ballpoint pen hovered over the page. 'And are you . . . *very* close?'

Gah, how embarrassing. Molly shook her head violently. 'Oh God no, nothing like that!'

The social worker smiled. 'No need to sound so horrified. He's not that repulsive.'

'We're just friends,' Molly reiterated.

'I'm giving that side of things a miss.' Joining in, Dex said firmly, 'It's all there in my notes. From now on it's just going to be me and Delphi.'

Gin Cottage was approved, the social worker left and Molly stayed on to help Dex unpack the rest of his belongings from the car. Not the garish yellow Porsche either; that had gone, been replaced by a practical Mercedes Estate.

'Look at this.' Having lifted the pushchair out of the boot, Dex unfolded it and click-snapped the levers into place with a flourish.

Her mouth twitched. 'How long have you been practising that?'

He looked proud. 'For weeks.'

'Very good,' said Molly.

'I know. If I'd bumped into me in the street three months ago I wouldn't have recognised myself. I've turned into Mr Sensible.'

In his head, maybe. From the outside he was as raffishly good-looking as ever, exuding dangerous amounts of charisma.

Once they'd emptied the car and finished unpacking the boxes, Dex took a bottle of champagne from the fridge and said, 'Well, this is it, we're officially in our new home. I hope you're going to stay for a bit and help us celebrate.'

'If you were really Mr Sensible you'd have a cup of tea.' Molly hoped the man she'd just vouched for didn't have a raging alcohol problem.

Reading her mind, he said good-humouredly, 'Don't panic, new leaf and all that. From now on I'm never going to have more than one drink a night.'

'Crikey.'

'I know.'

'Is that going to be difficult?'

'Compared with changing hideous nappies it'll be a piece of cake. Anyway, it's just one of those things.' Dex shrugged. 'Drunk in charge of a baby wouldn't be a good look, would it? Has to be done.'

Delphi, in her dungarees, was crawling determinedly across the tiled floor towards him. Watching as he picked her up and swung her into the air, Molly listened to her shrieks of joy and saw the look of love on his face. 'And she's so worth it.'

'She is.' Dex nodded then said, 'I know what I haven't shown you yet. Remember the time you saw Laura down here with Delphi? She borrowed the house keys without telling me why. She said it was a late Christmas present but wouldn't tell me what it was. And I was too busy to come down and find out.' As he spoke, he led the way out of the blue and white kitchen and up the stairs. 'I don't know what I thought she'd got for me. Some kind of lampshade, I suppose. Or a bit of furniture too big to fit in the Porsche. But it wasn't, it was something much better.' They'd reached the landing now. He stopped midway along it.

'She bought you that? Oh *wow*.' Having followed the direction of his gaze, Molly studied the stained-glass window at the far end of the landing. 'It's amazing.'

'Brrraaahhhh!' said Delphi, dribbling happily.

'She *made* me that. Did the whole thing herself. Even knocked out the old window frame and fitted it, can you imagine?'

'That's even more amazing.'

No longer smiling, Dex reached out and touched the expertly puttied-in frame. 'She was brilliant at DIY. A million times better than me.'

'It's beautiful.' Molly meant it; the stained-glass scene depicted a tiered garden with trees, shrubs and butterflies and a small lily pond in the foreground.

'It's where we grew up. That's the garden of our old house in Kent. It must have taken her hours,' said Dex. 'I can't believe she went to so much trouble, doing all that for me.'

'You were her brother.' Molly's heart went out to him. 'Why wouldn't she want to do it for you?'

He shrugged. 'I know, but it makes me feel bad. I bought her something I thought she'd like for Christmas and it turned out to be all wrong. So then I said I'd take it back and get it sorted . . .' He paused, visibly stricken with guilt. 'But I never got around to doing it, did I? So bloody typical of me. I bet Laura knew she'd never see her Christmas present, but she still bothered to do all this. That's the difference between us.' His voice cracked. 'Oh shit . . .'

'Hey.' He'd been doing such a good job of putting on a brave face, it was easy to forget he was still grieving. Molly said, 'She was your sister. You could have a million faults and she'd still love you to bits. When did you first see this?' she went on. 'Was it the last time you came down?'

Dex shook his head. 'No, not then. I didn't even come up the stairs that night. I only saw it this afternoon when I was carrying the cot up to the bedroom.'

'So you didn't know she'd done this for you when you decided to take care of Delphi. And why are you doing that? Because you love her and you loved your sister.' Molly paused. 'So there's absolutely no need to feel guilty. You stepped up and did the right thing when it counted.'

'You think I have?' He still didn't look convinced.

'Definitely.' She nodded.

'We're only on day one. It's bloody scary,' Dex said with feeling. 'I feel like a fraud. What if I can't do this?'

'Listen to me.' Molly rested her hand on his arm and felt the tension beneath the surface. 'Just take it one day at a time, and I guarantee you can.'

It was three o'clock in the morning and Delphi couldn't settle.

Which made two of them.

Dex closed his eyes briefly. *Oh God, what happens now?*

Molly had done a good job of reassuring him earlier but she was no longer here and the doubts were setting in. Last night in London he'd been lucky and Delphi had slept through, tricking him into thinking she had a proper routine and it would always be like that.

Tonight it was the opposite and he felt helpless. For the last two hours she'd been wide awake and fractious, and he had no idea what was wrong. Was she too cold? Too hot? Too hungry or too full? He didn't know, he just didn't *know*.

'Meh . . . mehhhh . . . MEHHHHH.' The gripes rose to a wail and Dex reached over to lift her out of the cot again. He'd read the books saying leave them to cry but it was killing him. What if she was missing her mum?

'Sshh, don't worry, it's OK.' It wasn't remotely OK but he murmured it anyway, attempting to soothe her with the timbre of his voice.

Delphi shook her head violently and jabbed him in the eye with her thumb. '*Ow.*' Dex rocked her from side to side and walked her the length of the landing, from the wall at the top of the stairs to the stained-glass window at the far end. He continued to pace and rock and murmur 'Ow . . . ow . . . ow-*ow*,' to the tune of 'YMCA', because it had been stuck in his head all day and appeared to be keeping Delphi from crying. Her huge dark eyes were fixed on his now, her right arm flung across his chest. Each time he stopped singing she began whimpering again. 'Ow . . . ow . . . ow-*ow*,' Dexter carried on. She definitely liked it. The idea that something so ridiculous could entertain another living being was like a tiny miracle. And unlike Molly and her mad dancing earlier, there was no one around to witness the ridiculousness. It was quite freeing, actually. Delphi wasn't going to be spilling the beans any time soon.

'Gahhh.' Her tiny starfish fingers flexed against his skin.

'Y . . . M . . . C . . . A,' Dex sang, and this time detected the first glimmer of a smile. Oh yes, success. *Hello, Wembley!*

'Gyaah,' bubbled Delphi.

'Y . . . M . . . C . . . A!'

'Kha-brrooogh.'

Holding her firmly with one arm, he did the letter-shaping gestures with the other. Delphi kicked and gurgled with delight as he danced up and down the landing, in and out of the bedrooms. OK, so the baby-raising books also warned you to maintain an atmosphere that was quiet and calm in order to soothe the infant back to sleep but he'd already tried that and it hadn't worked. At least this was keeping them entertained, cheering them both up.

And luckily Delphi wasn't fussy; she wasn't remotely bothered that he didn't know the words.

Forty minutes later he lay her down in her cot and said, 'That's it, sweetheart. Concert's over. The Village People have left the building.'

In response Delphi blinked up at him a couple of times, then closed her eyes and went to sleep.

Just like that. Spark out, in about three seconds flat.

Will you look at that? I'm a genius. I should write one of those How-to books.

The trouble was, he was now far too alert to fall asleep himself. Once he was properly awake, that was it. Covering Delphi with her pink elephant blanket, Dex made his way back to his own room. The interior designer had got the gist of him and decorated the bedroom accordingly, and the results were impressive: slate-grey walls, silver ceiling, black and white bedding, and concealed wardrobes running the length of the room.

Ironically, from now on there would be no female visitors to be impressed by it all. Not for the foreseeable future at any rate. Dex headed over to the window. There was an awful lot of nothingness out there. By day, the view over the village was perfect, like something the tourist board would use in their advertising posters, the ultimate depiction of Cotswold village life. It was out there, he knew, but right now it was like a blackboard that had been wiped very clean indeed. A few lights had been left on overnight in scattered houses, but that was all. The rest was just overwhelming, unremitting darkness.

It was four fifteen in the morning and everyone else in Briarwood was asleep. The silence was as heavy as a blanket, muffling every last sound.

Dex shuddered inwardly; what if he wasn't just the only person in the village to be awake? What if something cataclysmic had happened and he was the only person left awake in the whole *world*? This was a recurring dream he'd had as a child; it hadn't happened for many years now, but it used to completely freak him out.

Would a psychologist link it to abandonment issues, the death of his parents and the associated terror of being left alone?

Could that be why he'd slept with so many girls?

Dex considered this for a few seconds. No, fuck it, he'd just slept with so many girls because it was fun and he *could*.

But all the same, this silence was oppressive. What seemed peaceful by day felt alarmingly isolated at night. Had moving here been a terrible mis—

BRRRNNGG, BRRRNNGGGGGG.

Who the bloody hell was calling him at this time of night? Grabbing his mobile before the noise woke Delphi, Dex said, 'Yes?'

'Yay, Dex! Heyyyy!' He heard raucous male laughter and

pounding music. So the rest of the world wasn't asleep after all. Just over a hundred miles away, Kenny and Rob were in a nightclub having the best night ever.

'Dexy, mate! What's up? Listen, where are you? We're at Mahiki and you need to get yourself over here now!'

Dex exhaled steadily. 'I'm in Briarwood.'

'Bryard?' Kenny sounded baffled. 'Never heard of it. Is it new? Hang on, is that the place that just opened behind Harvey Nicks?'

'Ken, listen to me, concentrate. I'm not living in London any more. It's almost four thirty in the morning and I'm in my cottage in Briarwood. With Delphi.'

'Delphi.' Kenny was drunk; it took him a couple of seconds to absorb this information. 'Oh, that's your sister's kid, right? But who's looking after it? Can't you leave them there and still come up?'

Dex felt his jaw tighten; had Kenny always been this much of a prize idiot? 'No, I can't. Because I'm the one looking after Delphi. Who's a *she*,' he added pointedly. 'Not an *it*.'

'Hey, man, don't get mad.' Evidently still flummoxed, Kenny said, 'But you've got a nanny too, right?'

'No, no nanny. Just me.'

'Oh man, that sucks. So, who's in charge?'

'I am.'

'But . . . but . . .'

'Guess what? Some people actually think I'm capable of it.' Dex ended the call and switched off the phone.

Silence reigned once more.

Chapter 15

'OK if I sit by you?'

Amber looked up and saw the tall boy with the floppy brown hair who'd visited the café back in February – it must have been six or seven weeks ago now. Molly had forced him to take one of her business cards and there'd been no sign of him since.

And now he was back. Still good-looking in that clean-cut way of his and still absolutely not her type.

'Fine.' She nodded; he already had his hand on the arm of the chair next to hers. 'Didn't think we'd see you again.'

'I've been busy.' He shrugged and sat down. 'You're Amber, right?'

'Right.' Of course he remembered; he was the kind that would. 'I'm Sam. Hi.'

'Hi.' OK, now she was sounding like a parrot. 'Can I just say something?'

He hesitated. 'Go ahead.'

'Look, don't take this the wrong way,' said Amber, 'but if you're here because of me, don't go getting your hopes up.'

'Meaning . . . ?'

'I don't fancy you. Not at all. No offence.'

'Bloody hell,' said Sam. 'Are you always this blunt?'

She shrugged. 'Pretty much. Sorry, I just think some things are better said and got out of the way.'

'Fine.' A glimmer of a smile. 'Luckily I don't fancy you either. So that's good news, isn't it?'

Amber raised a sceptical eyebrow. Modesty aside, she was perfectly well aware of how pretty she was. Most boys were attracted to her. He was probably just saying it to get even.

'See that over there? Smashed on the floor?' Sam indicated something on the ground ahead of them.

Twisting on her chair to see what he was pointing at, Amber said, 'Where? What is it?'

'My heart, broken into a million pieces? Can't you see it? That must mean I'm OK.' He clapped a hand to his chest. 'Phew, lucky. Still in one piece.'

'You're hilarious.'

'Thank you. I know.'

Despite the fact that he was gently mocking her, Amber was intrigued. 'So what made you come back?'

He indicated the closed drawing pad on his knee. 'I want to learn how to draw cartoons and comic strips.'

'Let's have a look?' She opened the pad and flicked through the half-dozen or so pages with drawings on them. Oh dear.

'Well?' Sam was waiting for her reaction.

'You know how I'm a bit blunt?'

'I do.'

'Well, these aren't very good, are they?'

He surveyed her with amusement. 'I know. That's why I've come along to this evening class, to get better.'

But something told Amber that it wasn't.

Everyone else had arrived. Molly cheerily greeted them all,

introduced Sam to the rest of the class, wrote a list of drawing tasks on the board and pinned up a selection of photographs for people to use as the basis for caricatures and cartoons. Once they'd all started work, she would spend time with each student in turn, guiding them, offering help and suggestions and explaining how to create scenarios and particular effects.

'It's lovely to have you back!' Sitting down in front of Sam, she looked at the cartoon he was currently working on.

'It's OK,' said Sam, 'you can say it. I know it's rubbish.'

'It isn't. You've got some lovely lines going on here. Just too many of them. What you want to do is cut it down to the absolute minimum. Simplify.' Taking a fresh sheet of paper, Molly copied the scene he'd been attempting to convey. 'See? Pare it right back, exaggerate the expressions . . . and you don't need so many movement lines. Try again, let your hand relax and loosen your shoulders. Draw the lines faster . . . there, you see? So much better! Just enjoy it and don't get hung up on the tiny details. They're *your* characters; you can make them do anything you like . . . that's it, keep going . . . and again . . . well done!'

Amber smiled at the look on Sam's face. She'd seen it before, that moment of sheer wonder when Molly first showed her students that their work could be so much better than they'd ever imagined. It was revelatory and uplifting, like watching a five-year-old ride a bike for the first time without stabilisers.

He was still pretty rubbish mind, but that didn't matter. Molly's enthusiasm was infectious; her speciality lay in abolishing the fear that caused so many to tense up and fail before they'd even started.

'Hey, cool.' Sam's face was an absolute picture as he swooped and swirled across the page with his pencil. 'I can't believe I've never tried this before. Just holding the pencil more loosely makes a difference . . . oops, that's wrong.' He'd made a swoop too far.

Molly grinned at Amber and prompted, 'What do we say now?'

'It doesn't matter,' Amber recited to Sam. 'You aren't Michelangelo working on a three-ton chunk of Carrara marble. It's just a piece of paper. If you can fix it with a rubber, do it. If you can't, turn the page and start again.'

'That's right.' Molly gave a nod of satisfaction. 'And what else do we say?'

'Put some effort in,' Amber told Sam. 'Practice, practice and more practice.'

Molly smiled at them both. 'Exactly. And have fun.'

Twenty minutes later, Sam had completed his first caricature. He showed Molly. 'Well?'

'That's really good.'

'Who is it?'

'Um . . . Mick Jagger?'

'No!'

Amber stifled laughter.

'Oh, sorry,' said Molly.

Sam gave her a wounded look. 'It's meant to be Steve Tyler.'

'Well, it looks just like him. Both of them, in fact. They're practically twins anyway,' said Molly.

He peered across at Amber's drawing pad. 'Who are you doing? Is that Shrek?'

Amber looked innocent. 'Actually, it's you.'

'Thanks a lot.' He grinned.

She liked the way he took her teasing in his stride. 'No, it's Shrek. So are you going to be coming along every week from now on?'

'I don't know, depends what else is on. Maybe, maybe not.'

'Where do you live?'

'Cheltenham.'

'What's your name?'

'You've got a short memory. Sam.'

'I know that. Surname.'

'Why, so you can look me up?'

Rumbled. Amber shook back her magenta curls and said impishly, 'Maybe.'

'Sam Jones. But I'm not on Facebook.'

'Seriously? Why not?'

He shrugged. 'It's possible to live without it, you know.'

'How about BBM?'

'No.'

Shocked, Amber said, 'So how do you keep in touch with people?'

'Emails. Texts. Don't worry, I manage.'

They carried on drawing and chatting. For a while they talked about music. Then things moved on to the A levels he was taking in the next three months, his plans for a gap year before university and how his parents were coping with the prospect of him leaving home.

'My dad'll be fine. Mum's dreading it. How about yours?'

'Oh, I'm only in year twelve, I've got another year to go yet. But they'll miss me when I move out, I know that. There's only me,' said Amber. 'So they won't know what to do with themselves once I've gone.'

'And your mum runs the café. She seemed nice when I saw her.' Sam was now attempting a caricature of Prince Charles; he paused to peer at the photograph he was working from. 'What's she like?'

'My mum? She's the village agony aunt. If people have problems, she's the one they come to. It's that thing she has.' Amber searched for the right word. 'Empathy. It's like she always understands and never judges. Kind of the opposite of me,' she added with a grin. 'I'm not gentle at all and I'm *very* judgy.'

'Judgemental.'

'I also don't like it when people try to tell me I've said the wrong word. I prefer my way.'

'More of the judgy, less of the mental.' His mouth twitched at the corners. 'What's your dad like?'

'He's great. Always busy,' Amber amended. 'But fun too. We're just a really happy family. Sorry if that's not very interesting, but it's the truth. How about yours?'

Sam shrugged. 'Nothing too traumatic. Same, pretty much. Better than a lot of people.'

'How are we getting on here?' Having done the rounds of the group, Molly was back. She stood behind them, rested her hands on each of their shoulders and surveyed their work. 'Very nice, both of you.' She winked as Amber twisted round to look up at her.

'Don't do that. Don't even think it,' said Amber. 'I'm not his type and he isn't mine.'

'OK, so that's me told. In that case I want you to move your chairs so you're facing each other.' Molly took a step back and gestured with her arms. 'And I want you to draw each other.'

Sam frowned. 'What, our faces?'

'Whole body caricatures. As exaggerated as you want. And I wouldn't ask you to do this if you were each other's types,' said Molly. 'Because you'd probably end up being offended and having a massive row. But seeing as you aren't, you can draw away and be as mean as you like.'

'Brilliant!' Amber's eyes gleamed in anticipation.

'So come on.' Molly addressed Sam. 'What would you exaggerate in order to draw Amber?'

'Mad hair.' Sam made spiralling gestures around his head.

'Good. What else?'

'Giant gypsy earrings.'

Amber jangled them with pride; she always wore huge silver hoops in her ears.

'And?' said Molly.

'Bony shoulders. Big feet.'

Amber gasped at this slur. 'Hey, watch it, *Bambi*.'

'What's that supposed to mean?' demanded Sam.

'Your eyes! Those great long girly eyelashes. Like a *camel*.'

'Draw each other,' Molly said calmly, 'and try not to come to blows. Can you manage that, d'you think, or shall I pair you up with Greg and Toby instead?'

Sam looked at Amber. 'Would you rather do that?'

Amber smiled slightly. 'No.'

He shook his head at Molly and said, 'It's OK, we'll be fine.'

Chapter 16

The evening class was about to come to an end. Frankie, watching from the doorway, inwardly revelled in the sight of Amber and the good-looking boy sparring with each other as they compared their finished drawings. After all these weeks he'd come back. What's more, they seemed to be getting on well together. Was this a sign that Amber was finally growing out of her grunge-boy phase? No offence to all the grungy boyfriends she'd brought home over the last couple of years, *but please God make it so*.

'Mum, over here!' Having spotted her, Amber enthusiastically beckoned her over. 'Look what we've been doing!'

'Hello, nice to see you again.' Frankie beamed at the boy with the long-lashed green eyes, floppy hair and fresh complexion.

'Hi.' He smiled back at her.

'His name's Sam,' said Amber, showing off her artwork. 'See how I've given him a camelly kind of face?'

'Very good. You don't really look like a camel,' Frankie assured Sam. Then she burst out laughing at the sight of the caricature he'd drawn of Amber.

'Thanks a *lot*.' Amber tutted. 'You're only supposed to laugh at my picture of him.'

'I can't draw. I'm rubbish,' Sam said good-naturedly. 'But it's been fun.'

He was wearing really nice aftershave; such a novelty. 'They're both great. And having fun's what it's all about.' She smiled again at Sam and hoped she wasn't scaring him. *Was this how Carole Middleton had felt when Kate first introduced her to Prince William?*

'Actually, Mum, I was telling Sam about you being a kind of agony aunt, good with problems and stuff. And he's got one you might be able to help with.' As Amber said the words, Frankie saw the boy tense up and look momentarily panicked.

'Don't worry.' Amber's earrings jangled as she reassured him. 'I know it's hard to come out and say it. Want me to do this for you? The thing is, Mum, Sam's got this secret and he doesn't know how to deal with it. He likes dressing up in girls' clothes. Skirts and high heels and stuff.' Lowering her voice she added, 'And, you know, *lacy underwear*. I've told him it's fine, nothing to be ashamed of, but do you think he should tell all his friends?'

For the first few seconds Frankie had believed the story; her brain had shot into overdrive, ricocheting wildly from *Oh no!* and *Poor boy* to *How can I help him?* Then she'd realised it was just one of Amber's silly jokes and there was no need to worry after all.

What was interesting, though, was the way she and Sam both relaxed at the same time, as if the two of them had been simultaneously bracing themselves for whatever Amber may have been about to say.

Then again, that was the trouble with Amber; no one could ever know with certainty what might be about to come out of her mouth.

Frankly, was it any wonder the poor boy was nervous?

As he left Briarwood behind him, Sam's heart was racing. He'd covered his tracks, hadn't he? Left no clues. Two visits now and he knew he shouldn't be pushing his luck. But what he hadn't anticipated was how strong the pull would be.

Was this how it felt to be addicted to hard drugs? Knowing it was wrong and that you were dicing with danger but feeling the overwhelming need to go ahead and do it anyway?

Well, maybe once he was back at home he'd come to his senses. Realise that he should leave it now.

He'd already done what he'd come here to do.

Sam's heart quickened.

Hadn't he?

Facebook, Facebook, brilliant Facebook. What Amber loved most about it was the way it wasn't just a question of who you knew, but who your friends and their friends might know. Similarly, she might not go to school in Cheltenham but she knew some girls who did.

Bournside was by far the biggest; the odds were that Sam was in the sixth form there.

Except . . . after asking around a bit, it seemed he didn't.

Never one to give up at the first fence, Amber doggedly made her way through the other schools in the area; the independents, the boys only, the Catholic one . . . eventually she even double-checked that Cheltenham Ladies' College hadn't started taking boys.

But no one anywhere had heard of Sam Jones.

Which . . . and there was no getting away from it . . . was totally weird.

The other thing that had piqued her curiosity was the comment her mother had made in passing: 'Did you see the look on that boy's face when you said he had a secret? For a moment there he was terrified!'

'Maybe he really is a transvestite.' Amber had looked innocent.

Her mum had been appalled. 'Oh darling, don't say that. Of *course* he isn't.'

This had happened earlier, been said jokingly over dinner in front of the TV. Neither of them had thought any more of it at the time. But it was midnight now and Amber was beginning to have second thoughts. Adjusting the pillows propping her up in bed, she frowned at the screen of her laptop. Sam Jones. Samuel Jones. Could Sam be short for some foreign name that might solve the mystery?

The front door opened and closed downstairs, signalling her dad's return. He'd been working down in Dorset for the last two days.

Amber heard her mum say, 'You're home!' and knew they were hugging each other in the hallway.

'You didn't have to wait up for me.' Her dad always said it every time he got home late and her mum always waited up anyway.

'No problem. Hungry? There's pasta left, or cold chicken and potato salad.'

'Don't worry, I grabbed something at the services outside Winchester. Where's my girl anyway?'

'Upstairs.'

'Oh. Asleep?'

He sounded disappointed. There was something wonderfully comforting about overhearing yourself being discussed by people who loved you. Switching her laptop on to standby, Amber sang out, 'I'm still awake,' and heard footsteps bounding up the staircase.

'There you are.' Her dad appeared in the bedroom doorway. 'Hey, sweetie, missed you.'

'Missed you too.' Amber held out her arms for a kiss and

breathed in the scent of the aftershave he'd bought himself the other week, more lemony that the one she was used to, but still nice.

'Brought you a present.' He reached into his jacket pocket. 'A nice jar of fish eyes and some pickled pigs' ears.'

It wasn't that, of course. She watched as he produced a packet of Maltesers. Maybe it was childish but it was a long-standing tradition that whenever he came home he brought her a tiny present and told her it was something revolting.

'Pigs' ears are my favourite.' Amber held out her hand and he dropped the Maltesers packet into it. 'Thanks, Dad.'

'How's school? Get that essay finished?'

'Yeah, it took ages.' She moved her feet out of the way as he sat on the edge of the bed.

'But was it good in the end?'

'It was brilliant.' She grinned. '*Obviously*.'

'Glad to hear it. And so modest too. Now look at the time.' He gave her shoulder an affectionate squeeze. 'You should be asleep.'

She *was* tired. As he took the laptop away from her and placed it on the chest of drawers, Amber said, 'Dad, what should you do if you find out someone's been lying to you?'

He looked serious. 'Who is it? One of your friends?'

'Not really. Just a boy.'

'Daniel with the shark-tooth necklace?' He tried not to sound too hopeful.

'No.' Her parents weren't great fans of Daniel. 'Someone I've only met twice. He came along to Molly's class tonight.'

'And is he keen on you?'

'I don't know.' Amber shook her head. 'He *says* he isn't. But Molly and Mum think he probably is.' A huge yawn overtook her.

'Maybe he's just showing off, trying to impress you. But if you've only just met this boy and he's lying already, it's not a great start. I wouldn't trust him, if I were you.'

Another yawn, she was really tired now. As her dad reached the doorway Amber said, 'Don't worry, I already don't trust him.'

He gave a nod of approval. 'Good.'

In the changing room of his select West London health club, Henry Baron was in the process of placing his belongings in a locker when his phone went *ttting* to indicate the arrival of an email in his inbox.

Force of habit meant he couldn't bring himself to ignore it. It wasn't just that he was terminally conscientious; when you worked as a hedge fund manager, time was money and you never knew what you might be missing out on. Henry unzipped his sports bag, took out his phone and saw that it was a message from Dex.

OK, just a quick look. He opened the email, which said: 'And this is me introducing Delphi to my new girlfriend . . .'

The attached photo was of Delphi in an orange bobble hat and purple anorak pulling a comically surprised face as a result of finding herself nose to nose with a beady-eyed, tufty-chinned goat.

Henry didn't mind admitting – though only to himself – he'd had his concerns about his friend's ability to handle such a radical change of lifestyle. But so far, thankfully, Dex appeared to be managing to cope. He smiled, but his gaze was already being drawn to another character caught in the background of the photo. Her light brown hair was half blowing across her face but she was laughing at Delphi's expression as she passed behind him, carrying a tray of cups.

The door to the changing room was pushed open and Henry's squash partner stuck his head round.

'There you are! We're waiting for you.'

Henry said absently, 'I'll be with you in a sec.'

The door closed again and he enlarged the photo as far as it would go. Delphi and the goat disappeared off the bottom of the screen as he zoomed in on the woman whose face was almost hypnotically drawing him to her. She was around forty, at a guess, and wearing a red shirt and jeans. Her figure was curvy, her face lit up; her smile was . . . oh God, Henry couldn't believe he was even *thinking* this, but it was just magical. He didn't want to stop looking at her, which had to be the most ridiculous situation ever, because it wasn't as if he knew her or she was even someone famous . . .

OK, get a grip, switch off the phone, you've got a squash match to play.

An hour later, with the match won, Henry switched his phone back on and texted: 'Great photo. Where were you when you took it – some kind of zoo?'

See? Subtle.

The reply pinged back less than a minute later. 'No! Right here in the village at our local café. It's where that TV show *Next to You* was filmed, hence the goat. PS: Who isn't really my new girlfriend. Mainly because he's a boy goat.'

Yes. Henry experienced the kind of adrenalin rush he got when he took a major punt on a risky deal and saw it pay off. This meant if he *did* happen to find himself in Briarwood he might just decide on the off chance to call in at the café and there was a possibility the woman might still be working there –

Oh God, unless she didn't work there. He shuddered at the belated realisation that she might not, could in fact just have been a customer carrying a tray.

And there was definitely no way he was going to ask Dex, whose capacity for mischief was second to none.

OK. Think, think. He was possibly one of the few people who hadn't watched *Next to You*, but he'd heard of it. And it had presumably featured a goat . . .

Henry put *Next to You* + Briarwood + café into Google.

And up it came, Frankie's Café, a modest website welcoming visitors to Briarwood, explaining the history of the show and the opening times of the café. There were also photos of the house, of various items of *Next to You* memorabilia and of the tethered billy goat whose name was apparently Young Bert.

Best of all, there was a photograph of Frankie, who owned and ran the café and wasn't a Frankie of the Sinatra kind. It was her, this time aware that she was being photographed and visibly self-conscious about it, her shoulders a bit stiff and her smile fixed. But that just drew Henry to her all the more. He was the same, tensing up whenever a camera was pointed in his direction. Some people could relax and not let it bother them; some actively loved it, relishing the chance to preen and pose and show themselves off. Personally he found it as relaxing as root canal work.

It felt like another connection between them. Henry gazed at Frankie's face, taking in every last detail, feeling as if he knew her and knowing that he definitely wanted to. Was he going mad? It wasn't normal, surely, to be this affected by a photo of a complete stranger?

Nothing like this had ever happened to him before.

But she looked so perfect, so right.

'Haven't you even got in the shower yet?' Kenny, a towel fastened round his waist, was vigorously spraying his underarms with deodorant.

'Some of us have important business to take care of. It's called making money,' said Henry. 'Give me two minutes.'

'Coming for a drink?'

'Not tonight.' His mind was working overtime; how could he find out what he needed to know without arousing suspicion?

Luckily every problem had a solution. Henry fired off another text: 'OK, this could be a weird coincidence but the woman in the photo looks familiar – is she by any chance married to a guy called Bernard?'

As he waited, he could feel the perspiration drying on his skin. It wasn't the nicest sensation. Come on, Dex, hurry up . . .

Because for some reason he was finding he couldn't even jump in the shower until he had an answer.

Four long minutes later, it arrived: 'Not the same woman. Frankie runs the café and her husband's called Joe.'

Henry exhaled. That was it then, she was married. Just the answer he didn't want to hear.

Damn and blast.

In fact . . . *shit*.

Then again, so much for allowing himself to get his hopes up. This was pretty much the story of his life.

Chapter 17

'I've got a massive favour to ask. But I don't know if you can do it.'

'If it's help with your maths homework you're after, fire away,' said Molly. 'But I'm warning you now, the answer to every question you ask me will be seven.'

Amber, who was a whiz at maths, said, 'Luckily it isn't that.'

'Come on in, then.' Molly had a piece of toast in one hand and a pen in the other. 'So what's the favour?'

'OK, this is going to sound weird, but I've been trying to find out more about that guy from last night.' Having come over to the cottage straight from the school bus, Amber dropped her heavy bag loaded with textbooks on to the sofa. 'And basically, either his name isn't Sam Jones or he doesn't go to school in Cheltenham.'

Molly frowned. 'Hmm, that *is* weird.'

'I know! Me and my friends have been trying to work out what's going on, but they don't know what he looks like.'

'Got it.' Molly's expression cleared. 'So if he turns up at next week's class, you want me to take a sneaky photo of him. Or not even sneaky. We can make it part of the task. That's fine, we can do that.'

Was it being so much older that made Molly so patient? Amber said, 'Yes, but that's seven whole days away. How could you bear to wait that long? Don't you want to know *now*?'

Molly finished chewing a mouthful of toast. 'So how are you planning on doing this then? Taking a DNA sample from the pencil he was using last night? Tracking him through CCTV?'

'Right, here's the thing. Can you draw a picture of him?'

'What? No.' Molly put down her Berol pen and shook her head. 'No way.'

'Why not?'

'I just couldn't do it, not without something to work from. If he turns up next week I could ask him to sit for me . . .'

This *so* wasn't the answer Amber wanted to hear. She said, 'Could you do one of me? Now? If I wasn't sitting in front of you?'

Molly pulled a face, thought about it for a few seconds, and looked pained. 'Possibly. But only because I've known you for so long. And I still wouldn't do it.'

'Why wouldn't you?'

'It wouldn't be good enough.'

'Have you ever tried?'

'No!'

'Why not?' This was like being a high court judge.

'Because I know it wouldn't be good enough!'

'OK, don't panic. You mean it wouldn't be up to your usual standard,' Amber said soothingly. 'You'd end up with something not as completely brilliant as usual. But it doesn't have to be brilliant, it just needs to be similar enough to be recognisable.'

Molly still wasn't looking thrilled. It was evidently a pride thing. But at least she'd stopped shaking her head.

'Where's the harm in giving it a try? Just close your eyes and picture him.' Amber made her voice go all gentle and encouraging, like a hypnotist. 'Remember the eyebrows? And those eyelashes? And the way his hair falls forward? Think about the shape of his mouth . . . Just have a little go and see what you come up with. Even if it's just *slightly* recognisable, that's all we want . . .'

Molly opened one eye. 'Are you trying to do a Derren Brown number on me?'

'Yes. Is it working?'

'No.'

'Look, just have a go. One sheet of paper, that's all it takes. And it doesn't matter, does it, if it all goes wrong? It's not as if you'd be ruining a three-ton block of Carrara marble—'

'OK, stop, I'll do it.' Molly threw her arms up in surrender.

'Yay!'

'But I'm warning you now, I don't think it'll work.'

Work commenced on the portrait. As Molly had predicted, it wasn't easy. Conjuring up an image of Sam in her mind was one thing, but opening her eyes and attempting to transfer the details from brain to paper was quite another.

The first few goes were discarded. Amber ate Honey Cheerios out of the box as Molly drew pencil lines, erased them with her grey Staedtler rubber, heaved gusty frustrated sighs and crumpled attempt after attempt into a ball until the living-room carpet was awash with them.

'I can't do a straight portrait,' she said eventually. 'There's too much I don't know. Let me try a caricature.'

It took a while but after several more attempts she was getting there. Hardly daring to breathe, Molly gazed at the drawing board as the image began to take shape. As she'd predicted, it wasn't brilliant, nor was it instantly recognisable as so-called Sam, but it was similar enough to suggest it was him.

Which, with a bit of luck and a following wind, might be just enough to do the trick.

Amber hugged her when it was finished. 'Thank you so much.'

'OK, but I'm still not happy with it,' Molly grumbled. 'Don't tell anyone it came from me.'

Facebook was too public, in the end. Upstairs in her bedroom, having scanned the finished drawing into her computer, Amber emailed it instead to six of her friends along with a note saying: 'Just doing a bit of detective work, so don't mention this to anyone else, but does this picture remind you of anyone at all?'

Her phone began beeping with texted replies shortly afterwards. Her friends, while intrigued, were largely unable to help, although Aimee wrote: 'Looks a bit like a guy I met at a barbecue last year, can't remember his name though.'

Then Georgia sent a message that said: 'Ooh, you big old Sherlock Holmes you! Is it someone called Connor? Do I win a prize for this??'

Amber texted: 'Connor who? How do you know him?'

The message flashed back: 'Met him at Donna's boyfriend's party before Christmas. If it's him, don't bother asking Donna – she was trashed and doesn't remember a thing about that night!!'

Great. Amber sent the picture out to half a dozen more friends, widening the circle slightly. Then, because the endless beeps drove her parents demented when they were trying to eat, she left her phone on the unmade bed and went downstairs to join them for dinner.

Fillet steak with brandy and mushroom cream sauce and chips, her dad's favourite before he headed off to Norfolk.

'Found out anything more about your new admirer?' Her mum was looking all interested.

'Not really. His name might be Connor. But he isn't my admirer anyway.' Intrigued by the mystery though she was, Amber didn't want her mother involved; was there anything more cringe-making than parents encouraging you to get together with someone *they* liked? Changing the subject, she said, 'So, Dad, where are we going on holiday this year? Can we go to France again?'

After dinner they said their goodbyes. Once her dad had left, Amber headed back upstairs.

Her phone had been busy taking messages in her absence.

Basically the answers were:

'Nope.'

'No. Killer eyelashes though. What mascara does he use??!!'

'No idea but did you draw that picture???'

'Isn't that Sean Corrigan?'

'Is it Hugh Grant?????'

'Give us another clue, I like this game.'

And finally, a follow-up text from Georgia: 'Duh, I'm so stoopid! Not Connor. Sean. Got muddled because we were watching a James Bond film last night with that old guy Sean Connery in it. All this revision has shrivelled my brain to the size of a walnut, haha!!! Xxx'

Which was a blatant lie because Georgia never did any revision *ever*.

But things were looking up. Logging into Facebook, Amber keyed in the name Sean Corrigan.

God, there were loads. Hundreds of Sean Corrigans all over the world. Thank goodness she could narrow it down. Gloucestershire, typed Amber.

Oh. No results. That was a bit *too* narrowed down.

Maybe he'd been telling the truth about not being on Facebook.

Amber tapped her nails against the screen and considered what to try next.

Wiltshire. No.

Oxfordshire. Yes, Oxfordshire had a Sean Corrigan. Who was currently away on a gap year in New Zealand.

More nail tapping.

OK, try spelling it differently.

S-h-a-u-n C-o-r-r-i-g-a-n.

Gloucestershire.

Press Return . . .

And there he was.

Wow. Amber sat back in her chair. That was him, Shaun Corrigan, laughing into the camera. He was using privacy controls on his account, which was a bugger, but his school was listed as Deer Park School in Cirencester.

So, no Sam Jones. No Cheltenham. Why would he be lying about that?

OK, backtrack. It was Susie who'd known his name. Luckily she was discreet. Texting her, Amber sent the message: 'Yes, clever girl. How do you know him?'

A couple of minutes later, Susie's reply pinged up on her phone: 'He lives in Tetbury, across the road from my uncle. I met him at my uncle's New Year's Eve party. How about you?? He's not your usual type!!!'

Amber's heart was racing now. This private investigation malarkey was addictive. She wrote: 'Can't say. This is TOP SECRET, OK? Do you know his address?'

Another couple of minutes later and – *Ping*! – another reply. An email this time, containing a Google Earth link: 'My uncle's house is on the left, number seventeen, next to the postbox. Sean lives across the road at number twenty-two, the one with the yellow front door and white flowers in the garden.'

Amber opened the link and zoomed down to street view. She found the house, semi-detached and unremarkable.

The sensible thing to do now, of course, would be to wait as Molly had suggested and see if Sam-Sean-Shaun turned up at the café next week.

But what if he *didn't*? And what if he didn't turn up the week after that? What would she do then?

Another plan would be to send him a message. She could do that now, this minute. Just say something casual and non-heavy, along the lines of: 'Hmm, I thought you said you weren't on Facebook??'

And when you were as impatient as she was, it was a massive temptation. Ask a question, get an answer, no hanging around, simple as that.

Because it wasn't as if she found him remotely fanciable – if she did, she wouldn't dream of being so forward. But since she really didn't, she could just go ahead and ask him what he was playing at.

Except . . . *would* it be simple? And what kind of answer would she get? Because the down side of electronic communication was the time it gave the other person to think. And to come up with a convincing reply.

Whereas face to face would be so much more interesting.

Wouldn't it?

Amber smiled to herself as a possible plan began to unfurl. Tomorrow was Wednesday, which was good, she could do it then.

She couldn't wait a whole week for Mohammed to – possibly – come to the mountain. Far better for the mountain to get proactive and visit Mohammed.

Whose real name was Shaun Corrigan.

Chapter 18

The journey had taken a while; it was quite a trek. After leaving school, Amber had needed to catch two buses in order to get to Tetbury. A bunch of hilarious younger boys had sat behind her on the first one and made fun of her hair: 'So how d'you get it that colour, then? Just mashed up a load of pickled beetroot and splatted it on to your head?'

The second journey had been made to the accompaniment of two old dears moaning non-stop about young people today: 'And I know what's caused it too. Soft toilet paper. The country wouldn't be in the mess it's in now if we were all still using Izal.'

Honestly, geriatrics were weird.

The bus reached Tetbury at last and Amber jumped off. After all this effort Shaun Corrigan had better be home.

Parnall Avenue was easy to find and instantly recognisable from the street-view site. There was number seventeen, Susie's uncle's house. She walked past the postbox and paused to look across the road at number twenty-two. The front door was still yellow. The front garden was small but neatly maintained.

OK, no point hanging around. She crossed the road and made her way up the front path.

Rang the bell.

This was actually quite exciting now.

He'd bloody *better* be at home.

Moments later the door was opened and Amber found herself being smiled at by a slender green-eyed woman who had to be Shaun's mother. She was pretty, in her early forties, wearing jeans and a grey V-necked sweater beneath a striped apron. A delicious smell of casserole hung in the air behind her.

'Hello . . . ?'

'Uh, hi. Is Shaun here?'

The smile broadened. 'Yes, he is. Hang on, he's up in his room revising. Well, *allegedly* revising. Who shall I say's here?'

Why miss the look of surprise on his face? Where would be the fun in that? *Two can play at changing their name, Shaun Corrigan.*

'I'm Jessie,' said Amber.

Raising her voice, his mother called up the stairs, 'Shaun? You have a visitor! Jessie's here.'

They both heard a bedroom door open. 'Who?'

'Jessie's come to see you.'

Amber's heart was clattering; any second now, he'd see her. She could hear footsteps along the landing. The next moment she saw his trainer-clad feet on the stairs, then his jeans, then the rest of him.

And he saw her.

The blood drained from Shaun's face and he stopped dead, visibly appalled.

'What's going on? What the hell are you doing here?'

Bewildered by her son's outburst, his mother said, 'Shaun!'

'Charming,' said Amber.

'I mean it, go away.' He was shaking his head, still frozen on the stairs. 'You can't come here, you have to leave now. Just go.'

'Hang on.' Stunned by his reaction, Amber shot back, 'You were the one who lied to me!'

To the left of her, Amber heard his mother say faintly, 'Oh no . . .'

To the right of her, another door was pulled open and a male voice said, 'Dinner smells good. What time are we eating?'

And then it was Amber's turn for her world to implode and go into slow motion. Because the owner of the male voice was someone she knew.

Only too well.

It was her father.

'Oh God.' He stopped dead, closed his eyes and put his hands up to his face. '*Oh God.*'

If her heart had been clattering along before, it was now thudding ten times faster. More than anything, Amber wanted to run away but her legs refused to move. She was welded to the doorstep. Her father had been having an affair and she'd just caught him out. Chiefly because he was *wearing slippers*.

What were the rules for what happened next? She didn't have a clue.

'Amber. I'm so sorry.' Her dad sounded shaken, as well he might. 'How did you find me?'

Could she even speak? Only one way to find out. Amber cleared her throat and said, 'Um . . . I didn't. I wasn't looking for you. I was looking for him.'

She pointed to Shaun, who was looking as if he might actually be sick.

'What?' Her father stared in disbelief at the boy on the stairs who had just blown apart his double life. 'Tell me what's been going on.'

Time was now simultaneously speeding up and slowing down. There was a loud buzzing in Amber's ears.

'I didn't mean for this to happen. I don't know how she managed to find me.' Shaun was shaking his head at her father. 'I just wanted to know what they were like.'

'Oh Shaun . . .' His mother was looking increasingly distressed. His mother, *who was having an affair with her father*.

'How could you do this to Mum?' Amber's voice rose and cracked as she faced her father. 'How *could* you? How long's this been going on?'

Silence. Icy, tortured silence. Unable to bear it a second longer, she stumbled backwards and turned away.

'Amber, no, come back.' There was anguish in his voice. 'We need to talk. I can explain.'

But she couldn't even look at him. In his slippers, for God's sake. He was having an affair with another woman and wearing *slippers* . . .

'Don't come near me. I hate you.' Amber meant it. In the space of a few seconds everything had changed. How could she ever forgive him for this? 'You make me sick. You're *disgusting*. What about Mum?'

'Oh God, Amber . . .' She heard him call her name, fear mingled with desperation.

'Get away from me! I *hate* you. I never want to see you again!'

Her brain buzzing, Amber slammed the front door shut and stumbled into the street with no clue where she was going. Turn left at the end of the road . . . now turn right . . . or was it left? Oh God, this was like being trapped in a nightmare . . .

Fifteen minutes later she was back in the centre of town, where people were walking around and carrying on as if nothing had happened. Still in a daze, Amber made her way towards the bus stop.

Shaun was already there, waiting for her.

'Go away.' She stuffed her hands in her jacket pockets, refused to look at him.

'I'm so sorry.'

'I don't want to speak to you.'

'I didn't mean this to happen.'

'I bet you didn't. I've come along and spoiled everything, haven't I? The cat's out of the bag, thanks to me. Oh shit, I still can't believe it. I really can't. My mum's going to *die* when she finds out about this.'

'Look, it's not what you think . . .'

'No, don't go making excuses.' From not wanting to speak to him, Amber now found herself unable to stop, the words spilling out in a torrent. 'You have no idea what you've done. Because my parents are happy together, can you understand that? They love each other. They have the best marriage in the world, they really do. And now everything's *ruined*.' Her voice had begun to wobble; thank God there was no one else queuing at the bus stop. 'Your bloody mother has *no* shame; she thought she'd have an affair with a married man so she stole my dad . . .' Even while she was saying this, Amber knew she was concentrating her anger on Shaun's mother, when her own father was just as much to blame.

As they stood there staring at each other, it started to rain.

'You don't understand,' Shaun said helplessly.

'Oh, I do.'

'My mum isn't like that.'

'No? Take another look at her.' Amber felt the drops of rain hit her face. 'I think you'll find she is.'

'I already said I'm sorry. But you've got this wrong,' Shaun insisted.

'Did I? Did I really? You came over to Briarwood when you

knew my dad wouldn't be there because you were curious. You wanted to check out his family.'

Brakes creaked, the bus pulled up alongside them and the doors concertinaed open. The rain was coming down harder now. Amber narrowed her gaze at Shaun and waited for him to admit this much at least.

He exhaled, then said, 'His *other* family.'

The world tipped again.

'What?'

'You keep calling him *your* dad.' Shaun bowed his head, then lifted it again and said defiantly, 'But he's my dad too.'

'Hell-ooooo?' bellowed the bus driver. 'Anyone at home? Are we getting on or staying off?'

Amber could still hear Shaun's words swooshing through her head. 'He can't be.'

'He is.'

'Three.' The driver was starting a countdown. 'Two.'

'I feel sick,' said Amber.

'One,' the driver announced. 'Bye!'

The doors closed and the bus pulled away, leaving the two of them standing on the pavement in the rain.

Chapter 19

It was possible, Joe Taylor had discovered, to be essentially a good person but to end up in a situation that might – OK, *probably would* – cause others to think you were bad.

And he wasn't bad, he really wasn't. He'd just made one mistake a long time ago and had been paying the price ever since. The last seventeen years had been an exercise in damage limitation purely because he didn't want to hurt those he loved and make them miserable.

And, unbelievably, he'd managed it.

Joe closed his eyes. *Until now.*

It had been one of those unexpected, out-of-the-blue situations that you had no idea was about to happen. He'd been working in Bristol at the time. As a result of visiting the café across the road most days, he'd ended up bumping into Christina who worked at the firm of solicitors next door. Over the course of the next few months they'd become friendly, but only in the most innocent of ways.

Until a combination of events had conspired to change all that. A rare argument with Frankie had shaken him; being accused of not bothering to post a birthday card when he knew he *had* posted it had been unfair. And then, leaving work that day, he'd bumped into Christina in the street and asked how she was. In response she had promptly burst into tears. He'd taken her into the café and the whole story came tumbling out; her mother had been diagnosed with stage four cancer, she'd just handed in her notice at the solicitors in order to be able to care for her during her last months; she couldn't bear it, first thing tomorrow she was leaving . . .

She was all on her own in Bristol; how could he abandon her in such a terribly distressed state? Joe had driven her home to her flat in Clifton and they'd talked for hours, his own emotions heightened by the realisation that he would miss seeing Christina, miss her friendship.

And somehow tears and hugs had ended up leading to more. He'd wanted to make her feel better. It was wrong, of course it was, but for that brief period in time it hadn't *felt* wrong.

'Oh God, this is bad,' Christina wept afterwards. 'I'm so sorry. We shouldn't have done that. Your poor wife . . . it was all my fault.'

It had been a one-off event, never to be repeated, they mutually agreed. Tomorrow she'd be gone. Neither of them would say anything about this to another living soul. No one would ever know what had taken place here tonight.

Arriving home at ten o'clock that evening, he'd been greeted by Frankie throwing her arms round him. 'I'm so sorry. I never want us to argue again. I love you so much.'

The guilt had been overwhelming. But he'd known he was just going to have to live with it, in the sure and certain knowledge that it would never happen again.

'Shaun's got his phone switched off,' said Christina. 'Should I leave a message?'

Joe was sitting at the kitchen table with his head in his hands.

'Leave it for now. Amber's not answering hers either. I can't believe this has happened. Bloody hell, I don't even know *how* it has. What are we going to do?'

Christina licked her lips and put down the phone. 'I don't know. But I think you need to go to Briarwood, get there before Amber does.'

It was such an appalling prospect Joe couldn't even begin to process it. 'And then what?'

'Put it this way. Do you think Amber will keep quiet about all of this?'

Hopelessly, Joe shook his head. 'Not in a million years.'

'In that case,' said Christina, 'you're going to have to tell Frankie.'

Fifteen months after their last encounter, Joe saw Christina again. It was December and he was Christmas shopping in a mall in Bristol. One minute he was looking at silk scarves in John Lewis, the next he glanced up and saw her heading his way.

Joe's heart gave a jolt of recognition. She hadn't seen him; he could turn away and let her walk on by, but where was the harm in just saying hello? They'd been friends, hadn't they? *It was Christmas.*

'Hi.'

'Oh! Oh my goodness!' Christina jumped, her face registering a mixture of emotions when she saw who'd just greeted her. 'Um . . . hello, how are you?'

'Fine. Good.' Joe smiled and nodded at her reaction. Her fine blond hair was tied up in a high ponytail and she was wearing a heavy emerald-green coat over a black sweater and trousers. 'And you?'

'I'm . . . great, thanks. Just, you know, buying some things for Christmas.' She had armfuls of bags and a sheen of perspiration across her forehead.

'How have you been really?' He lowered his voice in sympathy. 'I mean, how did it go with your mum?'

Christina paused. 'Well, she died. Three months ago. Which wasn't a surprise; we knew it was going to happen . . . quite a tough time though.' Trailing off, she took a couple of deep breaths. 'Gosh, it's hot in here . . .'

'Give me your bags.' Joe held out his hands; it was hot in the store and she looked as if she might keel over. 'Take off that coat,' he ordered.

Nodding, she did as he said and briefly leaned against the glass-topped scarf counter. 'It's OK, I'll be fine. Thanks for asking about Mum. I miss her, but life goes on. Anyway, how's everything with you?'

'Good, good.' So much quivered, unsaid, in the overheated air between them.

'You and Frankie are still together?' She sounded as if she hated herself for asking the question.

It was his turn to nod. Without elaborating, Joe said, 'Yes, we are.'

For a moment Christina's eyes glinted with tears. She looked away, then down at the bulky coat in her hands. Shifting it so it was over one arm, she reached out to take back the bags he was still holding for her.

As he returned them, Joe inwardly debated whether a polite kiss goodbye would be OK or out of order. Best not. He wanted to, but he wouldn't. *Mustn't.*

'Nice to see you again,' said Christina, her smile over-bright. 'Happy Christmas!'

'You have a good one too.' Joe watched fondly as she turned to leave, to squeeze her way back through the December present-buying crowds. There was something on the left shoulder of her black sweater, as if a big bird had flown overhead and pooed on it. Since he knew Christina well enough to know she took pride in her appearance, he put out a hand and said, 'Hang on a sec, there's something on your shoulder that needs cleaning off.'

Christina stopped, twisted round to see what it was and instantly flushed deep red.

'Hey, it doesn't matter, we can get it sorted.' He was already pulling a handkerchief out of his pocket but Christina was backing away. In that split second Joe realised the splodgy white stain on the shoulder of her jumper hadn't come from a bird flying overhead.

And then he knew. He just knew from the look of panic and embarrassment and pain on her face. Because what other explanation could there possibly be?

In the very *next* split second he also knew he had the opportunity to let it go, to allow her to slip away. The choice was his. He could turn and pretend he hadn't made the connection. Carry on with his shopping, carry everything back to the car, drive home to Briarwood and Frankie and his familiar everyday uncomplicated life.

But when it came down to it, he found he couldn't.

'*Stop*. Christina . . . oh my God.' Catching up with her, fighting his way through the crowds, Joe reached for her arm. He heard himself say, 'We need to talk.'

Without another word they left the shopping mall, made their way past the fairy castle housing Santa's Grotto and the snaking queue of small children lined up to see Santa.

Small children.

Christina's red Mini was parked at the far end of the huge car park. Unlocking it, she piled her bags into the boot then sat in the driver's seat, trembling with emotion rather than cold. Her hands were tightly clasped in her lap.

Joe, sitting next to her in the passenger seat, said, 'It's obviously mine, then.'

She nodded jerkily. 'Yes.'

'You got pregnant and it didn't occur to you to tell me.'

'Oh Joe, of course it *occurred* to me.' There was despair in her eyes. 'I thought about it a million times. But what would it have done to you? You'd have been appalled. You had your life, you were happily married, this was *never* meant to happen . . .'

'I don't understand how it did. I mean, you said it would be OK . . .'

'I thought it would be, I was so sure the timing made it safe. Obviously it didn't. Please don't think I got pregnant on purpose,' said Christina. 'Because I really didn't, I can promise you that.'

There was a defensive edge to her voice. Joe believed her. OK, and now there were other things he needed to know. 'Boy or a girl?'

'A boy.'

'What's his name?' Not Joe, *please*.

'Shaun.'

'Is he . . . OK?'

'He's perfect. Actually, this is the first time I've ever come out without him. Any other day and he'd have been with me.'

'You didn't want a baby, but you went ahead and had it.' After a moment's pause, Joe said, 'Why?'

'I know. That wasn't part of the plan either. It was Mum, basically.' Her eyes were sheeny with tears again. 'She was in hospital, I was spending all my time there with her. She knew she didn't have long to go. One day she said the worst part of dying was never getting to meet her grandchildren. It was her biggest regret. She told me what a great mother I'd make and how she'd always dreamed of seeing me with a baby of my own.' Christina paused as a squabbling family trooped past the car. 'And that was it, really. It was her dearest wish and there I was, already pregnant. I had the power to make it come true.' Tilting her head and using the back of her hand to wipe her wet cheeks, she said simply, 'That's when I knew I was going to do it. She was my beautiful mum and I loved her so much. If I could give her one last fantastic present, I would.'

Joe nodded. It was a decision that had just made his own life a whole lot more complicated but he could understand her reason for making it.

'And did it make her happy?'

'Oh God, so very happy. You have no idea. For a few weeks I thought she was going to be miraculously cured, she was so excited. Even the doctors were amazed by how much better she seemed.' Christina smiled briefly. 'It turned out to be a blip, of course. But a fantastic blip. She came home from hospital, started knitting baby clothes, started coming along with me to all my antenatal appointments. It was a whole new lease of life for her. She was even there when I gave birth to Shaun. It was just the most amazing day. I have a video of her holding him in her arms. I'd actually done it, made her dream come true.' There was another pause while Christina rummaged in the glove compartment for a pack of tissues and wiped her nose. 'It didn't last, of course. We always knew it couldn't. She went downhill again and died when Shaun was three months old. But she got to meet him and she loved him so much. It meant everything in the world to her. And that's why I'll never regret doing what I did.'

They sat together in silence for a few seconds more.

Finally Joe said, 'What did you tell your mum about me?'

'The truth. Without any incriminating details. I just said you had someone else so we couldn't be together, but apart from that you were a really nice person.'

Hearing these words brought a lump to Joe's throat; he *had* always thought of himself as a nice person. If he hadn't been nice, he would never have gone back to Christina's flat and tried so hard to console her in the first place.

'And what did she say?'

'She said most men were useless buggers anyway and I'd manage perfectly well without one.'

He swallowed. 'Do you have a photo?'

'Of my mum?'

'Of . . . the baby.'

'Oh sorry. You mean in my bag? No, I don't.' Christina shook her head. 'Like I said, I've never needed to carry one before. Shaun's always been with me.'

'I want to see him,' said Joe.

She hesitated. 'Why? Don't you trust me? He's definitely yours.'

'It's not that. I just need to see him. He's my son.'

'Are you doing this to make me feel better, Joe? It's OK, you don't have to. We're fine.'

'That isn't it. I'm doing it to make me feel better. I have to see him.'

Her eyes widened. '*Now?*'

'Maybe. I don't know. Where are you living?'

'Chepstow. In my mum's house. I let the flat in Clifton go.'

Chepstow. Twenty-five miles from here . . . in heavy traffic . . . he couldn't manage that. Joe said, 'I can't, not today. Frankie's expecting me home.'

'Of course. It doesn't matter.'

'Tomorrow. I can tell her I have to work late. How about that?'

'Are you sure?'

'Absolutely.' He was sure. He also knew he was treading a dangerous line.

'OK. Great.' Christina looked as terrified as he felt, and as excited; her tentative smile was heartbreaking. 'Um . . . let me write down the address.'

She scribbled it on a scrap of paper. 'Shall I put my phone number too? Just in case you can't make it?'

'Yes, do that.' When she'd handed it over, Joe climbed out of the car. He didn't hug or kiss her; it would have felt wrong. 'I'll see you around six o'clock tomorrow.'

'Yes.' Christina nodded.

'There's something else I haven't told you.' It was no good; he had to say it now. 'Frankie's pregnant.'

A mixture of shock and disappointment flickered across her face. Followed by resignation. Finally she said, 'Right. Well . . . congratulations.'

Joe swallowed. 'Thanks.'

On the way home Joe recited Christina's address and phone number over and over again until he knew them off by heart. Then he ripped up the scrap of paper and threw the bits like confetti out of the car window.

You could never be too careful.

Back in Briarwood, Frankie welcomed him home with a kiss, her watermelon-sized bump pressed against his own stomach.

'Honestly,' she chided, noting the lack of bags. 'I thought you were meant to be getting loads of Christmas shopping done!'

'Too crowded, too hot, couldn't handle the queues at the tills.' That wasn't a complete lie, was it? 'The place was manic.'

'So does that mean I shouldn't expect any presents this year?'

'Don't worry.' Joe stroked her face; he loved her so much. 'I'll go again another time. How have you been today?'

'Great. Swollen ankles, indigestion, getting kicked from the inside. Couldn't be better.' Frankie's eyes shone. 'But it's all going to be worth it. Ooh, did you feel that?'

Joe nodded and placed his hand on the bump between them as their baby kicked again.

His baby.

One of his babies.

Oh God, what had he done?

The gabled house stood at the end of a cul-de-sac, large and detached, with a steeply sloping garden at the front and a For Sale sign outside.

The first thing Christina said when she opened the front door was, 'I should have said this yesterday, but don't worry about maintenance. Having him was my decision and I'll never ask you for a penny. I just want you to know that.'

Joe felt simultaneously guilty and relieved, because contributing money was something he certainly couldn't afford to do without Frankie finding out. Following his impulsive decision yesterday, he'd lain awake last night panicking about it.

'Thanks.' He wanted to hug her but didn't. 'It's not that I wouldn't want to help . . .'

'I know, it would make things too difficult. But it's OK, this is my house now. And Mum left me money too. Come along inside.'

'But you've put it up for sale,' said Joe.

'It's too big for us and the garden isn't suitable for children. I'm going to downsize, find somewhere nice and simple. The neighbours here are a bit old-fashioned. They don't approve of unmarried mothers.'

Joe immediately wanted to go round to the neighbours and

bang their narrow-minded heads together. How dare they disapprove?

'It's fine.' Christina saw the look on his face. 'A chance for a fresh start. It'll be an adventure. Anyway.' She pushed open the door to the living room and said, 'Ready to meet your son?'

Probably not, but Joe went ahead anyway. And the next moment it happened. There was Shaun, sitting in a blue bouncy chair, a small stuffed toy clutched in one hand as he slept. His hair was baby blond, he had cheeks like Winston Churchill and his bottom lip stuck out like . . . well, also like Winston Churchill.

In blue velour pyjamas with Postman Pat on the front.

My son.

As if aware that he was being watched, the lashes fluttered and the eyes opened. His gaze went instantly to his mother and he held out his arms. Christina unbuckled him and lifted him out of the bouncer. She kissed each pouty Churchillian cheek in turn and said lovingly, 'Hello, beautiful, you woke up! Someone's here to see you!'

Someone. It was only a figure of speech but the word cut through Joe like a razor. He was the father. Some men might choose to live their lives knowing they had children and happy not to meet them but this wasn't something he could do.

'Do you want to hold him while I get his bottle ready?'

'Won't he cry?'

Christina smiled. 'Only one way to find out. But he's usually very good.'

And he was. Joe picked him up and held him and in that moment knew there was no going back.

His voice cracking with a tidal wave of emotion, he said, 'My boy . . . my son.'

A month later, he was at Frankie's side when she gave birth –

after twenty-seven hours of fraught and painful labour – to Amber. Red-faced and bawling, she was checked and weighed by the midwife then wrapped in a white blanket and ceremoniously presented to Joe.

Exhausted and ecstatic, Frankie watched him take his daughter into his arms. 'Look at you!' she marvelled. 'You're a daddy!'

The midwife said cheerily, 'Taking to it like a duck to water, he is.'

'He's never even held a baby before,' Frankie told her with pride.

'Ah, your husband's a natural. That's a good sign.'

Unable to look at them, Joe concentrated all his attention on Amber. In the last four weeks he had managed to get over to Chepstow on six occasions. The other afternoon he'd given his son a bath. There were tiny resemblances between him and both of his children but they didn't look remotely alike. The overwhelming surge of love he felt for each of them, though, was exactly the same.

He didn't want to be in this situation but it had happened, it was happening now and it would carry on happening – he'd accidentally got himself on to a rollercoaster ride and could see no way of getting off.

'Look at us. We're a *family*.' Her fringe sticking to her forehead, Frankie beamed up at him. 'This is the happiest day of my life.'

He didn't want to lie to her, but what other choice did he have? Joe nodded and said, 'Me too.'

Promotion at work meant more travelling, more flexibility and more opportunities to spend time away from Briarwood. Joe made up for this by being an exemplary father when he was at home. He loved Frankie and Amber. He also loved Shaun. He didn't love Christina but he liked her a lot, respected her and really enjoyed her company. They were good friends and he told himself that as long as that was all they were, it would be OK. He wasn't cheating on his wife.

Christina's mother's house finally sold and she began searching in earnest for somewhere else to buy. When she found the place in Tetbury and saw how friendly the neighbours were, she went back the next day with Joe and together they looked over the house in Parnall Avenue.

The estate agent just assumed they were a couple, as did the owner of the house. It was easier to let them carry on thinking it than to launch into awkward explanations, especially as Shaun was now eleven months old and had started to say Da-da.

The offer was put in and accepted, the sale went through without a hitch and somewhere along the line the friendly neighbours learned that Joe's job required him to spend four or five nights away, on average, each week. It was a shame, of course, but that was life and sacrifices had to be made. As Christina pointed out, compared with soldiers serving overseas for months on end it was nothing at all.

They also explained that they weren't actually married but they *were* a committed couple devoted to their son.

Which was pretty much true.

Wasn't it?

Up until then, they had been careful to keep their renewed relationship platonic. Joe told himself that if it stayed that way, he needn't feel so bad about what he was doing.

But as time went on . . . well, it turned out they were only human after all. His feelings towards Christina deepened; from liking and admiring her, he grew to genuinely love her just as much as he loved Frankie. And after another year or so of struggling to keep their emotions under control, nature took its course. Because Christina loved him too and – among other reasons – it seemed unfair that she should be forced to live a celibate life.

From then on, Joe experienced more guilt, yet more happiness too. He felt simultaneously better and worse about the tangled web that his life had become.

But really, he had no other choice.

Chapter 20

Was this what having a panic attack felt like? Dex rang the bell again and felt perspiration prickle down his spine. When Molly opened her front door he held Delphi out towards her. 'It's no good, I've had enough of this. I can't do it any more. I'm not cut out for looking after babies.'

'Too bad.' Molly shook her head. 'Not my problem.'

'I'm serious. You have to take her.' He thrust Delphi into her arms and began to walk away, back down the path.

'I'm serious too. Honestly, you're such a waste of space. Here, catch.'

Dex turned just as she threw Delphi at him. Catching her like a rugby ball, he said, 'No, she's all yours,' and threw her back. They shouldn't really be doing this, not with a baby, but Molly needed to understand how desperate he was. 'And if you throw her at me again, I'm not going to catch her.' To prove he meant it, he raised his arms in the air and turned away. But Molly threw Delphi anyway. Too late, he realised he wasn't going to be able to reach her in time—

Dex sat bolt upright, jerked awake by the whoosh of adrenalin. Oh thank God it wasn't real, had just been a dream. Still in a state of terror, he took deep shuddering breaths and gripped the arms of the chair. There was Delphi, safe and well, fast asleep in her cot. He hadn't been hurling her through the air like a rugby ball, hadn't been about to let her fall.

Jesus Christ, though, it had certainly felt real. His heart was still hammering away in his chest. What was the point of a dream like that?

Dex checked his watch: of all the unearthly hours, it was five thirty in the morning. Delphi, who was teething, had had another terrible night. Three times he'd managed to get her back to sleep then returned to his own room, only to be woken again by more fretful sobs. On the fourth occasion he'd put her back down and sat on the hard chair next to the cot to wait and see if she stayed settled. That had been two hours ago and now he had a major crick in his neck.

Downstairs, because it might be a crazy hour but he wouldn't get back to sleep again now, Dex made himself a coffee and headed out into the garden. The sun was rising over the horizon, the sky was clear and it promised to be a stunning spring day. But that dream was still bothering him. What if it meant he was subconsciously tempted to absolve himself of the responsibility of looking after Delphi? Because there was no getting away from it; much as he loved her, she wasn't always the most scintillating company.

Dex paused to watch a spider busily weaving a web between one of the garden chairs and the yew hedge behind it. He used to make his way home from clubs as the sun was coming up. Now the whole day stretched before him and there was likely to be boredom involved. So far the highlight was whatever he decided to cook for his breakfast. Except his cooking skills were diabolical, which meant toast would probably be the safest bet.

Or a Farley's Rusk.

By eleven o' clock, cabin fever had well and truly set in. Five hours felt like five days. Dex scooped up Delphi, took her next door and rang the doorbell.

The sight of Molly with her hair twisted into a knot and secured with two pencils made him smile.

'What are you doing this lunchtime?'

'Why?' She blew kisses at Delphi. 'Want me to look after this one for a bit?'

If he was honest the thought had crossed his mind, but guilt over the terrible dream wouldn't allow him to do it. Besides, if Molly were babysitting, who would he go with?

'No.' Dex shook his head. 'I need to get out of this village for the day. The walls are closing in. Fancy coming out with us for something to eat?'

'Luckily,' said Molly, 'food is my favourite thing. Do I have time to change or can I just go like this?'

She was wearing pink pyjamas.

'I'll book us a table at the Avon Gorge Hotel,' said Dex. 'Wear whatever you like.'

By midday they were on their way down the motorway to Bristol. Molly, having showered and changed into a yellow sundress, watched Dex as he drove. Finally she said, 'What's the matter? You're still on edge.'

Dex shrugged and kept his eyes on the road. 'Honestly? I'm used to living in the city, going out to work, having fun. All the things the social workers kept warning me about when I told them I could do this. But now I'm here it's taking some getting used to.'

You had to feel sorry for him. 'Babies are hard enough to cope with when you've had nine months to get used to the idea of having them. Not that *I* have,' Molly amended. 'But I've heard other people say it enough times. It's bound to take a while.'

'I know.' He nodded in agreement.

'You're just having a bad day.'

'True.' Dex smiled briefly. 'Let's hope it turns into a better one.'

By the time they reached Clifton and found a parking space, the sky was blue and the sun was blazing down.

'Shall I carry the bag?' Molly pointed to the big holdall as he scooped Delphi out of her car seat.

'Leave it there. Let's live dangerously.' His mood already improved, Dex said, 'And to think I used to leave the house with just my wallet and keys. Now it's like packing to go to Australia. Nappies. Nappy cream. Wet-wipes. Bottle of milk. Bottle of water. Cans of food. Complete change of clothes in case she's sick. Another change of clothes in case something else happens. Soft toys, blanket thing, more nappies . . .'

'Microwave, rocket-launcher, frying pan,' said Molly. 'Trampoline.'

He smiled. 'It feels like that sometimes. Come on, let's go.'

The busy restaurant had tables out on the sunny terrace overlooking the gorge and Brunel's famous suspension bridge. The food smelled amazing, a wedding party was eating at one end of the terrace and the general mood was festive and celebratory. A waiter brought a high chair over for Delphi and Dex fastened her into it. Within minutes they had ice-cold wine, food had been ordered and Delphi was happily occupied chewing a piece of bread.

'This is more like it.' Visibly relaxing, Dex sat back and clinked his glass against Molly's.

'More like your old life,' she said.

'I guess.' He indicated the rest of the terrace. 'People I don't know, meaningless air kisses, superficial Sloaney types talking too loudly and laughing like donkeys.'

'WaaaAAHHHH,' squealed Delphi, frustrated by the high chair and doing her best to wriggle out of it.

'No.' Dex shook his head at her and handed her another piece of bread. 'Stay in the chair.'

'BRRRGGHH-YA.' Delphi hurled the bread into the air so energetically it reached the next table.

'So sorry!' Molly grinned at the brigadier-type and his starchy wife. 'Could we have our bread back, please?'

They didn't look remotely amused. Grumpy gits.

'Stay.' Dex pointed at Delphi. 'Honestly, if this was Crufts it would work. Why are babies more difficult than dogs?'

'*SSSKKKKRISSCCC.*' Delphi let out an ear-splitting dolphin shriek that caused diners all over the terrace to stop talking and turn their heads in disbelief.

'I'll have to take her out of there,' Dex sighed as she fought to escape the chair. 'She can sit on my lap.'

'Ridiculous,' sniffed the starchy wife at the next table. 'Bringing a baby to a restaurant when they can't even control it.'

Dex glared at the two of them as he unfastened Delphi and eased her — literally kicking and screaming — out of the high chair. Delphi repaid him by knocking over his glass of wine with her foot.

'No problem at all,' said the charming waiter, arriving with dry cloths. 'Let me just clean that up for you.'

'Thanks.' Molly gamely ignored the cold wine dripping off the edge of the table on to her knees. 'Can we have another glass of white, please?'

'Bbbbrkk,' Delphi trilled, beaming happily across at the flinty-eyed brigadier-type and his wife.

The table was dried, replacement wine was brought and their starters arrived. Holding Delphi on his lap with his left arm, Dex picked up his fork and dug into his twice-baked cheese and asparagus soufflé with—

'A-*tchoo!*'

Delphi's sudden sneeze caught them all by surprise. So did the amount of gunk that shot out of her nose and landed on Dex's plate.

Or more accurately, on his soufflé.

Oh dear. Any other time it would have been funny. Today it evidently wasn't. With a look of resignation, Dex produced a handkerchief and wiped Delphi's nose. For such a tiny one, it had done a lot of damage. He then pushed the plate away and said, 'I'll give that a miss.'

Molly said to the sympathetic waiter, 'Could he have another soufflé?'

'Of course, but I'm afraid there'll be a twenty-minute wait while it's cooked.'

'Don't worry, leave it. I'll just wait for my main course.'

Molly held out her arms. 'Dex, give her to me. She can sit on my lap.'

He shook his head. 'Thanks, but I'm fine. Doesn't matter. Right, let's just enjoy ourselves, shall we? Look at that.' He indicated the dramatic gorge beyond the terrace. 'What a view.'

'People have bungee-jumped off that bridge,' said Molly.

He grinned. 'Sounds like the kind of thing I'd do for a bet. Ever tried it?'

'No, but I've abseiled off a cliff.'

'Me too. How high was your cliff?'

It was nice to see him start enjoying himself at last. Molly took a sip of white wine and said, 'Just a bit higher than yours.'

The coup de grâce occurred ten minutes later, just as their main courses arrived at the table. A noise like a small erupting volcano emanated from the depths of Delphi's nappy.

'Oh my God.' Dex burst out laughing for roughly two seconds before the extent of the damage made itself hideously apparent. His face changed as the warmth and wetness sank in. He closed his eyes and said, 'Shit.'

Which was appropriate.

From across the table Molly could already see it had exploded out of the legs of the nappy and over the top of the waistband at the back. Maybe if Delphi had been wearing an all-in-one suit the worst of it might have been held in. But in a two-piece, containment wasn't an option. There were also ominous brown stains across the front of Dex's white shirt and jeans.

'WAAHHH,' bellowed Delphi, dropping the car keys she'd been playing with as Dex stared down at himself in horror.

Oh Lord, his *shirt*.

'Don't worry, I'll get the bag from the car.' Molly scooped the car keys up from under the table, jumped to her feet and ran through the hotel.

Back a couple of minutes later, the receptionist on the front desk said sympathetically, 'He's downstairs in the men's loo.'

'Thanks.' Clattering down the stairs, she hammered on the door.

'This is a nightmare.' Dex let her in. 'I don't know where to start.'

'It's OK, I'll help.'

'No.' He took the bag. 'It's my problem, not yours. Let me do it myself.'

He meant it. Molly leaned against the sink and watched him laboriously remove Delphi's poo-strewn clothes. It took an entire packet of babywipes to clean her up – while Delphi lay on her back, cheerfully oblivious, and gurgled at Molly.

At last she was presentable again, in a clean top and lime-green dungarees. Beaming, she pulled her thumb out of her mouth and said, 'Baaaa.'

'Baaaa to you too.' Molly scooped her up into her arms.

The door to the bathroom was pushed open and the brigadier-type barged in, stopping dead in his tracks at the sight that greeted him. His eyes narrowed at Molly.

'What the bloody hell's going on? For God's sake, what are you doing in here?' He then turned to Dex. 'And what d'you think *you're* doing with that brat?'

Dex replied evenly, 'Cleaning her up and changing her nappy.'

The man's grey moustache bristled in disbelief. 'What's the matter with you, man? Your wife's the one who should be doing all that. It's a bloody disgrace. And look at the state of your clothes. If you can't control your child you shouldn't bring it out to places like this. I've a good mind to report you to the manager.'

'Brilliant idea. You do that.' As he said it, Dex unbuttoned his shirt and took it off. Oh good grief, what was he going to do, challenge the man to a boxing match?

'Don't you dare touch me!' Evidently thinking the same, the brigadier-type backed away.

'Oh, do me a favour.' Dex, his eyes rolling with derision, stuffed the poo-stained shirt into the paper-towel bin. 'Right, we're off. You have a nice lunch with your wife and don't worry about us. Whatever you do, don't let it bother you that you've ruined our day.'

They left the bathroom, climbed the stairs and Dex beckoned for one of the waiters to follow them out of the hotel. On the pavement outside the entrance – because standing in reception bare-chested and wearing poo-stained jeans would be all kinds of wrong – he opened his wallet and began peeling off twenty-pound notes.

'It isn't that much, sir,' the Irish waiter protested.

'Those two miserable fuckers at the table next to us? Pay for their meal too.'

The waiter, who'd evidently heard them complaining, said, 'You don't have to do that.'

'I know, but let's do it anyway. Bastards.'

'I'll tell them you were here to celebrate your wedding anniversary.' He smiled. 'I hope we'll see you again, sir.'

'Thanks. And you may want to send someone down to the men's bathroom to empty the bin,' said Dex. 'It's got my shirt in it.'

It wasn't smelling great in the car, thanks to the present Delphi had left on Dex's jeans. As they drove along with all the windows down, Molly tried not to glance sideways at his lean tanned upper body. When they passed a clothes shop she said, 'We could stop and buy you a new T-shirt and jeans.'

He shook his head. 'No.'

'Why not?' In an effort to make things better, she said, 'Let's do that! It's not too late to find somewhere else to eat.'

'It is.' Dex paused. 'Sorry. You must be starving.'

'I'm not.' No sooner was the lie out of her mouth than her stomach rumbled.

There was a Burger King up ahead. He pulled in and handed her a tenner. 'I'll wait here. You have whatever you want.'

'Remember in *Pretty Woman* when Richard Gere said that to Julia Roberts? I always dreamed of hearing someone say it to me,' said Molly. 'And now they have.'

But Dex wasn't in the mood to be cheered up. 'Sorry. We'll do lunch another day.'

'Will you stop apologising? What shall I get you?'

'Nothing. Not hungry.'

He said it again when they arrived home. 'Sorry.'

'You'll look back and laugh about this one day,' said Molly.

But he was shaking his head; she'd never seen him so pissed off. 'Serves me right for thinking we could have a nice trip out of here. Spend a couple of hours having a good time.'

His eyes, normally sparkling with playful humour, were bleak with resignation. There was no hint of a smile. He'd been looking after Delphi without a break for weeks and now here they were, back in Briarwood.

'What are you going to do now?' Molly watched as he lifted a now sleeping Delphi out of her car seat.

'Me? Have a shower. Change into something that doesn't smell like a cowshed. Put the washing on, clean the bathroom. And then when this one wakes up we'll maybe watch a cartoon, play with some bricks . . . I don't know. The thrilling possibilities are endless.'

'Look, go up to London,' said Molly. 'See your friends, have a break. Leave Delphi with me.'

Dex had stopped shaking his head. The last time she'd seen a look of hope like that was when Joe and Frankie had presented Amber, back when she was ten, with a choice between the usual caravanning holiday in Wales or a trip to Disneyland, Paris.

'Really?'

'Why not? You're having a bad day. You need a bit of time off and I'm not doing anything else. I'll look after Delphi, you can meet up with your friends. Stay overnight and come home tomorrow morning.'

Dex's expression softened. He murmured something that sounded like, 'That's what friends are for.'

Molly said, 'What?'

'Something you said ages ago. You're a star. Only if you're absolutely sure, though.'

'Of course I'm sure. We'll be fine. Go on, have your shower now.' As he nudged the car door shut with his foot, Molly said, 'Don't take this the wrong way, but the sooner you stop smelling like a zoo, the better.'

He was back forty minutes later, thoroughly cleaned up, wearing black trousers and a dark grey shirt.

'See? You don't scrub up too badly.'

As she said it, Molly breathed in the clean citrus scent of his aftershave, so much nicer than before.

'I feel like a new mum, going out for the first time since giving birth.' Dex was restored to his normal playful self. He waggled Delphi's hands and kissed her on the tip of her nose. 'You be a good girl, OK? I'll see you tomorrow.'

Delphi stuck her fingers in his mouth and squealed with laughter as he pretended to bite them.

'Have fun,' said Molly.

'That's the plan.' Dex handed her the keys to his cottage. 'The spare room's all ready for you. Help yourself to anything. I'll see you tomorrow. And thanks again.'

'No problem.' Delphi was clamouring for another kiss; Molly held her up so Dex could oblige. The next moment, just as she was turning away, she belatedly realised he was about to give her a kiss on the cheek too. It was one of those completely-not-expecting-it moments; caught off guard, she jerked her head back round and managed to crack her forehead against his cheekbone . . . oh God, how mortifying, how juvenile. *OK, just pretend it didn't happen.*

'Right!' Flustered, she took a couple of steps back and yanked the door open. 'Off you go! Wave bye-bye, sweetheart. That's it, good girl, say bye!'

'Gaaahhh,' said Delphi.

Chapter 21

It was six o'clock and Frankie was making cheese on toast in the kitchen. Amber had texted to say she was staying for tea with one of her friends from school, and Joe wasn't due home tonight, so no need to cook a proper dinner. Instead she could have a snack in front of the TV, watch the programmes she wanted to watch, eat chocolate without having to feel guilty about it and maybe re-do the polish on her toes later in perfect peace.

The front door opened, Frankie jumped and the slice of cheese on toast slid off her plate on to the floor. Cheese side down, naturally.

She called out, 'Amber? Is that you?'

No reply. But Joe was in Norfolk so it couldn't be him, surely? Stepping over the slice of cheese on toast, Frankie pulled open the kitchen door.

It *was* Joe.

'Oh my goodness, you gave me a fright! What are you doing home? I was just making myself some . . .' Her voice trailed away as she saw the expression on his face. 'What's wrong? Are you ill?' She'd never seen him so pale and drawn. Was he about to have a heart attack? Why was he looking at her like that? Had he been made redundant?

Joe was shaking his head slightly. 'I'm not ill.'

'Is it your job then? Has it gone? Because it doesn't matter, we'll manage somehow, we can—'

'Have you spoken to Amber?'

'About what? She's over at Jess's.' Frankie's heart was racing now, her legs wobbly. 'Oh God, what is it? Don't tell me she's in trouble . . . please don't let it be drugs . . .' He was still shaking his head, as if he couldn't stop. Her mouth bone-dry with fear, Frankie croaked, 'Has she been expelled? Is she pregnant?'

'It's nothing like that. I love you, OK? You do know how much I love you.'

Time was slowing down. There was a loud buzzing noise in her ears. 'Just say it,' whispered Frankie. 'Oh God, just say it now. There's someone else, isn't there?'

Joe was rubbing his face with his hand; she could hear the dry rasp of stubble against skin. The desperate shake of his head gradually turned into a resigned nod.

'I love you more than anything. I swear I never wanted this to happen. But yes, there's someone else.' Frankie felt nausea rise in her throat, then realised he was still speaking. 'Two people, actually.' He paused as she let out an involuntary groan of horror. 'And Amber knows.'

How was she still able to drive? Somehow the automatic reflexes continued to function. Right now, reaching Amber was her number one priority; whatever it took, she would do it.

Frankie followed the satnav's instructions and reached the park in Tetbury. It was eight thirty, getting dark now. Getting chilly too. But there was the pond, there were the wooden benches between the flower beds and there was her daughter sitting where she'd said she'd be. With the boy beside her.

Joe's other child.

His son.

She pulled up, leaving the car's engine running and the headlights on. Twenty metres away, Amber rose to her feet and said something to the boy. He stood up too, heading off in the opposite direction and melting into the darkness.

Climbing out of the car, Frankie held out her arms and hugged Amber tightly to her.

'Oh Mum . . .'

'I know, I know. Sshh.' Stroking the wild aubergine curls, Frankie felt as if her heart would break on her daughter's behalf. Her own feelings were currently on hold. Amber, who had always idolised Joe, was her priority now.

'Shaun wanted to say sorry,' Amber mumbled into her neck. 'But I told him not to. He says it's his fault and I think it's mine.'

'Sweetheart, don't say that. It's not your fault.' Frankie's throat tightened. 'Or his.'

'Or yours either.' Her daughter stepped back. 'It's Dad's. Where is he?'

'At home, packing some things. He'll be gone by the time we get back.' *Would that upset her even more?*

'Good, because I hate him. I really do,' Amber said vehemently. 'I can't believe he's done this to us. I never want to see him again, *ever*.'

Dex rubbed the back of his neck and surveyed the scene before him. OK, this wasn't working out. He shouldn't be feeling like this. He'd wanted to escape, hadn't he? Leave the tedium of childcare behind for the night, meet up with his old friends, get laid, feel normal again?

That had been the plan, anyway. It was what he'd been desperate for, more desperate than he'd let on even to Molly. She had no idea how close to the edge he'd been feeling, and how guilty as a result. That couple at the table next to theirs had—

'Come on, keep up! Get that one down you and have another drink!' Rob and Kenny were back from the bar, voices raised to be heard over the music. The club was an old favourite; they used to come here all the time. But tonight Dex just felt wrong, out of place, as if something was missing.

Or someone.

'Drink.' Rob gave him a nudge.

Oh well. It had always worked in the past, hadn't it? Dex knocked back his beer, then the whisky chaser, shuddering slightly as the heat of the whisky hit his stomach.

'Pretty girls heading our way.' Kenny's eyes lit up. 'I wouldn't say no to the one in the red dress.'

Rob snorted. 'You wouldn't say no to anything in any kind of dress. You'll get what you're given.' He surveyed them as they approached. 'Bet you any money Dex goes for that one anyway. She's right up his street.'

The girl in the red dress was a stunning willowy brunette, but Dex's attention had been caught by her shorter blonder friend; if you blurred your vision and just took a quick look, she bore a passing resemblance to Molly.

Oh God, what was happening to him?

'Hiyaa!' The girl with the passing resemblance to Molly didn't sound like her at all; she had a voice like an overexcited budgie. 'Saw you looking at me! D'you come here often?'

'Not any more, no.' How many drinks had he had? Quite a few, if you added them all up.

'Me neither! So that's cool, isn't it? We're both here on the same night. That's, like, *fate*. I'm Stacey, by the way. Call me Stace.' She beamed up at him expectantly.

'Hello, Stace. Nice to meet you.' Dex took his car keys out of his jacket pocket and flashed her an apologetic smile. 'Have a great evening, OK? I'm off.'

Molly jolted awake, her heart leaping like a salmon. She'd definitely just heard the sound of footsteps on the stairs. Was it burglars? Oh God, not tonight of all nights.

It was pitch black outside, still the middle of the night. OK, now what? Run out and confront the intruder? Pretend to be asleep? But what about Delphi in her cot in the nursery across the landing?

The next second there was a tap on her door, which either meant it was an extremely polite burglar, or—

'Molly? It's me. Are you awake?'

And *breathe*. The frantic panic evaporated in an instant. She exhaled and collapsed back against the pillows.

'I'm awake. What are you doing back?'

The door opened and Dex came into the room. 'Can I come in?'

'You already have. It's fine,' Molly added as he hesitated. 'What's wrong?'

'I need to talk to you.' The bed creaked as he sat down. 'You can't imagine how I felt this afternoon. I really thought I couldn't do it. I was all ready to call the social worker and tell her I wanted my old life back.'

'You wouldn't have done that.' Dex wasn't completely off his head but he'd had a fair amount to drink, that much was obvious. The haze of alcohol fumes surrounded him like a Ready Brek glow.

'Wouldn't I? It's how I felt, I swear to God. All the baby stuff was doing my head in. That pair of miserable old gits at the restaurant today? I wanted to tip them into the river. I was *this* close to telling them what I thought of them.'

'So was I. But what did you do instead? Ended up paying for their meal. I wouldn't have done that for them,' Molly argued. 'Not in a million years.'

'You want to know why? Because I was ashamed,' Dex said bluntly. 'I used to *be* them. Before Delphi was born I bloody hated having my day ruined by other people's kids. It got on my nerves. I can't believe how horrible I used to be, but I was. All I cared about was me.' He stopped and threw himself down alongside her, gazing up at the ceiling. 'I know I said I could do this, but it doesn't come naturally, putting someone else first when you're not used to it. Giving up the life you used to lead. It's bloody hard.'

'Of course it is.' Molly nodded. 'You knew it wouldn't be easy.'

'And I was right about that. But guess what? Something weird happened tonight.' Dex tilted his head in her direction and raked his fingers through his hair. 'When I was back there, it felt all wrong. I missed Delphi. I didn't want to be in that club with those girls. They were just . . . a waste of space. But one of them looked a bit like you and all of a sudden it made me realise . . . well, stuff.' He gestured vaguely, searching for the right words and failing to find them. 'And then I started thinking about that thing earlier when I was leaving here and we bumped heads and you got embarrassed and, God, I did too, and that's *never* happened to me before . . . so I wondered if it had ever happened to you?'

The way he was looking at her and the tone of his voice was unsettling. He'd now rolled on to his side and was lying with his head propped up on one elbow. Talk about a surreal situation. Her pulse racing, Molly said, 'Lots of times. I'm very clumsy.'

Dex blinked, as if trying to work out if she'd deliberately ducked the question.

'Well, it was a first for me. And I had to come home. Because you're here. That was it, you see; I realised I'd rather be back here with you than in London with . . . *whoever*. Can I ask you something?'

'You can ask.' Oh help, was he drunker than she'd thought?

'Do you like me?'

OK, definitely drunker. 'Come on,' said Molly. 'If I hated you, I wouldn't have offered to babysit.'

'Because I like you,' said Dex. 'I mean, *really* like you.'

'You don't. Not in that way.'

'I do.' He was over-nodding now. 'In every way.'

Well, this was a turn-up. He'd had way too much to drink and was saying embarrassing things. Prompted, presumably, by the fact that she'd helped him out today. Thanks to the amount he'd had to drink – and an attack of gratitude – he appeared to be intent on making an impulsive, alcohol-fuelled pass at her.

Oh dear.

'Dex, go to bed,' said Molly.

He broke into a grin; she could see his teeth gleaming white, his dark eyes glinting with mischief.

'I'm pretty much already in this one. Can I kiss you?'

'No.'

'Please. To make up for the complete hash I made of it this afternoon.' Frustratedly he added, 'I can't *believe* that went so wrong.'

Molly's body was tingling; on the surface she was doing a good job of sounding sensible, but of course she found him attractive.

Because there was no getting away from it, he just *was*. Physically, he was pretty much faultless. And they got on well together. But taking it any further would be madness. They were friends, they were neighbours and Dex had already freely admitted that girl-friends were for Christmas rather than for life. He was an alpha male, a charmer, accustomed to bedding anyone who briefly took his fancy.

No way was she going to get involved, add herself to his list of conquests, become yet another victim of the inevitable subsequent brush-off.

Talk about catastrophic.

'You're not saying anything.' Dex's tone was playful, so convinced was he that she would give in.

Molly shook her head and said, 'I am now. I'm saying no.'

'What?'

'You're not my type. At all. Oh dear,' she added. 'After a meaningless quickie, were you? Bad luck. Looks like you should have stayed in London after all.'

Dex did a double take. 'Do you really mean that?'

'Yes.'

He sounded taken aback. 'I thought you liked me.'

'Not in that way. And I don't sleep around. Look, go to your own room now. Get some sleep.'

'I can't believe this.' He was frowning, genuinely perplexed.

Which helped. A lot.

'Sorry about that. It's a shock, isn't it, finding out you aren't irresistible after all?' This was getting much easier now; his utter certainty that she'd fall into his arms made Molly realise how right she'd been to resist his oh-so-generous offer.

'But—'

'Dex, give it a rest, *please*. Don't expect me to be grateful for a bit of attention. Don't pester me any more, OK? Maybe in London you're a superstar City-boy with girls falling at your feet, but down here in Briarwood . . .' She paused. 'Honestly? You just come across as a bit of a prat.'

Chapter 22

The beep of her mobile woke Molly the next morning. Not that she'd got a lot of sleep. The last few hours hadn't exactly been restful; giving Dex a piece of her mind had been bothering her ever since. Had she been too brutal in order to deflect attention from the fact that she did – against her better judgement – secretly fancy him? The answer was probably yes.

It had worked, though. In response he'd sat up and stared at her for several seconds, then said, 'Well, that tells me, doesn't it? Thanks for letting me know.' Before heading out of the bedroom and closing the door behind him without another word.

Molly flinched at the memory. Oh dear, and it had seemed like such a good idea at the time. Maybe she should apologise later.

Anyway. The beep had signalled the arrival of a text. Half wondering if it might be from Dex, she rolled over and retrieved her phone from the bedside table.

The time was ten past eight. And the text wasn't from Dex, it was from Frankie: 'Something's happened. I'm coming over.'

What? What had happened? What did that mean and how could Frankie send a message like that without giving even a clue?

Flinging back the duvet, Molly jumped out of bed and headed for the window. It was a grey and rainy morning, the last daffodils were being buffeted by the wind . . . and there was Frankie, not wearing a coat, starting to make her way across the green.

At least she didn't have long to wait to find out.

OK, better get home . . .

Molly threw on her clothes, peered around the door of the nursery and saw that Delphi was waking up. Scooping her up into her arms – *mmm*, so gorgeously warm and cuddly – she carried her along the landing. Then stopped in her tracks and turned to look out of the window again.

Any sense of remorse for the things she'd said last night to Dex promptly evaporated. What she saw made her want to punch him.

Without bothering to knock, Molly burst into the darkened bedroom and saw him lying fast asleep on his front. She gave his shoulder a shove and said, 'I have to go. Here's Delphi. And by the way, you disgust me. I can't believe you did that last night. As far as I'm concerned you're a repulsive human being and I'm *this* close to calling the police.'

'Ow.' His eyes still closed and his forehead creasing with the effort of waking up, Dex murmured, 'What?'

'You should be ashamed of yourself. I'm sure the social services would be interested to hear about it too. I thought you were a decent person.' Molly plonked her charge down on the bed next to him and said, 'Right, I'm off. So you'd better wake up and look after Delphi. She wants her bottle.'

'What time is it?' He sounded like a man with a headache. *Good.*

'Time you took a good hard look at yourself in the mirror and realised how ridiculous you are.'

Dex was still frowning and massaging his temples. 'Look, I'm sorry. Can you just—'

'No,' Molly cut in from the doorway. 'You're selfish. And pathetic. And you really need to sort yourself out.'

Molly reached her front door at the same time as Frankie.

'What were you doing over at Gin Cottage?' Frankie looked odd, her eyes wild, her face taut and pale grey.

'Babysitting, that's all. No funny business. Tell me what's happened to you.' Molly unlocked the front door and led the way into the kitchen.

'Quite a lot of funny business. Except it's not funny. Brace yourself,' said Frankie. 'Joe's been seeing someone else.'

'Oh God. Oh *no*.'

'He's left. I told him to get out of the house.'

Joe, of all people. 'And it's definitely true? He admitted it?'

'Under the circumstances he didn't have much choice.' Frankie had pulled out a chair, sat down at the kitchen table and was now playing with the contents of the sugar bowl. Eerily calm on the surface, she began spooning up granules then letting them cascade back into the silver bowl. Well, mainly into the bowl. A few grains scattered on to the tiled floor.

'Is it someone we know?' Molly couldn't believe this. And Frankie was being so matter-of-fact about it; she must surely be in a state of shock.

'No.' She was shaking her head.

'How did you find out?'

'I didn't. It was Amber. Completely by accident, poor darling.'

'But . . . is it just a fling? Or, you know, serious?'

'Oh, I think you can probably call it serious.' The ghost of a mirthless smile crossed Frankie's face. 'Ask me how long it's been going on.'

'How long?'

'Almost twenty years.'

'Twenty YEARS?' Molly shook her head and shouted, 'That's impossible!'

'Apparently not. You just have to be really good at lying and multi-tasking and covering your tracks.'

'You're in shock. I need to make you some tea.'

'Please don't, I've been drinking tea all night. It's practically coming out of my ears.'

Molly was stunned. She had a million questions and knew she was gaping like a goldfish. 'I just . . . oh God, I don't know what to say. Of all the men you could think of, I can't believe Joe would do that.'

Because basically, if you couldn't trust Joe, who could you trust?

'I know. And it gets better.' Still dry-eyed, Frankie corrected herself. 'I don't mean better, I mean worse. It's not just one of those affairs where you both occasionally sneak off and meet up. It's a whole double life. Their neighbours think they're married.'

Molly covered her mouth. 'No!'

'Oh yes. And they have a son.'

'What?'

'His name's Shaun.' Frankie spilled a bit of sugar and put the spoon back in the bowl. After a pause she went on, 'But when he came along to your evening class the other week he called himself Sam.'

'Oh my God!' Shaking her head in disbelief, Molly belatedly realised the part she'd played. 'That's why Amber asked me to draw him . . . she was desperate to track him down . . . I should never have done it.'

'Yes you should. If you hadn't, he'd still exist. Joe would still have another family. It's not the boy's fault,' said Frankie. 'He's grown up knowing they're the secret ones. He was curious, wanted to see what we were like. If you think about it, you can't blame him for that.'

Molly pictured herself in that situation. Of course she'd do the same.

'What about Amber? How's she taking it?'

'Not well. Understandably. She's pretty distraught, says she never wants to see her dad again.'

'And Joe's gone.'

'He's gone.' Frankie dipped her head in agreement. 'Yesterday I was married. Today I'm a single parent. Joe's living twenty miles away in Tetbury with his other family.'

Joe had another family. It was just the most astonishing situation imaginable. Molly closed her eyes briefly, envisaging Shaun's facial features. At the time there hadn't been any recognisable signs but now, looking back with hindsight, there were a couple of faint similarities . . .

Aloud she said, 'He doesn't look like Joe.'

'No. Apparently he takes after his mother. But . . .' Frankie hesitated and gestured at her own face.

'There's something about the jawline . . .' Molly ventured.

'Yes, that's it.' Nodding in agreement, Frankie said, 'I can see it too, now. And the chin.'

They sat there in silence for several seconds.

'I'm so sorry. I don't know what to say.' Molly tried and failed to imagine how her friend must be feeling. 'All this time and you had *no idea*.'

For a few seconds there was silence in the kitchen, then Frankie said slowly, 'Well, I wouldn't go as far as that.'

Molly stared at her. 'What? Oh my God, you mean you *knew*?'

'Not all of it. I didn't know the whole story.' Frankie exhaled and sat back, her fingers laced together and resting on the table in front of her. 'But honestly? It's not the biggest surprise in the world that there was something going on.'

'Seriously?' This was almost as startling as the story itself. 'But you never told me! I thought you and Joe had the perfect marriage.'

'So did everyone. I think that's what made it so impossible to say anything. You just don't want to . . . disappoint people,' Frankie said helplessly. 'Especially when they come to you with their problems.'

'You always seemed so happy though,' Molly protested.

'And a lot of the time I was. But there were clues.' Frankie took a deep breath. 'Things that got me suspicious.'

'Like what?'

'OK, years ago I found a lipstick under the passenger seat in the car. When I asked Joe about it, he said it must belong to one of the other sales reps he'd given a lift to. Which could have been true, who knows? So I let it go. But a couple of months after that, one of the other mums at Amber's school mentioned in passing that she'd seen Joe in Gloucester the day before with a blonde. And she was one of those smug mothers, you know?' Frankie pulled a face. 'The kind who'd love to think she might be stirring up trouble. So I just said straight away that the two of them worked together and had been there on a selling trip. I pretended I knew all about it. But Joe had told me he was working in Norwich that day.'

Molly winced in sympathy. 'Did you ask him about it?'

'I did. But Joe just shrugged and said how could it have been him? Because he'd been hundreds of miles away in Norwich. He didn't seem as if he was lying,' Frankie went on. 'He sounded completely believable.'

'So you just left it.'

'Yes. Was that cowardly?' With a grimace, Frankie said, 'Maybe it was. But I didn't want the other mother to be right. She would have loved that. And Amber was only eight or nine. We were such a happy family. It was easier to let it go.'

'And that was it? Nothing else?'

'Nothing major. Just the occasional tiny thing. A long blond hair on his shirt, one time. And he came home not long ago with a bottle of aftershave he'd bought for himself . . . which was weird because he'd never done that before, I was always the one who bought him aftershave.' Another sigh. 'OK, basically I always thought he might have been playing away. He was a travelling salesman, after all. It must be tempting when you're away from home . . . that's not making excuses, it's just being realistic. But what would have happened back then if I'd found out for sure? Amber loved her dad so much. And I loved Amber. I couldn't bear the thought of her life being ripped apart. And we were still great together . . . it's not as if it was a hardship to carry on. When you're doing it for the sake of your child, you'd be surprised. It's actually quite easy to turn the other cheek.'

God. 'Really?'

'Really.' Frankie saw her expression and said, 'I know what you're thinking, but you'd be amazed. So long as Amber was happy, nothing else mattered.'

Molly's mobile began to ring. She picked it up, saw Dex's name flashing up on the screen and switched it off.

'You thought Joe was having affairs.'

'I told myself they were meaningless flings. It didn't occur to me for one second that it could have been one long meaning*ful* thing. That's completely different. But now I know the truth, it's all over. He's lied to me every day for almost twenty years and that's too much. He says he loves both of us, just like he loves both his children. God, I still can't believe I'm *saying* this. I was so desperate to have another baby after Amber, and Joe was never so bothered about it. Now we know why.'

'I just can't imagine how you're feeling,' said Molly.

'Right now? Thirty per cent shock. Ten per cent stupid. Ten per cent terrified. And truthfully?' Frankie tipped her head back for a moment, then carried on counting on her fingers. 'Fifty per cent relieved, because it's happened at last and I don't have to pretend any more.'

'Oh God. Come here.' Molly threw her arms round her. 'This is the maddest thing I ever heard. But you'll get through it. As long as you're OK, that's the main thing.'

They hugged tightly, spilled sugar crystals crunching on the floor beneath their feet.

'Amber's the main thing. She's the one I'm worried about. You know how much she loves her dad.' Frankie checked her watch. 'I'd better get back before she wakes up. And I need to get the café ready for opening . . .'

'You can't work in the café today,' Molly protested. 'Do you want me to do it for you?'

'No, I need to keep busy. It'll take my mind off everything else. Well,' Frankie amended with a rueful smile, 'it won't, but it'll give me something to do. Thanks for the offer though.'

'Give my love to Amber.' When they'd shared one last squeeze, Molly said, 'You're being amazing, so brave. But any time you need me for anything at all, I'm here. Just give me a call.'

Chapter 23

It was midday and Amber's brain felt as if it was about to explode like a shot-at watermelon. Too many thoughts were careering around inside her skull, bouncing off the walls like brawling nightclub drunks. Fury and frustration were building up. Her dad had left home, gone to live with his *other family*. Her friends knew something was up but hadn't yet discovered what, and were bombarding her phone with nosy messages because there was nothing they adored more than a good old bit of gossip to brighten their day.

Right now Amber hated everyone. Her ghoulish friends. Her father. Shaun. Shaun's mother. And her own mother too, for not being as devastated as she should have been. Because an hour ago she'd come into the bedroom and said gently, 'Are you still asleep?'

Which had long been a standing joke between them – if Amber merely grunted *Uh-huh* it meant she wasn't ready to wake up yet – but today the last thing she was in the mood for was standing jokes. Still, she'd grunted *Uh-huh* and kept her eyes closed, and her mum had said, 'OK, sweetie, you stay there, I'm just opening the café.'

Opening the café? *Seriously?*

'Uh-huh.'

'Are you all right?'

What kind of a dumb question was *that*? 'I'm fantastic,' Amber had retorted. 'Never better.' Then, when her mum had hesitated in the doorway she'd added irritably, 'Go ahead and open up. I'm fine.'

And unbelievably her mum *had*. Even though she wasn't remotely fine, because how could she be? And how could her mum just head downstairs, open up the café and gaily serve coffee and sandwiches and stupid cakes to stupid strangers as if nothing had happened?

More hot tears leaked out of the sides of Amber's eyes as she lay there in the bed on her back. Her pillow was damp with them, her eyelids were puffy and sore and downstairs she could hear the faint chatter of customers and chink of china. Her mum was down there smiling and being lovely to people, carrying on as if today was just another normal day.

Not fair.

So not fair.

Amber rolled on to her side, reached for the tumbler of water on her bedside table and hurled it at the wall. Water sprayed through the air but annoyingly the tumbler didn't break.

'Aaaarrrgghhh.' Snatching up the pillow, she pressed it over her face and attempted to vent her frustration with a muffled shriek. 'Bastard . . . bastard . . . *fuck* . . .'

Was *anything* going to help?

Molly was putting the finishing touches to a Boogie and Boo strip when the doorbell went.

Opening the door, she saw Dex carrying Delphi on his hip. His hair was wet from the shower and he wore a grey T-shirt and old jeans. Delphi, in yellow dungarees, beamed at the sight of Molly – 'Brrahh!' – and offered her a chewed bit of carrot.

Having smiled at Delphi, Molly allowed her smile to drop away as she surveyed Dex and said evenly, 'Yes?'

'Look, about last night. Well,' he amended, 'this morning. I guess I need to apologise. So here I am. Sorry.'

She shrugged fractionally. 'Right.'

'I made a mistake,' Dex went on. 'A massive one. I misjudged the situation . . . thought maybe you felt the same way. I came back because I thought . . . well, anyway, it was one of those spur-of-the-moment things and it didn't work out. Obviously.'

'Obviously,' said Molly. What was really obvious was the fact that he'd never experienced rejection before. Which made her all the more glad she'd rejected him last night.

'I'd had a fair bit to drink.'

Her lip curled. 'I noticed.'

'Got out of the habit recently. If it's any consolation, I have a cracking hangover.'

Was he expecting sympathy? Molly gave him a so-what look and said pointedly, 'But you're still alive.'

Dex frowned. 'Is that supposed to mean something?' He gestured with his free hand before she could reply. 'Anyway, let me just say this. Sorry for getting it wrong and don't worry, it won't happen again. We're friends, we're neighbours, that's it. No more . . . whatever. From now on we'll leave it there.' He paused. 'Except . . . you don't seem to think we're even that. Look, I'm doing my best to apologise here. I know it's all a bit hazy, but I just wanted you to know how I felt. Did I really do anything so terrible?'

He had no idea, no idea at all. Eyeing him in disbelief, Molly said, 'Do you really think you *haven't*?'

★　★　★

'Aaaarrgghhh!' yelled Amber, this time without a pillow over her face.

That felt better. Get it out, let off some steam. 'AAAAAAARRRGGHHHH!'

Throwing back the tangled duvet, she leapt out of bed and retrieved the glass tumbler, hurling it against the door. What the hell, it *still* didn't bloody break. She tried again, aiming for her dressing-table mirror. Bingo, this time the mirror smashed *and* the tumbler cracked in half.

'WAAAAAAAAAAHHH,' Amber bellowed, reaching for the bottle of perfume her dad had bought her for Christmas. Then she was frenziedly throwing everything she could lay her hands on – make-up, the jewellery box she'd been given two years ago, her bedside lamp . . . 'AAAAGGGHHHHH!'

'OK, let me just say this. If you ever, *ever* do it again,' said Molly, 'I'll call the police.'

Dex was looking at her as if she'd suddenly sprouted horns. 'What?'

'You drove up to London.' Molly's mobile began to ring. 'Went out drinking with your friends.' Distracted, she glanced at the screen and saw Frankie's name. 'And then you got into your car and drove all the way back here while you were still drunk. Hi, what's up?'

'You said I could call anytime.' Her friend was frantic. 'Amber's upstairs having a meltdown. Can you come now and take over down here?'

'On my way.' Molly snatched up her keys and headed for the door, gesturing to Dex that she was leaving.

'Can I just—'

'Sorry, emergency, I have to go.' She locked the front door and set off across the village green without looking back.

'Brrrraaahhh,' Delphi called after her, indignant at having missed out on their customary goodbye kiss. A stab of remorse cut through Molly but it was too late to turn back; she had to get over to the café now. And Dex was still watching her, she could feel it. She was still furious with him and he was the one holding Delphi.

To whom she appeared to be in danger of becoming worryingly over-attached.

Maybe it was time to take a step back.

'Oh sweetheart, it's OK, we'll be all right.' Amber was in her arms and Frankie felt as if her heart would break. She held on to her daughter, rocking back and forth and patting her back as she'd done years ago whenever Amber had been upset. Right now she was sobbing like a baby, properly howling with misery, incapable of holding it in. Hopefully it would be cathartic.

They sat together for some time, on the bed, the front of Frankie's shirt growing steadily damper with tears as she continued to stroke Amber's hair and murmur soothing words of comfort. They might not work but at least she was saying them, reassuring her daughter that she was still loved.

At last the shuddering sobs died down, the flow of tears dried up and the tension leaked out of Amber's body.

'Sorry.' She wiped her eyes and said, 'Couldn't help it. Thought my head was going to explode.'

'Oh darling, it doesn't matter.'

'I feel a bit better now. Who's looking after the café?'

'Molly.'

'I'll have to say sorry to her too. Oh God, I just feel so . . . stupid. If Dad's lied about so many things my whole life, how do I know he's *ever* told the truth?' She paused, struggling to explain.

'Like when he used to call me his beautiful girl. He probably didn't even mean that.'

This thought had occurred to Frankie too. Fiercely she said, 'Of course he meant it. Because you *are* beautiful.'

'Does he like Shaun more than he likes me? He might do.'

Suddenly having to cope with the concept of sibling rivalry was evidently hard. Giving her a reassuring kiss, Frankie said, 'Your dad loves you with all his heart.'

'And what about Shaun's mum? Does he like her more than he likes you?'

Touché.

'I don't know.' Another question she couldn't answer. Frankie just knew she had to be strong for her daughter. 'But we're going to get through this, trust me.'

'How?'

'One step at a time.' All she knew right now was that seeing the hurt Joe had inflicted on Amber was having a powerful reciprocal effect on her own feelings for him. He was a lesser man than she'd thought and the love was evaporating like mist. *Which was a good thing.*

'What's the first step?' said Amber.

Frankie surveyed the wrecked bedroom and said with a brief smile, 'Probably clearing up the broken glass.'

On her way back home from the café, Molly saw in the distance that Dex was outside Gin Cottage, cutting back the overgrown wisteria at the side of the house.

As she approached, he glanced up and noticed her before looking away again. Awkward.

Drawing closer, she saw Delphi in her baby walker on the path and her heart did a squeeze of love. In turn spotting her, Delphi started waving her tiny starfish hands and shouting excitedly. Even more awkward.

Molly began to veer over to the left, away from Gin Cottage and towards her own. The next moment – oh help – Dex was opening the gate, closing it behind him so Delphi couldn't escape and making his way towards her with an air of purpose.

He wasn't smiling either.

And then he was digging into the back pocket of his jeans, pulling out a folded sheet of paper, holding it towards her.

'Here you go.'

What was this about? Unfolding the paper, Molly saw that it was a receipt from a company called ScooterGuys. Beneath their name was printed the shoutline: 'We drive you and your car home then scoot off back to base!'

The receipt was for three hundred and eighty pounds.

'Just so you know,' Dex said evenly, 'I don't drink and drive. Never have, never will. This is how I got home last night.'

'OK. Well, good.' She felt her cheeks redden at having wrongly accused him. 'Sorry.'

But the tension between them still hung in the air. Dex's eyes were glittering. He said, 'No problem,' in the tone of voice that clearly indicated there *was* a problem. 'But maybe next time you could check first, before accusing me of doing something I would never do.'

'Right, yes, I will.' The *other thing* still stood between them, as insurmountable as Becher's Brook. Molly hesitated; should she mention—

'Anyway, that's all. Don't panic, I haven't forgotten the agreement.' He turned away, heading back to Delphi who was watching them through the slats of the closed garden gate. 'Bye.'

Chapter 24

He'd started off with all the good intentions in the world, but caring for Delphi single-handed was turning out to be harder than Dex had ever imagined.

It was four weeks now since his trip to – and ill-fated return from – London. He and Molly were speaking to each other but the atmosphere between the two of them was still strained and set firmly to politeness-between-neighbours. It was killing him, but it wasn't his place to try and change it; he'd made a complete prat of himself and that was that. The rejection still stung but he had no choice other than to man up and deal with it.

Which he *had* been doing. But now he needed some form of distraction. The life of a celibate monk wasn't what he was cut out for.

Happily, thanks to Delphi's obsession with Young Bert, Dex appeared to have found himself a new babysitter.

'I think it's going to be her first word.' Outside in the garden behind the café, Amber had been watching with amusement as Delphi gazed rapturously at Young Bert and shouted, 'Go! Go!'

Dex said, 'She's either trying to say "goat" or telling him to clear out of here.' Personally, he couldn't see the attraction; with that bony skull, those pale beady eyes and the whiskery white beard, Bert reminded him of his old chemistry teacher from school.

'GO GO GO!' roared Delphi, clapping her hands at the little goat.

'She's a cutie.' Amber looked at Dex. 'I'm a brilliant babysitter, by the way. If you ever need one.'

'Really?' Dex was immediately interested.

'I've done loads around here. Haven't I, Mum?'

'Hmm?' Frankie was busy clearing and wiping down tables. 'Babysitting? Oh yes, she's done lots. Plenty of families can recommend her.'

'How about tomorrow evening?' said Dex.

'Friday? No problem. Five pounds an hour,' said Amber. 'What time would you be home, though? Because I have to be up early on Saturday.'

'Midnight?' said Dex. 'Half past?'

She gave him a pitying look. 'You can stay out till two, but no later than that.'

'Deal. Great.'

Frankie straightened up and said, 'There you are then, all sorted. Going somewhere nice?'

'I don't know yet.' Dex felt better already; the actual going out was the exciting bit. It didn't even have to be anywhere nice.

The Crown Inn was on the outskirts of Marlbury, the small market town eight or so miles from Briarwood. Serendipity had brought Dexter here tonight. Two years ago he'd heard and liked a song being played on the radio, made a note of the band and bought their album. He'd been one of a very select few to do so; they'd never been heard of since. Until yesterday, when he'd spotted a flyer on the noticeboard in the village shop, advertising a gig by the band at the Crown the very next night.

And now here he was, in a busy pub, watching them begin their set.

They were called The Games We Play, which Dex had thought an intriguing name for a band. With no photos on the cover of their CD, he'd had no idea what they looked like. Sadly, the female singer was a drippy-looking blonde and the drummer and guitarist were hand-knitted, straggly-haired hippy types. It shouldn't have mattered, but it did.

More to the point, they were playing as if they'd forgotten how to do it. The blonde girl was nervous, singing off-key and with her eyes closed.

God, what a let-down. This was awful. Should he get out now, escape while he still could? Or stay and hope they improved?

The first song ended and the applause was muted which was hardly a surprise. Scanning the audience, Dex noticed only one person clapping with enthusiasm. At the other side of the pub, her arms raised to show she meant it, was a girl around his own age with short red hair and sparkling eyes, wearing a blue top and cargo pants. She even stuck her fingers in her mouth and did a piercing whistle, which elicited a brief smile of gratitude from the drippy blonde.

Must be a friend or relative.

As if aware of his gaze upon her, the girl with the impressive whistle glanced over at Dex then looked away again.

The next song began. During the course of it he caught her looking at him twice more. When it ended, she once again applauded wildly. Definitely a supporter. Dex, leaning against the bar and noting that she was halfway down her drink, predicted that after two more songs she'd be heading over for a refill.

He was wrong. It took three. And then she materialised beside him, effortlessly attracting the attention of the barman and asking for another Bacardi and Coke.

'Hi,' Dex greeted her. 'Enjoying the set?'

The redhead nodded and said, 'Very much.'

'Know them, do you?' He indicated the band up on the stage.

'Why?'

'You were applauding as if they're your best friends.'

'Well, they're not.' She smiled. 'I just saw how terrified the singer was, thought a bit of encouragement would relax her. And it did. She's not so nervous now.'

'You're right. That's a very nice thing to do,' said Dex.

'Believe it or not, I'm a very nice person.'

She was attractive, well-spoken, had a sense of humour. He said, 'Here on your own?'

'I am. Is that allowed?'

'Of course. I'm just surprised, that's all. Are you a fan of the band?' If she'd also come along here tonight after having bought their CD last year, that would be a coincidence. It might even be fate.

'Never heard of them before. And just between us,' she confided, 'I'm quite hoping I won't hear them again.'

'See that lead singer?' Dex nodded at the drippy blonde on the state. 'She's my little sister.'

There was a pause, then the girl said, 'If that was true, *you'd* have been applauding enthusiastically.'

He smiled. 'Touché.'

Her eyes sparkled. 'My name's Amanda. Can I buy you a drink?'

'Hello, Amanda. No thanks.' This time it was Dex's turn to pause for a second, before taking out his wallet. 'Let me get you one.'

Amanda was thirty years old. She was single and worked as a

secretary. Up close, her eyes were grey, flecked with gold. When she went on holiday she liked to go either skiing or scuba-diving. She also didn't see the point of eating curries unless they were seriously, *seriously* hot.

The band reached the halfway point of their set and stopped for a break. Amanda and Dex applauded them off the stage then made their way outside for some fresh air. They grabbed one of the tables in front of the pub and Amanda chatted briefly to an elderly couple walking past with their spaniel.

When the couple had moved on, Dex said, 'So you're local?'

'Very.' Amanda indicated the row of houses across the street.

'That's where you live?'

'Number twenty-two, the one on the end.'

'Handy.' The moment he said it, Dex realised how it sounded. As she raised a quizzical eyebrow he said, 'OK, *cut*. I meant handy for you, living so close to the pub.'

Amanda smiled. 'There is that. It also has its drawbacks. Can get a bit noisy at chucking-out time. But when you just feel like popping out for a quick drink, catching up on local gossip and seeing who's around, yes, it can be very . . . handy.'

The playful way she said it told Dex all he needed to know. This was flirtation at its most subtle. Amanda was letting him know she found him attractive. He took a swallow of his drink and said, 'And who was around tonight? Anyone interesting?'

She inclined her head towards him. 'You know, I actually think there might have been.'

From inside the pub came the sound of a guitar being retuned. The barmaid, clearing glasses from the tables next to them, said, 'Sounds like they're about to start up again.'

Everyone else headed back inside. Dex and Amanda stayed where they were.

'Do you want to listen to the second half?' said Amanda.

'I don't mind. Do you?'

She was watching him intently now, her mouth curving up at the corners. 'I think we've done our bit, given them the encouragement they needed.' As the music began to play inside the pub, she listened for a moment and said, 'She's singing in tune now.'

'So there's no reason why we can't stay out here.'

Amanda considered this, then rubbed her arms. 'Except, it's getting a bit . . . chilly.'

'Let's go back inside then,' Dex said easily. He knew what was coming next.

'But then we wouldn't be able to talk, not properly.' She blinked and said, 'We could go over to my house, if you like. For coffee. How does that sound?'

A girl in a red Peugeot was driving past; for a split second Dex saw her blond hair and thought it was Molly. But no, of course it wasn't her. He watched the Peugeot disappear down the street and allowed his heart rate to return to normal. Then he drained his glass, smiled at Amanda and said, 'Coffee sounds great.'

It was ten o'clock; the coffee had been drunk. The lights in Amanda's sitting room were low and her intentions abundantly clear.

'Right, shall I just come out and say it?' She'd kicked off her shoes and was next to him on the sofa, her feet tucked beneath her. 'I'm a single thirty-year-old who'd rather not have her private life gossiped about. Which, in a town like this one, is easier said than done.'

'I can imagine,' said Dex. *Good news.*

'Plus, I'm not particularly interested in a full-time relationship.'

Dex nodded slowly to show he was listening and understood. *Better and better.*

'So what I'm saying is, you seem like a discreet kind of person . . .'

She waited. He nodded again, although seriously, how could she tell?

'. . . And I do have to be up early tomorrow, but if you'd like to spend the night here with me, I think we'd have a very nice time.'

'I think you could be right,' said Dex. 'Although I have to be up early too, so it's probably easier if I don't stay the whole night.'

Amanda paused and eyed him shrewdly. 'I'm not a marriage-wrecker. You told me you were single. Is that true?'

'Don't worry, it's true. I couldn't be more single if I tried.' Rising to his feet, Dex reached for her hand. 'That's why this idea of yours sounds pretty much perfect.'

Well, that had been nice.

Sometimes a bit of no-strings, honest-to-goodness, purely physical sex was just what you needed.

Or more than a bit, even.

Anyway. Very nice indeed.

Amanda's bathroom was done out in pale green marble. Stepping out of the shower, Dex towelled himself dry and dressed again, then headed back to the bedroom.

She was lying in bed, unashamedly naked, smiling up at him. 'You look cheerful.'

Dex grinned. 'So do you.'

'It's been like a really good workout at the gym. Only much more fun.' Amanda lifted her face to him for a kiss. 'Thank you.'

'You're welcome.'

'Well, you know where to find me if you ever fancy a rematch. And here's my number.' She passed him a Post-It bearing her name and number scribbled in felt-tip. 'Even though you haven't asked for it.'

'I was just about to,' said Dex.

'I was too impatient. Sometimes,' Amanda playfully nudged him with her foot, 'I'm too brazen for my own good.'

Chapter 25

Molly bumped into Amber in the village shop.

'How's things?' She gave the girl a hug, because the last few weeks hadn't been easy for Amber, who was still flatly refusing to see Joe. 'I thought you'd have come along to my class last night but someone said they'd seen you going out. Did you do something nice?'

'Nice enough, but it doesn't exactly count as going out. I was just babysitting. Delphi's adorable, isn't she? If you sing to her, she does this hilarious sitting-down dance, shuffling on her bottom and waving her hands in the air. It's *so* cute!'

'Oh, you babysat for Dex?' Molly experienced a jolt of envy coupled with loss; *she* had taught Delphi how to do the shuffle-bottom dance, they had done it together on her own living-room carpet. Not that she could have looked after Delphi last night, but it hurt to know that she was no longer being asked to babysit. On the surface she and Dex were polite towards each other but the chilly distance remained. Thanks to her cutting comments, the easy camaraderie between them had been killed stone dead.

'I didn't have to babysit the whole night,' said Amber. 'He was home by one o'clock.'

It was none of her business but she couldn't help herself. Molly said casually, 'And did Dex go somewhere nice?' *I'm not being nosy, just making polite conversation.*

'I don't know where he went, but I'd say he definitely had a good time.'

'Oh?' What did that mean?

'Put it this way. He went out smelling of that aftershave he always wears.' Amber's eyes glinted with mischief. 'Came back five hours later with damp hair and smelling of lemon shower gel.'

Right. So Dex had found someone who didn't reject his advances. Well, that was always going to happen, wasn't it?

With an effort, Molly forced herself not to feel jealous. She'd had her chance and turned him down, hadn't she? For *all* the right reasons.

In the long term, it was definitely for the best.

Leaving school that afternoon, Amber experienced that prickling being-watched feeling and saw a boy across the road observing her. When she paused, he slid down from the wall he'd been sitting on and headed her way.

Weirdly, she guessed who he was and what he was doing here just by the look of him. Clean-cut boys tended to have clean-cut friends.

'Are you Amber?'

She stopped walking. 'You already know I am.'

'OK, yes. Well, I looked you up on Facebook.'

Even his trainers were dazzlingly white. 'And who are you? Another long-lost brother?'

He shook his head. 'No. I'm Shaun's friend. Max. He asked me to come over and see you.'

'Why? To have a good laugh at me?'

'Of course not. Don't say that. Shaun's worried about you. He just wants to know if you're all right.'

Amber gave a snort of derision. 'Me? Oh I'm fine. Never better. My father's spent his life lying to me, and now he's living with his other family. Why wouldn't I be all right?'

'But it's not Shaun's fault, is it? And you were OK with him at first.'

She had been, on that initial fateful day in Tetbury. She'd been distraught and Shaun – her *half-brother* – had been apologetic. She'd had questions, he'd had answers. But since then, Amber's resentment had grown. If he and his mother hadn't existed, her life would still be normal, happy, trouble-free. Instead, she hated her father and was simultaneously repulsed and outraged by the fact that he was living with Shaun and Christina.

And, all right, also jealous.

'Look, I don't have to talk to Shaun if I don't want to. And sending you over here isn't going to make any difference, so don't bother trying it again. Anyway, I have to go now.'

'Fine.' Max pushed back his silky fair hair and took out his car keys. 'So that's that.' He flashed a rueful smile. 'Mission: abject failure.'

'Not my fault,' said Amber. Did he expect her to feel sorry for him? Apologise for wasting his petrol? *No chance.*

'Can I offer you a lift anywhere?' He pressed the key in his hand and a sporty blue Renault parked beside them emitted a high-pitched *woooop.*

One of those flashy types.

'No thanks. My boyfriend's waiting for me.'

'Right. Well, nice to meet you anyway. Can I just say one thing?'

'Go ahead.'

'Shaun's my best mate. He's a good person. As brothers go, you could do a lot worse.'

'Thanks, but still not interested,' said Amber. 'Bye.'

Doss was waiting for her, as arranged, outside the off-licence. 'All right?' He gave Amber a cider-tinged kiss on the mouth and said, 'Got any money on you?'

She was seventeen and the owner of the off-licence was an expert at spotting fake IDs. Amber gave Doss ten pounds of her babysitting earnings and waited on the pavement while he went inside to buy as much cheap alcohol as possible.

Doss wasn't his real name, of course. He'd been christened Daniel and had acquired the nickname as a result of not doing a stroke of work during his final years at school. Or since. But he was good company and really good-looking, thin and dark with Johnny Depp eyes and loads of tattoos. They'd been friends for months and on the couple of occasions he'd come to Amber's home, her father had palpably disapproved of him. Aware of this, Doss had been delighted when he'd heard about Joe's unravelled double life. He'd comforted her when she'd needed comforting and now they were a couple, hanging out three or four times a week. She enjoyed it when they spent a couple of hours together lying on the grass in the park, everything beginning to feel better. They drank strong cider, Doss told her Joe was a two-faced tosser and they talked about the upcoming music festivals they would attend this summer.

'Got 'em.' He emerged from the off-licence, the carrier bag clanking with cans, and took her hand in his. 'Let's go. We're meeting up with Beeny and some of his mates.'

Oh. Amber wasn't wild about Beeny, who didn't usually smell too fresh and could get quite tedious when he was stoned.

'Don't look like that,' Doss chided. 'He's cool.'

'I know.' He had a sweet dog, that was something in his favour.

'And he said he might have some stuff for us.'

Stuff that would make them as droney and repetitive as Beeny? Urgh, no thanks; it drove Amber nuts, the way he called everyone 'Maaaaaaan'. Changing the subject, she said, 'What happened to that earring I bought you?' Last week at the open-air market she'd picked out a silver hoop for him.

'Oh yeah, sorry. I kind of lost it.' He slung his free arm round her shoulders as they headed for the park. 'It, like, fell out.'

Chapter 26

It was her.

Oh my God, it actually *was* her.

Now that she was paying attention, Frankie could see it. The woman sitting at the corner table of the café was wearing a grey jumper, loose linen trousers and ballet flats. She was slender, unassuming, apparently in her sixties, with lots of wispy grey-blond hair falling around her face and light blue eyes hidden behind unflattering tortoiseshell spectacles.

Almost as if she were trying to be invisible.

And she was evidently doing a very good job of it. Frankie, behind the counter, listened as two families at adjacent tables competed with each other to be the biggest fans of *Next to You*. They were excitedly discussing favourite episodes, quoting lines from the show, attempting to mimic the characters.

Blithely unaware that Hope Johnson, one of the stars of the series, was sitting less than ten feet away from them.

To be fair, she wasn't recognisable unless you were openly searching for a resemblance. It had been eighteen years since she'd graced the nation's screens but the difference in her made it seem more like forty; she was like a faded shadow of her vivacious former self.

The banter between the visiting families, one from Cardiff and the other from Newcastle, continued to flourish. Photos were taken of the memorabilia and of the pictures hanging on the walls, and each of them in turn posed outside with Young Bert, who was used to it.

At last they left. It was almost four o'clock and Frankie began clearing the tables, aware that Hope Johnson was now surreptitiously eyeing the displayed memorabilia too.

Should she say something?

Or not?

Finally she ventured, 'Can I get you another cup of tea?'

Hope Johnson looked round. 'Oh . . . are you wanting to close up? Sorry . . .'

'No, no problem. Stay as long as you like.'

Tentatively, Hope said, 'Well, if you're sure . . .'

'Quite sure.' No one had heard of her for so many years; to be on the safe side, Frankie flipped the sign over on the door to say Closed. 'It's lovely to have you here.'

Hope looked like a startled faun in the forest. Her slender hands trembled as she handed her cup to Frankie. 'You know . . . ?'

'Who you are? Yes. Don't worry, though,' said Frankie. 'I promise you I'm discreet. If you don't want me to tell anyone, I won't.'

'Oh goodness.' Hope exhaled slowly. 'I can't believe you recognised me. No one ever does.'

'Well, I cheated a bit.' Bringing her a fresh cup of tea, Frankie said, 'One thing hasn't changed.'

'I can't imagine what.' The older woman remained utterly mystified.

'See that photograph up on the wall over there?' Frankie pointed to a close-up of Hope laughing with the director outside the front of the house. 'I took it myself, on the last day of filming. You'd just finished the final scene.'

Hope scrutinised it, peering through her spectacles. 'Ah yes, I remember that day.'

'Look again.' Frankie guided her attention to her hands in the photo, the right one close to her face. Then she nodded at Hope's own right hand, currently clutching the handle of her teacup.

'Oh my goodness.' Hope made the connection. 'My *ring*.'

It was a simple silver ring with bevelled edges and an unusual square tiger's eye stone set in the centre. There was a homemade quality to it, and an oddly masculine aspect that was at odds with Hope's narrow fingers.

'I dust the photos every couple of days, that's how I noticed. As soon as I saw your ring, I knew it was you.'

'Quite the lady detective,' Hope said with amusement.

'We've been running the café for the last twelve years,' said Frankie. 'So I pretty much know these photos off by heart.'

'Well. Hello. It's lovely to see you again.' Hope sipped her tea and surveyed her thoughtfully. 'I do remember you now. You haven't changed much. Unlike me.'

Seeing as she'd mentioned it herself, Frankie said sympathetically, 'Have you been ill?'

Hope's expression was rueful. 'You know, I almost wish I had that excuse. But no, no medical reason for it. I've just aged badly.'

Aaaargh, *that* was embarrassing. 'Oh sorry, I didn't mean—'

'No need to apologise. It's fine. You know, I always suspected it would happen . . . my mother was exactly the same. And when I found myself going down the same path, I just kind of . . . gave up. Some people carry on looking marvellous all their lives. Others 'don't have the genes for it.' Hope smiled briefly. 'On the plus side, I might be faded and wrinkly, but at least I'm still here.'

Since there wasn't much she could say to that, Frankie changed the subject. 'It must feel strange to be back.'

'Oh yes. I never imagined I'd see this place again.' Hope was gazing around the room, visibly moved now by the photos. 'Never thought I'd come back to Briarwood. I don't suppose . . . no, doesn't matter.'

'Say it,' Frankie prompted.

'Well . . . it's incredibly cheeky, but I wondered if I could see the rest of the house.'

'Of course you can!'

'Really? That's so kind of you.' Her thin face lighting up, Hope said earnestly, 'Just for a couple of minutes. I know how busy you must be and I don't want to be a nuisance.'

'Please, you wouldn't be at all. I wouldn't have this café if it wasn't for you. And my daughter won't be home before midnight,' Frankie assured her. 'You're welcome to stay as long as you like.'

And unbelievably, it was happening. After closing up the café and showing Hope over the house, they had gravitated to the kitchen, where a chicken casserole was bubbling in the oven. When Hope had commented on how good it smelled, Frankie had said, 'You're welcome to stay and have some,' not expecting for one moment that Hope would take her up on it.

But she had, and three hours later was still here. Frankie had opened a bottle of wine and they'd sat at the kitchen table, relaxing and chatting without interruption. At first they'd talked about the café, the fans who continued to visit Briarwood, and the phenomenon that had been *Next to You*. Then a question from Hope about Frankie's husband had brought *that* story tumbling out.

'How absolutely awful for you.' Hope shook her head in

sympathy. 'And you're being so brave. I would never have known . . . and you were so cheerful with those other customers in the café. It just goes to show. While I was watching you I thought you didn't have a care in the world.'

'I'm just keeping myself busy.' Frankie opened a second bottle and topped up their glasses. 'It helps. Well, that and the drinking.' Wryly she added, 'But rotten things happen to all of us, sooner or later. I'm just busying my way through it.'

'You're so brave. Maybe that's where I went wrong.' Tucking a loose strand of hair behind her ear, Hope glanced across the table as if making the decision to trust her. 'When it happened to me I ran away and did nothing at all. Probably the worst thing I could have done.'

'Where did you go?'

'A tiny village in southern Italy. Right off the beaten track, the kind of place the tourists don't visit. I hardly spoke any Italian. Nobody there spoke English. Which was what I wanted at the time, but it meant there weren't any distractions. All I had were my own thoughts, going round and round on an endless loop in my head.'

'How long did you stay there?' said Frankie.

'I never left.' Hope shrugged. 'I've lived there ever since. Bought a little place of my own after renting a room for the first year. Took in a few stray animals, got to know the villagers, learned the language. It's a beautiful place, up in the mountains. A good way of life.' Ruefully she added, 'I ran away and never came back. Until now.'

'That's understandable,' said Frankie. 'After losing William. Such a terrible thing to happen.'

Hope ran an index finger around the rim of her glass and said, 'I was the mad cat lady for the first couple of years. The villagers must have wondered what kind of nutcase they'd got themselves landed with. But I sorted myself out eventually.'

Frankie smiled. 'Good.'

'And I met my husband,' Hope went on.

'You got married? Wonderful!'

'His name was Giuseppe. He was a good man, a farmer. Kind, hardworking, steady. I don't think I loved him, but he loved me. And I liked him very much. We were company for each other. I made him happy. No children, just our animals and each other. He died two years ago.'

'Oh no.' Frankie's heart went out to her. 'I'm so sorry.'

'Thank you.'

'Life is unfair. So now you've been through it twice.'

There was that look again, from Hope. She was hesitating, weighing something up in her mind, wondering whether or not to come out with it.

'Look,' Frankie said hurriedly, 'we've had a few drinks. I don't want you to say anything you might regret. The last thing you want to do is wake up tomorrow morning in a cold sweat, wishing you'd kept your mouth shut.'

'But—'

'It would just make you feel terrible, really it would. And then I'd feel terrible too. Come on, let's change the subject.'

'God, you're so *lovely*,' Hope exclaimed. 'Is it just me or does everyone meet you and instantly feel as if they want to tell you all their secrets?'

'It does seem to happen,' Frankie admitted. 'I think it's my face. I do have this kind of agony aunt reputation around here.'

'I'm not surprised.'

Frankie grimaced. 'Not that it works with everyone. My husband spent eighteen years keeping a pretty big secret from me. Which makes it all extra humiliating.'

'OK, I'm just going to say it. I wasn't in love with William

Kingscott,' said Hope. 'I liked him as a person. We had this amazing on-screen chemistry, that's how the rumours about us started. And he developed a crush on me, but nothing ever happened. We were just great friends. The trouble was, the more we denied there was anything romantic going on between us, the more everyone thought we were lying, covering up this amazing love affair. I was upset when he died, of course I was, but I wasn't utterly devastated.'

Frowning, Frankie puzzled over this. 'But you disappeared, went to live in Italy . . . you *were* devastated . . . oh, OK.' The unspoken sorrow in Hope's eyes, combined with her own intuition, caused the clouds to clear. 'I see, I get it now. You were devastated, but not by William's death.' She paused, gazed at her and said slowly, 'It was someone else.'

'You're good.' Hope dipped her head in wry acknowledgement. 'Yes, that's right. Phew, this feels a bit weird, actually. I've never told anyone before. Well, apart from my cats.'

'And they were Italian cats,' said Frankie, 'so they wouldn't have understood.'

'Exactly.' A brief smile. 'Sometimes the language barrier has its uses.'

'So who was it? One of the other actors from the show? Oh listen to me, here I go again.' Frankie flapped her hand by way of apology. 'Not my business, don't tell me.'

'It's OK, I want to now. No, he wasn't one of the actors. Nothing to do with the production,' said Hope. 'He was a wonderful man, the love of my life.' Her eyes softened. 'But there could never be any future for us. It wasn't possible.'

'Why not? Was he married?' Frankie's eyebrows shot up. 'Oh my God, was it *my* husband?'

They both burst out laughing at the same time. Hope spluttered wine into her sleeve and rocked back in her chair.

'Ha ha, wouldn't *that* be a soap-opera twist? No, it wasn't Joe. And he wasn't married. There was . . . another reason we couldn't be together. The last time I saw him was just after we'd finished filming the final episode of *Next To You*. I felt as if my life was over. I'd already decided to disappear when the accident happened and William was killed. So that was it; as soon as the funeral was over, I was gone.'

'And what happened to . . . the other one?'

'Who knows? Never saw him again. Never likely to. He wasn't, shall we say, the type to hang around.'

'But you met him while you were filming? So does that mean he was from around here?'

Hope said simply, 'Yes.'

Wow. 'And is he still?'

She shook her head.

Frankie's thoughts were racing. 'Well, I was here then. Would I have known him?'

'I don't know. Possibly. Probably.'

'It's none of my business. You don't have to tell me. Maybe it's better that I don't know.'

'His name was Stefan,' said Hope.

'Oh my God. Really?' Frankie's mouth fell open. 'Stefan the gypsy? Stefan Stokes?'

Two spots of bright colour glowed on Hope's face. 'So you do remember him.'

'I do. I mean, I don't have to remember him. He's still here.'

It was Hope's turn to be shocked.

'He is? But . . . I went into the woods.' Her hands were trembling. 'The caravan . . . there's nothing there any more. It was all gone, the pathway completely overgrown. He always told me he could never stay in the same place . . .'

'He never could.' For years Stefan had moved around the country, sometimes joining his extended family of Romany travellers, at other times preferring to be alone. 'Until his daughter had a daughter of her own,' Frankie explained, 'and decided to put down roots. He came back eight years ago and this time he stayed.'

Hope said breathlessly, 'Is he . . . well?'

'Very well. The caravan's moved,' said Frankie. 'When the Hanham-Howards bought Finch Hall they offered him a pitch on their land in exchange for keeping an eye on the grounds. Oh wow, this is amazing,' she exclaimed. 'It's like something out of a film! And he's still single. I could take you over there now!'

'No, no . . . it's no good, there's no point, that would just make things worse.' Her hand pressed to her chest, Hope said, 'He's a Romany, that's why we could never be together in the first place. His family would never have accepted him marrying an outsider. Oh crikey, I can't stop *shaking*.' She held her fingers outstretched. 'I came back, but I didn't expect this. I really didn't expect him to be here.'

'It's good news,' said Frankie. 'Wouldn't you like to see him again?'

Hope's eyes glistened as she considered the question. Finally she said, 'Is he still as handsome as ever?'

How old was Stefan? He had to be sixty. But yes, there was no getting away from it, tall and tanned, with those flashing dark eyes and sculpted cheekbones, Stefan Stokes would always be handsome.

Frankie nodded. 'Yes.'

Her smile sad, Hope visibly deflated. 'Of course he is. And look at me.'

'Why? I don't know what you mean.'

'Oh come on, I'm not blind, I do occasionally see my reflection in the mirror. When I can't avoid it,' Hope said with resignation. 'I know what I used to look like.'

'But—'

'That was then and this is now. Some people age well and I'm not one of them. Trust me, I'd be such a disappointment to Stefan. And I'd find that hard to bear.' Finishing her drink, Hope checked her watch and pushed back her chair. 'Anyway, time I was going. It's been lovely to see you again, and thank you so much for . . . well, everything. But I have to be off now.'

She was like a terrified gazelle. Discovering that Stefan was in the vicinity had completely unnerved her; now she couldn't get away fast enough. Frankie waited while she called the taxi company and asked to be collected and taken back to Cheltenham, where she was booked into a hotel.

'It's been wonderful to see you too,' she told Hope.

'Please don't tell anyone I was here. I mean it,' Hope begged her. 'Not a soul.'

'I won't, I promise. You're still *you*, though.' Frankie couldn't help herself, she had to give it one last try. 'I honestly don't think Stefan would be disappointed.'

'But I can't afford to take that risk. I just couldn't bear it.' They were at the door now. Hope was still trembling at the thought that Stefan could be nearby.

'You can wait in the house until the taxi arrives,' Frankie offered.

'No, it's OK, I'll just lurk in the shadows.' On the doorstep, Hope kissed her on each cheek and said, 'They'll be here any minute.' She half-laughed. 'I've been in such a jitter I forgot to ask about Stefan's family. I can't believe his daughter's living here now. And his granddaughter! What's her name?'

'Addy,' said Frankie. 'She's nine. A complete character.'

Hope's smile was wistful. 'How wonderful. And whereabouts are they?'

It was pitch black outside. From where they were standing, the houses clustered around the village green were randomly lit up. Frankie pointed to the brightest, the Saucy Swan, with its multi-coloured fairy lights sparkling in the trees outside. 'Over there. Lois runs the pub.'

When Delphi flatly refused to sleep, Dex had discovered the trick was to put her into the pushchair, tilt it back into almost-flat mode, tuck her up in a blanket and take her for a turn around the village until she dozed off. It was probably the wrong thing to do, but what the hell, it did the job. And sometimes he stopped for a chat with whichever of the villagers happened to be occupying the tables outside the Swan. Like tonight he'd sat down with Stefan Stokes, Lois's father. Following their first unpromising meeting all those months ago, the two of them had become friendly. Tonight they'd discussed astronomy, about which Stefan was hugely knowledgeable, and the best ways to get unsleepy babies to sleep.

'When Lois kept us up, we just added a few drops of brandy to her bottle.' Stefan's eyes had flashed with amusement at the memory. 'Everyone did it back then. I suppose you'd be reported if you tried it now.'

Lois, who'd come out to collect empty glasses, said, 'Yes, funnily enough, giving alcohol to very small children is kind of frowned upon these days.' She shook her head at Dex. 'Just ignore him.' Pointing at Delphi, still wide-eyed in her pushchair, she added, 'And you, young lady, stop playing silly beggars and go to sleep. Give your dad a break.'

'BRRRRRRRRAAAHHH,' said Delphi.

If anything, she was even more awake now. Stefan and Lois had headed back inside the pub, leaving Dex to resume his walk around the village. He made his way past the entrance to the churchyard, then paused outside Frankie's house to gaze up at the sky. He'd never studied the constellations before but Stefan had pointed a few out to him. Could he recognise them again without help?

'GAAAAAH,' Delphi grumbled in protest because they'd stopped moving.

'Sshh.' Dex rocked the pushchair back and forth and continued to stare at the stars. How could the shapes be so obvious one minute and impossible to find the next? Where was—

He turned his head, realising there was a figure in the shadows by the church gate. Blinking, readjusting his vision, Dex saw a thin older woman standing next to the wall.

'Sorry.' She sounded flustered. 'I didn't mean to startle you.'

'No problem.' Dex smiled at her concern. 'I was just looking at the stars, trying to find Orion's belt.'

After a moment the woman stepped out from beneath the branches of the yew tree overhanging the lychgate. Moving towards him, she turned her head up to the sky and pointed. 'There it is. See it now? Three stars in a row.'

'OK, yes, got it. Thanks.'

'And there's the Plough.' She pointed again and drew the shape in the air with her finger until he found it.

'You know your stuff,' said Dex. He'd never seen her before but she was definitely coming in useful. 'I'm just a beginner.'

'We were all beginners once. I was taught by someone who loved the stars. Now I love them too,' the woman said simply before turning to Delphi. 'And is this your daughter?'

The advantage of Delphi's hair growing longer was that she

was no longer mistaken for a boy. Being asked if she was his daughter invariably made Dex's heart swell with pride. 'She is.'

Well, kind of.

'She's a beauty. Aren't you, hmm?'

'KYAAHHH.' Delphi beamed and kicked her feet in the air.

'Hard work too, I bet. But worth it.' The woman bent over and waggled Delphi's outstretched fingers.

'Definitely worth it.' Wondering who she was and what she was doing here, Dex was about to ask when the twin beams of a set of headlights swung across the green and a car rounded the corner.

As it approached them, the woman said, 'Ah, that's my taxi,' and straightened up, signalling to the driver with her free arm.

Dex watched as she climbed into the passenger seat and waved at Delphi. 'Bye then. Nice to meet you. Don't forget Orion's belt!'

'I won't.' He knew he probably would. 'Goodbye.'

Delphi, copying the woman's wave and opening and closing her hands like tiny starfish, chirruped, 'Baaa!'

Chapter 27

At three o'clock on Friday afternoon, Henry gave in at last and called Dexter.

He'd held out for long enough, hadn't he? Alarmed by the strength of his reaction to the photograph of Frankie, he'd actually forced himself not to visit Dex for a few weeks. To prove that he wasn't a crazed stalker, basically. And also in the hope that the feelings might subside.

Well, that mission had been semi-completed; he'd managed to stay away, but the feelings were still there. In the meantime, his friend Dex was probably thinking he'd been abandoned, which wasn't good.

Dex picked up the phone and Henry said, 'Hey, how are things with you?'

'Fantastic, never better. I'm sitting in the doctor's waiting room, feeling like the world's most evil torturer.'

'Why?'

'Because Delphi's on the floor playing with a plastic giraffe and thinking everything's fine. What she doesn't know is that in a few minutes I'm going to be the one holding her down while she gets stuck with a hypodermic as big as a knitting needle.'

Henry smiled. 'You heartless bastard.'

'I know. Anyhow, speaking of bastards, when are we going to see you? I thought you were coming down to visit us.'

In London, in his office on the thirty-seventh floor, Henry swung round on his swivel chair and gazed through the windows at the city spread out below him. There was the invitation; how could he turn it down?

'That's why I'm calling you now. How about this weekend? I thought of maybe driving down tomorrow.'

'Hey, great. That's brilliant. I'll introduce you to the locals.' Dex sounded cheerful. 'You'll love the pub, there's some mad characters in there.'

'Can't wait.' Henry's mouth had already gone dry. 'Shall I see you around midday?'

'Oh, hang on, better make it a bit later than that. I promised to help someone out tomorrow, give them a hand in the café.'

Just the mention of the word *café* gave Henry a massive jolt. 'You mean the place with the goat?'

'Ha, that's the one.' Amused, Dex said, 'This is Briarwood, remember. It's the only café we've got. Anyway, I'll be there for a few hours. Maybe you could turn up around five?'

'Whatever.' Talk about a golden opportunity. Henry, who had no intention of waiting until five, said, 'I'm easy. See you when I get there.'

When he'd hung up, Henry swung his chair round in a circle and did an inner, triumphant air punch. Tomorrow he'd meet her. He'd get there early and offer to help out in the café alongside Dex.

What could be more perfect than that?

★   ★   ★

'Delphi Yates?' The motherly receptionist beamed at Dex and said, 'You can take her through now, love. Dr Carr's ready for you, second door on the left.'

But were they ready for Dr Carr? Dex was already feeling a bit sick. What if he fainted at the sight of the needle? Scooping Delphi up, he carried her out of the waiting room and down the corridor. He knocked on the door, pushed it open . . .

And came face to face with Amanda.

They stared at each other for several seconds.

The last time he'd seen her, she'd been naked. Today she was wearing a neat olive dress beneath a white medical coat. He was tempted to say, 'I hardly recognise you with your clothes on.' Then again, perhaps not.

Finally he said, 'You're Dr Carr.'

'I am.' She wasn't smiling.

'You didn't tell me you were a GP.'

'No, well, it's not compulsory.' Glancing at Delphi, on his hip, Amanda said coolly, 'There appears to be something you forgot to mention too.'

Dex gave Delphi a squeeze as he sat down and settled her on to his lap. 'Don't worry, I'm still single. I'm Delphi's guardian. It'll all be there in her notes.'

He waited while she brought the relevant pages up on the computer and read them through.

'Right.' When she'd finished, Amanda visibly relaxed. 'Well, now I know why you had to rush off home. Can I ask, are you registered with me as well? Because if you are, we should switch you to one of the other doctors in the practice.'

'I'll do that.' Dex nodded; God, who'd have thought registering with a new doctor could be such a minefield?

'OK, so Delphi needs her Hib/Men C jab. Let's get that done, shall we?'

Amanda launched into professional mode. Dex held Delphi and did his best to distract her while the hypodermic was plunged into the soft squidgy bit of her upper thigh. Delphi's happy care-free smile turned in slow motion into a howl of disbelief and she struggled to escape.

Dex, attempting to console her, was horrified to feel his own eyes prickle with tears. He knew he was doing this because it had to be done, but would Delphi forgive him and ever trust him again? And God, how embarrassing that Amanda was seeing him like this . . .

'Never easy, inflicting pain on a baby.' She smiled at him and blew up a disposable rubber glove; within seconds, Delphi had stopped crying and was shrieking with laughter as she tried to grab the inflated fingers.

'So, anyway. This doesn't have to be awkward,' said Dex.

'Apart from the slightly awkward fact that I gave you my number and you haven't called it.' Amanda efficiently disposed of the syringe in the sharps box and washed her hands.

'Still have it though.' For once he hadn't thrown the piece of paper away; flipping open his wallet, Dex triumphantly produced it. 'I was just waiting for the opportunity.' Was this true? Actually, it probably was.

'Well, good. Glad to hear it.'

'Why did you tell me you were a secretary?'

'Occupational hazard of being a medic.' Amanda grimaced. 'It's just easier. As soon as anyone finds out you're a doctor, they start asking you about their clicky necks and headaches and asym-metrical breasts.'

'I wouldn't do that,' said Dex.

'Even better news. Well, nice to see you again.' Checking her watch, she said, 'My next patient will be waiting.'

'Let's hope you haven't slept with them too.'

'Especially seeing as she's eighty-six years old with chronic bladder trouble.' Amanda smiled and said, 'Bye. Call me.'

'Gaaaaaahhh,' burbled Delphi.

Dex said, 'I will.'

It was one o'clock on Saturday and the sun was blazing down. Having arrived in Briarwood two hours earlier, Henry was having a curate's egg of a day.

The good news was that Delphi was enthralled by him, following him around like a besotted puppy and endlessly fascinated by his face, his hair, his teeth, his voice.

The other items of good news were that it was great to see Dex again, the village itself was charming and the villagers friendly.

The bad news, the very, *very* disappointing bad news, was that Frankie Taylor, the woman who'd occupied his thoughts for the last few weeks, wasn't among them.

Ironically, he'd learned with a sinking heart, she was in London. Even more ironically, for the first time ever.

'That's why I'm here, helping out,' Dex had explained when he'd finished introducing Henry to Amber. 'I was in here with Delphi the other day, chatting to Frankie about London. I couldn't believe it when she said she'd never been. Can you imagine? And I told her she should go.'

Brilliant. Just perfect. Thanks a lot. Henry did his best to look only mildly interested.

'Then Mum said she'd love to but she couldn't,' Amber chimed in, 'because how could she leave me to run the café on my own?'

'So I offered to give Amber a hand,' Dex said cheerily.

There was such a thing as being too helpful. 'And she's gone up there for the day?' said Henry.

'The whole weekend! Her and her friend Molly.' Amber rolled her eyes. 'They're going sightseeing during the day, then off to a club at night. I told Mum she was too old to go clubbing but it's like she's on some kind of mission to humiliate me.'

'It's about time she had some fun,' said Dex.

'Fun? It's embarrassing. She's threatening to dance.' With a mock shudder, Amber said, 'Except she calls it *having a bit of a bop*.'

'Here we are, found it!' The door to the café swung open and a curvy woman in a tight pink dress burst in, carrying what looked like a couple of wooden gates in each hand. When she saw Henry holding Delphi, she stopped dead in her tracks and said, 'Well, hello, my day just took a turn for the better. Who have we here?'

Assuming she meant the baby, Henry said, 'This is Delphi.'

'I know *that*.' Amused, the woman said, 'I was talking to you.' *Help.*

'Don't frighten him,' Dex chided. 'His name's Henry and we used to work together. He's down here for the weekend.'

'Better and better. You're a sight for sore eyes, aren't you?' Handing the gates to Dex, the woman reached for Henry's hand and shook it, hanging on for a good few seconds after the shake was over. 'I'm Lois. How very lovely to meet you. I hope we'll see you in the Swan this evening.'

'Lois runs the pub,' Dex explained. He added, 'And I don't know if you'd noticed, but she's not shy.'

Henry, who *was* shy, managed to claim his hand back at last. To cover his confusion he pointed to the gates and said, 'What are they?'

'We're building a cage.' Lois regarded him for a second, then broke into a red-lipsticked grin. 'It's my daughter's old playpen. Dexter was going to tether Delphi to a stake in the garden, like Young Bert. I said I'd dig it out so he could pop her in this instead.'

The next thing Henry knew, he was out in the café garden with Lois, slotting together the sides of the pen and tightening the screws she'd rather disconcertingly put for safekeeping inside her mauve satin bra. He found himself on the receiving end of a barrage of personal questions: Was he married? Any kids? Did he want any? What, soon? Did he ever think of leaving London? And what did he do to keep himself in shape?

Dex, coming outside and watching from a distance, said, 'You're scaring him, Lois.'

'No I'm not. Am I?' She patted Henry's arm and gave it a little squeeze. 'Don't be scared, I'm just interested. I like to know things about people. If you don't ask, how else are you going to find out? And let's face it, we don't get many like you around here.'

'You mean the colour of my skin?'

'Ha, I meant the fact that you're so handsome. Your eyes,' said Lois. 'That voice. Those muscles. The whole damn package.'

Now what was he supposed to say? Oh God, and had she deliberately unbuttoned her dress so more of her cleavage was on show?

'Hang on,' Dexter protested. 'Are you saying he's better looking than me?'

'Now, now, you're both perfect specimens. But this one has the shoulders, the build, like a big burly rugby player.' Henry flinched as Lois gave his shirt-clad arm an appreciative rub. 'He's definitely more my type.'

Back at the pub, between serving customers, Lois inwardly cringed at the show she'd put on earlier for Dexter's friend. Honestly, what was she like? Sometimes she despaired of herself. Other people got plastered and ended up being embarrassing, but she somehow managed to do it when she was sober. It just seemed to happen, as if she were mentally programmed to play the part of the bawdy *Carry On* barmaid, over the top in every way, jaunty, cheeky and flirtatious. She could feel herself doing and saying things that really shouldn't be said but it was almost impossible to stop. Even when – like this afternoon – it was perfectly obvious that the poor man, Henry, would far rather be left alone.

She didn't even know why she did these things; it was like some kind of compulsion to prove to the world that nothing scared her. It was a front, a barrier she put up against all men to show that she was more than a match for any of them.

And sometimes, Lois thought ruefully, it worked just a little too well. When it came to men like Henry, without meaning to but unable to help herself, she succeeded in terrifying the life out of them.

Hairy Dave from the garage approached the bar. 'Same again, two large ones.' As always, he leered at her chest and added with a chuckle, 'Any time you like, love. You know that, don't you?'

Ergh, in his dreams. But he single-handedly drank enough to practically keep the pub in profit, so Lois rolled her eyes and said good-naturedly, 'Yes, Dave, I do. Dream on.'

Because wasn't she as bad as him, in her own way?

Chapter 28

The soles of Molly's feet were on fire. Sightseeing was hard work and they'd done more than their fair share today. Buckingham Palace, the London Eye, the Houses of Parliament, Knightsbridge, the Serpentine . . . so many places Frankie had never seen in real life were being ticked off the list. Together they'd navigated the Tube, greeting and smiling at their fellow travellers and being summarily blanked in return. She'd warned Frankie from past experience that this would happen but Frankie had refused to believe her and done it anyway. So many thousands of people crammed together like sardines and still not speaking to each other, refusing even to acknowledge each other's existence.

But that had been during the day. It was night-time now and the unfriendliness of the city was no longer so apparent. As darkness had fallen and the lights had come on in the West End, London had begun to look magical, like something out of a film. The bridges strung across the Thames glittered like necklaces, illuminated tourist boats chugged through the water and the trees along the banks were lit up with white lights. It was a warm night and people thronged the pavements outside bars and cafés.

Was this how it felt to live here, or did you stop noticing, after a while, the endless bustle, the busyness and anonymity of it all?

Frankie, evidently thinking the same, said, 'You could walk these streets for weeks and never bump into anyone you know.'

Molly nodded in agreement and the next moment was knocked sideways by a man hurrying past with headphones in his ears. 'But you can bump into lots of people you don't.'

Not everyone, though, was unfriendly.

'Sorry, I can't stop looking at you. You just have the most amazing eyes.'

The trouble with being paid compliments like that was Molly never knew how you were supposed to react. They'd been in this club on Charlotte Street for a couple of hours now and Adam had been talking to her for the last forty minutes. Chatting her up, actually. Quite charmingly, too. He was easy to talk to, an advertising executive who lived in Notting Hill and owned a chocolate Labrador called Fredo.

'He's the love of my life, my best friend.' His grey eyes creased at the corners as he talked fondly about Fredo. 'Such a character. Do you like dogs?'

'Oh yes.' Molly nodded.

'I knew you would.' His smile broadened as he rested his hand on hers. 'I could never be attracted to a girl who didn't love dogs. Here, let me get you another drink . . .'

'Let me just check my friend's all right.' Swivelling round, Molly searched the crowds and saw that Frankie was on the dance floor with the man she'd been talking to earlier. Frankie wasn't out on the pull but she'd decided earlier to pretend to be. They were in London where no one knew them; for one night only she had the chance to be whoever she wanted, rather than poor old Frankie whose husband had been cheating on her for the last twenty years. When this one had asked her if she was divorced she'd simply said yes as if it had all happened years ago and couldn't matter less. And now she was laughing and chatting as they danced together. She was learning how to be single again, practising the long-forgotten art of flirtation.

Although to be honest the dancing could probably do with a bit of work.

'Here you go.' Adam pressed another drink into her hand and said, 'Cheers.'

'Cheers,' said Molly.

They clinked glasses and he smiled at her again. 'You're amazing. I'm so glad this happened tonight. Imagine if one of us had gone to a different bar.'

'You don't mean that.' She shook her head. 'It's just another line.'

'You think?' The smile became a grin. 'But am I saying it well?'

'Saying it very well.'

'Well, maybe that's because it's true.'

'Smooth,' said Molly. 'Very smooth.'

'I also like that perfume you're wearing.' Moving closer, Adam inhaled. 'What is it?'

They'd gone mad in Harrods' perfume hall this afternoon, squirting themselves with dozens of different scents with names they'd never encountered before. It had been hard not to.

Molly said, 'It's kind of a mish-mash,' and he laughed again.

'See, how many girls would say that? I like everything about you. Come on, let's have a dance.'

The music had slowed down. Where was the harm? She let him draw her on to the dance floor and slide his arms round her waist. OK, this was promising. Adam was a good dancer, he had rhythm, he was fun and easy to talk to. The last thing she'd expected to happen tonight was encountering someone she might actually want to get involved with, but maybe the universe had other plans. Every couple had to meet each other for the first time somewhere. What if this was their first time? Imagine if they were to get married and have children and live happily together for decades to come and one day their granddaughter would sit on her knee and say, 'Come on then, Granny, tell us how you and Grandpa got together, did you know straight away that he was the one for you?' And Adam would laugh and say, 'It was for me, but your gran played it very cool and pretended not to find me irresistible. We met in a club in North London and—'

'Hey.' Adam's voice cut in, interrupting her fantasy. 'What are you thinking?'

As if she was going to tell him *that*.

'I'm thinking how much my feet hurt.'

'That's so romantic.'

'True though.'

'And there's me, marvelling that you have the most beautiful eyes I've ever seen.'

Yeah, right. '*Okaaaaaay.*'

'And a perfect nose.'

'Ha.' Molly shook her head. 'Are these your best chat-up lines?'

'As for your mouth,' Adam murmured, 'it's just so . . . kissable.'

'You don't actually know that for a fact though.' He was a smoothie, but a playful one. It was a bit of fun, nothing more. Entering into the spirit, Molly said, 'It's just a guess.'

'But an educated one. I'm not just a pretty face, you know. I bet you're a fantastic kisser.'

'I'm not. I'm terrible, completely disastrous. Like a camel.'

Adam laughed and stopped dancing for a moment. 'I'll bet cold hard cash that isn't true.'

'Ah, but what if it is?' Molly resumed dancing, her arms around his waist.

He said, 'OK, this is killing me now. I have to know.'

She pretended not to hear him.

'If you're playing a game with me,' Adam breathed in her ear, 'it's working. I'm liking you more and more. My God, you're *dangerous*.'

And then he was tilting her chin, turning her face up to meet his. For a split second Molly considered making the kiss comically disastrous to make him laugh. Oh, but she didn't want to. Imagine if they did end up getting married; the very first kiss should be a thing of beauty, shouldn't it? Something to be remembered with fondness, rather than for its similarity to being attacked by a rabid camel . . .

Their lips made contact and Adam pulled her closer. Hmm, this was nice, although the way his other hand was wandering over her bottom was a bit presumptuous. Molly reached down to move it away and—

'You bastard, you complete BASTARD!' shrieked a woman two inches from her ear.

'Oh shit, no,' Adam groaned as a pair of furious arms came between them, yanking them apart like a pair of mating dogs.

Which they definitely *weren't*.

'What's going on?' said Molly, although it was pretty obvious.

'Well, hello, Adam's *granny*, you're looking incredibly well,' sneered a woman with super-thick false lashes and a mane of waist-length white-blond extensions. 'Considering you're eighty-five and at death's door.'

Oh God, everyone around them had stopped dancing and was staring avidly. Molly said, 'Maybe he lied to you, but it's nothing to do with me. I don't even know him!'

'Ha, I'll bet. Girls like you make me *sick*, you should be ashamed of yourself. Sleep with someone else's boyfriend, then go running off to the papers, that's all your sort do—'

'Will you tell her?' Stunned, Molly appealed to Adam who was keeping well out of it. 'Seriously, this isn't *fair*.'

'Shut up shut up SHUT UP,' the blonde bellowed in her face. 'And keep away from my boyfriend!'

'But I wasn't—' Molly gasped and failed to jump out of the way in time as the contents of a wine glass scored a direct hit on the front of her dress.

Chapter 29

Molly froze.

Her white dress.

Red wine.

All over.

'Oh fuck.' Adam grabbed hold of his girlfriend's arms. 'You shouldn't have done that.'

'Ha!' White-blond extensions flying, his girlfriend jabbed a finger at Molly and shrieked back at him, 'And *you* shouldn't have been doing *that!*'

Molly stared down, aghast at the state of herself. She looked like a murder scene and red wine was dripping from the ends of her hair.

'Maybe that'll teach you to keep your filthy hands off my boyfriend,' the blonde yelled as Adam hauled her away. Aiming a wild slap at his head she added, 'And I bloody hate you too!'

Adam snapped back, 'You stupid bitch, look what you did to her dress.'

'Oh my God.' Back from the ladies' loo, Frankie stopped dead at the edge of the dance floor. 'What *happened?*'

Cat fights weren't Molly's scene. This was a nightmare. She

turned and headed for the exit, dripping red wine all the way out of the club. On the pavement, yet more people turned to stare. One of the bar staff came after her.

'Adam sent me out to say sorry and give you this.' The boy handed her a wad of notes.

On closer inspection it turned out to be less of a wad, more a select few; he'd evidently valued her dress at sixty pounds.

Luckily she'd found it in the Top Shop sale reduced to thirty. *Win.*

'Tell Adam he and his girlfriend deserve each other.' As Molly folded the notes, a flash went off and she saw the barman had just snapped her on his phone. 'Hey. What was that for?'

'Sorry. I just like taking photos to show my mum. Bye.'

He disappeared back inside the club and seconds later Frankie came rushing out with her jacket slung over her arm.

'I had to get it back from the cloakroom. Are you OK? I can't believe she did that to you.'

'He lied to her, told her he was visiting his grandmother in hospital. Come on, let's go.' Fed up with the attention they were getting, Molly crossed her arms across her drenched chest.

As they made their way back to the hotel, Frankie said, 'Honestly, and to think I'd wondered if we'd see any celebrities in London.'

Molly's footsteps slowed. 'What does that mean? Was there someone famous at the club? Damn, I didn't even see them.'

'Are you joking?' Frankie was giving her an odd look.

'Why? No. Who did I miss?'

'Are you serious? Don't you ever watch *Mortimer Way*?'

Molly shook her head; *Mortimer Way* was one of the soaps she'd never got hooked into.

'The one who chucked wine over you,' said Frankie. 'She plays the hairdresser in it, the one who's married to a transvestite.'

'Oh, great.'

'She just got out of prison for kidnapping her husband's boyfriend.'

'In real life?'

'No, on the show. I don't often watch it,' Frankie said hastily. 'Just catch it every now and again.'

Back at the hotel, Molly filled the bathroom sink, attempted without success to scrub the wine stains out – well, you always have to try, don't you? – and chucked the ruined dress in the bin.

The signal wasn't brilliant on her phone but a spot of Googling eventually informed them that the actress's name was Layla Vitti. She was in her early thirties with a string – if not a tug-of-war rope – of disastrous romances behind her. She infamously fell for men who treated her badly and broke her heart. And now Adam appeared to be another one she could add to the list.

'Why did she have to ruin *our* evening?' Molly grumbled. 'Why couldn't she chuck red wine over her cheating boyfriend?'

'Some women are like that. Never blame the man. What was he like, anyway?' Having kicked off her shoes, Frankie began unzipping her own dress. 'You looked as if the two of you were getting on so well.'

'We were.' Molly grimaced. 'That's because he forgot to mention he was a lying scumbag. Oh look, this was supposed to be your big weekend. It's only one o'clock and there's plenty of other clubs still open. Why don't I change into something else and we'll go out again?'

'Honestly, I don't think I can be bothered. What's the point?' Reaching for her pyjamas, Frankie said drily, 'Knowing our luck, if we tried it we'd only end up meeting someone worse.'

★   ★   ★

'Oh no, are you off?' Lois looked desolate.

Henry didn't want to leave either, but it was eight o'clock on Sunday evening and there was still no sign of Frankie from the café. The situation was getting ridiculous now. He and Dex had spent last night here at the Saucy Swan while Amber and her boyfriend had babysat Delphi. This afternoon they'd come over to the pub again, this time bringing Delphi with them, and had eaten one of Lois's stupendous Sunday roasts.

'I am.' Henry took out his car keys and realised she was going to kiss him. Since there was no escape, he braced himself and prepared to submit with good grace.

'Well, make sure you come back and see us again. *Soon.*' Earrings jangling and rose perfume wafting, Lois clasped his head in her hands and planted a smacker on his mouth. 'Ha, your face! Sorry about that, couldn't resist. Your fault for being so damn gorgeous. Did you enjoy the food?'

'Very much.' He nodded; this much was true.

'She's a fantastic cook,' Dex said appreciatively. 'That's why we come here every week.'

'Just one of my many talents.' She winked at Henry.

Lois was definitely a character. She was also terrifying. Covering his embarrassment, Henry turned to Delphi, who didn't terrify him.

'Bye, gorgeous. See you soon.'

'Hear that?' Lois beamed. 'He's missing me already.'

'Wawawawa WAAA.' Delphi, babbling away on Dex's lap, reached up for a kiss from Henry.

'Wawawa to you too.' Henry scooped her into his arms and allowed her to grab hold of his ears – *ow* – while she planted a kiss on his cheek.

'Ah, look at you two.' Lois was watching them fondly. 'You'd make a lovely daddy.' Her eyes glinting with mischief, she said, 'I'd be up for it if you wanted. I'm only thirty-seven, in case you're wondering. Still got plenty of eggs left.'

Fifteen minutes later, in his car, Henry was considering the last two days. They'd been great, and he'd really enjoyed seeing Dex and Delphi again, but his mission had been ultimately unsuccessful. He hadn't achieved what he'd set out to do this weekend.

Oh well, too late now. Couldn't be helped.

The traffic lights at the junction ahead turned red and he slowed to a halt. In the opposite direction, a yellow Fiesta also stopped. As Henry sat waiting for the lights to change, he saw a small creature amble into the road in front of the Fiesta. Was it a rat? A hamster? A hedgehog, maybe? He was a townie, he didn't know. More importantly, had the people in the other car spotted it? Because if they hadn't, they could be about to run over whatever it was.

The lights changed and Henry buzzed down his window to warn them. At the same time, the Fiesta's passenger door burst open and a girl in a red T-shirt and white jeans leapt out. Running in front of the car, she bent and scooped the animal up into her arms. Henry saw the long ears and realised it was a baby rabbit. The girl, aware that he was watching, grinned across at him as she carried the rabbit over to the field opposite and shooed it off to safety.

Warmed by the vignette, Henry smiled and drove on.

'OK, this *really* hasn't been my weekend.' Climbing back into the passenger seat, Molly said, 'Do an animal a favour and how do they repay you?'

'Oh no!' Frankie was trying hard not to laugh.

Molly said sadly, 'I hate wildlife,' and gazed down at the stain on her white jeans where the terrified rabbit had weed down her leg.

The email pinged into Molly's inbox while she was busy sketching out ideas for Boogie and Boo. Glancing across at her computer screen, she saw that it was from Liz, an old friend from school. The subject line said HAHAHAHAHA which probably meant it was one of those jokey emails people liked to forward to everyone in their address books. Ignoring it, Molly continued working on the strip.

Two hours later, stopping to make herself a mug of coffee, she idly clicked on the email to open it. 'Hiya! Just saw this online and got the shock of my life – the girl's the spitting image of you! How spooky to think you've got a doppelgänger!!!'

There was a link to click on. Liz just *loved* sending these round robins; at a guess, opening the link would reveal a hilarious photo of a toothless geriatric in a bikini.

Molly took a gulp of coffee and pressed the button.

The photo popped up on the screen and she almost choked.

Oh shit, it *was* her. The link had been to one of the more scurrilous tabloids. For once Liz hadn't been joking.

Stunned, she read the caption: 'Layla makes a splash!' This was above two photographs, one of which she hadn't even realised had been taken. In the first, Layla Vitti was clutching the empty wine glass, yelling and being half-heartedly held back by Adam. Molly felt sick; she was there in the photo too, but her face was partially hidden behind Adam's shoulder.

Unlike in the second photograph, which was the one that had been taken outside on the pavement. Full frontal, as it were, with her wine-splattered white dress and face both on show.

Oh God, oh God, *why me*?

The accompanying piece went: 'Fiery actress Layla Vitti made a surprise appearance at Bellini's Club last night, catching the latest love of her life, car salesman Adam Burns, in the arms of a mystery blonde. The encounter ended messily with red wine being flung at Layla's rival, who promptly fled. Pictured here outside the club following the dramatic showdown, the humiliated girl appeared close to tears.

'We say: Oh dear, Layla, that's not very classy, is it?

'We also say: We'd love to know the identity of the mystery blonde with the wrecked dress. Contact us if you know who she is.'

Molly shook her head vigorously. Noooooo, please don't. Hadn't she already suffered enough?

Also, what a cheek, she bloody *hadn't* been close to tears.

Hastily she typed out a reply to Liz's email: 'Ha, how funny, it really does look like me, except she was in London and I was at home here in Briarwood, eating Chinese and watching TV. Looks like I had a better time than she did – bet she wishes now she'd stayed in too! Love Molly xxx'

There, send.

Would other people recognise her? How many readers did this newspaper have, anyway? Hopefully only a few who actually knew her.

To be on the safe side, she'd better give Frankie a quick call, to warn her too. And if anyone asked if the girl in the photo was her . . . Molly shuddered at the prospect. Well, they'd just have to insist it wasn't.

Deny, *deny*.

Chapter 30

If you were a single man in search of attention from the opposite sex, Dex had discovered, you could do a lot worse than pay a visit to the supermarket with a cute baby in tow.

The only drawback was the attention didn't always come from the kind of female you might have had in mind.

'Ahhh, innee a bootiful boy? Oh yes you are, oh yes you are!' A rotund granny in a pink crocheted cardigan leaned across the trolley and beamed at Delphi, who gazed back in astonishment at the massive wart on the end of her nose.

'Thanks.' Dex attempted to steer the trolley past her before Delphi reached out to grab the wart, but the woman had blocked him in.

'Woss 'is name then?'

'Um . . . actually, she's a girl. Called Delphi.'

'Ha, bloody funny name, that is,' she cackled. 'Like one of the Seven Dwarves.'

It was a minefield, navigating the aisles, aware that every woman you encountered could choose to swoop on Delphi and strike up a conversation about the length of her eyelashes, the dangers of E numbers, the cost of nappies or the best washing-up powder to get stains out of clothes. Last week a girl surrounded by small children had invited him back to her house for coffee, flirtily assuring him that he needn't worry, she was quite safe now, she'd had her tubes tied after falling for the sixth.

Another, when Delphi had got stroppy and hurled her bottle of water on to the floor, had said, 'Oh no, poor baby, is he trying to make you drink that horrible stuff?' Turning to Dex she'd pointed helpfully to the contents of her own trolley and said with enthusiasm, 'You want to give her some Fanta, it's all my kids'll drink. They love it!'

And today as he'd been leaving the shop he'd been stopped by the sweetest little old lady who'd cooed besottedly over Delphi and exclaimed how beautiful she was for several minutes before turning to him and saying sorrowfully, 'You have to make the most of them while you can, love, before they go off and leave you. Five children I've got, and seventeen grandchildren, and I haven't seen any of them for years.'

This was, of course, unbearably sad. Until five minutes later when, as Dex was returning the empty trolley to the front of the shop, he saw her again, being ushered along by a middle-aged woman who was saying patiently, 'Come on then, Mum, let's get home now, shall we?'

Which was unbearably sad in quite another way.

Right, they were home now. As he pulled up, Dex saw a car he didn't recognise outside Molly's cottage. A gleaming burgundy Mercedes, no less. His heart did a double thud in his chest; had she got herself a new man?

Then he saw two people on the doorstep, ringing Molly's doorbell. As he lifted Delphi out of her baby seat, they turned and came down the path.

'Hi there! Wow, cute kid!' The woman looked faintly familiar and was wearing a fitted leopard-print dress and towering heels. Eyeing Dex with appreciation, she said, 'Cute dad too. You married?'

'Never mind that now.' The older man with her shook his head. 'We need to get on.'

'Right, sorry.' The woman swung back round to Dex. 'We're trying to get hold of Molly Harris. This is her place, right? But there's no one in.'

Dex checked his watch – ten past eight – and pointed across the village green. 'She'll be over there. She does an evening class on Monday nights. And it's Hayes,' he added, 'not Harris.'

'Whatever,' said the woman with the blond hair extensions. Dimpling, she said, 'So anyway, what's *your* name?'

Her grey-haired companion said impatiently, 'Will you give it a rest? We're here for a reason, remember.' Addressing Dex, he said, 'Where are these evening classes held, exactly?'

OK, he definitely recognised the woman from somewhere. Was she on TV or something? Intrigued, Dex lied, 'It can be tricky to find. Why don't you let me show you?'

The man opened the boot of the Mercedes, lifting out a bouquet of cellophane-wrapped lilies and a vast gift bag. 'Fine.' He handed the bag to the woman. 'Here, you can carry that.'

The woman's name turned out to be Layla. She had a spot of trouble with her spike heels sinking into the soft earth as they crossed the village green. When they reached the café, she paused to check her reflection in the glass door. 'Am I OK?'

'Show me your teeth,' ordered the grey-haired man. She obediently bared them at him like an orang-utan and he tutted. 'Lipstick on the top left. Sort it out.'

Dex hadn't the least idea what was going on but he had no intention of missing out on a moment of it. As soon as Layla had finished rubbing the fuchsia pink lipstick off her bleached teeth with a tissue, he pushed open the door and said, 'This way.'

'Right, here we go.' Layla braced herself and peered through the doorway. 'Oh, cool, she's *running* the class. You ready?' She turned to check with her companion.

The grey-haired man thrust the flowers into her free hand. 'Do it.'

And then she was sashaying into the café, making her flamboyant entrance, and Molly's pupils were turning to see whose heels were clacking their way across the tiled floor. One boy in particular, a slumped teenager in a grey hoody, did a double take and almost fell off his chair.

Finally Molly, who'd been drawing expressions on faces on a flip chart at the front of the class, looked round and dropped her felt pen. Dex, leaning against the door with a quizzical Delphi on his hip, silently marvelled at the fact that she had gone bright red.

If she'd been drawing a caricature of herself, her cheeks would be radiating heat rays like the sun.

'So sorry, everyone, for the interruption, but I'm here on a mission.' Layla's voice carried effortlessly across the room. 'This is something I just *have* to do. Darling, I can't believe I've found you!' Spreading her arms wide, she approached Molly who appeared to be frozen in horror. 'I've come to apologise. It was a silly misunderstanding and I was so wrong to do what I did . . . but isn't that men for you? They rip your heart to shreds . . . I couldn't believe it was happening to me all over again. So anyway, I'm sorry. From the bottom of my heart. These are for you . . .' She handed the flowers and the bag to Molly. 'And I just hope and pray you'll forgive me. Here, do you like lilies? They're my favourites. And look in the bag – go on!'

The grey-haired older man, Dex realised, was now taking photos. The teenager in the grey hoody was videoing the scene on his phone. The rest of the class was agog.

'I thought he was single.' Molly's face was still scarlet, her tone clipped. 'He was the one in the wrong. You should have chucked your drink over him, not me.'

'I know, I *know*,' Layla exclaimed theatrically. 'But that jacket he was wearing? I'd bought it for him only the week before, from Prada! It cost a bomb!'

'So it was easier to throw it at me because my dress was so much cheaper?'

'Oh look, that's why I had to track you down! I felt so terrible about it! I've come all this way to say sorry and make it up to you. Here . . .' Since Molly still wasn't opening the bag, Layla did it herself, pulling out another white dress and a lilac leather handbag with silver trim. 'These are for you. And I really hope we can be friends. Oh, come here and let me give you a big hug!'

'There's no need, I'm fine—' But it was no good, Layla was grasping and determined; Molly was forced to give in and let her get on with it. When the grey-haired man from the newspaper had taken his photos, Molly said, 'So how did you find me?'

'Someone recognised you from the paper and gave us a call.'

'Name?'

'Hang on, let me think, I know it.' Layla screwed up her eyes then opened them again and said brightly, 'Alfie!'

Molly rolled her eyes and looked over at the teenager in the hoody as he slid lower in his chair. 'Well done, Alfie. Thanks a lot.'

'Sorry, Miss. They said they'd pay me twenty quid.' He turned to the grey-haired man and said hopefully, 'Are you from the paper? D'you wanna buy my cartoons?'

Having cast the briefest of glances at the sketches visible on Alfie's A4 pad, the man said dismissively, 'No.'

Chapter 31

Public relations exercise done and dusted, Layla and the long-suffering photographer had left the café and headed back to their car. Since it was practically eight thirty, Molly wrapped up the class and despatched her students. Eyeing Dex with suspicion, she said, 'Why are you still here?'

'Thought I'd wait for you. We can walk back together.' Still intrigued by the incident, he said, 'Sounds like you had quite an eventful weekend.'

'And I suppose you're dying to hear all the gory details.'

Of course he was.

'Hey, don't be so defensive. I'm on your side.' This much was true; he'd genuinely hated the distance that had come between them. Hopefully tonight might be his chance to sympathise and get them back on to the old easy footing.

Molly hesitated and Delphi stepped into the breach with a cheery, 'BRRRRRRRRAAAHHH!'

It did the trick; babies blowing raspberries was always a crowd-pleaser. Molly smiled and said ruefully, 'That's what I should have said to Layla's boyfriend on Saturday night. Honestly, what a prat.'

'Here, let me do that.' Passing Delphi over to her, Dex finished stacking the chairs and put the flip-chart easel away in the cupboard. 'And it's OK,' he added over his shoulder. 'I'm not going to pressure you. You don't have to tell me if you don't want to.'

This, he'd discovered, was a tactic that almost always did the trick. And luckily it wasn't failing him now.

'Oh God, it was so embarrassing,' Molly blurted out. 'This guy just started chatting me up in the club. I really thought he seemed nice – which just goes to show how stupid I am. We talked for ages, he told me he was an advertising executive, he said it had been years since he'd found someone he really hit it off with. And he kept paying me compliments. I mean, I knew he was just doing it to be flirty but a bit of me thought maybe some of them were true. I can't believe I'm telling you all this.' She shook her head at him. 'Talk about gullible. You must be laughing your head off.'

'I'm not. I wouldn't.' Dex took the keys, locked up and led her outside. 'So then what happened?'

'We were on the dance floor. Slow-dancing. Adam kept wanting to kiss me.'

'And?' The thought of it made him tense up. It wasn't jealousy, Dex decided; probably more to do with already knowing the encounter didn't end well.

'So I was joking about being rubbish at kissing . . . and he bet me I wasn't rubbish. So then he said he had to find out which of us was right. By then Layla was already there, watching us.' Molly paused to disentangle the handful of hair Delphi had grabbed and twisted between her fingers.

'Stay still. I'll do it.' Moving closer, Dex carefully loosened and separated the strands from Delphi's sticky determined grip.

'Well, you pretty much know the rest. The next thing I knew,

I was covered in red wine and Layla was screaming at me because as far as she was concerned I was deliberately targeting her boyfriend. Everyone was staring at us. I didn't even know who she was, for God's sake. I was just mortified. Bloody men.'

Dex tried not to think how many times he'd been the cause of similar upsets. It wasn't as if he'd ever deliberately set out to make girls miserable but sometimes these things just happened. Without thinking, he said aloud, 'Sorry.'

Molly gave him a look. 'You weren't there.'

'I know. I'm apologising on behalf of bloody men everywhere.'

'Ach, I just felt so *stupid*.'

'Well, you shouldn't.' Dex debated putting a reassuring arm around her shoulders; deciding not to risk it, he gave her a friendly nudge instead. 'He's the one to blame.'

'But I'm the one who's ended up looking like a pillock in the paper. And now it's going to happen again with the photos they took tonight.' Molly shuddered. 'I didn't want to do that. But kicking up a fuss would only have stirred up more trouble, made everything worse.'

'And she gave you stuff,' Dex agreed. 'If you'd refused to accept it, you'd have ended up looking bad.' As it was, Molly had left the flowers in the café for Frankie.

'I know. Oh well. I'm an idiot.' She shook her head resignedly. 'You'd think I'd be used to it by now.'

'Hey.' His heart went out to her. 'You didn't do anything wrong.'

'I'll keep telling myself that.'

'*I'll* keep telling you.' Feeling brave, Dex said, 'Look, do you have stuff to do or would you like to come over for a glass of wine?'

For a second, Molly didn't reply. Oh God, was she trying to come up with an excuse? But he'd missed their old easy relationship *so much*.

Then she smiled and said, 'Thanks, I'd love that. Can it be a big glass?'

'As big as you like.' Dex felt as if he'd won an amazing prize. 'That red tub in Delphi's room with all her toys in? You can use that if you want.'

'You think you're joking,' Molly warned. 'But I might.'

He gave her another nudge. 'So does this mean we're friends again?'

This time she nudged him back. 'Maybe.'

Thank God.

'Good. I'm glad. Missed you.'

'Well, you would,' said Molly. 'I'm very missable.'

He wanted to hug her. *He definitely wasn't going to hug her.*

As they reached the cottages, Dex took out his car keys and opened the boot of the car. 'I need to get everything inside. It's OK,' he waved Molly away, 'you take Delphi in. I'll bring these.'

When he'd unlocked the front door, Molly said, 'Her nappy's pretty wet. Shall I take her up and change her?'

'Thanks, you're a star.' He paused to watch her make her way up the staircase with Delphi beaming at him over her shoulder. What a great bum Molly had. *OK, don't even think that.*

Turning, Dex headed outside and collected the first of the carriers from the car. Back in the kitchen, he discovered the ice cream was melting and some of the other frozen food was starting to defrost. Unpacking the bags, he began stowing everything in the freezer. As usual he'd bought more food than there was space to store it so fitting everything in was like a game of sub-zero Tetris.

He was doing battle with a bag of frozen peas and another of roast potatoes when someone behind him coughed to let him know they were there and an amused voice said, 'So *officially* I'm dropping by to make sure Delphi's OK after her inoculation, but what I'm actually wondering is if you might be interested in an evening of wild sex, seeing as I happen to be in the vicinity.'

Shit, *shit*. Dex rose, turned and said, 'Hi, nice to see you—'

'I would have rung the bell,' Amanda went on, 'but the front door was wide open and I saw the supermarket stuff in the boot of the car. And I know I was meant to wait for you to phone me, but this was just a spur-of-the-moment decision. I was visiting another patient in the next village. You don't mind, do you?' She raised a playful eyebrow. 'If you aren't in the mood for wild sex, just say the word. I won't take offence.'

Such a clear, confident, *carrying* voice.

'The thing is, I'm a bit . . .'

'Hey, it's fine, I can give you a hand with this. Let me help. Shall I go and get the rest of the bags out of the car?'

'Um . . .' He was hopelessly out of practice with situations like this, had lost his lightning-fast reflexes. Amanda was already heading outside. All he needed to do was explain to her that he had other plans and—

'OK, well, this is slightly awkward,' said Molly from the top of the stairs.

Oh fuck, she'd heard. Well, of course she had. Dex turned to see her standing there with Delphi, who was ready for bed in her fuzzy blue sleepsuit.

'It isn't.' He shook his head. 'I'll just tell her you're here.'

'Dex, it's fine. I'll go.'

'But—'

'Look, she's obviously offering you a far more exciting evening than I am. It's not a problem. You just go ahead and carry on. I didn't realise you two were having a thing.' As she spoke, Molly came down the stairs and handed Delphi over to him. At that moment Amanda reappeared in the front doorway, weighed down with three carriers and a multi-pack of nappies.

'Oh hello!' Unlike him, Amanda recovered at the speed of light. 'I didn't realise anyone else was here! Just popped by to check that Delphi hadn't been off colour after her last inoculation—'

'We're just friends,' Molly told her. 'I live next door. Really, it's OK, I was about to leave anyway.'

So the options were no sex with Molly or sex with Amanda, and Dex was actually torn. Before he could react, the decision was made for him.

'Were you? Oh well, in that case,' Amanda said brightly to Molly, 'bye!'

Back at home, Molly sat cross-legged on the sofa with an A4 sketch pad on her lap. So Dex was having a clandestine relationship with Dr Carr. And if she was going to leave her silver Peugeot parked outside Gin Cottage, it wasn't likely to stay clandestine for much longer.

Not that there was anything wrong with that; they were two single people and there was no reason why they shouldn't see each other. Although it rather looked as if Dex's vow not to sleep with women in his home was about to bite the dust.

Then again, had anyone ever thought for a minute that it wouldn't?

Well anyway, good luck to them. Molly's stomach tightened as she doodled a quick sketch of Amanda Carr with her geometrically perfect hair, pert nose and crisp white shirt, always so calm and in control. They were probably close in age, but Amanda was the proper grown-up. She had a stethoscope.

With mixed emotions, Molly exaggerated the slightly pointed chin and narrow mouth for witchy effect. Perhaps it was the grown-upness that had attracted Dex's interest. Maybe this was what he wanted or needed from a partner in order to stop him endlessly sloping off in search of the next conquest.

Molly closed her eyes and opened them again. Did this mean it was a relationship that might actually last? If she was honest, she didn't want it to be. The reason she'd spurned Dex's drunken advances had been because he was, by his own admission, such a player, such a hideously bad bet. They were next-door neighbours and she had taken the executive decision that they were infinitely better off as genuine friends than as two people who'd got themselves entangled in a messy fling that hadn't worked out.

Especially as she sensed it wouldn't be Dex who ended up getting emotionally shredded when it didn't end well.

Which was all fine and perfectly sensible, but it was still going to be a kick in the teeth if he were to promptly ditch his bad-boy ways and end up living happily ever after in Gin Cottage with Delphi and the uber-efficient Dr Amanda Carr.

Molly added vampire teeth and wrinkles to the sketch of Amanda. Ashamed of herself, she then tore the page into tiny shreds. It was absolutely none of her business. They could do whatever they liked. Amanda Carr was a smart, attractive, professional woman with a great figure. It wasn't as if they were rivals, for heaven's sake.

It was just slightly embarrassing that the last time they'd seen each other, she'd been lying on her back naked from the waist down while Dr Carr had snapped on surgical gloves and given her a smear test.

Chapter 32

The postman had delivered the parcel a couple of hours earlier but it wasn't until mid-afternoon when the café emptied that Frankie had the chance to open it. Ripping off the tape, she unfastened the end of the Jiffy bag and pulled out something soft and squishy wrapped in white tissue.

The moment she pulled the tissue paper apart she knew what it was and who had sent it. The dress, made of scarlet viscose and modestly styled with a Peter Pan collar, long sleeves and randomly scattered white polka dots, had been worn by Hope during the much-loved Christmas episode of *Next to You.*

Wow.

There was a handwritten note with it. Unbelievably touched by the gesture, Frankie saw from the address at the top that it had been sent from Hope's late mother's house in Devon. It said:

Dearest Frankie,

I found this packed away in a trunk in my mum's attic and thought you might like to add it to the collection of memorabilia in your café. Call it a thank you for dinner and our lovely chat. Obviously I'd rather keep my involvement out of it so if anyone asks, maybe you could tell them you bought the dress at auction from another collector on eBay. Or if you prefer, you can sell it on eBay – since it's my gift to you, you can do with it whatever you like!

Anyway, it was wonderful to see you again. I'm so glad I plucked up the courage to revisit Briarwood. Thank you also for your continuing discretion.

Warmest wishes,

Hope

Gosh, how incredibly generous of her. Even if it presumably counted as a form of bribery. Running her fingers over the silky matte viscose, Frankie jumped as the door swung open and a couple of tourists entered the café. She folded the letter up small and slipped it into her pocket.

'Oh my goodness.' The woman's eyes widened at the sight of the instantly recognisable dress on the counter. 'Is that a copy of the one from the show?'

'It's the original.' Frankie smoothed the edges of the white collar like a proud mother.

'How *amazing*.' The man was gazing at it as if it were a holy relic. 'Where did it come from?'

'I got lucky.' Discovering that sometimes lying came quite easily to her, Frankie said happily, 'Picked it up on eBay. Isn't it great?'

It was a private party, held in one of those houses bordering the Downs in Bristol, the kind of imposing five-storey Georgian property you could never imagine being lived in by just the one family.

But this one was. And rather endearingly, the request to have Molly there drawing caricatures of the invited guests had come from ninety-three year old Muriel Shaw. Having made contact via the website, computer-savvy Muriel had booked her for the evening. Now, having met her, Molly had gained new understanding of the word *matriarch*.

The ground floor of the enormous house was open-plan and wooden-floored, enabling Muriel to bomb around it on her mobility scooter with her small dog Wilbur perched in the basket attached to the front. The party was being held to celebrate her birthday and she'd organised every last aspect herself. Hugely intelligent and charismatic, with white hair pulled back in an elegant chignon and bright blue eyes that missed nothing, she was overseeing operations, greeting guests, knocking back mojitos and dazzling everyone with the diamond necklace she'd treated herself to as a reward for having reached the grand age of ninety-three.

'Don't worry about trying to make me pretty,' Muriel told Molly while she sat regally for her own caricature. 'Just so long as you make Wilbur look good. He's the one who matters.'

And when she surveyed the end result she said happily, 'My nose is bigger than that, but you got my teeth off to a tee. I'm glad you've drawn me looking like I'm having fun.'

For the next two hours, Molly drew the great-grandchildren, the various members of the huge extended family and other assorted guests. Finally a hand came to rest on her shoulder and a male voice said, 'I think you should stop for a rest now, take a break before your hand seizes up. Let me show you where the food is.'

Glancing up, her heart did a little skip of interest. Wow, talk about impressive. He was in his early thirties, tall and rock-starry with longish blond hair and slanting emerald-green eyes. He wore a black shirt, cool jeans and a leather beaded choker around his tanned neck.

'Thanks.' Molly followed him through to the drawing room where the buffet was laid out. She covertly admired his long legs and athletic build. He was well-spoken and polite, with elegant hands and good teeth. 'Are you one of the family?'

'I am. Muriel's my grandmother. She's incredible.' He smiled and added, 'I don't know how she does it.'

When he'd finished piling food on to her plate, he said, 'I'll get you a drink. Where would you like to eat?'

From experience, Molly knew that if she mingled with the guests, they'd ask her to sketch them. 'Outside, maybe? Just somewhere quiet? It's OK, you don't have to keep me company.'

'I'd like to.' He led the way out into the garden, found an empty table with candles flickering in multi-coloured glass jars. 'That is, if you don't mind.'

'I don't mind.' *In fact, hooray*. 'I'm Molly, by the way.'

His eyes glinted. 'I know you're Molly-by-the-way. Muriel told me.' Solemnly he held out his hand. 'My name's Vince.'

'Hi, Vince. Nice to meet you. And I agree with you about your grandmother. She's an amazing lady.'

'My parents weren't too thrilled when she picked out that diamond necklace.' Vince's tone was rueful. 'They like to save money, while Gran prefers to spend it. But as she pointed out, if my grandfather were still alive, he'd have bought it for her, so why shouldn't she get it for herself?'

'And how did you feel about that?'

'I was the one who said she definitely should. In fact, I drove her to the auction rooms.'

'Good for you.' Molly was all in favour of that.

'Not at all. It's her money, she can do what she likes with it.' Vince shook his head. 'My mother thinks a diamond necklace is a ridiculous waste of money when Muriel might not have long left to wear it. As far as I'm concerned, all the more reason to buy it now.'

Molly swallowed a mouthful of smoked salmon blini. 'I think so too. And what do you do?'

'Guess.'

He looked so cool. 'Musician.'

He smiled briefly. 'Architect.'

'Really?'

'I know. It's the clothes.'

'And the hair.'

'I'm sorry. I just put on whatever makes me feel comfortable. Most architects do wear proper clothes.'

'Is there a proper uniform?'

'There is.' Vince nodded. 'I sometimes have to wear a suit to work. I'm happier when I don't.'

'You're making me wonder now,' said Molly, 'if there's a caricaturist's uniform I should have been wearing all these years.'

'And what do you suppose that would look like?' He sounded interested.

'Big red clown shoes, probably. With baggy trousers and a spinning bow tie.'

Vince laughed and let her carry on eating. They chatted for a while longer and Molly found herself liking him more and more. Which, given her history, undoubtedly meant he had to be either gay, married or an extraterrestrial alien.

Eventually a middle-aged couple came over and begged her to draw them before they had to leave. She went back inside to work for another hour. At ten o'clock in the evening, Muriel sailed across the parquet floor on her bright red mobility scooter and said, 'Darling, can I ask you a few highly personal questions?'

'Fire away.'

'Are you single?'

Crikey. Molly nodded. 'Yes I am.'

'So does that mean you'd be open to the idea of going out on a date?'

'Depends who with.'

'OK, I'm going to let you in on a little secret.' Muriel leaned forward and clasped her arm. 'My grandson Vince, he's a little shy. I have no idea where he gets it from. Certainly not me.' The fabulous diamonds flashed under the light from the chandelier. 'But there we go. He's the loveliest boy – well, man. He just lacks confidence. I spoke to him earlier and it's obvious he likes you and finds you attractive. Well, why wouldn't he? Look at you! Anyway, I told him he should ask you out but he said you might not want to go. So I'm here to make discreet enquiries on his behalf, because being ninety-three can make you kind of impatient.' Her eyes were birdlike as she scrutinised Molly's face for a reaction. 'So what d'you think, hmm?'

The hilarious thing was, Muriel's head was tilted to one side and so was Wilbur's, at exactly the same questioning angle. The difference between them was that Muriel was drinking a Manhattan and Wilbur was wagging his tail.

'Well,' said Molly, 'this is a first.'

'What can I tell you? More than anything, I just want my grandson to be happy. He deserves to be,' said Muriel. 'He's a good person, I can promise you that. No nasty secrets. He's intelligent, handsome, kind . . .' She trailed away, waiting to see if she'd succeeded in her pitch.

Molly smiled. Basically, how could she refuse? 'If he asked me out,' she said, 'I'd say yes.'

'Good girl. You won't regret it.' Muriel triumphantly reversed her scooter and executed a tight turning circle in order to head off. 'Have you drawn him yet?'

'Er, no . . .'

'Excellent, I'll send him over. Bye-eee!'

Perhaps understandably, it took Vince a while to pluck up the courage to return. Personally Molly was amazed he hadn't done a runner.

'Hi again,' he announced when she'd finished a caricature of one of Muriel's neighbours. 'I'm back. My turn now.'

'No problem!' Molly carried on as if everything was *fine*. 'Take a seat!'

'OK, so it's pretty obvious my grandmother's been meddling. I can tell by the look on your face.' He nodded when she pretended to look mystified.

'Oh.'

'Look, I'm sorry. I love her to bits but she's incorrigible. I begged her not to say anything but there's just no telling her. She's already forced you to agree to go out on a date with me, hasn't she?'

'I wouldn't say forced.' Molly realised she was going to have to put him out of his misery. 'She wanted to know if you asked me out, would I say yes.'

'And?'

'I said yes.'

'You don't have to.'

He was a nice person. More to the point, this time it wasn't just her own possibly flawed opinion; she had a cast-iron guarantee from Muriel.

Anyway, why shouldn't she go? It would be an adventure. Work had taken over recently. Fishing-mad Graham had been her last boyfriend, which meant she'd been single for almost a year now.

Crikey, that was ages. How had she only just realised it had been so long? What had initially been a deliberate decision to steer clear of men for a bit had somehow stretched into twelve whole months.

At this rate she was in danger of turning into the village spinster.

Aloud, Molly said, 'I'd really like to,' and saw Vince exhale with relief.

'Sure?'

'Sure.'

'You're not just saying that?'

'I'm really not.' She began to sketch him as the smile spread across his face and he visibly relaxed. Goodness, he was *so* good-looking. He resembled a rock star, yet the stellar outer package concealed an inner, less confident personality. That was actually a very attractive quality in a man.

'You've just made my night,' said Vince. 'My grandmother has her uses.'

'She could come along with us if you like.'

He grimaced at this. 'No, she couldn't. Much as I love her, that would be weird. How about next Wednesday, are you free then?'

'I am. But I live in Briarwood; it's quite a way from here.'

'Not a problem. Give me your address and I'll pick you up at eight, We'll go out to dinner.'

'Where?'

'Somewhere nice, don't worry.'

Molly made him stop talking then, and swiftly completed the

caricature with his mouth in an exaggerated smile. As she was showing him the finished result, they heard the squeak of wheels on polished floorboards.

'Very good. That nose is exactly right.' Muriel studied the drawing with satisfaction then said loudly, 'And how about the other thing?'

Molly kept a straight face. *So subtle, so deft.*

'All I can think is, you must have paid her an awful lot of money,' said Vince. 'She said yes.'

'I didn't offer her a penny.' Muriel looked smug. 'This girl's got her head screwed on the right way. All she had to do was meet you to know you were a good bet.'

Just before midnight there was a firework display on the Downs, in Muriel's honour. 'That'll wake 'em all up,' she chuckled as chrysanthemum bursts exploded into the sky. And to her delight it wasn't long before a police car pulled up, the officers alerted by disgruntled neighbours who didn't appreciate the disturbance.

'Miserable sods,' Muriel unrepentantly pronounced. 'Some people just don't know how to have fun.'

Molly left the party at one o'clock. Muriel and Wilbur went with her to the front door.

'Darling, you won't regret it.' The diamond necklace reflected rainbow shards of light as she reached for Molly's hands. 'Vince would be any girl's dream man. He's a genuinely nice person . . . housetrained, charming, even knows how to cook. I'm telling you, he's a catch.'

'And you missed your vocation,' said Molly. 'You should have been a matchmaker.'

'Darling, I've been matchmaking all my life. I have a talent for it.' She patted Molly's cheek. 'And I have a good feeling about you.'

As she climbed into her car, Molly experienced a squiggle of excitement about her upcoming date. See? Dexter wasn't the only one with a bit of romantic excitement in his life.

After a couple of alarmingly false starts, it appeared the time had finally come to start de-spinstering herself.

Chapter 33

Amber lay back, the long grass tickling her shoulders and the nape of her neck. The heat of the sun was melting over her closed eyelids. In the distance, over on the main stage, one of her favourite bands was playing. She'd been looking forward to seeing them but couldn't be bothered now to get up and make her way over there. She was just too comfortable.

'Hey. You OK?' Doss gave her hip a nudge with his foot.

'Yeah.' Amber opened her eyes and saw him standing over her, his face advancing and receding like waves on the shore. She giggled and said, 'Stay still.'

'I am still. You're stoned.'

'Little bit, maybe.' Bit drunk, bit stoned, whatever. A fly buzzing around her head landed on her left shoulder and she batted it away, missing and hitting herself in the chest instead. 'Ow.'

'Hahahaha.' That was enough to set Doss off; he cracked up laughing and couldn't stop. As the clouds swirled overhead, Amber joined in. The clouds were dancing along to the music from her favourite band. She might not be able to stand up but she could waggle her arms . . . ha ha, and make sure she didn't whack herself in the face . . .

The band played on, the smell of frying onions drifted across from the burger stand and Amber's stomach gave a rumble of hunger. She hadn't eaten anything today, which was probably why the cider had gone to her head.

'I'm starving,' she told Doss.

'Me too.'

'I want a burger.'

'I want a private helicopter and a holiday in Vegas.'

'Not Vegas, that's too far.'

'Yeah. Ibiza, then.'

'I'm still hungry. Shall we have a burger?'

He pulled a face. 'Have you seen how much they cost? Rip-off.'

'But we need to eat something.' Amber dug in the pocket of her jeans and eased out her last ten-pound note; she already knew she'd have to pay for his too. 'Will you go and get them?'

Doss looked over without enthusiasm at the snaking queue. 'Why can't you?'

'Because my legs won't work.'

'You're such a lightweight.' He took the money from her and loped off. She lay back down again and watched a bird soar overhead, lazily changing direction as if it were writing its name in the sky. She was only a lightweight because smoking spliffs was new to her, unlike Doss who'd been doing it for years. Her stomach rumbled and she pressed her hand against it to make it stop . . . sshh . . . God, she couldn't *wait* for him to come back with the burgers.

'Hi, Amber.'

Amber's eyelids, which had been drooping, snapped open. Two faces were gazing down at her. Shaun Corrigan and his friend Max.

'Hi.' If she said it with enough lack of enthusiasm, hopefully they'd get the message and go away, leave her in peace.

'Are you OK?'

'Just perfect, thanks.'

Shaun crouched down next to her. 'Sure?'

'Like you care.'

'Don't be like that. I do care. You're my sister and you look pretty wasted.'

'Thanks. You look like you work in a bank.' He didn't, not really, but he and Max certainly looked cleaner and shinier than most of the other festival-goers. 'What are you doing here, anyway? Wouldn't have thought it was your thing.'

'Hey, we like music. And it's free. We weren't spying on you, by the way. We were just sitting over there and Max spotted you a while back. Was that your boyfriend with you?'

'Yeah, he's just gone to get a couple of burgers.'

'So you've been smoking dope?'

Oh God. Bored, she said, 'Spare me the lecture.'

'Dad said you'd always been really anti-drugs.'

'Did he? Maybe that was back when he was *my* dad.'

'He's still your dad.'

Amber shook her head. 'No no no, he's all yours now.'

'He really misses you,' said Shaun.

A knot tightened in her chest. 'Well, I don't miss him.'

They sat there without speaking for a while, listening to the band playing on the faraway stage. Then the music stopped and Shaun said, 'You must be in the middle of exams. How's it going?'

'Honestly? Really bad. I'm going to fail all of them. Haven't done any revision. Can't be bothered. And guess whose fault that is? Your father's. You can tell him that too. When I don't pass any of my AS levels, I hope he feels guilty.' Amber gazed steadily at Shaun. 'Because it'll all be thanks to him.'

'He's so proud of you.' Shaun looked shocked. 'It's going to really upset him.'

'Oh no, how terrible, what a *shame*.'

'Shall I tell him about the drugs too?'

Amber paused; that wouldn't be such a great idea. 'No, don't say that. He'd only tell Mum and she'd get all stressy about it.'

'OK. But take care, all right? Look after yourself.'

'I always do.'

'I'm glad we bumped into you.' Shaun's voice softened. 'It's nice to have a chat. Look, can we swap numbers? Then maybe we could text each other. You know, not loads, just every now and again.'

Her instinctive reaction was to say no. But actually it had been kind of nice to see him again. In a weird way. And she'd enjoyed telling him about her exams, knowing he'd be passing the information on. It was actually a neat way of worrying her dad, causing him a bit more pain. Which he *deserved*.

'OK.' Amber took out her phone and Shaun took out his, which was a newer model than hers. Who'd paid for that, hmm?

Once the numbers had been exchanged, Amber said, 'How did your exams go, then?'

'Good, thanks. I need two As and a B to get a place at Birmingham. I should be fine.'

'Great.' Amber hadn't meant to sound sarcastic but it came out that way. She shook her head. 'Sorry, I mean it *is* great. And I bet you worked hard for it.'

'I did.' Shaun nodded.

'So how does it feel to have a full-time father? A bit weird?'

He smiled briefly. 'A bit.'

Max, who'd stayed quiet up to now, said, 'Here comes your boyfriend.'

'Oh thank God, I'm *starving*.' Twisting round, Amber saw Doss loping across the grass towards them. 'Anyway, you'd better go.' She instinctively knew it would be awkward; Shaun and Max were a different species, a million miles from Doss.

'This is Shaun and his friend Max. They're just leaving.' As she said it, Amber saw that the bag he was carrying was too heavy to be burgers. She pointed to it. 'What have you got in there?'

'OK, right, the queue was too long at the burger van, yeah? So I went off to find another one and there were these guys who'd brought along too much cider so they were offering it to people for a really good price.' Proudly Doss pulled out a couple of plastic litre bottles filled with cloudy amber liquid that looked as if it had been dredged from a stagnant pond.

'What was the really good price?'

'Tenner.'

Amber wanted to yell at him but she couldn't, not in front of Shaun and Max. She wanted to cry. Aloud she said, 'I don't like cloudy cider.' It was going to be disgusting, she just knew it.

'Hey, be cool. You'll grow to like it,' said Doss. 'You just have to give it a chance.'

Shaun said, 'But you told us you were starving.' He was frowning at Amber now, looking concerned.

'I'm fine. I'm not really that hungry.' Embarrassed, she shook her head.

Doss said defensively, 'This is way better than a couple of stupid burgers.'

Ignoring him, Shaun said, 'Do you want me to get you one?'

'No, no, definitely not.' That would be the ultimate humiliation; she could already see he was wondering what she was doing with Doss, who couldn't have chosen a worse time to act like a prat.

'Sure? Because I can, it's honestly not a problem.' He had his wallet open now; there were a couple of ten-pound notes visible.

'Let him buy you a burger if you want one.' Doss rolled his eyes slightly as he said it, as if she was making a big fuss about nothing.

'No. I'm not bothered. We'll just drink this.' Taking one of the plastic bottles from him, Amber unscrewed the top and took a defiant swig. Urgh, it was dry and sour and repulsive. She wiped her mouth, which was doing its best to shrivel up in disgust, then turned to Doss. 'Actually, it's not bad. Come on, let's move away from here, find somewhere else to sit.' As they made to leave, she waved her free hand at Shaun and Max and said, 'Bye!'

Chapter 34

When he saw her on the doorstep Dex whistled and said, 'Wow, look at you.'

Pleased, Molly did a little curtsy. Well, was it really so wrong to want to show off your scrubbed-up appearance and angle for the odd compliment? She was looking nice this evening and a bit of an ego boost was always good for the soul. 'I know, it's a shock. I came to ask if I could borrow a bit of milk.'

'Come in, no problem. Have you run out?'

'No, I just opened a new carton but it doesn't smell very fresh.' She wrinkled her nose. 'And the shop's shut.'

Dex grinned. 'You dress up really smart in your house to eat a bowl of cereal.'

'Ha ha. I'm going out,' Molly announced with pride. 'On a date. But when he brings me back home later I don't want to invite him in for a coffee and then only have stinky milk to put in it.'

'A date.' Dex raised an eyebrow. 'Who with?'

'Someone I met the other night. Someone nice.'

'Glad to hear it.' He opened the fridge and took out the milk. 'And is this one single?'

Oh well, that was to be expected. And he was currently doing her a favour. Molly said with dignity, 'Yes he is. And yes, I double-checked.'

'You're looking great.' She saw Dex take in the purply-blue cotton shift dress, the dark blue glittery flip-flops, the hair fastened back at the sides with silver combs and the extra-careful make-up. As he poured a pint of milk into a jug he added, 'You smell nice too. What is it?'

This time it wasn't a mish-mash from Harrods' perfume hall. 'Just a cheap one from Next.'

'I like it.' He moved nearer to her neck and inhaled the light, clean scent. 'Very much. And it doesn't smell cheap.'

'Good.' Having Dex this close was making her stomach go funny. For a moment their eyes met and the look in his made her heart race.

'Lucky him,' said Dex.

'I know.' Could he hear her heart frantically thud-thud-thud-ding away?

Dex smiled and said, 'There you go, then. Is that enough?'

'Tons.' Molly took the jug from him and jumped as his phone, on the worktop next to her, emitted the shrill *ddrringgg* that signalled the arrival of a text. Glancing down at it, she saw Amanda's name flash up on the screen, and the words: 'Be with you by eight xxx'.

'All going well with you two, then?' Since Dex had seen her looking, there was no point in pretending she hadn't seen the message.

'Pretty well. She's good company. Is this your date?'

A car had pulled up outside. Molly checked through the window. 'Yes, that's him. He's early.'

'Keen. See you later.' Dex held the door open for her. 'Have fun.'

Her stomach did the washing-machine swirl again and she said brightly, 'You too.'

Was Dex watching her now? Having deposited the borrowed milk in the fridge, collected her bag and keys and greeted Vince with a kiss on the cheek, Molly smiled as he held the car's passenger door open for her like a proper gentleman. And Vince was looking incredible too; he was definitely the kind of date you'd be proud to be seen out with.

Acting as if she *wasn't* being watched, which was actually more difficult than you'd think, she managed to climb in without tripping over or flashing her pants. Did they look like a glamorous couple in a TV advert? Oh please let the answer be yes.

'Sorry I was early,' said Vince. 'I'm always early for everything.'

'It's fine. I was ready. And you weren't that early anyway. Only ten minutes.'

Vince grimaced. 'More than that, if we're being honest. I've been sitting in the car in the pub car park for the last twenty minutes.'

'Really?' Was he joking?

'No.' He looked rueful. 'More like half an hour.'

It had been a nice evening. Better than nice, Molly chided herself because that didn't sound over-enthusiastic. Vince had taken her to a charming French restaurant in Malmesbury; having done his internet research he'd narrowed the choices down until he'd found the perfect one. The food had been amazing. So had the wine, although Vince was driving so it had been left to her to drink most of it. But they'd had a good time, the conversation had flowed easily enough and when Vince had excused himself to pay a visit to the men's room, one of the two middle-aged women at an adjacent table had leaned across and said to Molly, 'I hope you don't mind me saying this, dear, but ooh, your boyfriend is so *handsome*. We've hardly been able to tear our eyes away!'

'He's like someone in a Hollywood film,' her friend rhapsodised, plump hands clasped in ecstasy.

Which had been lovely to hear, but at the same time slightly appeared to imply, Molly felt, that they couldn't work out what on earth he was doing with her.

'Is he a famous actor?' The first woman looked hopeful.

'No.' Molly shook her head. 'He's an architect.'

'Ooh, well, that's good too. You make sure you hang on to this one, dear. Men like that don't come along very often, do they? You don't want to let him slip the hook.'

'It's only our first date,' said Molly.

'All the more reason to hold on tight,' stage-whispered the second woman as Vince made his way back across the restaurant towards them. 'Think of the beautiful kiddies you could have.'

Anyway, they were home now, back in Briarwood. And she had fresh milk. Molly turned to him.

'D'you want to come in for a coffee before heading back?'

'Great,' said Vince.

'Hey, over here,' Dex called as they climbed out of the car. 'How was dinner?'

He was sitting at a table in his front garden, with the front door open behind him. On the table was a can of beer. Beside him was some kind of metallic tripod affair glinting in the dim light.

'Dinner was fantastic. What are you doing?'

'Stargazing. Look.' Dex patted the tripod with pride. 'I bought myself a telescope.'

'I wouldn't have thought it was your kind of thing,' said Molly.

'Me neither, but it's brilliant. I didn't realise there was so much out there.' He spread his hands wide and looked up. 'It's all so . . . *big*.'

'Yes, galaxies and universes do tend to be a bit on the large side.'

'Hi, I'm Dex.' Rising to his feet, Dex greeted Vince. They shook hands and he gestured to the other chairs. 'Join me. There's cold beer or wine in the fridge . . . or coffee. Here, take a seat, it's too nice to stay indoors. Look how clear the sky is.'

Was he doing this on purpose? Purely for his own amusement? Oh well, too late, Vince was already pulling up one of the chairs, examining the undoubtedly expensive telescope Dex had bought on a whim and would probably be bored with by the end of the week.

'OK,' said Molly. 'Vince has to drive so we'll have coffee, thanks.'

'The only thing is, could you make it in your kitchen and bring it over?' Dex's eyes glistened in the darkness. 'Only I lent someone some milk earlier and now I've run out.'

Vince finally left an hour later. Staying where he was while Molly walked her date back to his car, Dex listened to the low murmur of their voices. He couldn't make out what they were saying and wasn't able to see them either; Molly had ensured the branches of the juniper bushes hid them from view.

Then the car disappeared down the lane and she rejoined him.

'I'll have this.' She sat back down and poured the last of the beer into her own empty glass. 'What was that about, then?'

'Sorry?'

'Forcing us to sit out here with you. Asking Vince all those questions, every last detail about himself. It was like being inter- rogated by the secret police.'

Oh, so she'd noticed then.

'I was just interested to meet him, find out what he was like. Are you going to see him again?'

'Yes I am.'

Really? How will you manage to stay awake? Dex didn't say this out loud but it hadn't taken him long to decide that Vince didn't possess the sparkliest personality in the box.

'What are you thinking?' Molly was on the defensive, prepared to rail at any hint of criticism.

Sensing it was the wisest thing to do, for once in his life Dex managed to keep his opinion to himself. 'I like him. You've done well there, got yourself a good one.'

It was the right thing to say. She visibly relaxed and exclaimed proudly, 'I know! And he's so handsome!'

'Not bad, I suppose. Not as good as me.'

'He's handsomer than you.'

'What?' Dex clutched his chest in shock as if she'd just fired an arrow at his heart.

'These women in the restaurant told me how gorgeous he was, like something out of a Hollywood movie. And they were right, that's exactly what he looks like.'

'What am I, then? Stig of the Dump?'

'You're very good-looking too,' said Molly. 'But in more of a real-life way.'

Ouch. Dex reminded himself that at least he had the ability to make people laugh. 'So you've hit the jackpot with Vince,' he said playfully. 'Can't imagine what he sees in you.'

She lobbed the ring-pull from the beer can at his head then kicked him under the table for good measure. He caught her ankle between his bare feet and held it there for a couple of seconds before letting go.

'So when's the next date?' He asked the question as if they were just good friends, because that was what they were.

'On Saturday.'

'*What?* But that's—'

'It's OK,' Molly broke in, sensing his alarm, 'I know, I'm not going to miss that. We'll be going out afterwards,' she explained.

Dex felt himself partially relax. It wasn't ideal, but it would have to do. It was Delphi's birthday on Saturday. She would be one year old.

On a day when emotions would inevitably be heightened, he'd hoped – OK, taken it for granted – that Molly would be there at his side to help him through.

Chapter 35

It was the kind of thing Frankie might have been tempted to do, but she wouldn't have felt comfortable instigating it off her own bat. Sometimes, though, fate intervened and the opportunity that presented itself was just too perfect to pass up.

Fat Pat was the local carpenter in Briarwood. He wasn't remotely fat, he just liked to go to fancy dress parties done up as Fat Pat from *EastEnders*. Last night Frankie had emailed him a description of what she required and he'd dropped by this morning to explain why he was unable to do it.

'Sorry, love, not going to be able to help you.' He held up his heavily bandaged right hand. 'Near as dammit chopped a couple of fingers off yesterday, you never saw so much blood in all your life, and the doc reckons I'm not going to be able to work properly for weeks. Which leaves me stuck barking orders at those two useless sons of mine while they try and do the jobs we've already got booked.'

'Oh no, poor you.' Frankie offered him a slice of walnut cake which he scooped up in his massive left hand. 'Don't worry. Thanks for letting me know. Does it hurt?'

'Like you wouldn't believe.' He shook his head and grimaced.

'Anyway, with what you're after, I reckon Stefan might be worth a try. He could do it for you. Don't look so shocked,' he chuckled, 'I wouldn't be saying it if I could manage it myself. But I can't, so I'm thinking he's the best man for the job instead.'

Which wasn't why Frankie had been looking shocked, but never mind.

And as a suggestion, it actually made a lot of sense. When Fat Pat had left, she drank a cup of tea and mulled it over. *Was* this fate? If Hope Johnson was to be the topic of conversation, might Stefan suddenly blurt out the whole heartbreaking story and conclude in desperation, 'If only there was *some* way I could find her again?'

Well, there was one way to find out. And it was only nine o'clock in the morning; she could go now, before opening the café.

It was the start of a beautiful summer's day. Swinging the bag as she went, Frankie made her way on foot across the village and out the other side. She came to the river, crossed the wooden bridge and followed the path along the riverbank.

It was officially private land, but generations of Hanham-Howards had allowed this part of their estate to be walked on by the general public. And in Stefan's case, they'd given him permission to live on it too. If there were laws against it, no one had ever said anything. For the last seven years the caravan had remained there in the natural clearing that Stefan had, over time, patiently coaxed into a wild garden. The scene was picturesque and it all seemed idyllic but Frankie didn't envy him in the winter.

He was sitting on the steps of the caravan now, enjoying the morning sun and watching the birds hopping around on the grass in front of him. As Frankie approached, she saw him hold out his hand and one of the tiny birds flew up to take seeds from his outstretched palm.

Stefan inclined his head and said, 'Morning,' as she slowed to watch.

Frankie smiled. 'It's like something out of a Disney film.'

'They visit me every day. We've got to know each other pretty well.' Realising she'd come here to see him, he said, 'What can I do for you?'

He was lithe and tanned, wearing a pale yellow shirt and narrow jeans. His watchful dark eyes missed nothing and habitually gave nothing away.

'I asked Fat Pat to do some work for me but he injured his hand yesterday and is going to be out of action for a bit. He suggested you for the job.'

'Which is?'

'I need a glass-fronted display case to hang on the wall in the café.' She opened the carrier bag and took out the red dress. 'It's for this.'

True to form, not so much as a flicker. Stefan Stokes's expression remained utterly inscrutable. He'd make an awesome poker player.

'Right. Well, I can do that. Hold it up for me?' He surveyed the dress for a couple of seconds and said, 'OK, got the size. How soon would you need it?'

'Whenever. Gosh, thanks.' Was he truly inscrutable or did he genuinely not remember the dress? Actually, did he own a TV? Had he ever even *seen* the show? 'It's from the Christmas episode of *Next to You*.'

But Stefan simply nodded and said, 'Won't take long. I'll paint the whole thing black; that'll show it off best.'

'Oh yes, great idea. Thanks very much.'

'No problem.' He returned his attention to the birds waiting to be fed. 'I'll have it done for you by the end of the week.'

★　　★　　★

266

The imperious rattle of the cot's bars signalled that Delphi was awake. Seven thirty, pretty civilised. Sliding out of bed, Dex crossed the landing and pushed open the door to her room.

Delphi was wearing her pink bunny-printed babygro and standing up in her cot, waiting like the Queen. She beamed and jiggled the bars again, babbling excitedly at the sight of him.

'Hello hello hello, beautiful girl!' As Dex lifted her out of the cot she wrapped her bare arms around his neck and gave him a kiss. 'It's your birthday! Happy birthday to you!'

'BabababaBA.' Delphi responded by drooling lovingly on the side of his face. It was what people called their first birthday but it wasn't really, was it? It was the second. Surely your first birthday was the day you were born.

In an instant, Dex was transported back to that night exactly a year ago when he'd turned up at the hospital in the small hours and met Delphi for the first time. He remembered with absolute clarity the rush of love he'd felt for her, and the look of pride on Laura's face as she'd watched them together. She'd become a mother and created something both perfect and priceless. It had been the happiest day of her life.

Dex's throat tightened at the brutal unfairness of it all. Laura should still be here. That she wasn't alive to celebrate her beloved daughter's birthday was just so terribly *wrong*. She was missing it all, would continue to miss every birthday to come, would never witness the first steps, the first words, the first *anything* . . .

Unless she was watching down on them as well-meaning people often liked to suggest. In which case, being the perfectionist she was, the chances were that Laura was clutching her head in her hands and yelling in desperation, 'Oh God, look at you, you're doing it ALL WRONG.'

Was he?

Dex had no idea but suspected he probably was. The authors of the many books he'd read on the subject had seemed as confused as he was, to be honest, and loved to contradict each other.

Anyway, all he could do was his best.

'Your mum loved you so much,' he told Delphi. They headed along the landing, pausing as they always did to admire the sunlit stained-glass window Laura had made.

'Bralamagablahhh,' Delphi pressed her tiny starfish hand against the coloured glass.

'Come on then, let's get some breakfast first. Then you're having a bath,' said Dex. 'You want to look nice for your party.'

And later on this morning when Molly came over, they'd give Delphi her presents and video the occasion for posterity. Laura might not be here but he was determined her daughter was going to have a happy day.

Frankie watched as the guests spilled out into the garden. Thankfully the sun had continued to shine. It had been her idea for Dex to hold the party here at the café and he'd jumped at it, paying her to lay on the kind of buffet he could never have put together himself. He'd also ended up inviting most of the village so it was just as well the garden was big enough and the weather was good. There were children of all ages being entertained by a magician, a band was playing, adults were drinking champagne and Young Bert had coloured ribbons tied around his horns.

It wasn't your average one-year-old's birthday bash, that was for sure.

Next to her, having left the pub for an hour, Lois murmured, 'Bless him, he's doing his best for that baby. Can't have had an easy time of it, these past few months.'

'I know. He's doing really well.' They both watched as Dex helped Delphi to tear the flowered wrapping paper off a present from Mary, one of Briarwood's oldest residents, and affect delight when it turned out to be a large pair of pink hand-knitted leggings.

'They're perfect. Just what she needs. I don't know how you do it,' Dex told Mary as he gave her a kiss on the cheek. 'Thank you so much.'

Mary, beaming with toothless pride at the compliment, clutched his forearm with a gnarled hand and said, 'Ah, she's a fine babby, I'll do her a romper suit next. And if you ever want a nice jumper for yourself, my love, you just say the word. I'm good with my needles, always have been . . . ooh, I've got a big bag of orange wool going begging if you fancy it. With your colouring you could really carry it off.'

Frankie hid a smile; Delphi had already received enough lovingly hand-knitted items to see her through early childhood. With his open friendly manner and ability to charm, Dex was quite a hit with the older inhabitants of Briarwood.

Then Lois said, 'Here's my dad,' and Frankie turned to see Stefan making his way towards them. Her face lit up when she saw what he was carrying under his arm.

'This the kind of thing you had in mind?' He showed her his handiwork, a black-framed, glass-fronted case exactly the size she needed.

'Stefan, that's just perfect. You're so clever. How much do I owe you?'

'Twenty pounds? Is that too much?'

'Are you mad? Twenty pounds isn't enough. Look at all the work that's gone into it . . . and that beautiful wood . . .'

Stefan shrugged. 'But I already had the wood, only needed to buy the glass.'

'Forty,' Frankie insisted, opening her handbag.

'Thirty, then. No more than that.' Money was of little importance to him.

'What are you putting in it?' said Lois.

Frankie said, 'The red dress Hope wore during the Christmas episode. It's going up on the wall in the café.'

'Oh, I know the one you mean.' Lois nodded. 'With the white spots like snow. Where'd you get it?'

How she wished she could tell them the truth. But she mustn't. And Stefan was giving no sign that he was paying close attention.

'I picked it up on eBay. Here,' Frankie pressed the money into his hand. 'And thank you again. If I ever need anything else I'll know where to come.' She smiled at Stefan, longing to know what was going on behind that unreadable exterior.

'No problem. Any time.' He held up the neatly wrapped present he'd also brought along with him. 'I'll give this to Delphi.'

When he left them and made his way over to Delphi and Dex, Lois said fondly, 'I bet I know what it is. Same as he made for Addy on her first birthday. And me on mine.'

Together they watched as the paper came off to reveal a wooden box with shaped openings carved into the sides. Opening the lid, Delphi tipped out the wooden shapes and instantly – enthusiastically – attempted to cram the star through the oval hole.

'Hours of fun,' said Lois.

'Imagine how long it must have taken him to make it,' Frankie marvelled. 'Your dad's an amazing man.'

'I know.'

Over on the buffet tables, a couple of serving dishes were almost empty. Frankie said, 'We're running low on sandwiches. I'd better go and make some more.'

'You don't want to be stuck in the kitchen missing the party.

Come on,' Lois gave her a nudge. 'It won't take long if I give you a hand.'

They stood companionably side by side and began a mini production line, Lois buttering and de-crusting, Frankie piling on the fillings and cutting into triangles.

'It's such a long time since your mum died.' Emboldened by the fact that she didn't have to make eye contact, Frankie said casually, 'Does he never get lonely?'

'Dad? Oh, who knows? He says not, but he must do.' Slicing and spreading like lightning, Lois's hooped earrings jangled as she shook her head. 'And you know what he's like, typical man, never says much. I'd be thrilled if he met someone else, but he just never makes the effort. He says there were only two women he ever loved and that was enough . . .'

'*Two?*'

'Mum was one. They just adored each other. They got together when they were seventeen; it was love at first sight for both of them, a beautiful thing.'

The hairs at the back of her neck were zinging. Frankie said, 'And the other one?'

Oh God, it was probably going to be Lois.

'I don't know who it was. He only talked about her once, a couple of years ago.' Lois stopped spreading and said thoughtfully, 'No idea what made him come out with it like that. I'd just asked him if he thought he'd ever find someone else and he told me he had, once.'

Zinnngggg.

'But you've no idea who? He didn't give you any clues?'

'Nope.' Lois resumed buttering. 'He said they'd loved each other but couldn't be together.'

'Why not?'

'Haven't the foggiest. Unless she was married.' Another shrug. 'It's the only reason I could think of.'

'What about the Romany thing?' Frankie's hand shook and she sprinkled far too much chilli sauce over the prawns. 'Would that make it difficult?'

'You mean if she didn't have Romany blood? Pfft, it's really not the end of the world. These things happen. Look at me!' Lois pointed through the window at her adored seven-year-old daughter. 'Addy's father wasn't a gypsy. He was a complete *dickhead*,' she curled her lip, 'but that's something else altogether.'

'So you don't think your dad would have a problem with getting . . . you know, involved with a . . .'

'Civilian?' Her dark eyes flashing with mischief, Lois said, 'I honestly don't think there'd be a problem.'

Which was good news in one way but something of a puzzle in another. Because did that mean Stefan had significantly relaxed his views in the last decade? Or did it signal that he'd only ever used the Romany aspect as an excuse – a get-out clause – in the first place?

And why was Lois now giving her that oddly speculative look? OK, time to change the subject. Frankie said brightly, 'Well, anyway, let's hope everything works out! There, are we all done now?' They'd refilled the silver serving dishes and anyone helping themselves to the extra-chillied sandwiches was going to get a mouth shock. 'Shall we take them through? Thanks *so* much for your help!'

Chapter 36

There she was. *There she was.* Henry, who'd just arrived and begun to panic slightly when he hadn't been able to spot her, exhaled with relief as a door swung open and Frankie appeared holding a vast tray of sandwiches. At last. It was like the final piece of a jigsaw slotting into place, making the puzzle complete. She was wearing a pink sundress and several silver necklaces, and a broad smile as she turned and talked to someone behind her . . . oh help, it was lascivious Lois from the pub. And she'd spotted him . . .

'Henry, you're late!' Her face lighting up, Lois rushed over and greeted him with a big kiss; if he hadn't turned his head in the nick of time it would have landed smack on his mouth. As it was, he knew he now had an extravagant crimson lipstick print on his cheek. Laughing, Lois said, 'Shy boy, so sweet. I've been wondering when you'd get here. Dexter told me you were coming down for another visit. Hey!' Reaching out, she stopped Frankie in her tracks. 'Here he is, the one I was telling you about. This is Henry. Henry, this is Frankie. You missed her last time.'

On the outside, Henry remained normal. Inside, multi-coloured cartoon hearts and stars were shooting out of his eyes. At least, he hoped it was only on the inside. But it was happening, she was here and so was he. *At last.*

Frankie's smile was warm. 'Hi.' Up close, her eyes were clear blue with a darker blue outer edge, her lashes were blond-tipped and there was a faint dusting of freckles over her nose. She was perfect. And she smelled perfect. This was one of those moments he knew he'd never forget.

'Hi,' said Henry. Then he said, '*Oof,*' and clapped his hands to the front of his trousers as the icy contents of a pint glass hit him square in the groin.

'Oh, sorry!' The small girl with tangled dark curls who'd tripped over a chair leg and drenched him, yelped, 'It was an accident, I didn't mean to!'

'Addy, don't worry, sweetheart, we know that.' Frankie gave Lois's daughter a reassuring hug as Lois said eagerly, 'No problem, I'll get some kitchen towels and mop it up.'

Which was a truly alarming prospect. Gazing down at himself in dismay, Henry saw that the glass had contained Coca-Cola, which wasn't ideal when you were wearing cream chinos.

'It's fine,' he told Addy, 'it doesn't matter. These things happen.'

'Here we are!' Lois was back with a roll of kitchen paper, tearing off sheets in readiness.

'Please, let me do it.' Henry took them from her then said, 'I should have brought a spare pair of trousers.'

'Let me take you over to the pub,' Lois offered with enthusiasm, 'and sort you out.'

Which was the very last thing he needed.

Wishing the ground would swallow him up, Henry stammered, 'N-no, really, it's OK . . .'

'This is my café. I'll do it.' Taking control, Frankie pointed to the door and said kindly, 'Come on, we'll have you as good as new in no time.'

Now this was an offer he couldn't refuse. When they'd left the party behind them, Henry said with feeling, 'Thanks.'

'That's OK.' She grinned at him. 'I saw the look of horror in your eyes.'

'You did?' As he followed her up the stairs, Henry hoped she couldn't mind-read as well.

'I don't know if you've noticed, but Lois isn't exactly backward at coming forward. Right, this is mine so it isn't ideal but it'll have to do for now.' In the bathroom, Frankie took a fluffy lime-green bathrobe off the hook behind the door and passed it to him. 'I'll start running the water, you take your trousers off.'

Henry retreated to the privacy of the landing, removed his trousers and put the bathrobe on. It was far too small for him and looked ridiculous of course, but it was Frankie's so he wasn't going to object.

In the bathroom, she took the trousers from him and dunked them into the sink, where the hot water was foaming with hand-washing liquid. Over her shoulder she said, 'How's your underwear?'

OK, so this was a question he hadn't expected to hear today. Particularly from Frankie herself. 'Fine. Er, fine thanks.' His trunks were slightly damp but Henry had no intention of taking those off too.

'Lois has told us all about you,' Frankie went on. 'She's a teeny bit smitten. I'd thought maybe you felt the same until I caught that look on your face.'

'Yes, well. She's a bit . . . full on.'

'I know.' Her smile was sympathetic. 'Not your type, then?'

Henry shook his head slowly. How would she react if he were to say, 'It's you, can't you see that? You're the one, *you're my type*.'

He wasn't going to say it, obviously. He wasn't completely mad. As she rinsed and expertly wrung out his trousers, he said, 'No, she's a great character, but not really . . . my cup of tea.' Oh God, what did he *sound* like? Why had he started channelling Noel Coward? 'Anyway, thanks for rescuing me.'

'Otherwise who knows what she'd be doing to you now! Right, all done. Spin dryer next.' As they headed back downstairs, Frankie said, 'What are you, six foot five? If you weren't so tall you could have borrowed a pair of trousers from someone else, but the legs wouldn't be long enough.'

'Much as I love this dressing gown,' Henry said gravely, 'I think I'd rather wait until my trousers are dry before rejoining the party.'

'No problem at all.' In the utility room, Frankie put the trousers through a spin cycle then threw them into the tumble dryer and switched it on. 'There, they'll be done in no time.' Ushering him across the hallway and into a charming blue and cream living room, she said, 'You just make yourself comfortable in here. Put the TV on if you want. Can I bring you a drink?'

'No thanks. I'm fine,' said Henry.

Frankie dimpled. 'OK, I'll bring you your trousers in twenty minutes.'

There appeared to be some kind of party going on. When he pulled up outside his old home, Joe could see and hear the music, the voices, the garden full of people behind the house.

Which meant it probably wasn't the ideal time to pay a visit, but that was hardly his fault, was it? Amber had blocked his number from her phone and Frankie appeared to have turned hers off. But he'd had to come; his conscience wouldn't allow him not to. He was here because there was a situation that needed to be resolved.

Almost everyone was out in the garden. There were balloons bobbing everywhere, people dancing, children running about. Seeing that the door leading from the café to the house was ajar, Joe made his way through to the hallway. The kitchen was empty but the living-room door was closed and he could hear what sounded like the TV coming from inside. Amber was probably in there, keeping out of the way of the party going on outside.

Joe turned the handle and opened the door. Having braced himself to come face to face with his daughter, he was even less prepared for the sight of a complete stranger – a huge Afro-Caribbean hulk of a man at that – stretched out across the sofa wearing Frankie's lime-green dressing gown and watching athletics on the TV.

'Who are you?' Joe demanded, torn between shock, outrage and – if he was being *completely* honest – a thud of fear. 'What are you doing in here?'

After a beat of silence, the huge man wearing his wife's lime-green dressing gown said, 'I could ask you the same thing.'

'This is my house.' *Shit, look at his muscles. And also, what the hell did Frankie think she was playing at?*

'Is it?' The visitor raised a mildly interested eyebrow and stayed where he was. 'So that makes you the ex-husband.'

'Not ex. We're still married. You're wearing my wife's dressing gown.' The words were coming out of his mouth but Joe couldn't quite believe he was saying them. Did he *want* to be beaten to a pulp by someone with the physique of Lennox Lewis?

'I know. I didn't just break in and steal it, if that's what you're wondering. She gave it to me to wear.'

'Here we are, all done – ooh!' Swinging open again behind him, the door bounced off Joe's shoulder. Then Frankie came into the room and saw him. 'Joe! What's going on?'

His shoulder hurt a lot but if he rubbed it he'd look like a wimp. Joe said evenly, 'I need to talk to you.'

She looked surprised. 'Why?'

'In private. It's important.' He saw the pale trousers she was holding, saw the hulk in the dressing gown get up from the sofa.

'Thanks. I'll leave you to it.' Taking the trousers from Frankie, the hulk said, 'But if you need me, just give me a shout, OK?'

When he was gone, Joe said, 'Who is he?'

She shrugged. 'None of your business.'

'I'm just asking. Being polite.'

'He's a friend.'

'What kind of a friend?'

'A very nice one. And don't look at me like that, Joe.' Defiantly she said, 'I'm moving on.'

'But . . . you're not the type to move on.' He hadn't meant it to sound like that; the words were coming out all wrong.

Frankie looked as if he'd slapped her. 'Maybe I am now.'

'Look, I'm sorry.' They couldn't argue; it wasn't why he'd come over here. 'We need to talk about Amber. She won't speak to me.'

'No? Goodness, how strange, I wonder why that could be?'

Joe gave her a look; the old easygoing Frankie would never have made a comment like that. 'Shaun bumped into her at a music festival. They talked for a bit. She told him she was going to fail all her exams. Apparently she's not even trying to do well.'

'OK, I'll have a word with her about that.'

'Then there's the rest. I wasn't told this but I overheard Shaun yesterday, talking to a friend. He said Amber was out of it when he saw her. Drinking rough cider and smoking dope.' He shook his head at Frankie. 'We need to do something about this. Make it stop, sort it out.'

She bridled. 'Are you saying it's my fault?'

'I'm saying you can't just sit back and let it happen. She won't take my calls.'

'Wait here.' Frankie abruptly turned and left. Returning shortly afterwards, she pulled Amber into the room after her. Joe's heart contracted at the sight of the daughter he loved so dearly, then squeezed tighter still with sorrow and pain when he saw the look on her face.

'You tricked me,' Amber murmured icily to Frankie.

'Sorry, darling. Your father insisted. He wants a word.'

Amber's eyes flashed with a mixture of satisfaction and disdain. 'No thanks.'

Joe said evenly, 'Shaun told me about your exams. He said you hadn't done any work for them.'

'And why would you care about that?'

'Amber, I'm your dad.'

'Not any more.'

'I also heard about the drinking, the drugs.'

'Ha, I knew it.' Her jaw was set.

'He didn't tell me, I heard him talking to one of his friends about you.'

'Making excuses for your perfect son?' Amber's tone was jeering. 'Protecting him?'

'If you're taking drugs, it's my business.'

'It's not your business, it's just your *fault*.'

The living-room door banged shut behind her.

'I'll speak to her later,' said Frankie. 'You can go now.'

Joe wanted to say sorry, he wanted to take her in his arms and tell her he still loved her. But he knew he couldn't.

Without another word he turned and left.

Chapter 37

Frankie found her daughter out in the garden, drinking orange juice and listening to the band.

'Has he gone?' said Amber.

'Yes. Sweetheart—'

'Oh Mum, don't look so worried, none of it's *true*.'

Frankie's stomach was in knots. 'But why would the boy – Shaun – say it?'

'Because he believed me! I did it on purpose, don't you get it? Because I just wanted to make Dad think I was messing everything up and I knew Shaun would tell him. Ha, and it worked.' Beaming, Amber said, 'Good! Except I really should have warned you. Sorry, I didn't think he'd actually turn up.'

'So . . . but Shaun said—'

'Mum, I told him what I wanted him to hear. I said I'd done *no* revision and was going to fail *all* my exams. But you know that's not true, don't you, because you've seen all the work I've been putting in – there's no way I'm going to let it go to waste. And that day at the festival him and his friend were watching me from a distance. You should have seen them, all clean and shiny looking, it was hilarious, they were so out of place. When they came over to talk to me I thought it would be funny to pretend to be all spaced out. I wanted to hurt Dad and that seemed like a good way to go about it. But you know the truth, Mum. You *know* I don't do drugs, and I wasn't drinking either. Doss bought a bottle of cider but it tasted horrible. Ha, I fooled those boys though.' Her eyes dancing, Amber said, 'I'm a better actress than I thought.' She assumed a dopey, heavy-lidded expression, clutched Frankie's arm and said slurrily, 'I'm gonna fail all those exams and I don' even care, right?'

She looked and sounded convincingly out of it. And she'd always been so anti-drugs. It made perfect sense. Trusting her, believing her, Frankie exhaled with relief. 'Well, thank goodness for that. You had me worried there for a minute.'

'Ah, sorry, Mum.' Amber gave her a squeezy hug. 'But you don't have to worry about me. I'm fine.'

'Ooh, and I need to apologise to you!' Reaching out to stop Henry as he and Molly made their way past, Frankie said, 'I'm so sorry about that little misunderstanding earlier.'

Henry smiled and shook his head. 'No problem at all.'

Molly said, 'What misunderstanding?'

'When Joe turned up just now, he found Henry in the living room wearing my dressing gown and no trousers.'

'Ha!'

'Henry was brilliant,' said Frankie. 'Played it *very* cool.'

Henry said modestly, 'Well, as cool as I could manage in a small green dressing gown.'

'After you left the room, Joe asked me what was going on.' Her cheeks flushing, Frankie said, 'I hope you don't mind that I kind of hinted there might be a bit of . . . you know . . .'

He shook his head. 'It would have been a waste of a perfect opportunity if you hadn't.'

He had a lovely dry sense of humour, Frankie decided, and a charming manner.

'We missed you last time you came down here,' said Molly. 'Heard all about you though.'

'Actually, I've seen you before,' Henry told her. 'From a distance, on the day you came home from London. There was a baby rabbit in the middle of the road. You jumped out of a car and rescued it.'

'I did! We were stopped at the traffic lights! Were you the one heading the other way? That rabbit did a wee all down the front of my jeans! Oh wow,' Molly exclaimed, gesturing at his chinos. 'And you've just had the same problem . . .'

Watching them, Frankie said, 'You know what this means, don't you? You're practically twins.'

Molly's phone buzzed to signal the arrival of a text from Vince: 'Hi, how's it going? What time do you want me to pick you up? And shall I wear a blue shirt or a green one?'

She hesitated. It was five o'clock and the party was still in full swing.

Next to her, Dex said, 'Problem?'

'Just wondering how long you're all going to be carrying on here.'

'Well, I wasn't planning on kicking everyone out right away.' Dex was busy videoing Delphi, who was modelling yet another hand-knitted present, this time a fluffy yellow hat with ear flaps that made her look like a just-hatched chick. 'If people are still having fun, no reason why we can't keep going. Oh, you've got your date tonight. When do you have to leave?'

'Not yet.' Molly pulled a funny face at Delphi, who was clapping her hands against Henry's. She'd send a text back to Vince and say eight o'clock would be fine.

'CacacacacaCAH,' Delphi babbled happily as she grabbed Henry's fingers. 'GagagagaGAH . . . DadadadadadaDAH!'

'Oh wow, listen to that, clever girl!' Molly turned excitedly to Dex. 'Has she ever said Dada before?'

'No.' Dex smiled drily. 'And it would have been nice if she could have said it to me instead of Henry, but it's a start.'

Their eyes met and Molly's heart went out to him. It was quite an emotional moment, hearing Delphi say the word for the first time, even if it was to the wrong person. And on her birthday too.

'Dada.' Molly attracted Delphi's attention and pointed to Dex. '*Dada.*'

'Dadadadada.' Delphi curled her arm around Henry's neck and plonked a slobbery kiss on the side of his jaw.

Then Molly jumped as an amused voice right behind her said, 'Genetically unlikely.'

'Hi.' Dex stopped videoing Delphi and Amanda brushed past Molly as she moved towards him and greeted him with a kiss on the mouth.

Well, *that* got everyone's attention. All around the garden people turned to look and eyebrows were raised at this new and gossip-worthy turn of events. Molly felt a tiny bit as if she'd taken a step on to ground that was no longer there.

'I decided there's no reason to keep quiet about us any longer,' Amanda told Dex with a grin. Turning to survey the sea of interested faces, she announced, 'Don't worry, everyone, he isn't my patient and neither is Delphi now. It's allowed! We're completely legal and above board, two single people who get on together very well indeed. And look who else I'm here to see!' Holding out her arms, she removed Delphi from Henry and scooped her up into the air. 'Happy birthday, little one!

Don't you look beautiful in your fluffy hat? Such a pretty girl!'

Delphi had been the centre of attention all afternoon, but seeing Amanda holding and hugging her in such a proprietorial fashion was making Molly feel even weirder than witnessing the kiss between Amanda and Dex.

A tiny twist of – what was it? Jealousy? – speared her chest as she watched Delphi pucker up her tiny rosebud mouth and plant a kiss on Amanda's cheek.

'Aahh, thank you, that's lovely,' cooed Amanda.

'MamamamaMAH,' said Delphi.

The tiny twist in Molly's chest became a Sabatier knife. Unable to watch, she turned her attention to the phone in her hand. OK, Vince would be waiting for a reply.

Her fingers trembling slightly, she texted: 'Come over now!'

'By the way.' Lois drew her father to one side and murmured, 'Don't say anything to anyone else, but it's only fair to warn you. I think Frankie's interested.'

Stefan frowned slightly. 'Interested in what?'

'In *you*, Dad!' Lois grinned at his look of dismay.

'Surely not.'

'I'm pretty sure she is. She was giving me the third degree earlier, asking all sorts of questions about you and your romantic history.' Wryly she added, 'So that didn't take long. But you should have heard her and seen the way she was looking at me when I talked about you. She was *desperate* for details.'

'Oh God,' sighed Stefan. 'I wondered if there was something a bit weird going on when she turned up at the caravan to see me. But I didn't realise it was that.'

'Well, why would you? You're only a man.' Lois, who adored her father, was familiar with the shortcomings of the opposite sex; you didn't run a pub for as long as she had without learning how hopeless they had the capacity to be.

'Are you sure you're right?'

'Dad, I'm always right. Frankie's husband left her. She's on her own and frantic to feel whole again. And wanted. And . . . attractive. She needs another man in her life to replace Joe and it looks like you're the one she's set her sights on.'

'Well, this is awkward.' Stefan looked worried. 'I mean, she's a perfectly nice woman but I just don't . . . there isn't any . . .'

'I know, Dad. That's why I'm warning you,' Lois said sympathetically. 'Do you want me to say something to her? Kind of let her down gently, let her know you aren't interested?'

'No, no, don't.' Evidently mortified at the prospect, Stefan said, 'Please don't do that. I'll just make sure I stay well out of her way.'

Chapter 38

Molly had never been so glad to see someone. Keeping an eye out for Vince, she'd watched as Stefan slipped away from the party, then saw Vince's well-polished car pull up outside the café. Ten minutes ago, Amanda had said, 'So I hear you've got yourself a boyfriend? That's fantastic!' In the manner of a competitive mother being over-delighted that her toddler has managed to do its first ever poo in the toilet.

Molly nodded. 'Yes, his name's Vince.'

'I know, I've been hearing all about him from Dex. And is he nice?'

'Really nice.'

'Well, that's great! I can't wait to meet him. Dex was telling me it's been quite a while since your last boyfriend.'

It had been a year ago exactly, in fact. The last twelve months had been something of a sexual desert. The only person she'd shared a bed with was Dex, and that had lasted all of ten minutes.

Molly wondered if he'd told Amanda about that, the infamous over-confident, drunken fumble?

Actually, probably best not to mention it.

Meanwhile, Amanda was waiting for a reply.

'Yes.' Another nod of agreement. 'It's been some time.' *Thanks for reminding me.*

'Well, if you need anything in the contraception department, just give the surgery a call and book an appointment.' Amanda surveyed her with the confident air of a woman entirely in control of her own contraceptive requirements. 'We'll soon have you fixed up!'

Anyway, Vince was here now, looking thrillingly handsome in a dark blue linen suit and pale green shirt, pausing beside the car for a moment to take out a handkerchief and wipe away a smudge of something on the gleaming paintwork.

'Is that him?' Joining her, Frankie whistled and said, 'Wow.'

'I know.' Molly experienced a rush of pride; he *was* a physically perfect specimen. It felt a bit weird to be thinking about it, but she probably should get some contraception sorted out.

Not through Amanda though, brrr.

Having greeted Vince and led him through to the garden, she introduced him to the other guests along the way. Finally they reached Dex and Amanda. Vince shook Dex's hand and said, 'Good to see you again.'

Dex said easily, 'You too.'

'And I'm Amanda. Hello!' Having greeted him, Amanda linked her arm proprietorially through Dex's. Eyes sparkling, she turned to Molly. 'I have to say, well *done.*'

Right in front of everyone, as if to signal her amazement that Molly could have landed such a prize. *OK, please don't start talking about contraceptives again.*

Molly blurted out, 'Actually, we only came back to say hello and goodbye. We're heading off now.' They'd seen and admired him, that was enough.

'We don't have to,' said Vince. 'The table's booked for eight so we don't need to leave before seven twenty.' He paused to consider. 'Maybe seven fifteen to be on the safe side.'

OK, he'd been a little bit like this the other evening; being punctual was evidently important to him. Molly said, 'Yes, but I want to go home first, get changed and freshen up.' Oh God, *cringe*, had she really just said that? She'd never used the words *freshen up* before in her life.

'Ah, didn't realise.' Vince checked his watch, mentally recalculating the timings. 'In that case, let's go.'

Amanda raised a groomed eyebrow as if discreetly reminding her not to get carried away and have wild sex without protection. Then she broke into a wide smile. 'Have a great evening. And listen, we're practically neighbours now. We should get together!' She turned to Dex. 'Why don't we invite them over for supper next weekend?'

'Sounds like a plan.' Dex, as easygoing as ever, went along with it. 'Why not? I'm getting pretty good at cheese on toast.'

This was his new culinary masterpiece. Molly said, 'Only because I taught you to add Worcester Sauce.'

'Wash your mouths out, you two.' Amanda affected horror. 'I'll be in charge of the food and it isn't going to be anything like that. Trust me, I'm an excellent cook.'

'Really?' Dex looked impressed.

'Absolutely.' Her smile was both playful and provocative. 'Just another of my many talents.'

Bleurgh, definitely time to go.

'You don't need to do this,' said Frankie when she saw Henry at the sink with his shirtsleeves rolled up, elbow-deep in suds, washing all the glasses that hadn't been able to fit into the dishwasher.

'Not a problem.' He dismissed her protest with a shrug. 'I enjoy it.'

It was eight o'clock; the party was finally over, the band packed up and gone now, the last few guests drifting away.

'Always nice to see a man getting domesticated.' Frankie picked up a clean tea towel and began polishing the glasses dry. 'Are you staying down here tonight?'

Amused, Henry nodded through the window at Dex and Amanda.

'With the lovebirds, you mean? I'll hang around for the next couple of hours, then I think I'd better head home, give them some privacy. It's been a good day though. I've enjoyed it.'

'Me too. *Whoops.*' A wet glass slipped from Frankie's grasp and toppled sideways on the edge of the drainer. Demonstrating lightning reflexes, Henry caught it before it could hit the floor.

'Here you go.' He handed it back to her.

'Well held.' She smiled; he was so obviously a sportsman.

'Mum? I'm off now.' Bursting into the kitchen, Amber gave her a hug. 'I'm staying over at Nicole's tonight, be back tomorrow afternoon.'

For the first time, Frankie experienced a wobble of doubt. She'd always trusted Amber implicitly. 'What are you going to be doing?'

'Oh, nothing much, just injecting hard drugs into my veins and knocking back bottles of neat gin. That's a joke, by the way,' Amber said patiently. 'What we're *actually* going to be doing is making salted caramel popcorn and watching girly DVDs. And I need to be home by lunchtime tomorrow because I want to do tons of revision and at least two practice papers. But if Dad asks, whatever you do, don't tell him that. And don't panic either, because you definitely don't have to worry about me. OK, Mummy?'

'Now you're making fun of me.' Frankie secretly loved it when Amber teased her like that. She relaxed and hugged her in return. 'OK, darling, I'll see you tomorrow. Have a lovely time.'

'I will. Bye!' Amber waved to them both and danced out of the door.

'Your daughter's a credit to you,' Henry said when she'd gone.

Frankie glowed. 'Thanks.'

'So what are your plans for this evening?'

'Mine? Feet up, cup of tea, telly on . . . then I'll probably doze off and manage to spill tea all over the sofa.' She pulled a face. 'I live a very rock 'n' roll lifestyle.'

Henry rinsed another glass and said suddenly, 'Because if you felt like going out for a drink or something to eat, we could do that . . . I mean, if you wanted to, I'd be up for it . . .'

Frankie looked at him in amazement. Crikey, had she just been asked out on a *date*?

'Oh well, that's really nice of you, but . . . gosh.' Panic, panic. 'Look, thanks, but I'm not ready for any kind of . . . you know, *thingy*.' Which sounded completely ridiculous and pathetic but the words were tumbling out of their own accord, an instinctive reaction not even pausing to involve her brain.

'Sure, sure, no problem. Fair enough. Forget I said anything.' It was comforting to realise Henry was as eager to put it behind him as she was, an erroneous blip to be deleted as fast as possible.

'Thanks.' Frankie shot him a grateful smile. 'And look, it's not you. It's definitely me.'

'And I shouldn't have asked.' His embarrassed-but-relieved expression gave her the first inkling that he was far shyer than he appeared.

Who'd have thought it was possible for someone so outwardly imposing to lack confidence?

One of the last remaining guests came into the kitchen at that moment and asked Henry, whom he'd earlier been tapping for free financial advice, if he could take his contact details. Henry dried his hands, opened up his wallet and gave him a business card. When the man had thanked him and left, Henry fumblingly pulled out another card and murmured, 'Just in case you ever need . . . or want to ask anything . . . I'll just leave one, shall I? You can always throw it in the bin as soon as I'm gone.'

Their hands brushed as Frankie took the business card and she experienced a tiny, just detectable *swoosh* of adrenalin.

'Of course I won't throw it in the bin,' said Frankie.

Henry didn't speak, just looked at her with an unreadable expression in his dark eyes. The *swoosh* happened again, ten times harder.

Frankie looked away, winded. Blimey, where had *that* come from?

Chapter 39

Dex and Amanda had urged him to stay longer but Henry knew perfectly well only Dex had meant it; it was obvious Amanda wanted him all to herself. As soon as Delphi had been settled down in her cot, leaving him the lone gooseberry in the house, he'd made his excuses and left.

It was eight fifteen and the sun was now sinking lower in the sky behind him as Henry accelerated on to the slip road and joined the eastbound carriageway of the M4. Well, talk about an eventful day. As he'd been on his way down to Briarwood earlier, he'd heard a positive-thinking expert on the radio declaring that people just needed to instigate events if they wanted to change their lives for the better. 'Never regret the things you've done,' the Positive Thinker had forcefully announced, 'only the things you didn't do.'

Which had sounded bloody terrifying, frankly, but the quote had stayed with Henry, dancing around inside his head and repeating itself, like an annoying song stuck on replay.

So what had he done? Decided to take the risk, make the leap, act on impulse and see if the saying was true.

Which meant he'd met Frankie, spoken to her, and discovered she more than lived up to his expectations.

He'd then gone on to clumsily ask her out.

And been briskly rejected.

Even then, though, he'd kept the faith – the ridiculous, *ludicrous* faith – and had followed up with an even clumsier move, forcing a business card upon her when it was so painfully apparent she wasn't interested.

What a muppet. God, what must she have been thinking while he was floundering around, making a fool of himself like the dorkiest teenager? His hands gripping the steering wheel, Henry tortured himself with the memory of all the stupid things he'd said and done, and how tactfully and sweetly Frankie had handled his unwanted advances.

And it was all his own fault.

So much for taking the advice of so-called experts on the radio. He wouldn't be making *that* mistake again in a hurry.

Silence. Silence. And yet more silence.

Frankie, draped across the sofa, switched on the TV and flicked through a few channels. Turning it off again, she looked at her cup of tea. It had gone cold and scummy.

How was it that some evenings whizzed by, while others crawled along like a constipated snail? And had *any* evening ever passed as slowly as this one? Frankie exhaled with frustration; she was here in an empty house, feeling more lonely than she could remember feeling before. Amber was away. Molly was off out somewhere with Vince. Joe was in Tetbury with Christina. On a boredom scale of one to ten, this was a twenty. God, and the hours were stretching endlessly ahead . . . she wished now that she'd taken Henry up on his offer.

As usual, she'd managed to say no when she should have said yes.

And it was too late now to change her mind.

Wasn't it?

OK, don't even think it. Of course it's too late. Frankie rose from the sofa, went into the kitchen and took a bottle of wine from the fridge.

Twenty minutes later, the thought was still buzzing around inside her brain.

What if it wasn't too late?

What if it wasn't?

Next to her on the sofa, her mobile rang and she jumped a mile. Was it Henry calling to see if she'd changed her mind?

OK, pretty unlikely, seeing as he didn't have her number.

'It's me,' said Joe. 'Have you spoken to Amber?'

Oh brilliant, this was all she needed.

'Amber's fine. She hadn't taken any drugs, just pretended she had, because she knew you'd find out.' It was only fair to tell him. Frankie added, 'She's also doing tons of work for her exams.'

'And you believe that?'

She bristled. 'Yes I do. I'm her mum and I know when she's telling the truth.'

'Hmm. And who was the guy wearing your dressing gown?'

Ah, so that was the other reason Joe was calling.

'I told you. He's a friend.' Her glass was empty. She made her way back through to the kitchen for a refill.

'Look, just go steady, OK?'

'What does that mean?'

'You know what it means. Everyone's watching you, waiting to see what you do next. There's no need to make a complete fool of yourself.'

Bristling didn't *begin* to describe what she was experiencing now. Frankie surveyed the icy bottle of wine in her hand; if Joe had been here, she'd have happily hit him over the head with it. 'You mean there's no need to make any *more* of a fool of myself, seeing as how my husband's had another family tucked away for the last twenty years and I'm already the laughing stock of the whole village?'

'I'm talking about dignity now. I'm trying to help you out here and you're getting defensive,' said Joe. 'Which just goes to show, you know I'm right.'

God, how she hated it when he used his ultra-reasonable voice. 'You're a lot of things,' said Frankie, 'but I've run out of money to put in the swear box.'

She hung up *hard* and poured more wine, the neck of the bottle t-t-tinging against the rim of the glass as her hand trembled with rage.

Have some dignity. Don't make a fool of yourself. Sit at home on your own, don't rock the boat and definitely don't have any fun, was that what Joe expected her to do?

Well, sod him. And sod that. Frankie glugged back more wine and listened to her heart flailing against her ribs. Then she crossed the kitchen and picked up the business card Henry had left on the dresser.

She punched out the number and listened to it ring at the other end. This wasn't the kind of thing she did.

Well, maybe it was time for a change.

Then the ringing stopped, the answering service asked her to leave a message and Frankie realised she hadn't thought this through.

'Hi, it's me . . . um, Frankie . . . sorry, I was just wondering if you'd like to come over after all, but if you aren't picking up your phone it probably means you're driving . . . so you're on your way back to London . . . OK, don't worry, I left it too late. Never mind, bye!'

All the out-of-the-blue bravery had poured out of her. Hanging up, Frankie let out a wail of despair and howled, '*Oh fuck.*' Then her heart did a double thud as she glanced back at the phone and saw that she *hadn't* hung up; it was still recording her message. Yelping, 'Sorry!' she jabbed the button again, made sure it was properly off this time, and buried her head in her hands.

Pulling in at the motorway services, Henry listened to the message on his phone. Was this how it felt to get a call telling you you'd won the Lotto?

He called back and heard Frankie say cautiously, 'Hello?'

'It's me. Am I still OK to come over?'

'Really?' Her voice rose. 'Of course! I didn't realise you were still here, I thought you must be on the M4 by now.'

How far away was he from Briarwood? If he turned round at the next junction and raced back, how long would it take? He definitely couldn't tell her where he was.

'Just wait there.' A ridiculous smile spread across Henry's face as he put the car back into gear. 'I'm on my way.'

It was nine thirty when the doorbell went.

Her heart hammering, Frankie opened the door and said, 'You were on the M4.'

'I'm here now,' said Henry.

'This is mad.'

'I know.' He smiled slightly and nodded in agreement.

'Sorry about saying fuck earlier. I thought I'd turned the phone off.'

'I like it that you said fuck. Made it easier to phone you back.' He paused. 'And drive back.'

Frankie exhaled. The weirdest thing was happening. Somehow

their individually messed-up approaches had succeeded in balancing each other out. First Henry had made a clumsy advance, then she'd matched it. The playing field was level now, the initial layers of pretence stripped away.

'Where's your car? I didn't hear it.'

'I didn't know if you'd want it outside your house. I parked it in the lane behind the church.' He hesitated then added, 'I didn't know if it was too late to go out. But we still can if you want.'

'Well, it is a bit late.' She could feel herself nodding in agreement, a weird kind of nod like one of those toys with springs in their necks. 'Probably easier to stay here. I have wine. Or, you know, coffee.' Was offering wine implying that she expected him to *stay* stay? Oh Lord, this was a minefield.

But a thrilling one.

'I don't mind,' said Henry. 'Either. You decide.'

His eyes were mesmerising. Frankie took another wine glass down from the glass-fronted cupboard, then switched the coffee machine on. 'I tell you what, I'll do both. Then it's up to you.'

As she made the coffee and filled the glass with wine, she'd never been so aware of someone standing behind her. What was he thinking? Did her bum look big? Could he tell how she was feeling right now?

'So Amber's out for the night?' Henry broke the silence.

'Yes.' *He already knew that.*

'And you're not expecting any other visitors this evening? Oh *God*.' He shook his head in despair. 'That's the kind of thing a murderer would say. Sorry, sorry. I'm not a murderer.'

'Good.' Frankie smiled. 'And no, no other visitors. Are you nervous?'

Henry nodded. 'Very. You?'

'Oh yes. Here, take these.' She passed him his drinks and led the way through to the living room. 'Actually, put them down. Is it OK if I just do something?'

Because the sooner it happened, the sooner they could get the awkwardness out of the way. Frankie, her heart going into over-drive, waited until he'd placed the glass and the cup on the coffee table. Then she went straight over to him, wrapped her arms round his neck and kissed him full on the mouth.

Wow, wow, look at me, look what I'm doing.

Also, even more wow, this is fantastic.

The doorbell rang and they froze. Oh, for crying out loud.

So much for no other visitors.

'I don't know who it is,' Frankie whispered. 'But I can't not answer it.'

'What shall I do?'

'Stay here. It's fine, I'll get rid of them.'

She closed the living-room door behind her and crossed the hallway. Who on earth could be ringing the doorbell at this time in the evening?'

'Hi,' said Lois. 'Sorry, did I startle you? You look like you've seen a ghost!'

Chapter 40

Lois, of all people. Henry's biggest and most ardent fan.

'I just wasn't expecting anyone. Gave me a fright.' Frankie patted her palpitating chest; at least that much was true. 'What's up?'

'It's Addy's bracelet, she left it here this afternoon. Turquoise and silver beads on elastic, only worth a couple of quid but you know what girls are like. She begged me to come over and get it back.'

'I haven't seen it anywhere.' Frankie shook her head; Addy was adorable but she certainly picked her moments.

'It's OK, she told me where it is. She was worried Young Bert might make a grab for it so she took it off and brought it into the house. It's in the little silver dish on top of your mantelpiece.'

'Oh right. Well, wait here and I'll go and fetch it!' Frankie held out her hands like a traffic cop to indicate that Lois shouldn't move, and backed towards the living room. 'I'll just get it for you now!'

But Lois, apparently oblivious to body language, was following her. Oh no, she wasn't going to be happy when she saw—

No one. No one at all. The room was empty. Just the one cup

of coffee on the table and no sign of Henry anywhere. Jesus, where had he gone? Was he secretly Derren Brown?

'Here it is.' Frankie scooped up the bracelet and practically threw it at Lois. 'Safe and sound. There you go!'

'Thanks.' Lois paused and surveyed her thoughtfully. *Why?*

'Right! Busy at the pub tonight? Well, it's Saturday so of course you're busy!' She was attempting to herd Lois out of the room but Lois wasn't moving.

'OK, I don't want to make you feel in any way awkward, but there's just something I need to say while I'm here. Dad isn't really interested in . . . you know.'

Baffled, Frankie said, 'He isn't interested in what?'

A deep breath, then Lois said sympathetically, 'Well, *you.*'

Frankie spluttered and covered her mouth. 'Excuse me?'

'Look, it's all right, no need to be embarrassed. After you'd asked me all those questions about Dad, I figured out why you were wanting to know. So I'm just telling you now, it's not a situation that would ever . . . happen. But don't worry, this is just between us. I won't breathe a word to another living soul.'

When she'd shown Lois out of the house, Frankie closed and double-locked the front door after her.

Back in the living room she said, 'Lois has gone. Where are you?'

'Well, I'm not hiding up the chimney,' Henry replied. 'I'm not Santa.'

Her stomach jittering, Frankie drew back the French window's full-length curtains. There he was, standing behind them with a full wine glass in each hand.

She'd known he was there, obviously. There hadn't been anywhere else to hide.

Henry solemnly raised his right hand and downed the contents of the glass in one.

Frankie took the other and did the same.

'So this business about her father . . .' she began. 'I don't have a crush on Lois's dad.'

He nodded. 'And you're telling the truth, because if you weren't you'd be all "Um . . . er . . . look, um . . ." and getting in a flap about it.'

She grinned because he was so right. 'How can you know that?'

'It's how I'd be.' Henry shrugged his massive shoulders and said simply, 'We're the same.'

And he was right; beneath their wildly differing exteriors, they were. This time Frankie experienced the electrifying *swoooosh* of attraction without physical contact . . . which had the effect of making her yearn for that contact all the more.

But at the same time she knew she had to be honest.

'OK, I need to say something. What I told you before still stands; my husband humiliated me and I'm only just starting to get used to being single again. There's no way I'm ready for any kind of relationship. God, listen to me,' she half-laughed at her own presumption. 'As if that's going to bother you. But anyway, I'm just saying, there wouldn't be any . . . involvement.' Her cheeks were on fire now. 'I can't believe I'm even saying this. Sorry.' He lived in London, for heaven's sake. They'd met for the first time this afternoon. Whatever had possessed her to think he'd be even remotely interested in an actual relationship?

Henry was shaking his head, doubtless finding it hilarious that she should be ordering him not to get any romantic ideas about a frumpy older woman whose husband had cheated on her for years.

Finally, somehow managing to keep a straight face, he said, 'It's fine. Come here.'

And Frankie did.

OK, this was embarrassing. Molly, whose body was apparently playing some kind of childish trick on her, was trying so hard not to yawn she was in danger of actually dislocating her jaw.

'How are the carrots?' Vince indicated the vegetables on her plate. *Was that so she knew which ones he meant?*

'Great. Brilliant.' Oh no, she'd managed to suppress the last yawn and now another one was building up. This was awful, she'd already done it twice; they just kept happening, completely beyond her control.

'Everything OK?' He looked concerned as she tried to subtly cover her mouth.

Poor Vince, what must he be thinking? Molly nodded brightly and said, 'Fine!'

But it was no good, the yawns were still *in* her, waiting to come out. Hurriedly finishing her meal while Vince talked about the meeting he'd had yesterday with a new client, Molly then pushed back her chair and said cheerily, 'Back in a bit!'

In the otherwise empty ladies' loo, which was plush and spacious, she did three enormous yawns in a row. But were they properly out of her system? It didn't feel as if they were. Right, yawns happened when your body was in need of more oxygen. It therefore stood to reason that exercise was what she needed to sort herself out. When athletes were running races in the Olympics, did they stop for a yawn halfway round the track? No, they did not. And seeing as there was no one else in here . . .

Molly had been jogging furiously on the spot for a couple of minutes when her phone rang.

Oops, please don't let it be Vince calling from the dining room to ask where she'd got to. Relieved to see Dex's name flashing up instead, she answered without thinking things through.

'Yes?' Oh dear, *properly* out of breath.

'Molly?'

'What?'

'Am I interrupting something . . . important?'

'No.'

'You're panting,' said Dex.

'I'm not.'

'Yes you are. Like a dog. Are you sure you and Vince aren't . . . ?'

'Quite sure, thanks very much. I was just *laughing*.'

'Laughing at what?' The doubt in his voice signalled she'd made the right decision; admitting she'd been jogging in order to combat a fit of the Unstoppable Yawns would have been more than Dex could resist.

'It's just Vince telling me funny stories . . . we've been having such a brilliant time.' Molly did a little ha-ha chuckle as she said it, as if the memory of all the funny stories was in danger of setting her off again, tipping her over the edge into full-blown hysteria.

'Right.' Dex paused. 'Well, that's excellent.'

See? Even now he was doing it, sounding ever so slightly surprised. Her breathing restored to normal, Molly said, 'Why are you calling me, Dex?'

'Amanda wants to fix a date for dinner next week. She needs to organise her work diary, schedule cover at the health centre. So how about Wednesday evening?'

'No, sorry, can't manage Wednesday.' She could, but why should Amanda be the only one important enough to have schedules that needed scheduling?

'Friday, then?'

'Hang on, let me ask Vince. I know he's pretty busy this week.'

At least the yawns had stopped. Covering the phone, Molly returned to the restaurant where Vince was waiting. 'Hey, Dex and Amanda want to fix a date for dinner. How about next Friday?'

'Great.' Vince nodded. 'Where have you been?' he added jovially. 'I thought maybe you'd squeezed out of the bathroom window and run off!'

Praying Dex hadn't overheard that bit, Molly unclamped her hand from the phone and said into it, 'Friday's fine for us.'

'Perfect.' Dex sounded amused. 'Can I ask you something?'

She stayed cool. 'Ask away.'

'Were you out of breath because you were busy squeezing through the bathroom window?'

He was a nightmare. With ears like a *bat*. Molly said, 'Bye, Dex,' and hung up.

Chapter 41

Wow. Just . . . wow.

Anyone looking at her now might think she was sleeping but beneath the closed eyelids Frankie's brain had never been more awake.

Tonight she'd had the first ever one-night stand of her life, for no other reason than that it had been a way of getting her own back on Joe. Even though he'd probably never find out.

OK, so it hadn't just been for that reason. The pyrotechnics of physical attraction had been there too, spiralling out of nowhere and catching her by surprise. After almost twenty years of marriage, it had been a while. And instead of being all coy and sensible and insisting that nothing could possibly happen until they knew each other better, she'd deliberately ignored her prim and proper other self, cast caution to the wind and just gone ahead and fallen into bed with someone she'd only met a few hours ago.

They'd had sex, imagine that!

She'd got naked – *completely naked, oh my!* – and slept with a physically beautiful man who had actually wanted to sleep with her.

And she didn't even know his surname.

Her prim and proper self was shocked at such impulsive and wanton behaviour. She would also have wanted the sex to be disappointing, in order to teach her a lesson.

Oh, but that was the thing, it *hadn't* been disappointing. Quite the opposite in fact. It had been amazing, spectacular, possibly the most fantastic sex of her life.

Frankie's eyes stayed closed but she felt the beaming smile spread unstoppably across her face. Did that make her a shameless, loose-moralled trollop?

It did?

Yay!

And now it was five thirty in the morning, already sunny outside, and Henry was stealthily easing himself out of his side of the bed. Suddenly, what had seemed so wild and wonderful last night began to feel less so.

'Are you creeping out on me?' Frankie turned her head and smiled to show she was joking. Kind of.

'Hi. No.' He shook his head. 'Just thinking it might be an idea to leave early so I'm not spotted. You told me last night this was a one-off. I don't want you panicking, feeling trapped, wondering how on earth you're going to get rid of me. And I have a squash game booked for nine o'clock,' Henry added. 'So I do need to get back.'

That was a lot of reasons, fired out at warp speed by someone evidently terrified of finding themselves faced with a one-night stand suddenly blurting, 'I know what I said yesterday but I've changed my mind now – I want you to be my boyfriend *pleeeease?*'

'Right. Yes.' Not that she *would* have said it, but he didn't know that. Nodding vigorously, Frankie said, 'Definitely a good plan, leaving now. Makes sense.'

'And don't worry, I won't tell Dex. No one's going to know about this.'

'Great. It'll be our secret.'

'Come here.' Having not made it out of the bed, Henry pulled her towards him. 'Last night was . . . great.'

'Yes.' He was so lovely, *really* lovely, but she couldn't tell him that. They'd both wanted no-strings sex, hadn't they? And got it. Who could ask for more?

'I'm glad I came down to the party yesterday.' He kissed her, after a moment's hesitation, on the cheek.

'I'm glad too.' OK, awkward. Last night had been electrifying, about as intimate as it was possible to get, and now he was kissing her as if she were his ancient maiden aunt.

Well, what else could she expect? Frankie's heart sank at the realisation that her Cinderella moment had been and gone. He'd done what he'd come back here to do. Now it was time for him to make his escape.

Henry drove away from Briarwood for the second time in under twelve hours, his brain in a whirl. Yesterday had been unbelievable. Imagine being a teenager with a crush on Beyoncé, fantasising that during her concert she might beckon him up on to the stage, dance with him, sing to him and invite him to a party afterwards.

Then imagine it all coming true.

OK, so Frankie wasn't Beyoncé, but meeting her had meant *more* to him, it really had. For them to have ended up spending the night together had been beyond his wildest dreams, a million times more of a result than he could ever have hoped for.

Luckily he'd managed not to frighten her to death by telling her this. Imagine how it would have made her feel.

No, he'd just been lucky enough to be in the right place at the right time. As she'd told him herself – twice – she was in no position to be interested in any kind of emotional relationship.

And that was OK, he understood that. Just as he'd known the only way to behave this morning was to keep things casual, play it ultra-cool.

Let's face it, he'd do whatever it took, anything at all not to scare Frankie off.

'You're here!' Molly stared at Vince, standing on her doorstep on Friday evening with a navy holdall in his hand. Had the clocks gone forward without anyone telling her? 'It's only six o'clock. I thought we said seven.'

'I know. I left work and came over early for a reason.' He lifted the canvas holdall and said, 'What was it I said to you last week about your car?'

'No idea. Oh, hang on, you told me it was dusty.'

'I did.' Vince nodded. 'And I also showed you those scratches and rust spots. Remember?'

She belatedly remembered; it hadn't been the most riveting conversation of her life. 'Yes.'

'And?' said Vince. 'Have you done anything about them?'

'No.' Cars weren't really Molly's strong point. As long as they started and stopped when she wanted them to, that was as far as her interest extended.

'You see? I guessed you wouldn't have. But these things are important. They need to be done. Rust spreads like bindweed,' said Vince.

'Crikey. Does it?' He was looking so handsome. And so serious.

'Yes it does. And if those scratches on the paintwork aren't dealt with, they'll become rusty too.'

'Oh dear.'

'Cars need to be looked after.' He gestured for her to follow him down the path. 'It's not rocket science.'

Molly knew it wasn't rocket science. It was just the kind of stuff that was so boring to actually do. Startled, she watched as Vince unzipped his holdall and pulled out a cellophane package containing something white. Opening the package revealed a set of coated-paper overalls which he proceeded to put on over his shirt and trousers.

'Crikey, what's that for?'

'To protect my clothes.' Having zipped it up, Vince gestured to the baggy all-in-one suit with elasticated bits at the wrists and ankles, and a hood that covered his hair. He looked like one of the scary government scientists in *E. T.*

'Right.' Molly hesitated while he took various pots and cloths and brushes out of the holdall and lined them up on the ground in a neat row. 'Well, shall I go in and start getting ready?'

'Or you could stay and watch,' Vince suggested. 'Then I can explain everything, take you through it step by step and teach you how to do it yourself.'

Frankie's neighbour Eric, in his eighties now, had been struggling recently to exercise his old Labrador so the villagers were helping him out. This evening it was Frankie's turn to take Bamber for a walk.

It also gave her the opportunity to address something else that needed sorting out.

Along the way, she passed Molly and Vince outside Molly's cottage.

'You look like one of those scene-of-crime forensics experts,' she told Vince.

Molly said, 'He's showing me how to treat the rust on my car.'

'Gosh.' This was startling news.

Vince, kneeling beside the wing on the driver's side, looked up and said, 'And how about you? Do you take proper care of your car?'

Frankie hesitated. 'Umm, I put it through a car wash the other week.'

'And did you wax it afterwards?'

She shook her head. 'Well . . . no.' Why was Molly giving her that look behind Vince's back?

'You see, you really should. It's important,' said Vince. 'If Molly had looked after her car, it wouldn't be in the state it's in now. Prevention's better than cure.'

'Right. Wow, I'll do it in future, definitely.' OK, *now* she knew why Molly had been giving her that faintly desperate look; it was a signal to get away, escape while she still could.

Luckily she had a dog to walk and misconceptions to straighten out. Leaving the village, Frankie and Bamber made their way down to the riverside path. Dragonflies were dancing over the surface of the water, iridescent flashes of colour catching the sun as they darted this way and that. As she followed the bend in the river, the caravan came into view and there was Stefan, occupying his usual position on the top step.

When he saw her, would he disappear inside the caravan?

She didn't have to wait long to find out. Less than twenty seconds later he did as she'd fully expected him to. Just as he'd discreetly altered course and veered away when she'd approached the village shop the other morning as he'd been leaving it. And just as he'd taken to walking in the other direction around the green so as to avoid passing her house.

Frankie smiled briefly. Poor man, he must be terrified; did he think she might be about to launch herself at him and declare passionate undying love?

Reaching the caravan, she tapped on the door and called, 'Hi, Stefan, can I have a quick word?'

He opened the door with visible trepidation. 'Hello . . .'

'OK, no need to look so worried. Just listen.' She was going to get it all out in one go. 'Lois was wrong, I don't have a crush on you, I don't even secretly fancy you a tiny bit. If I *did*, there's no way in the world I'd be able to stand here and talk about it like this. So you can stop panicking, OK? Just relax. You don't have to try and avoid me, because I'm not chasing after you. Lois doesn't often make mistakes, but this time she did.'

Silence.

At last Stefan said slowly, 'Well, you're right about not being able to say it if it wasn't true.'

See? This was the lesson she'd learned from Henry. 'I know. It stands to reason. If I liked you, I'd be blushing and stammering.' Frankie shrugged and spread her hands. 'And look at me! I'm not!'

'OK, I believe you. Well,' he exhaled, 'that's a relief. No offence.'

'None taken. Also, you're way too old for me. No offence,' she added with a grin.

'That's exactly what I told Lois!' All the tension had gone from his face now. From behind him came the sound of a whistling kettle coming to the boil 'Look,' said Stefan, 'I'm just making a pot of tea. Would you like some?'

'Great.' Glancing down to check on Bamber, Frankie saw he'd curled up and fallen asleep at her feet.

'All the excitement's been too much for the old boy.' With a compassionate smile, Stefan said, 'Leave him there, he'll be fine. Come along inside.'

The interior of the caravan was immaculate, a miracle of space-saving organisation and a mixture of modern and traditional. The floor was polished wood strewn with handmade rugs. The solid fuel stove gleamed. The seating was covered in crimson plush velvet, there were curtains and cushions in rich jewel colours and paintings hung on the walls. There was also a bathroom, a bedroom, a well-stocked bookcase and a small area containing a workbench and box of carpentry tools.

'Here.' Stefan passed her a mug of tea and a slice of fruit cake then sat down on the banquette opposite. 'So how are you coping without Joe?'

Talk about straight to the point. Frankie shrugged. 'Not so bad. It takes some getting used to.'

'It does.' He nodded in agreement. 'Is that why you were asking my daughter about me?'

'Kind of. Well, you've been on your own for a long time. I wondered how it felt.' His gaze didn't waver as she looked to him for an answer, even if it had only been half the question.

'Like you said, you do get used to it. It becomes the new normal. After my wife died, I had Lois to care for. She became my number one priority.'

'And she told me there was someone else too, many years later. Someone you loved but couldn't be with. That must have been heartbreaking.' Ooh, risky tactics, but this could be her only chance and she wasn't going to waste it. Frankie ploughed on: 'Why couldn't you be together? Am I allowed to ask?'

Stefan turned his attention to the open doorway where, on the top step, a blackbird had landed. He threw a tiny morsel of fruit cake towards it and watched as the blackbird hopped forward, took the crumb in its yellow beak and flew off. Quietly, without looking back at Frankie, he said, 'She had a reputation to maintain. People were interested in her personal life. Professionally, it wouldn't have done her any good. They would have expected more for her . . . someone better, the kind of partner she deserved. Basically, it would have had a negative effect on her career.' He was shaking his head now. 'And I couldn't have borne that responsibility. I'm proud of who I am, even if others aren't. I couldn't have allowed them to belittle and laugh at her for choosing to be with me.'

Frankie was lost for words. So Lois had been right; the reason he'd given Hope hadn't been the correct one. He'd ended the relationship in order to protect her public image and glittering career.

Except there had, subsequently, been no glittering career to protect. Hope had removed herself from the public's eye and never acted again anyway. Imagine, all that self-sacrifice for nothing.

Talk about pride and prejudice.

But much as she longed to tell Stefan everything, she still couldn't. A promise had been made to Hope and she had to honour it.

Aware that she was pushing her luck, Frankie said, 'What was her name?'

Because if she could make *him* say it . . . well, that would be different. And there had to be a chance, surely, that Stefan suspected she already knew the answer to the question.

Like now, with those shrewd, watchful eyes of his, still giving absolutely nothing away.

He shook his head again, just fractionally. 'It doesn't matter.'

'But it might.'

'Sshh. If I've never told another living soul, not even my own daughter, why would I suddenly tell you?'

The conversation was at an end; a metaphorical door had just been politely but firmly closed in her face. A man of his word, Stefan would go to his grave without giving away Hope's secret.

'Good point.' Finishing her slice of fruit cake, Frankie said, 'This is fantastic, by the way. Did you make it?'

A glimmer of a smile as Stefan drained his mug of tea. 'I make things out of wood, Frankie. That's what I'm good at. The cake's from Marks and Spencer.'

Chapter 42

Molly couldn't wait for this dinner party to be over. It was like being trapped in one of those dreams where you're taking an exam and don't even understand the questions let alone know the answers.

Not that Amanda and Dex were firing questions at them and laughing when they got the answers wrong, but it was how she *felt*. Wrong-footed. Defensive. Protective. And embarrassed, because she'd had such high hopes for Vince and it had been so lovely to proudly introduce the handsome new man in her life to her friends.

But glossing over his tendency to be precise, pedantic and a tiny bit humourless was no longer possible. Dex and Amanda were being careful not to give any outward indication of this but they had to be thinking it. The exterior of Vince might be perfect but personality-wise he was never going to set the world alight. He was well-meaning but boring. Bordering on downright dull. Every time he'd opened his mouth to speak, Molly had found herself tensing up, silently willing him to be dazzling and witty, to say something capable of making the rest of them sit up and reassess their opinion of him.

Oh, but it just hadn't happened. Never *ever* had she so longed to be a ventriloquist, capable of putting words into Vince's exquisite mouth.

And the food, as promised, was sublime. Which should have helped but somehow made things worse, simply by highlighting Amanda's many achievements and emphasising the differences between them. The starter had been perfectly seared scallops on puy lentils braised in red wine. For the main course, she'd effortlessly prepared and served meltingly tender fillet steaks with peppercorn sauce, sautéed potatoes and broccoli. Even the broccoli, tossed in lemon juice and butter, was delicious.

And now she was bringing out twice-baked raspberry soufflés with whisky cream. Even a tiny disaster along the way would have been comforting, but none had happened. Disasters simply weren't a part of Amanda's world; she was beautiful and super-intelligent with a model's figure . . . *and* she could bake perfect, non-collapsing soufflés. Twice.

Digging in, Molly said, 'This is amazing,' because there was no point in pretending it wasn't.

Amanda smiled. 'Yes, Dex did happen to mention your chocolate sponge experiment.'

Oh great, cheers Dex, thanks a lot. The other week she'd heard about a cake recipe you made in a mug in the microwave. When Dex and Delphi had called round, she'd made it, boasting about how brilliant it was going to be. She still had no idea what had gone wrong but the end result had resembled chocolate concrete.

Which, needless to say, had caused Dex *hours* of amusement.

'We did try to eat it.' He was grinning now at the memory. 'Nearly ripped my teeth out.'

'Oh dear. Molly hasn't cooked anything for me yet,' said Vince. 'Now you've got me worried.'

Was that meant to be a joke? It was impossible to tell.

'By the way,' Vince turned to her, 'Muriel was asking after you yesterday. She'd love it if we could go and see her soon.' Placing his hand over Molly's, he added, 'She's just thrilled we're getting along so well together. I think she wants to welcome you properly into the family.'

OK, *whoa.*

'That sounds serious.' Dex raised an eyebrow.

Molly was shaking her head. 'We're not getting *married* . . .'

'I know, she just wants to introduce you to everyone. She really likes you.' Vince gave her fingers a squeeze. 'So do I.'

Molly flushed as Amanda said, 'Oh, this is all so romantic!'

Help, though. It wasn't romantic, it was *wrong.* She adored Muriel, it had practically been love at first sight, but you couldn't maintain a relationship with a man just because he had an amazing grandmother.

'It's dark now. Clear skies tonight.' Pointing out of the window, Vince said to Dex, 'Still keen on the old star-spotting?'

'I am.' Dex nodded. 'You should give it a go, you don't know what you're missing.'

Vince, who had been less than enthusiastic last time, said, 'I don't think it's really my thing, to be honest. But if you want to get it out, I'll happily take a look at your telescope.'

As Dex met Molly's gaze, his mouth twitched. In return she silently defied him to make a joke about it.

'What?' Aware of Dex's suppressed laughter, Vince looked mystified.

'Sorry.' Dex shook his head apologetically. 'I just crack up every time I think about Molly and that microwaved chocolate cake.'

★ ★ ★

'Thanks for this evening.' On her way back from the bathroom ten minutes later, Molly found Dex in the kitchen opening another bottle of wine. 'It's been great. But we're going to have to head off now.'

'Why? It's only eleven o'clock.'

'I know.'

He put down the wine and lowered his voice. 'Are you OK?'

'I'm fine.' How could she begin to explain to Dex, of all people, the confusion currently going on inside her head? 'Just . . . tired.'

'Vince and Amanda are still out in the garden. I showed Vince my telescope.' Dex's eyes glittered. 'He was most impressed.'

'Don't make fun of him.'

'OK, I won't. And you mustn't marry him.'

Time slowed down. There was some indefinable emotion quivering in the air between them. Then Molly felt her throat tighten at the realisation that she was completely misinterpreting it. Dex was happy with Amanda, who was an alpha female, super-confident and in absolute control of her life. They were a matching pair, the perfect couple. He was only saying it because he felt compelled to warn her that Vince wasn't her type, just in case she hadn't figured this out for herself.

In a nutshell, she'd tried to find herself a decent man . . . and failed miserably. Yet again.

'Promise me you won't,' Dex murmured, his head close to hers.

'Oh please, why would I even want to get married? I hardly know him,' Molly protested. 'I'm not *that* desperate—'

'Come on, you two!' Amanda was calling from the hallway. 'How long does it take to open a bottle of wine? There you are.' She appeared in the kitchen and tugged at Molly's arm. 'Come outside and keep us company! Vince has been telling me *all* about the best way to treat rust on cars! He's such a sweetie, isn't he? Heart of gold.' Adopting another of her stage whispers, she added, 'You haven't popped along to the surgery yet, by the way. Is everything . . . sorted out?'

As Amanda said it, she pointed her index finger none too subtly in the region of Molly's pelvis.

'What?' Dex was now staring at it too. 'What's wrong? Are you ill?'

Honestly, couldn't doctors get struck off for this kind of talk?

'She's not ill,' Amanda cheerily assured Dex. 'Just friendly chat between two girls about certain girly matters that need to be taken care of.' The way she slid her arm around Dex's hip and pressed her thigh against his pretty much spelled it out for him. 'Ooh, while I think of it, we haven't had any photos. Here.' She produced her mobile and pressed a few buttons before handing it over to Molly. 'Could you take a couple of me and Dex?'

The two of them looked so glamorous, so completely right together, laughing and holding jokey poses as the flash went off.

'Here you are, I wondered where you'd all got to.' Joining them in the kitchen, Vince said, 'Is that an eight megapixel camera? Here, mine's ten megapixels, let me take some too.'

Then, when all the fun, playful snaps had been taken, Amanda said, 'Come on, your turn now.'

And Vince stood like an army captain with his back ramrod straight and his arm resting stiffly on Molly's shoulder while Amanda took the photos.

'Now loosen up, have some fun,' she ordered, gesturing encouragingly.

Vince said, 'It's OK, we're fine as we are.'

When Amanda returned his phone, he checked the results and

showed them to Molly. 'I'll get the best one printed out and framed and we can give it to Muriel. She'll be thrilled.'

Molly nodded and smiled and wanted to die a little, because in the photos they looked like a pair of shop mannequins in a nineteen-fifties department store.

Oh help, it was no good, when the time was right she was going to have to break it to Vince that this relationship couldn't go on.

Chapter 43

There it was, the name on the gate. She was here. And what an extraordinarily beautiful place it was.

Frankie clicked open the gate and made her way along the narrow winding path. The events of the last few months had definitely made her braver, more of a risk-taker, more proactive. Rounding the last bend in the gravelled path, lined with wild flowers on either side, she saw the cottage ahead and prayed it wouldn't be empty.

More to the point, she hoped it was occupied by the person she'd come here to see.

It had taken less than two hours to travel from Briarwood to this tiny, tucked-away valley in the Blackdown Hills, not far from Honiton in Devon. The cottage couldn't be more secluded if it tried, which was probably why Hope had felt able to come back and live in her late mother's home. *If she was still here*, Frankie reminded herself. The return address had been written on the parcel containing the polka-dotted frock but that had been weeks ago; there was no guarantee she hadn't moved on.

She knocked at the faded pale blue front door, which had no bell.

Nothing. Her heart sinking, Frankie tried again.

Then she heard the sound of footsteps and a hesitant female voice behind the door said, 'Who is it?'

Definitely Hope, thank goodness.

'Hi, it's Frankie Taylor. From the café. In Briarwood.'

'*What?*' Hope sounded stunned. 'What's going on? Are you alone?'

'I am, I promise. Don't worry, everything's fine.' Frankie heard the chain go across before the door was opened a couple of inches.

Hope peered out at her, then past her. 'You haven't brought him here?'

'No! I wouldn't do that to you. I haven't breathed a word to him,' Frankie assured her. 'Not to anyone.'

The door closed in her face. The chain was unfastened. Then Hope reappeared, trusting her finally. 'Well, it's lovely to see you again, but I can't imagine what this is about.'

'There was something I wanted to tell you. I wrote a letter.' Frankie opened her bag and took out the addressed envelope. 'But I wasn't sure if you'd still be here and I didn't want to run the risk of it getting lost or being read by someone else.'

'Come in.' Hope led the way through the cottage to the wraparound balcony at the back, overlooking the valley and the brook at the bottom of the sloping country garden. There was a sunbleached wooden bench and a table, a jug of lemonade and one tumbler, a battered paperback, a wide-brimmed straw hat and a half-empty packet of liquorice.

'Amazing view,' said Frankie, shielding her eyes in order to admire it.

'I know. I can sit out here for hours. Here, take a seat.' Plumping up an eclectic collection of cushions, Hope said, 'I'll fetch another glass while you make yourself comfortable.'

When she'd done so, Frankie handed over the envelope and allowed her to read the letter in silence.

As she learned what Stefan had said about having to end the relationship with the woman he'd truly loved, tears welled up in Hope's eyes and dripped off her chin, landing on her baggy grey linen trousers and soaking into the material.

Then she wiped her eyes with the backs of her fingers and managed a wobbly smile. 'Thank you. For finding out and for letting me know. I can't believe he did it for me, to protect me. I honestly had no idea. As for my career . . . oh dear, what a waste of time it was, trying to save *that*. He was just so proud, I suppose. Didn't he realise he was a million times more important to me than any stupid acting job? And I wouldn't have cared what anyone else thought. Stefan should have *known* that. Men can be so blind . . .'

'It's the pride thing.' Frankie nodded in agreement.

'Such a waste. Oh well, I'm still glad I know now.'

'I didn't tell him about you. But I so badly wanted to. I wish you'd let me.'

'No.' Hope shuddered and indicated her face. 'We've been through all this before, remember? I'd still be a disappointment.'

'I honestly don't think you would be.' How to convey to this insecure, once-stunning woman that Stefan simply wasn't that shallow? That when he was creating things from outwardly unprepossessing pieces of wood he took delight in seeking out and revealing its hidden beauty? 'But if you wanted to, you could always tidy yourself up . . .' *Oh God, that sounded terrible.*

Hope said ruefully, 'It's OK, I know what you're saying. But there's a world of difference between a bit of a tidy-up and a whole-head transplant.' Grimacing down at the rest of herself she added, 'A whole-head-and-body transplant, more like.'

Back at the gate, having bid Hope a fond farewell, Frankie waited for her lift to show up.

It was ironic that Henry and Hope had never met but between

them had conspired to change the way she was living her life.

For the last fortnight Henry had been in her thoughts and she'd found herself longing to see him again. But only a shameless floozy would take the initiative and make the first move, wouldn't she? Even if she had already demonstrated just how much of a floozy she could be.

The sound of a car engine in the distance reached her and Frankie smiled in anticipation. If Stefan and Hope's love story had taught her anything, it was that you only had one life to live and sometimes risks were worth taking. Two days ago she'd sent Henry a text suggesting that if he wanted to meet up again he should call her. When he had, she'd asked him outright how he'd feel about spending Saturday night with her in a hotel in Devon?

Her treat, obviously.

And guess what? It had turned out that he liked the sound of that idea very much indeed.

When she'd explained that she just needed to pay a brief visit to a friend living nearby, Henry hadn't minded at all.

If it hadn't been for Henry, would she have come all this way to see Hope?

If it hadn't been for Hope, would she have been brave enough to extend the invitation to Henry?

Basically, no, she probably wouldn't.

And here he was now, coming to pick her up on a hot and dusty roadside in the middle of nowhere, in order to whisk her back to the charming country hotel she'd booked in nearby Honiton. Frankie felt her heart expand like a marshmallow as the car slowed and the driver's window buzzed down.

'Hi.' Henry lowered his RayBans and flashed her a dazzling white smile. 'You're gorgeous. Fancy spending the night with a tall dark stranger in a four-poster bed?'

'Would that be you?'

'It most certainly would be.'

'Right. Just checking.' Frankie loved it when he gave her that look. 'In that case, yes please.'

'Hop in, then.' When she'd jumped into the passenger seat he gave her hand a brief squeeze and said, 'How was your friend?'

She hadn't told him about Hope and, perhaps sensing that discretion was called for, Henry hadn't pressed for details.

'She's fine. It was really nice to see her again.' Frankie had been most struck by the realisation that both Stefan and Hope spent endless hours of their lives sitting in solitude outside their homes, taking in their respective views of wild flowers, weeping willows, and a stretch of grass sloping gently down to a small river . . . Imagine how much happier and better the view would be if they could enjoy it together.

Well, she'd done her best. Maybe in time her words to Hope would sink in and have the desired effect.

'Good. Glad it went well.' As the car snaked along the narrow sun-dappled lane overhung with trees that almost met in the middle, Henry said, 'I've never been to Devon before. I like it.'

Frankie nodded in agreement. 'It's beautiful.'

'It's not the only one.' Glancing sideways at her as the breeze through the open windows whipped strands of hair across her face, his expression softened. 'Maybe I shouldn't be saying this, but I think we're going to have a fantastic weekend. And I'm so glad you contacted me.'

See? It was simply a matter of being brave, daring to take that risk. Frankie tilted her head back and felt the sheer elation of the moment rise up. Aloud she said, 'Me too.'

Chapter 44

'Bababa ... dadada ... mamamama ... BREEEGH!'

'Don't do that.' Dex shook his head at Delphi, who was chattering away in her high chair and banging her spoon on the tray by way of punctuation.

'TatatataGAH!' Beaming and kicking her bare legs, she flung a spoonful of porridge across the table.

'No.' He took the spoon from her and gave her his unamused look, causing Delphi to shriek with laughter. Dex said, 'Not funny, OK?'

In response she jammed her fingers into the bowl, scooped out two handfuls of porridge and slathered it all over the front of her favourite Bob the Builder T-shirt.

'*No.*' Dex made a grab for the bowl but Delphi was too quick for him; with a full-body sweeping gesture she sent it flying across the kitchen. Which wouldn't have been so bad if it had been a thick-porridge day but this morning he'd added too much milk and the resulting goo was now splattered across the window, the wall and the floor.

'Ha-ha-HA!' Delphi let out a whoop of delight.

There was no getting away from it; on some days, small

children could be a complete and utter pain in the neck. Lifting her out of the chair and holding her at arm's length, Dex stepped on a splat of porridge on the floor and skidded. In order not to drop Delphi he ended up clutching her tightly to his chest, which meant they were both now smeared with the stuff.

For fuck's sake . . .

'Bwwwwaaaah!' As a *coup de grâce* she blew a triumphant porridgey raspberry in his face.

Great.

The phone rang and Dex thought: *Just leave it.* But then he saw who was calling. It was Phyllis, Laura's kindly old neighbour in London, who'd supplied him with that glowing character reference when he'd been applying to become Delphi's guardian.

Right now, he was kind of wondering why he'd ever bothered. In a parallel universe at this moment, he could still be living a trouble-free, porridge-free, baby-free life.

Keeping the phone out of Delphi's sticky reach, he pressed reply and said, 'Hello, Phyllis. How are you?'

'Ooh my goodness! How on earth did you know it was me?' Phyllis had never got to grips with twenty-first-century technology. 'Hello, could I speak to Dexter please?'

'This is Dexter.' His voice softened. 'It's OK, your name comes up on my phone when you call me.'

'Well I never. Like magic, isn't it?' Phyllis marvelled. Then she lowered her voice a fraction and said, 'The thing is, I've got a friend of Laura's turned up here and he wants to have a long talk with you. He didn't know she'd died, love. So he's quite shocked and upset.'

Molly was in Cheltenham spending a happy hour stocking up in the art supplies shop when the text came through from Dex:

'Need to see you. It's urgent. Can you come over as soon as you get home?'

She sent a message back: 'I'm in Cheltenham. Back by three, is that OK? What's happened?'

He replied: 'Tell you when I see you. Hurry please. x'

Was it the *please* that did it? Or that tiny lone kiss? Molly felt a squeeze inside her ribcage and prayed the reason he needed to see her wasn't because Amanda had just informed him she was pregnant and they were getting married.

Although after all that banging on about contraception this would have its funny side in a *Schadenfreudey* kind of way.

She carried her wire basket over to the till and watched as the assistant rang up the various technical pens, pencils, erasers and sketch pads. She'd planned on doing a bit of clothes shopping while she was here, but Dex's messages had got to her; she'd head straight back instead.

And no, of course it wouldn't be amusing if Amanda was pregnant; the tiny hairs along her spine prickled in alarm at the thought. It would be horrendous.

Alarm, a whispering inner voice enquired, *or jealousy*?

OK, never mind about that. Molly hastily dismissed the snide inner voice as she stuffed her debit card into the card machine and tapped in her number.

Let's find out what the problem is first, shall we? One step at a time.

Dex was waiting for her. Pulling up outside the cottage just after midday, Molly was struck by the taut muscles and controlled anxiety in his face. He was wearing a navy polo shirt and jeans, and carrying a sleeping Delphi whose head was resting in the crook of his neck.

'Thanks for coming back.' The expression in his dark eyes was unreadable.

Jumping out of the car, Molly said, 'What's wrong? Is she ill?'

'No, nothing like that.' He led the way inside Gin Cottage and began pacing the living room, breathing deeply and evidently psyching himself up to begin.

'She's fast asleep.' Molly pointed to Delphi, snoring gently on his shoulder. 'Why don't you put her down in her cot?'

But Dex shook his head; he was holding on as if he couldn't bear to let go. 'I don't want to.'

'Tell me what's happened. It's something to do with Delphi.' Molly belatedly realised her fingernails were digging into her palms; his tension was catching.

'I got a call from Phyllis this morning. She lived next door to Laura in Islington . . . well, she's still there . . .'

'I remember. You told me about Phyllis.' Molly nodded. 'In her eighties, used to make cakes for you.'

'That's the one.' Dex tilted his head so his cheek was resting against Delphi's downy hair. 'Anyway, someone called Matt turned up on her doorstep this morning. He'd tried Laura's house first and the new people sent him next door. He asked Phyllis where Laura was and she had to tell him what had happened.'

'Poor guy,' said Molly. 'That must have been a shock for him.' In view of Dex's reaction she already had an inkling as to what this might be about.

'It was. A hell of a shock. Then he got a bigger one,' said Dex, 'when Phyllis started going into detail and talking about Delphi. From the sound of things, that's when he really freaked out. He hadn't known Laura was pregnant.'

Oh God, *oh God*.

'Is he the one?' Molly's mouth was dry. 'Is he Delphi's father?'

Dex shrugged and carried on pacing, a muscle jumping in his jaw. 'I don't know, but there's obviously a chance. He wants to see her. I spoke to him on the phone. He's coming down here this afternoon to talk to me and to meet Delphi. Oh God, every time I think about it I feel sick. She's mine now.' His voice cracked as he said the words. 'I can't bear the thought of someone else turning up and taking her away.'

'He might not want her.' What else could she say to lessen the terror? 'Lots of men don't.'

'I know that. I know. But he'd have got out of there the moment he found out, if that was the way he felt. He'd have cut and run.' Dex was shaking his head now. 'But he didn't, did he? He's driving down from London to see us. Phyllis had already given him the address. He's definitely interested.'

'OK, interested is one thing, but actually wanting to take on a baby . . . that's on a whole different level. That's *major*,' said Molly. 'So many men couldn't handle it.'

Dex closed his eyes briefly. 'But what if this one wants to? Just because the odds are against it doesn't mean it isn't going to happen.'

'OK, have you called your social worker? Asked her what you should do?'

'No.' He shook his head. 'I don't want her involved. You don't know what she might say.'

It was like having symptoms of a serious illness and not going to the doctor because you didn't want it to be true. Lovely though Dex's social work team were, they would undoubtedly tell him Delphi had a right to know her biological father. If this man decided he wanted to care for her full time, could anyone refuse him that?

'What made him suddenly turn up today?' said Molly. 'After all this time?'

A muscle was twitching like a metronome in Dex's jaw. 'He's been in Australia. That's where he lives now.'

Australia. So if he won guardianship of Delphi, he could take her to live with him on the other side of the world.

'Have you talked to Amanda?'

Their eyes met and something unspoken passed between them. Like the social workers, Amanda was part of officialdom.

Another shake of the head. 'No,' Dex said slowly. 'Only you.'

Matt-from-Australia was due to arrive at five o'clock and Dex's stomach was in knots.

By three o'clock the shortlist for their plan of action had comprised two possible alternatives: leave Briarwood for a few months and hide, or bury Matt-from-Australia in a shallow grave in the back garden and quickly put down a patio.

By three thirty Dex had come up with a third option. It definitely wasn't the kind that would be approved of by social workers but what they didn't know wouldn't hurt them.

When this much was potentially at stake, he'd go with anything that might do the trick.

'Hiya!' Tina greeted them with a beaming smile. 'Come along in, excuse the mess, we're just back from the school run . . . you two, stop fighting and *share* the biscuits.'

Dex and Molly followed her into the house. Dex liked Tina, who lived next to the village shop and was always cheerful, despite having seven children whose decibel levels would have driven a lesser woman to drink.

'I need a favour,' Dex told her. 'Someone from social services is coming over in a bit to do one of those review updates and they're interested in seeing how Delphi interacts with other children. So I was wondering if we could borrow George for a while.'

'Of course you can! Borrow as many as you like!' Tina stepped over a couple of school-age ones stretched out on the floor playing with the dog and watching TV. She scooped George up and said, 'Hey, baby boy, want to go on a play-date with Delphi?'

George regarded his mother with pale, blond-lashed eyes; nothing much bothered him. Placid and largely silent, so long as he had food to eat, he was a happy lad. Only a week separated him and Delphi but whereas she was dark-eyed and dainty, George was as bald and chubby as a baby hippo.

'BRRREEEEEE!' Delphi gleefully reached over to grab one of George's ears by way of greeting.

'Thanks,' said Molly, holding out her arms and taking him from Tina. 'And don't worry, we'll look after him. He'll be back before seven, is that OK?'

'No problem.' Tina blew a kiss and gave her son a wave. 'Bye-bye, baby boy, see you later. Have fun!'

'Oh dear. Poor George.' Molly stepped back to admire her handi-work. 'He doesn't look as if he's having much fun.'

'Sorry, George,' said Dex. 'We wouldn't be doing this if we didn't have to.'

George eyed them balefully from his position on the sofa. The pink smocked dress that was too big for Delphi was a bit tight on him. He was wearing frilly white ankle socks and his fair hair had been coaxed into a little topknot and secured with a bright pink scrunchie. The next moment, as if accepting his fate, he broke into a placid smile and examined the white lace trim around the hem of his dress with interest.

'Good boy, George.' Dex nodded approvingly. 'I mean, good *girl*.'

Molly said, 'If he grows up to be a transvestite, it'll all be down to us.'

Chapter 45

Molly had left, taking Delphi with her. Dex watched from the window and waited for Matt to arrive. George, after eating a couple of biscuits and watching an episode of *In the Night Garden*, had fallen asleep on the beanbag. OK, it was unlikely that Matt would turn up demanding a DNA test today, but if he asked for one any time soon, they'd just have to borrow George again. It was the only way.

And yes, it might be wrong and illegal and morally indefensible but Dex knew he would do it; he'd do anything, *risk anything* to prevent Delphi from being taken away from him.

Especially to Australia.

At ten to five a car drew up outside. Matt climbed out of the driver's seat, well over six feet tall and broad shouldered, wearing a plain T-shirt and jeans. Not particularly good looking but not bad looking either, just average. Mid-brown hair, fairish freckled skin, no immediate resemblance to Delphi – but then, with her dark hair and eyes, Delphi took after Laura; appearance-wise she was all Yates.

Dex mentally braced himself; this was like all the times in the past when he'd lied to the girls in his life, only a million times more important. *OK, here we go . . .*

'Dexter. Thanks for seeing me.' Matt shook his hand and said, 'I just can't get over it. What a shock. I couldn't believe it when Phyllis told me about Laura. Such a tragedy. And then to hear about the *baby* . . .'

'Yes. Come in.' Having left George fast asleep in the living room, Dex led Matt into the kitchen and switched on the coffee machine. 'When did you leave for Australia?'

'Just under two years ago. I've been working on a cattle station in the outback. In Queensland. I'm not the greatest at keeping in touch with people at the best of times . . . but if I'd known she was pregnant . . . well, oh Jesus, I had no *idea* . . .'

'But if Laura had wanted you to know, she could have found a way to contact you. She was just happy to be a mum. It's all she ever wanted. She was such a great mother,' said Dex. 'And Delphi's fine. She's fantastic, doing really well. She's changed my life. I love her, I'm her legal guardian, the adoption's going ahead, it's all on track, she's calling me Dada . . . as far as Delphi's concerned, I'm her father—'

'Right. Can I see her?' Matt was giving him an odd look.

'Of course you can.' Dex realised he'd said too much too fast, so desperate was he to stake his claim. 'She's asleep. Come on through.'

At the sound of the door opening, George opened his pale blue eyes. He looked more than ever like a baby hippo in drag. Overcome with emotion, Matt gazed at him in silence and covered his mouth with his hand.

'Delphi. Come here, sweetheart. Come to Daddy!' God, it felt weird, saying the words to George. Reaching down, Dex scooped him up into his arms. 'There's a good girl. And look, someone's here to see you!'

A ribbon of shiny drool dangled from George's bottom lip and

Dex left it there; the only saliva he didn't mind cleaning up was Delphi's.

'Here she is, then.' Swinging round to Matt, he said, 'This is Delphi.'

George blinked and dribbled a bit more as he stared blankly at Matt.

Matt stared back for several seconds. The ribbon of drool lengthened, like a miniature silver bungee.

Dex held his breath.

At last Matt said evenly, 'I don't know what's going on here, but this isn't Delphi.'

'What?'

'It's not Delphi.' He shook his head.

'Yes it is.'

'Oh come on.' Matt took out his phone, pressed some buttons and held it up so Dex could see the photograph on the screen.

Shit. When had that been taken? Just a few weeks before Laura's death, presumably. There was Phyllis sitting on her pristine pale blue sofa, proudly holding Delphi on her lap.

Beautiful elfin-featured Delphi, with her sparkling dark eyes, delicate cheekbones and irresistible beaming smile.

Phyllis had evidently – oh so helpfully – shown Matt her precious framed photograph and he'd taken a picture of it.

Dex felt sick. So much for their grand plan. What was going to happen now?

'Who's this?' Matt pointed at George.

'He belongs to a friend.'

'*He?*' His eyes widening in disbelief, Matt said, 'So where's Delphi?'

'She's . . . next door.'

'Am I allowed to ask why?'

'Because she means everything in the world to me,' said Dex, 'and I panicked, I couldn't bear to lose her. The thought of someone turning up out of the blue and staking a claim, taking her away . . .' His throat tightened at the prospect, 'Well, it's enough to make you do something desperate. So we did.'

'Right.' Matt nodded thoughtfully. 'I can see that it would. But I'd like to see the real Delphi now, if that's all right with you. By the way,' he added as Dex turned to leave, 'if that means you think I'm her father, I'm not.'

Molly and Delphi were on the floor building a tower of wooden blocks when the doorbell began to ring.

And ring and ring and rrringgggggg.

Her heart leaping with terror, Molly jumped up and pulled the front door open. She'd never seen Dex looking so happy. Wasting no time, he said, 'It's OK, everything's fine, he's not the dad.'

'WAAAAH!' Her shriek of relief would have been ear-splitting had it not been muffled by Dex flinging his arms round her. All the pent-up fear dissipated in a whoosh of release as they clung to each other. Then Molly pulled back in order to look at him and they both began to laugh.

'All that worry,' she told Dex, 'for nothing. No one's taking Delphi away from you.' Whoops, for a split second there she'd almost said *us*.

'I know.' He was shaking his head in wonder. 'I still can't believe it. Come here.' And he was hugging her again, too overcome with relief to speak. The next moment, somehow, they were kissing. It just felt so natural, so right, his warm mouth on hers—

'DadaDA!' Having crawled across the hallway, Delphi clung to the leg of Molly's jeans in order to pull herself to her feet. Tugging energetically at the hem of her shirt, she demanded to be lifted up and allowed to join in. 'DadaDADADA.'

Since what was carrying on over her head clearly wasn't a good idea, it was a timely intervention. Molly picked her up, planted a big kiss on Delphi's cheek then passed her over to Dex who did the same.

'Oh, my baby girl.' For a moment his eyes swam as he hugged her to him and was rewarded with a poke in the ear. 'Ow.'

'Bladada.' By way of apology, Delphi stretched out her delicate hand and trustingly stroked his cheek.

'I love you too,' Dex murmured, before collecting himself. 'Come on, let's go. Matt's waiting for us. I left him in charge of Transvestite George and I don't know which of them's more scared.'

'Now I can see it.' Matt held out an index finger and watched as Delphi grasped it. 'My God, she looks just like Laura. Those eyes.' He turned back to Dex. 'She looks like you too.'

In a corner of the living room, Molly changed an uncomplaining George out of the dress and girly accessories and turned him back into a boy. She stayed out of the conversation as Dex took Matt through the details of Laura's sickeningly sudden death.

Then it was Matt's turn to explain his and Laura's relationship. 'We worked together years ago and stayed friends afterwards. It was mainly thanks to Laura we kept in touch. I'm not brilliant at that sort of thing.' He pulled an embarrassed man-face. 'But we always picked up where we'd left off. Laura was great. We got on really well, enjoyed catching up with each other's lives. It was a platonic relationship.' He paused. 'Then a few years back, Laura talked about wanting children and not having any luck with finding herself a man. She asked me if I'd help her out.'

Dex had gone very still. 'In what way?'

'In the way friends do. You know what I'm talking about,' said Matt. 'Laura was happy to take the responsibility and be a single mother. She just wanted a donor to . . . well, donate.'

'When was this?' said Dex.

'Four years ago. We tried for a few months, but it never did happen.' Matt shook his head. 'Poor Laura, she was disappointed, she'd been desperate for her wish to come true. But then I was offered a job in Alaska, so that was that. I was out there for a year. When I came back we met up, but didn't . . . you know. I'd started seeing this other girl so it wouldn't have been appropriate. And then not long after that I went out to Australia. When you're living that kind of life, it's easy to lose touch with friends. Before you know it, they've moved on. I lost my phone with all the numbers in it . . . I just assumed everyone else was as busy as I was.' He paused, lost in thought. 'You tell yourself you'll catch up at some stage, whenever you get back. I finally came home last week and thought it would be great to see Laura again. Didn't have her number any more, so I just turned up on the off chance at the house. But the door was answered by a teenage boy who hardly spoke any English. I thought Laura must have moved away, and knew she'd always been friendly with Phyllis next door. So I went to ask her where Laura was living now.' He stopped abruptly, closed his eyes and took a deep breath. 'I couldn't believe it when she told me what had happened. Couldn't *believe* it.' He rubbed a hand across his forehead. 'Still can't. Laura was such a good person.'

'I know.' Dex nodded. 'She was.'

'And then Phyllis started talking about Delphi. Well, you can understand why I was shocked. Pleased in one way, because it meant Laura had had the baby she was so desperate for. And devastated because she'd died, leaving Delphi without a mother. So if you thought I was the father,' Matt went on, 'that means you have no idea who it is.' This had evidently only just occurred to him.

'None at all. A one-off, Laura told me. Anyway, I'm adopting her.' Dex was firm. 'Right now, I'm her uncle. But I'm going to be her dad.'

'Wow. That was the other shock.' Matt shook his head. 'When Phyllis told me who was taking care of Delphi now.'

'What does that mean?'

'Well, I know we've never met before, but Laura used to talk about you.' Grimacing apologetically, Matt said, 'No offence, but she told me what you were like.'

From the other side of the living room, Molly watched and wondered how Dex would react to this less than complimentary observation.

'It's OK.' Delphi was attempting to take off his watch; Dex unclipped it and fastened it around her ankle, currently her favourite place to wear several thousand pounds' worth of Switzerland's finest. 'I used to be a complete . . . idiot.' Now that Delphi had begun imitating sounds, he was having to learn to censor himself. 'And I never imagined I could do this. The first time I talked properly to Molly was just after Laura died.' He glanced over at her as he spoke, and a lump sprang into her throat at the memory of that night. 'I told her I couldn't do it, that there was no way I could look after a baby.' He paused, a world of emotion in his eyes as he held her gaze for a long moment. 'She was the one who told me I could.'

'And I was right,' said Molly. *Mustn't cry, mustn't cry.*

'Eventually. Well, not even that. One day at a time,' said Dex. 'But we're getting there. And I'm doing something I never thought

I could do. Delphi's changed my life and I had no idea it was possible to feel this way about someone who can't even speak. She just means everything in the world to me. Sorry, I know it sounds pukey. I'm not used to talking like this.' He leaned forward and waggled Delphi's bare foot with the oversized Breitling watch dangling from her ankle. 'I just love her so much.'

'Has she turned you into a better person?' said Matt.

Dex shrugged. 'I don't know about that. I hope so.'

Matt turned to Molly. 'Is he?'

She nodded. 'Yes.'

'Well. That would make Laura very happy,' said Matt.

Dex nodded. 'It would. And she was the one who wanted me to be Delphi's guardian.' With a brief smile he dropped a kiss on Delphi's tangled dark curls. 'My big sister always did like to think she knew best.'

Molly left Dex and Matt sharing their memories of Laura. As she carried George on her hip across the village green, she said, 'And don't tell your mum about the dressing up, OK? It's our secret.'

'Here he is!' Greeting them at the door, Tina took George from her and smothered him in kisses. 'The prodigal son, home again. Did he behave himself?'

'Good as gold,' said Molly.

'He always is. And how did the assessment go with the social worker?'

Tiny fibs weren't too terrible, were they? 'It went well. Fingers crossed, everything's going to be fine.'

Tina looked pleased. 'Ah, I hope so, I really do. Dex deserves it. We were only talking about him yesterday, me and the other mums at the school gate.'

'Oh?' Molly smiled, picturing the scene. Of course the other mothers would discuss Dex; he was the most enthralling addition to Briarwood in years.

'Yes! We were saying it's just like one of those Hollywood romcoms, you know the kind. Handsome Jack-the-lad giving up the city high life and moving to the sticks to look after a baby.' Her eyes dancing, Tina said, 'And to begin with he doesn't have a clue what he's doing and all sorts of things go wrong, but after a while it gets better . . . and then he ends up getting together with the girl who helped him through it!'

'Oh gosh.' *Crikey.* Molly felt herself growing pink at the thought of all those people at the school gate gossiping about her and Dex.

'And there are setbacks along the way, of course there are, because you *always* have to have setbacks in movies like that. But everyone knows they're perfect for each other and the whole village is rooting for them . . . and then in the end something *really* romantic happens and that's when they realise it's proper love and happy-ever-after time . . .'

Wow. The memory of their recent kiss had come rushing back.

'. . . for City-boy Dex,' Tina was doing happy-ever-after jazz hands now, 'and Dr Amanda the fantastic village GP!'

Molly saw Matt's car leave just after eight o'clock that evening. Moments later her doorbell rang.

'You didn't come back,' Dex protested, following her into the living room.

'You didn't need me to.' She sat back down at her drawing board and uncapped her pen. 'And I had work to catch up with. Anyway, panic over. I'm glad it went well. He seemed really nice.'

'He is. We've been talking about Laura. And . . . all sorts of stuff.

He wants to stay in touch, be a kind of honorary uncle to Delphi. You know the sort of thing, turn up every couple of years or so with unsuitable presents.' Dex paused. 'Look, I've just put Delphi to bed. Do you want to come over for a bit? I thought we could open a bottle, celebrate the fact that Matt isn't her father, she's still ours.'

Ours. It was only a figure of speech but it hit Molly like a knife in the heart. She shook her head and concentrated on the job in hand, capturing Boogie on a surfboard. 'I really need to get this done. Can't miss my deadline.'

'Oh. Right.'

There was a bit of an awkward silence. Aware of his gaze fixed on her, Molly didn't look up. 'And you can tell Amanda about it now. No need to mention the illegal baby-swapping bit.'

'True. Well, I'd better get back to Delphi.' Dex moved to the door. 'Thanks anyway. For helping out with the whole illegal baby-swapping bit.'

'No problem.' Molly carefully cross-hatched the underside of the surfboard. 'Bye.'

When the door closed behind Dex a lump sprang into her throat, her skin prickled with shame and she had to force herself not to burst into huge sobby tears.

Oh God, this is so stupid . . .

An hour later, a different car pulled up outside Gin Cottage and Amanda jumped out, her short hair gleaming and her perfect figure more perfect than ever in a strapless aquamarine dress and matching heels. Glancing up and spotting Molly lurking like a troll behind the bedroom curtain, she waved and flashed her a saucy, cat-got-the-cream smile.

Basically, because she *had*.

Molly flinched at this last uncharitable thought, which surely made her a despicable person. Since learning the other item of news this afternoon, she should really be feeling more sympathetic than this.

God, how she wished Tina hadn't told her now.

But that was the trouble with gossip; once heard, you couldn't un-know it.

When Vince's name flashed up on her phone at nine thirty, Molly was tempted not to pick up. The relationship wasn't going anywhere; he was a genuinely nice person but niceness wasn't enough. It would be kinder to stop it now.

Which meant she probably should get the deed done and answer the phone.

'Vince, hi. Look—'

'Hello, darling, it's me, Muriel! Listen, I'm here with Vince . . . remember we talked about how much we loved *Mamma Mia* and you said you'd tried to get tickets for the show here in Bristol but they'd all sold out? Well, they must have released a few more because Vince is on the website now and there are three available for the stalls on Thursday evening! But the page is on a timer and we have to book it now or we'll lose it . . . so is Thursday OK for you?'

'Um . . .' Oh God, she'd *really* wanted to see *Mamma Mia* at the Hippodrome.

'Thirty-seven seconds left,' said Muriel. 'Thirty-six . . . oh please say you can make it, Molly. It'll be such fun . . . thirty-three seconds before it times out . . .'

'Yes, I'll come!' Molly blurted out. Oh dear, now she was officially a bad person.

'Really? Hooray, I'm so glad! We'll have such a great night!'

Then again, having heard the unalloyed joy in Muriel's voice, maybe it was allowed.

'Hear that, Vince? We're on,' Muriel said excitedly. 'Go on, do it. Book those tickets now!'

Chapter 46

Never had a fish been more out of water. Poor Vince, he was like a fish in the middle of the Gobi desert.

But it was a crowded, noisy desert. The audience at the sold-out show at the Bristol Hippodrome was having the time of their lives; everyone was up on their feet, singing and dancing and clapping along with their hands in the air. Muriel, in the aisle seat, was loving every minute and Molly, next to her, could feel her joy. And then, to her right, there was Vince. Doing his level best to join in and failing utterly, his awkwardness palpable. Attempting to move in a dance-y way was evidently mortifying for him. He simply couldn't relax, let go of his inhibitions and have fun.

To look at him, anyone would think he'd be a brilliant dancer. But he wasn't.

Some people just weren't the type.

'That was amazing,' sighed Muriel, once they were back at her house on the Downs. 'Did you love it?'

'I did.' Molly smiled at her across the kitchen table. 'Thanks so much for inviting me along.'

'Darling, thanks for coming.' As Vince left the room in order to reply to an urgent message on his phone, Muriel leaned forward and lowered her voice. 'I don't think it was quite Vince's cup of tea, bless him.'

'I noticed.' Molly pulled a face.

'But wasn't it lovely of him to come with us, despite it not being his thing? That's Vince all over, he's such a caring, thoughtful person. Want some?' Muriel held up the silver hip flask she'd just used to add a dash of brandy to her coffee.

'No thanks. Driving home.'

'Not staying over?' Muriel tilted her head helpfully in the direction of Vince's flat.

Yikes. 'I really have to get back,' said Molly.

'You couldn't ask for a better boyfriend, you know. He's kind . . . generous . . .' There was a touch of desperate saleswoman creeping into Muriel's voice now. 'He'd never let you down. Vince isn't one of those who'd mess you around.'

Oh dear, this was awkward. And they both knew it. Molly hesitated and said, 'I know he wouldn't.'

'He's been paying into a private pension scheme since he was twenty-one.'

'That's . . . great.'

Cutting to the chase, Muriel said, 'OK, call me a nosy old bat if you like, but do you think there could be a future for you two?'

Oh dear, here we go.

Molly said gently, 'I don't think so. Sorry.'

'Me too. Bugger.' Muriel heaved a sigh and added another slosh of brandy to her cup. 'Well, that's a real shame. But it can't be helped.' Ruefully she went on, 'I just want to see my grandchildren settled before I die. But that's never going to happen, is it? It's like trying to squash an octopus into a jar.'

They heard Vince coming back down the staircase, finishing up his business call. Molly drained her coffee and said, 'I'd better be off.'

Hugging her goodbye, Muriel whispered, 'Oh well. Thanks for trying, darling. We'll get there in the end. I'll find him a nice girl if it's the last thing I do.'

'There, all sorted. Oh, are you off?' Vince looked disappointed as Molly reached for her bag and keys. 'Well, it's been a wonderful evening.'

She couldn't bring herself to do it now; it would be too cruel. Molly took the decision to leave things as they were, just for tonight. She'd come over and tell him tomorrow.

'I know.' She waved goodbye to Muriel and left the kitchen with Vince; giving him a quick kiss, she said, 'Thanks again. It's been great.'

'What are you doing here?' Molly's heart sank when she opened the door the next day and saw Vince. 'Didn't you get my text? I said I'd come over to you.'

'I know you did.' He was smiling down at her. 'But I thought I'd surprise you instead. I've booked a table for dinner at the Manor House.'

'But—'

'And we're also going to take a look at these!' Having led the way into the kitchen, with a triumphant gesture he produced a handful of travel brochures from behind his back. 'No arguments, this is my treat. You were saying you'd always wanted to visit Venice, so that's where we're going to go!'

Aaargh. 'Oh but—'

'Unless there's anywhere else you'd prefer. Florence . . . Paris . . . Timbuktoo?'

He'd said *Timbuktoo* in a comedy voice. Oh help, here we go. Molly held up her hand to stop him in his tracks. 'Vince, wait. Hang on. Was this Muriel's idea?'

'No!' He paused. 'Well, she may have mentioned it, but I'd already thought about doing it myself. We deserve a break, don't we? A few days away, so we can get to know each other better . . .' He faltered at the expression on her face.

'I'm sorry, Vince. I can't go away with you.' This was why she'd been putting it off; this was the bit Molly hated. 'I can't see you any more. You're lovely, but it just doesn't feel right.'

'What?' He looked stunned.

'It's not your fault. It's me.' *Oh no, was she really coming out with that old line?* 'You deserve someone better than me. There's a girl out there who'll fall madly in love with you and truly appreciate everything you do for her.'

Silence. At last Vince said. 'But it's not going to be you?'

Molly slowly shook her head.

'Oh.' He gazed blankly at the brochures in his hand.

'Sorry.'

'But . . . my grandmother really likes you.'

Was he trying to break her heart? 'I like her too. But you'll find someone else.'

'People always say that.' Putting the glossy brochures on the kitchen table and straightening them so the edges were lined up, Vince said sadly, 'But I never do.'

Vince left the cottage and started up his car. Well, that was that. So much for pinning his hopes on Molly to be the one.

And he was thirsty too. Annoyingly, as a rule he made sure to keep a bottle of mineral water in his car for emergencies. But yesterday Muriel had drunk it on their way home from *Mamma*

Mia and this morning he'd forgotten to replace it. And he could hardly go back to Molly and ask for a glass of water now.

It was seven o'clock; the village shop in Briarwood was closed, as was Frankie's café. The only place open was the Saucy Swan. Driving around the green, Vince pulled into the pub car park.

It was a warm sunny evening and all the outside tables were occupied but inside the pub it was cool, dark and almost completely deserted.

'Hello there!' The friendly barmaid greeted him with a broad smile. 'And what can I get you?'

'Just water please.'

'Still or sparkling?'

'Still.' He didn't like water with bubbles in it.

'And is Molly coming over?'

The sound of her name made Vince flinch. 'No. No, she won't be.'

'Oh! Is everything . . . OK?'

Vince looked at the barmaid and remembered that she was actually the landlady of the pub. Louise, was that her name? He'd seen her at Delphi's birthday party at the café.

'Not really.' He paid for the bottle of water and drank half of it down in one go.

'Oh dear, sorry to hear that. Not your decision?'

Vince looked at her. It was Lois, that was it, not Louise. Big hair, big earrings, plenty of crimson lipstick and sooty-black mascara. Suddenly, completely out of the blue, a massive wave of emotion welled up and he shook his head.

'Hey, it's OK. Don't worry.' She rested her hand on his. 'I'm not being nosy and I don't gossip.'

He exhaled slowly, paying closer attention to the dark eyes and compassionate smile. It wasn't like him to confide in a virtual stranger but Molly's rejection this evening had felt like the last straw.

'It's happened before.' Pausing to drink more water, Vince realised his hand was trembling. 'And I don't know why. No one can ever give me a proper answer. They tell me I'm a good person and I haven't done anything wrong, but they just don't want to see me any more. I mean, am I *that* ugly?'

'Are you kidding?' Lois shook her head in disbelief. 'You're the opposite of ugly. Come on, look at you. You'd give Brad Pitt a complex.'

'But I always end up on my own. I was going to take Molly away on holiday with me and she wasn't interested. What's that?' said Vince as she put a small glass tumbler in front of him.

'Whisky. It'll make you feel better. My treat.'

'I'm driving.'

'One is fine.'

Not a great drinker, Vince tried it. The whisky was surprisingly nice. He said, 'Thanks very much,' and watched as Lois turned away to serve another customer. She was wearing a black dress printed with huge pink roses. The neckline was ruffled and elasticated so as to expose her tanned shoulders and impressive cleavage. She looked over-the-top and brassy, like a parody of a good-time girl, in her bright pink court shoes with scuffed heels. But she was being kind to him and there was a warmth to her character that was making him want to stay and talk some more.

If he went home now, what would he do? Nothing.

Apart from bear the brunt of his grandmother's unspoken disappointment.

Again.

'You've finished your drink.' Lois was back and the other

customer had headed outside, leaving them alone once more. 'Would you like a coffee?'

'No thank you.' Vince stared at the empty tumbler, then raised his head and gazed steadily at her. 'I'll have another Scotch.'

Chapter 47

'I thought I'd better give you a call,' Lois whispered into the phone. 'Let you know.'

'Oh God.' At the other end of the line she heard Molly heave a sigh. 'I thought he'd just go straight home. How is he?'

'Bit drunk. Not too bad. Not causing any trouble.'

'I can't believe this. He isn't the getting-drunk type.'

'He's drowning his sorrows. So you're not interested in coming over, talking things through with him?'

'No,' said Molly. 'Look, I'm sorry, but there's really no point. It's over.'

'Am I allowed to ask why?'

'You know what? I don't even know the answer. On paper, he's perfect in every way. Vince is kind and thoughtful and hand-some . . . he even treated the rust spots on my car. But he just isn't right for me.'

'OK.' Lois softened. 'Well, these things happen. I'm sure he'll live.'

'Damn, he's got his car with him. You'll have to call a taxi to take him home. Don't let him drive.'

Watching Vince through the doorway, Lois said, 'Don't worry, I won't.'

It was one o'clock in the morning. Lois was wide awake in bed, staring up at the ceiling with her brain in overdrive.

At eleven thirty the rest of the customers had left. The taxi she'd ordered for Vince had been a no-show. She'd finished clearing the bar and cashing up for the night and still it hadn't arrived.

'It's all right, don't worry about me.' Somewhat the worse for wear but not wildly so, he'd said, 'I'll sleep in my car.'

'You can't do that. Look, you can have the spare room.'

Upstairs, he'd stood in the doorway and watched her pull out the sofa bed. Lois had taken sheets and a duvet out of the airing cupboard and said, 'This won't take me two minutes to make up. Are you hungry? Thirsty? Anything else you want, just say.'

'Really? What I want more than anything is for someone to want me.'

Lois turned to look at him and saw the expression on his face. His chiselled, oh-so-handsome face.

And that particular expression.

'You mean Molly?'

'No.' He shook his head. 'Wow, this isn't a situation I'm used to. You're not the kind of woman I'd usually go for. *At all.*'

'Thanks.'

'But you're actually very attractive . . . sexy . . . God, sorry, listen to me. I shouldn't be saying this.'

Lois's heart was racing now. 'You can say it if you want to.'

'Can I?'

'Yes. You know, you're not so bad yourself.'

Ooh, *bold.*

They gazed at each other in mutual astonishment. Vince was swaying slightly. Lois's mouth had gone dry. *Where had this come from, bursting out of nowhere?*

The next moment they'd launched themselves at each other and begun to kiss. Just like that, with virtually no warning at all. The adrenalin had coursed through Lois's body and there had simply been no stopping them. Out of the spare room with the unmade-up sofa bed and into her own bedroom . . .

And now it was an hour and a half later. The alcohol had caught up with Vince and he was fast asleep, out for the count beside her. But not before they'd done it twice. *Twice!*

It had been a while for both of them, it turned out. His relationship with Molly, Vince had admitted, hadn't got that far. Which Lois was glad about. Although when she'd confided that she hadn't slept with a man for the last two years, she'd known he hadn't believed her. This came as no surprise; when you looked like she did, everyone tended to assume you were a good-time saloon girl, always up for a bit of fun with anyone who happened to show a passing interest in you.

Oh well. She was used to it. Whereas in reality the number of men she'd slept with was almost laughably small. And they hadn't been the most charming characters either. She'd always managed to go for the brash swaggering bullies who ended up treating her like dirt and on more than one occasion had become physically abusive. It wasn't until a couple of years ago that she'd begun to find decent, polite, *gentle* men attractive. The drawback being that, thanks to her own brash exterior and upfront manner, she always seemed to scare the decent gentle types rigid; the moment she demonstrated the smallest amount of interest they ran a mile.

Until tonight.

In the darkness, Lois broke into an unstoppable smile. Talk

about a turn-up for the books. Vince was everything she could have dreamed of. And somehow, miraculously, he had decided he liked her too. Well, enough to spend the night in her bed, which was an excellent start.

She wasn't stupid, she knew the situation wasn't ideal, what with Vince having arrived here fresh from being dumped by Molly, but never mind that now. The basic attraction was there, she just knew they'd be perfect for each other.

Sliding closer to him as he slept peacefully beside her, Lois revelled in the blissful warmth of his body and, still smiling, felt her eyelids begin to close. Little by little she could win him round, she was sure of it.

Life was looking good . . .

Lois's internal alarm clock woke her, as it always did, at six thirty. Easing herself out of bed, she washed, brushed her teeth, tousled her hair, applied a touch of smoky eyeshadow and mascara, made two mugs of tea and slid back under the covers.

Mmm, he even smelled gorgeous.

Lightly running her fingers across his torso, she leaned over and murmured huskily in his ear, 'Good morning . . .'

Vince's eyes snapped open. He sat upright like those toy snakes that burst out of a tin. The look on his face when he realised where he was made Lois wish she hadn't witnessed it.

Talk about abject horror.

'Oh God, what's the time?'

'Six forty-five.'

'I have to go. I'm late for work.'

This wasn't true; he'd told her last night he didn't have to be at the office until nine. It was also a million miles from the romantic fantasy she'd concocted about them waking up in each other's arms and Vince whispering between kisses, 'Well, good morning to you too, isn't *this* a nice surprise?'

And maybe, *just maybe*, wondering aloud if it might be permissible today to phone in sick.

Instead, a small part of her soul shrivelled with shame as he rocketed out of bed, grabbed his discarded clothes and stammered, 'I'm s-so sorry, I've never done anything like this before.' The next second he'd locked himself into the en-suite bathroom and Lois just knew he was struggling to get dressed, Benny Hill style, faster than the speed of light.

When the door opened again, she was waiting for him.

'You don't have to apologise. We had a nice night together, didn't we? And there's still plenty of time before you have to leave. Why don't you let me cook you a full English?'

'Really, no.' He was unable even to meet her gaze.

'But I've already made you a cup of tea. Look, it's here!' *Oh God, listen to me, I'm practically begging.*

Vince blurted out, 'You don't understand.' He gestured at her, then at himself, then the bedroom. 'This isn't the kind of person I am. I got drunk last night and did something I never do.' He was now visibly hyperventilating with fear. 'Please don't tell anyone.'

'I won't.' Lois held the mug of tea out, forcing him to take it. Politeness winning over panic, he glugged the tea down in one go, his face flushing red with pain when he realised just how scalding hot it still was.

'Right, I have to go now.' He fumbled in his jacket for his keys, palpably relieved to locate them.

'I enjoyed last night.' It sounded completely pathetic but she couldn't help saying it.

'Um, me too, thanks for everything. You're very . . . nice.' He darted forward and jabbed a kiss at her cheek like a panicky woodpecker.

It made Lois, who never cried, want to cry.

'I am, actually. Nicer than you think.' She managed a brief smile to mask the pain of rejection.

'I know, I know.' Vince, clearly longing to be gone, said, 'You won't mention anything to Molly, will you?'

It was evidently killing him that he'd made such a complete fool of himself, getting drunk and ending up having sex with the kind of woman who wouldn't normally feature on his radar.

Lois shook her head. 'Don't worry. I won't.'

After he'd left, she went to wake Addy who slept at the other end of the landing. While Addy was brushing her teeth and Lois was downstairs making breakfast, Molly phoned.

'I just saw him driving out of the car park. Everything OK?'

'Fine. The taxi didn't turn up last night so I made up the bed in the spare room.' *Well, this much was true.*

'Thanks.' Molly sounded relieved. 'So he wasn't any trouble?'

'No trouble. He was a bit drunk and a bit upset, but that's all.'

'Poor Vince, I feel bad about that. He's a good person and finishing with someone's always horrible.' Sounding resigned, anxious, Molly said, 'What I really hate is when they won't take no for an answer, like Graham last summer. Remember when he brought me that massive fish?'

'Don't worry, I don't think you'll have that problem with Vince.' Having watched from the bedroom window as he'd screeched out of the pub car park at fifty miles an hour, Lois was enveloped in a wave of sadness. 'I'm pretty sure we won't be seeing him again.'

Chapter 48

Amber liked loud music but this music was so loud it felt as if it was being injected directly into her brain. The floorboards were vibrating beneath her feet, her head was pounding, someone had spilled a drink down the back of her shirt and someone else had just staggered backwards and trodden on her foot.

'*Ooow*,' wailed Amber but no one could hear her above the noise. The party was being held in a squat belonging to Carter, a friend of a friend of Beeny's. Well, *belonged* probably wasn't the right word. It had been occupied by him and a few others, and tonight they'd invited over what felt like everyone they'd ever met.

It was impossible to count how many were here, because of all the different rooms in the place; it was dark and crowded and disorientating. One thing was for sure though, the invited guests didn't like to wash much.

Also, Doss had given her a drink that hadn't just been beer; when she'd started stumbling around, losing her balance and bouncing off walls, Beeny had said, 'Ha-ha, there was a ton of vodka in that too!'

She'd laughed because everyone else was laughing, but then Beeny had rolled her another spliff and when she'd shaken her head he'd curled his lip and said, 'What's the matter, Lady Amber? My stuff not good enough for you?'

Beeny had changed; she really didn't like him any more, but he was Doss's friend so they still had to hang out together.

'Shut up, Beeny, leave her alone.' Phil, another new friend of Beeny's, put a reassuring arm round her. 'Lady Amber don't have to smoke your crappy skunk, man. Not if she don't want to.'

That had been twenty minutes ago but she'd now managed to lose sight of everyone she knew. It was time to go and find them. Hazily, feeling as if she was having to crawl through the fuggy smoke that hung in the air, Amber made her way up the broad curving staircase. Swaying and knocking against the newel post, she mumbled, 'Sorry,' which was such a Lady Amber thing to say. Phil was the one who'd started calling her that, apparently because she sounded posh compared with the rest of them. OK, up the uncarpeted stairs and along the landing. Wow, so many doors, *so many* . . . let's start with this one . . .

When Amber realised what she was seeing she stopped dead in her tracks. There was no furniture in the bedroom other than a dirty mattress on the floor with people huddled around it. Phil had been kneeling with his back to her; when he turned, Amber saw the syringe in his hand. Then her horrified gaze took in the fact that one of the people on the mattress was Doss.

Someone was shouting, 'What's going on?' and it took her a moment to realise the words had come from her.

Doss had his shirtsleeve rolled up and a tourniquet wrapped round his skinny upper arm. Shaking her head in disbelief, Amber yelled, 'What are you *doing*?'

'Oh Christ, can someone get fucking Lady Amber out of here?' This came from a stringy-haired girl she'd never even spoken to before.

But Doss was holding out his other arm, beckoning to her, his own voice soft and hypnotic. 'It's OK, babe, it's all cool, you have to try this. It's, like, the most amazing stuff.'

'Are you mad? It's heroin!'

'Yeah, but you're saying that like it's a bad thing.' His dark eyes glowed with love and warmth as he closed his fingers around hers. 'But once you give it a chance, you'll see what I mean. Go on, babe, try it, Phil's got loads and he'll let you pay him back.'

So this was why Doss had borrowed her last fifteen pounds – and why he'd never repaid the twenty he'd borrowed the other week. It also explained those bruises she'd seen on his inner arm. Oh God, this was a nightmare. There'd been the occasional mention of other drugs before now, but she'd had no idea it had come to this. Amber's brain was still fogged but her eyes were wide as she stared from Doss to Phil.

In turn, Phil flicked the upturned syringe with a grubby fingernail and said, 'Seeing as it's you, darling, I can do you a hit for a tenner.'

Lunging wildly at him, Amber smacked the syringe out of his hand. The next moment she was being dragged backwards and there was a searing pain in her ear.

'You stupid cow!' The stringy-haired girl was hauling her across the floorboards by her hair. 'How fucking *dare* you?' She was surprisingly strong. Behind her, Amber glimpsed Phil reaching for the fallen syringe and heard Doss say, 'Just go ahead and use it anyway, it'll be fine . . .'

'*Owwww.*' The pain in Amber's ear was excruciating. The door was opened and she was flung out, her head bouncing off the opposite wall. The girl with stringy hair and a bony but equally strong male with a skull tattooed on his throat shoved her towards the top of the staircase. A blast of fetid sour breath hit her in the face as he snarled, 'Just fuck off, OK? And don't come back.'

Outside it was eleven o'clock, pitch black and raining heavily. Amber stumbled down the driveway in a state of shock, clutching her ear. When she pulled out her phone, the lit-up screen was smeared with blood from her hands.

OK, think, *think*. Where was she? The house was in the depths of the countryside . . . there were no lights visible in any direction. *Oh Mum, help me, I don't want to be here any more.*

Fingers trembling, Amber pressed *Home* and listened to it ring. And ring. Oh God, if her mum was already in bed she might not even hear the phone downstairs.

When the answering machine kicked in, she whimpered, 'Mum? Mum . . . are you there?'

Nothing. Ending the call, she wiped blood and rain from the screen and saw how little battery she had left. Hardly any at all. This was a nightmare. Woozily she tried to work out where she might be. Was it somewhere between Tetbury and Stroud? Stumbling into a wall, she fell to her knees and in desperation rang a number she hadn't rung for months.

Still nothing. Her father's mobile was switched off. And blood was dripping steadily from her ear, soaking into her shirt. Blinking rain out of her eyes . . . or were they tears? . . . Amber felt the rough stone wall end and a wooden gate begin. Groping her way along it, she came to a rectangular plaque. By holding the phone close to it, she was just able to make out the letters carved into the wood. Morton . . . Morton Farm . . .

Only four per cent battery power left now. Her hands shaking, she scrolled through the numbers. There was Shaun's, given to her ages ago and never rung either. But if he was at home, it meant he was relatively close. And he was her brother. The battery went down to three per cent and with a whimper of fear she pressed *Call*.

'Hello?' It was Shaun's voice, he sounded surprised. 'Amber?'

'Shaun?' *Thank God*. At the sound of his voice she began to cry. 'D'you know where my dad is?'

'He's away tonight, up in London. What's wrong?'

'Oh Shaun, I've got no battery left and I don't know where I am. I want to go home . . .' Behind her, she heard footsteps and the sound of someone bellowing her name.

'Tell me what's going on,' Shaun said urgently.

'It's a p-party at Morton F-Farm.' The tears were clogging her throat. 'I don't like these p-people. I don't like Doss any more. Can you help me? I'm not far from you, I don't think.'

'Who are you calling?' It was Phil, looming up out of the darkness. 'Is it the police? Come on, Lady Amber, you don't want to spoil our night, do you?'

'*Nooo!*' Amber shouted as he grabbed her roughly by the arm.

'Hey, don't worry.' Snatching the mobile from her grasp, Phil said into it, 'It's OK, she's fine.' Ending the call, he saw Shaun's name on the screen and visibly relaxed, before switching the phone off. Then, shoving her in the direction of the farm, he said, 'I'll look after you. Come back inside with me.'

Frankie was upstairs but she wasn't asleep. Or alone. With Amber spending the night with another of her schoolfriends, she'd invited Henry down from London. And the last hour or so had been . . . wonderful.

Now, as they lay in bed with their arms around each other, she heard the distant sound of the phone beginning to ring. Disentangling herself, she said, 'I'll have to answer that.'

Downstairs she reached it just before the answering machine could kick in. Who would be calling at this time of night?

'Hello?'

'Hi, look, this is Shaun. Um, have you heard from Amber?'

Shaun? The boy's voice hit her like a football in the chest. 'No. Why?'

'Sorry, it's just that she called me and sounded pretty upset. I don't want to worry you, but she was crying and then I heard someone else say she was OK, but she didn't *sound* OK, and now her phone's off.'

'Oh God. And she called you?'

'She was trying to find Dad. I mean . . . her dad. But he's away in London and his phone's switched off too.'

Amber was in enough of a state to try and reach *Joe?* Frankie felt herself begin to panic. 'OK, what should I do? Shall I try and contact her friends? She told me she was staying at Emma's house tonight.' So *that* had obviously been a lie.

'She's at a party with Doss. At Morton Farm, Amber said, but I can't find out where that is. She thinks it's near Tetbury. Mum's here,' Shaun went on hurriedly. 'She says we can drive around and start looking for her if you want.'

Frankie covered her mouth. Henry, coming downstairs behind her, said, 'What is it? What's going on?'

'Tell your mum thanks, that's very kind. But we'll come over.'

'I want to help,' said Shaun.

'We'll pick you up,' Frankie told him.

'Right. The address is—'

'It's OK, I know where you live.' Hadn't she and Molly driven past the house in hats and dark glasses the week after Joe had left Briarwood?

★　★　★

The roads were empty. Henry, who had insisted they take his car, drove like the wind. Within twenty-five minutes they'd reached Tetbury.

When they turned into Parnall Avenue, there they were, waiting for her outside number 22. Joe's other family. Shaun and his mother.

'I've found it.' Shaun waved his phone at them. 'Amber got it wrong; she thought it was Morton Farm. But it's Horton Farm . . . I remembered it was taken over by squatters a while back. And when I looked it up on Twitter, someone's mentioned going to a party there tonight.'

'Right. Let's go and get her. This is my friend Henry,' said Frankie as Shaun jumped into the back seat.

'And I'm Christina.' His mother was slender and blonde, her gaze compassionate as she looked at Frankie. 'I've heard about the things that go on at Horton Farm. I want to come along too.'

They were both mothers. If Shaun were the one in trouble and Christina needed help, Frankie knew she'd be there in a flash. *You just would.* She nodded at Christina and smiled briefly at the woman who had shared her husband for so many years. 'Thanks. Yes, why not? Let's all go.'

Chapter 49

Horton Farm was dilapidated, the land around it hopelessly overgrown. The rain was coming down harder now and there was no one outside. But there were lights on in the property and they could hear thudding music and loud voices.

Frankie's stomach was in knots as she and Shaun approached the front door. Had they completely overreacted? Would Amber be absolutely fine and utterly mortified to see her mother on the doorstep? Would her friends tease her so much she'd never live it down?

Frankie and Shaun knocked on the door and waited. Finally it creaked open a few inches and a dead-eyed girl with unwashed hair surveyed them with suspicion.

'What?'

Frankie managed a friendly, unthreatening smile. 'Hello, we're looking for Amber.'

'Who?'

'My daughter. She's seventeen. Curly dark red hair.'

The girl's lip curled with derision. 'Nope, don't know her.' And the door was slammed shut in their faces. On the other side, they heard bolts being wrenched across.

'Right.' When they went back to the car and told the others what had happened, Henry said, 'Well, we tried asking nicely.'

Sensing Frankie's terror, Christina said reassuringly, 'Don't worry, it's going to be fine.'

Oh, but was it? Frankie felt sick. *Please don't let anything bad happen to my baby girl . . .*

This time all four of them made their way up to the farmhouse. Henry led them around the side of the building until they reached the back. Finding a door, he tried the handle. Locked. Then Frankie spotted a tiny broken window and pointed to it.

'That'll do.' Henry stuck his hand through the hole in the glass and opened the window from the inside. 'Except it's too small for me to get through.'

'Let me.' In jeans and trainers, Christina climbed up on to the narrow window ledge and eased her way through. Within seconds she'd unlocked the door from the inside.

'Jesus, it smells in here.' Henry grimaced at the stench; they were in a narrow, empty utility room with dirty plates and abandoned lager cans littering the floor. Opening the next door would take them into the main house. Stealthily turning the handle he said, 'OK, let's go.'

The music was bone-shakingly loud, the air thick with smoke and unwashed bodies. There were hundreds of people in various stages of intoxication, some barely coherent. They turned to stare at Henry, six foot five inches and sixteen stone of honed Caribbean muscle, accompanied by a preppy student type and two older women who clearly didn't fit in.

'What's going on? Who are you?' A filthy hand gripped Shaun's arm and he shook him off.

'Where's Amber?' said Frankie and the owner of the hand said, 'How the fuck should I know?'

'Right, no sign of her downstairs.' From his great height, Henry had a better view amongst the throng. Pointing to the staircase he said, 'We'll try up there.'

'Hey, man, get away from that door.' At the top of the stairs, two more people attempted to stop Henry in his tracks. Pushing them effortlessly to one side, he led the way. Frankie's heart thudded as she caught her first glimpse of filthy mattresses on the floor, one of them occupied by Doss. There were syringes scattered around, pieces of crumpled tinfoil, an unfamiliar smell . . .

'Oi, get out,' bellowed a man wielding a syringe. That was when all hell let loose. Someone tried to hit Henry. Then more people launched themselves at him. Like a great bear, he shook himself free and yelled, 'Where's Amber? She's not in here . . .'

'Come on, let's try the other rooms.' Christina seized Frankie's arm and pulled her outside. 'Call her name, see if she hears you.'

'Amber? AMBER?'

Shaun came running out of the room, his breathing ragged. 'Someone just said was she Doss's girlfriend, the one covered in blood. She's in one of these.'

Covered in blood? Oh God.

'Amber!' Shaun burst in through another door and bounced back out again. 'No, not in there.'

Frankie tried the next one but the room was empty. *Oh my baby girl, where are you?* She took a lung-bursting deep breath and bellowed, *'AMBER?'*

Then they heard, faintly, someone whisper, 'Mum . . .'

'In there.' Christina zoned in on the voice and pointed to the third door along. Attempting to get in, Frankie said breathlessly, 'It won't open . . .'

'Henry!' shouted Christina, and Henry came flying out of the first room. 'The door's locked and she's inside.'

'Out of the way,' Henry ordered, readying himself. The next moment he swung round at dizzying speed, his leg kicked out and the door crashed open on its hinges.

Sick with fear, Frankie stumbled into the room. There was another grey mattress on the floor and there, huddled on it and sobbing as if her heart would break, was Amber. Spattered in blood but alive. Gazing brokenly up at them, she held out her arms to Frankie and sobbed, 'Oh M-mum . . .'

Well, what an evening. Here they were, back in Tetbury, all of them crowded into the living room of 22 Parnall Avenue. Bonded together, Frankie realised as she rubbed Amber's back, in the most peculiar way.

Then again, it might be peculiar but it was also quite moving. Both she and Christina had shed tears of relief that Amber was all right.

Amber had sobered up now and was shocked and repentant. Her hooped silver earring had been ripped out, slicing straight through her earlobe, hence the alarming amount of blood all over the right side of her previously white shirt. Having phoned a friend who was a plastic surgeon, Henry had ascertained there was nothing to be done about it just now. When the inflammation had subsided, the repair would be carried out under local anaesthetic, so there was no need to visit A&E tonight.

Which was a relief as far as Frankie was concerned because all she could do at the moment was hug and comfort her beloved daughter and pray she'd had a big enough fright to make her want to change her ways.

'I'll tell you one thing,' said Shaun. 'I'm going to take up karate again.' He looked at Amber. 'Honestly, it was so brilliant. Henry was like Superman, the way he kicked that door open. I used to go to karate lessons when I was little but I gave up after yellow belt. Well, this time I'm going to keep on going all the way to black. That's a handy skill to have.'

'Thanks.' Tears of gratitude filled Amber's red-rimmed eyes as she turned to Henry. 'Sorry I was such a nuisance. Thank you so much to all of you.'

'Christina was brilliant too,' Frankie chimed in, because it needed to be said. Holding her hands not far apart, she went on, 'There was the tiniest broken window, just *this* wide, and she climbed through it. Otherwise we wouldn't have been able to get into the house.'

'Oh don't, it was nothing.' Christina dismissed the words with a shrug as she handed round mugs of tomato soup. Smiling at Amber, she said, 'We're just so glad you're all right.'

At that moment they all heard the front door being unlocked. It was one o'clock in the morning and Joe, having responded to a text from Shaun, had driven back from London in record time.

Frankie gave her daughter's hand a squeeze. Amber was their number one priority; she was all that mattered now.

Joe burst into the living room, his voice cracking as he saw Amber on the sofa. 'Oh, my girl . . .'

Fresh tears rolled down Amber's cheeks and she rose clumsily to her feet, arms outstretched like a child. 'Dad . . . oh Daddy, I've missed you *so much*.'

'Here.' Christina offered Frankie the box of tissues. 'I think we're all going to need one of these.'

Later, they learned from Amber that from this night on, Doss was well and truly out of her life. She never ever wanted to see him again. Shamefacedly she admitted how much of her savings he'd spent on drugs. He was selfish, a loser and a leech.

'He might be sitting in a cell right now,' said Frankie, because after leaving Horton Farm they'd called the police to let them know what had been going on. Hopefully the farmhouse would be raided and the drug pushers arrested. Amber didn't want to make any complaints about the way they'd treated her, she just wanted to put the whole terrifying experience behind her and move on.

When he'd heard the full story, Joe looked at Henry and said, 'And how did you happen to be around to be involved?'

'He's Mum's new friend,' said Amber. With a ghost of a smile she added, 'Well, that's what I'm guessing. Is that right, Mum?'

Frankie glanced at Henry and nodded. 'Yes, he is.'

'Good, I'm glad.' Amber exhaled and rested her head on Joe's shoulder. 'That means we have our own superhero. I call that pretty cool.'

Later in the kitchen as they prepared to leave, Christina murmured to Frankie, 'I haven't had the chance to say this before, but I'm so sorry about everything. I honestly never meant for any of it to happen.'

There was no grief left, miraculously. No bitterness, no pain. Nodding slowly, Frankie said, 'I know you didn't. It's OK.'

'Thank you. And I'm glad Amber's made up with her dad.'

'Me too.'

'He's missed her so much.' Christina glanced over at Amber and Shaun hugging each other out in the hallway. 'You know what? She's had her big scare and her difficulties and none of us can blame her for that. But from now on, I think she'll be fine.'

'I think so too. It's as if you know her.'

'I feel as if I do.' Her smile fond, Christina said, 'I've listened to her dad talking about her for the last eighteen years. She's welcome here any time, by the way, if that's OK with you.'

Gosh, this was weird. 'Same here,' said Frankie, meaning it.

'Whenever Shaun wants to come over, that's fine. He's a lovely boy, a real credit to you.'

'Thank you. And Amber's wonderful too.' Christina said warmly, 'Between us, I think we've done well with our children.'

When they left shortly afterwards, Frankie didn't embrace Christina; that would have been too Disney for words. But she felt as if the next time they met, she might.

Chapter 50

Something was happening and Molly wasn't at all sure she liked it.

Actually that wasn't true; it was the fact that she *did* like it that was causing all this internal kerfuffle and angst.

They were outside in the garden of Gin Cottage, in the shade of the juniper trees. It had been Dex's idea to commission a portrait of himself and Delphi. A proper portrait in oils, not a dashed-off caricature. And Molly had been delighted, had agreed at once without realising quite how much eye contact would be required and the degree to which it might affect her.

Nor was it helping that Dex was currently entertaining himself by doing subtle movie star poses, every now and again raising an eyebrow, twitching the corners of his mouth, gazing at her with the kind of glittery amusement that indicated he was perfectly well aware just how off-putting it was.

'Stop it,' said Molly when he did it again.

'I'm giving you my Brad Pitt look.'

'Well, don't.'

'OK, let's try Ryan Reynolds.' He altered the angle of his jaw, the tilt of his chin, and drawled, 'Hey, baby, how are you?'

She shook her head. 'You sound like Joey from *Friends*.'

Dex half-lowered his eyelids and slowly nodded, Joey-style. 'Except he'd say, "How're you doin'?"'

'OK, can you stop talking now,' Molly ordered. 'I have to concentrate and you need to keep still.'

So he stopped talking, but every now and again when she looked up at him to study the precise shape of his mouth he would purse his lips just slightly and blow her a barely perceptible kiss.

Bastard.

Inwardly, it was having quite an effect on her, even though she knew it didn't mean anything at all; it was just a bit of fun, his way of passing the time.

Outwardly she rolled her eyes and said, 'You're hilarious.'

When she'd finished his mouth, Dex said conversationally, 'Speaking of hilarious, how are things going with you and Vince?'

Molly concentrated on getting the line of his left eyebrow exactly right. Oddly, Lois didn't appear to have told anyone about Vince spending the evening in the Saucy Swan drowning his sorrows because their relationship was over. The inhabitants of Briarwood still thought they were a couple and somehow she'd found herself perpetuating the myth, going along with it.

OK, not *somehow*; she knew perfectly well why she had. The way she was feeling about Dex these days simply wasn't . . . appropriate. And maintaining the pretence that she and Vince were still together made the situation a whole lot easier to handle. Because he had Amanda and the two of them were the perfect couple. More to the point, thanks to Tina, Molly now knew why. And like it or not, once you'd been made aware of something like that, what else could you do but wish them well?

Only someone completely heartless would want to break them up.

Anyway, hence the white lies.

Call it self-defence.

And Dex was still waiting for an answer. Molly mustered a bright smile and said, 'Everything's fine! Vince has gone over to Toronto for a couple of weeks. He's working out there on a new hotel his company's building.' Thankfully this bit was true.

'Great. Will you miss him?'

'Of course I'll miss him.'

'Right.' Dex surveyed her for a moment. 'Can I ask you something? Do you ever find Vince a bit . . . dull?'

For heaven's sake, talk about *blunt*. Trust Dex to say exactly what was on his mind.

'He's not dull. He's just quiet.' Pointedly Molly added, 'And sometimes quiet is a good thing to be.'

'Touchy,' said Dex.

'Maybe I am.' And even though she wasn't seeing Vince any more, the dig still annoyed her. 'Different people like different things. Some people would find Amanda too full on for their liking.'

'I suppose they might.' Refusing to rise to the bait, he winked at her. 'Don't get cross. I only asked. There's nothing wrong with people being quiet, I just didn't think it'd be your thing.'

'Well, maybe you're wrong.'

'So, how about you?' Dex sounded interested. 'Do you ever wish you were more upfront, more full on? Like Amanda?'

'No.' Molly shook her head; she was exactly as upfront as she wanted to be. 'I really don't.' She raised an eyebrow. 'Do you wish you were as good-looking and intelligent as Vince?'

'Oh yes. All the time.'

You see? It was answers like this that left her torn between wanting to burst out laughing and give him a slap.

'Dada.'

They both turned to look at Delphi, who had been asleep on the rug on the lawn and had now woken up. She rolled over on to her front, stuck her bottom in the air and levered herself to her feet. Arms outstretched for balance, she took a couple of unsteady steps and stopped, then staggered across the grass to Molly, who was closest.

'Yay, good girl!' Molly clapped her hands and caught her before she could fall. 'You're so clever! Now go to Daddy!'

'Dadada.' Delphi beamed and tottered over to Dex, who lifted her into his arms and covered her cheeks with kisses.

'Hello, hello, beautiful. Come and sit with me and let's get painted, eh?'

'Dada.' Balancing on his left leg, Delphi clutched his face and planted a dribbly kiss on his face, and Molly's heart melted. They loved each other so much. Putting down her paintbrush, she took a few quick photos to help her during the times when Delphi wasn't in the mood to stay still.

But for the next few minutes Delphi obligingly stayed where she was, settling on Dex's lap and playing with his watch. Working fast, Molly focused on the curve of her cheek, the inquisitive angle of her head and the way the corners of her mouth lifted with delight when she managed to open the clasp on the watch strap.

She was also tinglingly super-aware that while she was concentrating on Delphi, Dex was in turn watching her, his attention unwavering. Each time she flicked a glance in his direction and found his gaze still upon her, adrenalin whooshed through her veins.

Dry-mouthed, Molly wiped the brush with a turps-soaked cloth then dried it on the leg of her jeans. If this carried on, completing the portrait was going to be like some kind of emotional torture . . . painting his face while longing to touch it with her fingers . . . oh God, how had she managed to land herself in a situation like this?

A bee buzzed lazily around Delphi's bare feet and Dex brushed it away. Delphi gave him back his watch and began playing with the daisy-shaped metal fasteners on her turquoise dungarees instead.

'I haven't seen the dungarees before.' Desperate to change the subject away from the torment that was going on in her head, Molly said, 'Are they new?'

He nodded. 'Amanda bought them for her.'

Oh. *Shrivel.*

'And she bought the T-shirt too. Didn't she?' Pointing to the yellow T-shirt sporting a lime-green dragon on the front, Dex said to Delphi, 'It was a present, wasn't it? From Amanda.'

Delphi, her dark eyes shining and her bare feet kicking happily against his knee, said, 'A-*mama.*'

Engulfed with sadness, Molly had to look away. Because this was the reason she couldn't interfere. Her feelings towards Dex may have changed – OK, *had* changed, practically hurtling out of control – but there was nothing she could do about it, not now she knew the truth about Amanda.

And it was all thanks to Tina, George's mother, that she'd found out. Elaborating on the serendipity of the pairing of Amanda and Dex, Tina had confided, 'My friend Kaye told me. She's been trying for a baby for ages without any luck. Anyway, she had tests done at the hospital and it turned out she's got this problem with her womb that means she can't get pregnant. So Kaye was pretty upset about it, obviously, and burst into tears in the doctor's surgery, and it was Dr Carr she was seeing.'

'Right.' Molly's throat constricted at the mention of Amanda's name; without even knowing what Tina might be about to say, she had a premonition it wasn't going to be good news.

'And Dr Carr — Amanda — was so brilliant. She gave Kaye the hugest hug. Then she said she knew how she felt because she had the same thing wrong with her. The exact same problem.' Tina's eyes shone with compassion at the thought of it. 'I mean, wasn't it nice of her to share that? Kaye said she was so kind, it really made her feel better. And when you think about it, that's why it's so fantastic that Amanda and Dex have got together. She wants children and can't have them . . . and Dex already has Delphi! You can't ask for a happier ending than that, can you? It couldn't be more perfect if it tried!'

Hmm, for some people perhaps . . .

Dragged back to the present, Molly realised Dex had just said something and was waiting for an answer. 'Sorry, what was that?'

'I don't know, you artistic types.' He shook his head with amusement. 'So wrapped up in your work, it's like you're in another world.'

Molly wished she was in another world; this one was rubbish. 'I know, sorry. I'm listening now. Say it again.'

'You looked a bit sad, that's all. I wondered what you were thinking.'

Why did men only ever ask you that question when you couldn't give them an honest answer? Molly wished she could tell Dex that what she was really wondering right now was did he know his girlfriend couldn't have children of her own? But if Amanda hadn't told him . . . well, there was no way in the world *she* could. Seeing as doctors weren't allowed to blab about their patients' medical conditions, presumably the reverse also applied.

'I'm not sad. Just concentrating.' Molly sat back and playfully waggled her paintbrush at Delphi to make her smile. 'Like a true artist.'

Never mind that Tina and Kaye had both breached the confidentiality agreement, she wasn't going to be the one to further spread the news.

Because, knowing her luck, she'd definitely be the one who ended up in court.

Chapter 51

The doorbell rang at seven o'clock and Frankie hurried out of the kitchen to answer it. She was here. The plan she'd never imagined would work out was coming together at last. Well, hopefully it was.

As she pulled open the front door, the wide brim of the straw hat was raised and the huge dark glasses removed. Frankie saw the face of her visitor and gasped.

Oh my goodness . . .

'Well? What do you think?' Hope managed a nervous smile and said, 'Will I do?'

Four days ago, Frankie had taken the call. After weeks of struggling to boost her own confidence and pluck up the courage to take action, Hope had announced, 'Right, it's time, I'm going to do it,' and they'd arranged for it to happen today.

'Come along in. You look . . . well, I hardly recognised you!' Ushering her inside, Frankie wondered how best to handle this. In an effort to impress, Hope had undergone a bit of a makeover. And she wasn't at all sure it was in her best interests.

'I know.' Her tone self-deprecating, Hope said, 'Quite a

difference, eh? I did what you said and went to the hairdresser. For the first time in I don't know how many years!'

The hair was fine, the hair was actually an improvement. Trimmed into shape, flatteringly coloured and subjected to lashings of deep-conditioning treatment, it was lovely. Similarly, the clothes were perfectly acceptable, understated but flattering pale blue layers of cotton top, overshirt and three-quarter-length skirt. A manicure and pedicure had also been carried out, and finished with a somewhat startling shade of flamingo pink polish.

Seeing her looking at them, Hope waggled her hands. 'And I had my nails done! They have a girl working at the hair place who does them!'

'Great,' said Frankie, because it wasn't the nails that were the problem either. Oh Lord, how was she going to say this?

'And then when I told them I was trying to make myself look better, less decrepit, they insisted on doing my face for me too! Such sweet girls, so enthusiastic and keen to help.'

They'd definitely been enthusiastic. Faintly horrified by the amount of make-up they'd managed to slather on Hope's face, Frankie took in the details: heavy matte foundation, powder, blusher, *awful* shimmering highlighter, too-dark lipliner, too-bright lipstick, eyeshadows, eyebrow pencil, kohl, mascara . . .

Finally she said, 'And . . . how do you think you look?'

'Me? Oh well, I'm a walking disaster when it comes to make-up. *Completely* hopeless! I haven't worn any since we made the last episode of the show! I always used to think it made me look weird, but everyone else kept telling me it was fine. So now, all these years later, it's bound to feel strange.' Hope nodded with determination. 'It's just a question of getting used to it. When the girls finished with me this afternoon they said I looked gorgeous, bless their hearts.'

Whereas in reality she looked like a small middle-aged drag queen channelling Katie Price. Hesitantly Frankie said, 'I just wonder if maybe we should tone it down, perhaps wipe some of it off . . .'

'Ooh no, I couldn't do that, no *way*! Those poor girls worked so *hard*, it took them ages to get me looking like this. Anyway, the whole point of wearing make-up is to boost my confidence,' Hope concluded brightly. 'Without it, I'd be all the way back to square one!'

Yikes. The make-up hadn't been badly applied, there was simply way too much of it. Frankie realised she was going to have to let her go out wearing it and just hope for the best.

'OK. Well, are you ready?'

'No.' Hope took an audible breath. 'But I'm going to do it anyway.'

'Come on.' Picking up her own RayBans and praying this wasn't all about to go horribly wrong, Frankie said, 'Let's go.'

Evening sunlight dappled through the branches of the trees as they made their way down to the river. Hope was glad to have Frankie with her, providing emotional support and showing her the way.

But they were here now. The emotional support was about to run out. As they reached the water's edge, Frankie pointed to the curve in the narrow path and said in a low voice, 'Round the next bend, then you'll see the caravan in the clearing ahead of you.'

'I think I'm going to be sick.' Hope's mouth was bone-dry; if anyone wanted to experience something a million times worse than stage fright, all they had to do was try this.

'You'll be fine. Take those off.'

Hope dutifully removed the floppy-brimmed straw hat and huge dark glasses she'd worn as they'd made their way down here.

Frankie held out a hand. 'Shall I take them home with me?'

'No.' Was she mad? If Stefan rejected her outright, she was going to need her disguise more than ever.

'OK. Good luck.'

'Thanks.' Hope watched as Frankie turned and walked back the way they'd come. This was exactly how it had felt being dropped off at boarding school at the age of eleven.

OK, time to be brave. She took a few deep breaths and peered around the side of the bushes. There was the caravan – *God, the very same caravan* – facing the water.

Fifty metres further along the path, the angle altered enough for her to glimpse Stefan sitting on the top step. Her heart had never raced so fast in her life. Tightly clutching her hat like a security blanket, Hope forced herself to keep on putting one foot in front of the other. How she was still managing to walk, she had no idea. Oh Lord, and there he was, she could see him properly now. Wavy dark hair combed back from his face, the familiar angular profile . . . those perfect lines, carved into her memory and almost eerily unchanged.

Hope's heart sank at the irony that in comparison she should have changed so very much.

He was wearing a red shirt and narrow black jeans. A knife blade glinted in one hand and he held a piece of wood in the other while he worked to carve it into some intricate shape; it was something Stefan had begun to do after giving up smoking all those years ago and the habit had evidently stuck.

As the distance between them decreased, Hope felt her courage shrivel and fade. He hadn't glanced up yet, hadn't lifted his head in her direction. She could still turn and leave.

Alternately her thundering heart could give out and she could drop dead on the spot. She was watching his tanned, skilful hands at work now. Or she could walk straight on past him without stopping and keep her own gaze averted, fixed on the river—

'So you came back then.'

The words, quietly spoken, stopped Hope in her tracks. She hadn't had time to avert her gaze, had been too fixated on Stefan to implement the plan. Which was how she knew, for a fact, *knew without doubt*, that he hadn't looked at her.

Not even for a nanosecond.

In which case, how could he possibly know?

Her own voice barely audible, she croaked, 'Sorry?'

And then he did turn his head to look at her and the world stood still, frozen in time. Their eyes met and Stefan said, 'Oh Hope, do you think I haven't been waiting for this moment?'

Those gentle dark gypsy eyes were utterly hypnotic.

'But . . . but . . . how did you know it was me? Did Frankie tell you?'

'Frankie? No.' He shook his head. 'I just knew.'

'How could you? You didn't look up, not even once.'

Stefan put down the knife and the piece of wood he'd been carving. He rose to his feet and moved towards her, as lithe and beautiful as a panther. 'Peripheral vision. I saw you coming down the path, recognised your walk. The way a person moves doesn't change.'

'Oh.'

'It's good to see you again.'

Hope's heart was clattering away in her chest. 'You too.'

Stefan shook his head. 'Oh, my love. You don't know how much I've missed you.'

'Same.' The word came out as a croak; it was all she could manage.

'Hope.' He raised his left hand, gently touched the side of her face with the backs of his fingers.

She trembled in response. What a feeling. 'You sent me away, said we couldn't be together. But you were wrong. We could have been.'

'I know, I know that now.' He exhaled sadly. 'With hindsight. But at the time I thought I was doing the right thing. You had your glittering career . . . how could I get in the way of that? I wouldn't have been able to live with myself.'

Hope gazed up at him. 'And it never once occurred to you that you were fifty thousand times more important to me than my so-called career? The one I gave up anyway, because without you in my life I didn't want to do it any more?'

'I know. But at the time I didn't believe it. I thought I was setting you free to conquer Hollywood. Because it would never have happened if we'd stayed together, that's for sure. We'd have been mocked, laughed at. And I couldn't bear the thought of that happening. To either of us.'

Her throat aching, her eyes shimmering with sorrow for all those lost years, Hope whispered, 'How about now?'

Stefan placed his hands on her shoulders, fixing her with the full intensity of his gaze. 'I never stopped loving you. Not for a single second. And now you've come back. We've wasted too much time, Hope. You're my whole world, you always have been . . .'

In response, she threw her arms round him and found his mouth with her own, quickly covering it with butterfly kisses. Each renewed contact filled her with joy; it was what she'd dreamed of doing for so long. *Oh Stefan, Stefan, I'm never letting go of you again . . .*

When the kissing finally ended and they clung to each other, still trembling with emotion, he stroked her hair and whispered, 'Why do you have all that stuff on your face?'

Ah. So he'd noticed, then.

'My desperate attempt to impress you. From now on I'm going to wear it every day. Believe me, you wouldn't want to see me without it.' Fizzing with joy, as exhilarated as if she'd drunk three glasses of champagne, Hope heard the words spill out of her mouth. No more hiding the truth; from now on, honesty was the only way. 'I haven't aged well, you see. All this make-up is to give me confidence.' She grimaced. 'And to stop you running away in terror. Without it, I'm a complete fright.'

Stefan shook his head. 'That's crazy.'

'But true. If I'd come down here to see you with my face bare, I'm telling you now, you'd have pretended you hadn't recognized me. You would have sat there and let me walk on by.'

'Never.'

'You would have done.'

'If you really think that, you don't know me at all. Think back,' Stefan instructed, 'to when we used to meet up after you'd spent the day filming. What was always the first thing you'd do?'

Hope remembered, of course she did. She'd used pale pink, rose-scented cleansing cream to remove the make-up from her face. And Stefan had watched her do it, had lovingly told her she was becoming herself once more.

With a helpless gesture, she said, 'But that's when I was young. My face . . . it's different now.'

Without speaking, Stefan led her by the hand up the steps into the caravan. Opening a cupboard, he took out a glass jar filled with palest pink cream.

Hope's eyes widened at the sight of it.

'Don't worry.' Stefan smiled slightly. 'It hasn't been sitting in that cupboard for the last twenty years. I was showing my granddaughter how to make it the other week.'

She took the jar from him, unscrewed the lid and breathed in the smell. That was it, exactly the same old Romany recipe Stefan had used before.

'Marshmallow root, wild roses and angelica.' She remembered him telling her the ingredients.

'That's right.' He nodded and passed her a box of tissues.

Hope watched his expression as she applied the delicious-smelling cream to her face, massaged it into her skin and carefully wiped it off with the tissues. When the last scraps of make-up had been removed, she felt the knot of fear in her chest unfurl and relax.

Stefan was smiling at her. Properly smiling. Everything was going to be OK.

'Better.' He nodded approvingly. 'So much better. You look like yourself again.'

'Old and wrinkly.'

'Beautiful. The most beautiful girl in the world.'

'Girl . . .' Hope pulled a face, echoing the word in disbelief.

'You'll always be a girl to me.' He paused, touching her upper lip with the tips of his fingers, tracing the outline of her mouth. Then he took her in his arms once more and Hope wondered if it was possible to die of joy. He felt just the same; the smell of his skin miraculously unaltered.

Her life felt as if it had just changed irrevocably; she never wanted to be apart from him again. Thanks goodness she'd plucked up the courage to return to Briarwood.

At long last she was back where she belonged.

Chapter 52

'Well, this is going to get the tongues wagging,' Lois said cheerfully as she climbed into the passenger seat.

Yesterday Dex had overheard her on the phone, booking her car into the garage in Marlbury. When he'd asked her how she was planning to make the eight-mile journey home afterwards and Lois had said she'd get a taxi, he'd offered to pick her up instead. Now, having been aware of the frequent curious glances of the woman at the garage's reception desk, he said, 'Does she know you?'

'Her son's in the same class as Addy. Nothing she likes better than a bit of gossip. She just said, "Doesn't Dr Carr mind you two being so . . . friendly?"'

Amused, Dex took another look at the woman still covertly watching them. 'But I don't even recognise her. How does she know who I am?'

'Because everyone knows you.' Lois rolled her eyes at his ignorance. 'You're a hot topic at the school gates, didn't you realise that? When you first moved down here, all the mothers got completely overexcited because you were single, eligible and pretty damn gorgeous to boot. Nowadays they pretend they don't fancy you any more, they're just delighted to see you settling down with Dr Carr.'

Settling down? Dex wouldn't have called it that. Taken aback, he said, 'We're just seeing each other, that's all. It's very casual.' And mainly at Amanda's instigation. The thought that so much more was being read into the relationship was alarming.

'Oh, but you know what I mean. It's going really well, isn't it? And she's such a great doctor. They all want you to stay together.' Lois gestured expansively with her braceleted left arm. 'The whole fairy-tale happy ending.'

'Fairy tale?' echoed Dex. 'Why would it be a fairy tale?'

But Lois was no longer looking at him; she was staring directly ahead, her one visible cheek uncharacteristically flushed. The silence stretched between them. Dex, who had spent the last week or two idly wondering if the time was coming when he should make the inevitable break, sensed that something significant was up. Finally he repeated, 'Why fairy tale?'

'Look, I wasn't thinking. I shouldn't have said it. That's me,' Lois shrugged. 'Queen of the foot-in-mouth situation.'

'Tell me.' He couldn't begin to imagine what was going on.

'You should ask Dr Carr.'

'Ask her what? Come on, Lois. Just say it.' Switching off the ignition, he said, 'We're not moving until you do.'

Another hesitation, then she reached her decision. 'Fine then. Maybe you do have a right to know.'

'I think so too,' said Dex. 'Fire away.'

'It's just that you've got gorgeous Delphi, and you're single. And so's Dr Carr, and she can't have children.' Evidently still embarrassed by her faux pas, Lois said, 'Which is why you two getting together and becoming a proper family would be so perfect.'

'She can't have children?' Dex felt as if he'd been winded. Not because he wouldn't want to be with someone unless she was capable of giving birth, but by the burden of the responsibility this revelation created.

'Sorry,' said Lois.

'How do you know?'

'She told one of the other mothers at school. Everyone knows.' Lois nodded at the key stuck in the ignition. 'Can we go now?'

Dex restarted the car. 'Don't worry. Thanks for telling me.'

She looked rueful. 'You kind of forced it out of me. I'd make a rubbish spy. I'm usually good at being discreet.'

'You run a pub. I'd imagine you have to be.'

'So am I allowed to ask? Are you in love with her?'

'With who?' For a split second Dex was caught off guard; he'd been thinking about Molly, wondering if 'everyone knows' meant she was aware of it too. 'Oh, you mean Amanda?' *God, no, of course I'm not.* But he could hardly say that aloud. Discreetly sidestepping the question he said, 'So does the whole village think we should be together?'

'Not quite all. I didn't say I did. To be honest, I always thought you and Molly could have had a bit of a thing going on.'

Aware of her gaze upon him, it was now Dex's turn to keep his eyes fixed on the road ahead as they made their way back to Briarwood.

'Little giveaway twitch there,' Lois murmured. '*Did* you two have a thing going on?'

He shook his head fractionally. 'Never happened.'

'Did you try?'

'Yes.'

'And?'

'She wasn't interested.'

'That surprises me. I thought she might have been.'

'Well,' said Dex, 'you were wrong. And now she has Vince.'

Perfect, car-polishing Vince . . .

Another pause, then Lois said, 'Yes. Do you like him?'

Dex was getting better at keeping his thoughts to himself, not getting caught out. It was always nice not to end up looking like a complete idiot. Aloud, he said, 'Vince is a nice guy. Not sure he's right for Molly, but she seems to think he is.'

Lois nodded in agreement. 'Oh well, there you go.'

And they drove the last few miles in silence, each alone with their thoughts. You can't always get what you want.

At the Crown Inn in Marlbury, Dex waited at a table by the window for Amanda to arrive home from work.

It was no good, he wasn't looking forward to the ensuing conversation but it had to be done. And ironically, this was where he'd first met her, when they'd bonded over the awfulness of the band playing up on the tiny stage that evening.

And now he was back, here to end the relationship. Not pleasant, but pretty much the only way to go. For both their sakes.

There was her car now, the sporty silver Peugeot slowing to a halt outside her house. Watching through the window as Amanda jumped out of the driver's seat and locked the door with an electronic flourish, Dex drained his coffee and braced himself for the ordeal ahead.

Amanda's initial delight at seeing him soon faded once they were inside her house and she learned the reason for the unexpected visit.

'What? But why?' Her eyes widened in disbelief.

'Because . . . it's not fair on you.'

'Oh please, don't give me that.' Amanda shook her head. 'It's the oldest line in the book. Everything's been great, hasn't it? We're great together! You can't say the sex hasn't been fantastic.'

'I know, but—'

'You won't get better than me.' There was an edge to her voice that made Dex realise why he was going through with this; natural self-confidence was one thing, but there was a limit to the amount he could truly be comfortable with.

'Maybe not, but it'll just have to be my loss.' A degree of guilt meant he had to be gentle with her. 'And I'm sorry, really I am, but it's for the best. You'll thank me in the long run. It's better to make the break now, for your sake.'

'Is it someone else?' They were in her immaculate kitchen; Amanda crossed to the sink and filled a glass from the tap.

Dex hesitated and shook his head, wondering if she was about to chuck the cold water at him. 'No . . .'

'Rubbish, you're lying. Of course there is. You've got the next one lined up, ready to go.'

'I haven't, I promise.' Oh God, he wished he had.

'But we're perfect together!'

'On paper, yes. But it has to feel right too.' The amount of practice he'd had at this over the years, you'd think he'd be better at it by now. Unconsciously pressing his hand to his chest, Dex said, 'It has to feel one hundred per cent, properly right.'

She gripped the glass. 'And there's nothing I can do or say to make you change your mind?'

Another shake of the head. 'No. I'm really sorry. About everything.'

'Right. Well.' Pride kicked in, thankfully. Amanda wasn't the type to beg. She drank the water and put the empty tumbler in the sink. 'In that case, what a shame. I'll miss you. And Delphi. Where is she now? Let me guess, you left her with Molly while you came over here to do the evil deed.'

'Frankie's looking after her.' It hadn't felt right to ask Molly, under the circumstances. To be kind, Dex said, 'Delphi's going to miss you too,' even though he didn't think she would. 'Look, I know how you must be feeling, but we can't stay together just because of Delphi . . . that'd be crazy.'

'Is that what you think? That we should break up now before Delphi's old enough to find it traumatic?'

'I didn't mean it that way,' Dex said with compassion. 'I'm talking about you not being able to have children and Delphi filling the gap, and that being the only reason for us staying together.'

Amanda tilted her head to one side and surveyed him for several seconds. Finally she said, 'Excuse me?'

'Someone told me.' Dex wasn't going to name names. 'Apparently everyone knows.'

'Everyone knows what, exactly?'

'That you can't have children.'

'Really? How interesting. You'd think someone would have told me that,' said Amanda. 'Seeing as it's my womb.'

What?

'OK, I'll tell you what I heard.' Having listened to Lois expanding on the situation, Dex did his best to recall it accurately. 'One of your patients came to see you at the surgery, upset because they were infertile, and you told them you had the same problem, the exact same thing wrong with you.' He gestured helplessly. 'That's about it. That's all I know.'

Amanda nodded slowly, her frown clearing. 'Right. Got it. And that's how it happens, is it? Chinese whispers around the village? One of my patients was having problems conceiving because she was suffering from something called endometriosis. I have the same condition myself. I told her that. But endometriosis causes lots of symptoms and it doesn't mean you can't have children, just that you might have difficulties. God, I had no idea she'd misunderstood what I was saying to her. So . . . everyone's been feeling sorry for me, have they? Thinking I'm infertile?' The corners of her mouth twisted into a rueful smile.

'Seems that way,' said Dex.

'And there's you with Delphi . . . well, no wonder all the mothers kept telling me how pleased they were that we'd got together.'

'Were they saying that?'

'Oh yes, all the time. It was extraordinary. Well, now we know why.'

'I guess so,' said Dex.

'And that's what scared you,' Amanda continued, visibly relieved. 'But there's no need to be scared. My symptoms are only mild, the chances of me not being able to conceive are really low . . . in fact, pregnancy is one of the best ways of alleviating the problems! So there's really no reason why we can't carry on seeing each other and—'

'Hang on, no, sorry.' Dex hastily held up his hand to stop this train of thought in its tracks. 'I've said everything now . . . I still think we'll leave it as it stands.'

A wry look, then Amanda said with good humour, 'Oh well, it was worth a try. And I still think there's someone else you've got your eye on. Would you like me to take a wild guess as to who it might be?'

In the pit of his stomach, he felt the knot tightening. 'No,' Dex said steadily.

'Sure?' Amanda's smile was brave, but tinged with sadness. 'Because I bet I could.'

Chapter 53

The finished painting stood on the easel in the centre of her living room, covered with an old lilac pashmina, all ready for the big reveal. Molly, leading the way into the room, wondered if non-artists could ever begin to imagine the sensations she was experiencing now. It was always a nerve-wracking moment. Each time, while the sitter was studying the painting, she was watching them for signs – microsignals, sometimes – that they either loved the end result or were disappointed with it.

'This is exciting,' said Dex, with Delphi on his hip. 'You'd better have made me look like Johnny Depp or there's going to be big trouble.'

By accident rather than design, he was wearing the same white shirt as in the painting, with different jeans. His hair was a fraction longer now, his tan deeper as a result of the blazing heat of the last few days.

'Oh no, that's a shame, you should have said Johnny Depp before,' said Molly. 'I've given you more of a Jeremy Clarkson look.' And reaching forward she pulled away the tatty pashmina to reveal the painting beneath it.

'TAAAGH!' Not remotely interested in what was on the canvas,

Delphi let out an excited squawk and made a grab for the still-billowing pashmina. Molly exhaled with relief and let her have it to play with because Dex was happy, she could already tell, with the end result.

'Well, I have to say, Jeremy Clarkson never looked better.' Moving closer in order to study the fine detail, he shook his head in appreciation. 'Seriously, this is amazing. Look at Delphi . . . look at me. You've made us look more like ourselves than we do in real life.'

'Thank you.' Anxiety over, Molly basked in the warm glow of satisfaction, the knowledge of a job well done. 'The aim is to make you look like who you really are. I think it helped that there's such a connection between the two of you. The way you interact with each other. It's like . . . you can feel the love.' OK, stop now, that just sounded over the top.

But it was true.

Delphi was wriggling to be put down. Lowering her to the floor, Dex said, 'Watch what she does now. It's her new trick.'

Molly's heart gave a squeeze of love and they both watched as Delphi sat on the rug and covered herself in the pashmina like a mini version of E.T. out on his trick or treat adventure. Then Dex returned his attention to the painting on the easel, examining it closely for some time.

At last he smiled at her and said, 'Aren't you clever?'

Modesty aside, sometimes you just had to come out and admit it. 'Yes, I am.' Molly nodded. 'I'm really pleased with it.'

'Waaah!' From beneath the pashmina, Delphi waved her arms at them like a small, attention-seeking ghost.

'Thank you. It's even more perfect than I'd hoped.' Digging in his jeans pocket, Dex said, 'Here, I got you this . . .'

'Why?' Molly saw that he was holding out a small flat leather case. 'You already paid me.' He'd insisted on paying her usual commission fee in advance. She had offered to do it for nothing but Dex, typically, had refused to hear of it.

And now he was rolling his eyes in amused exasperation. 'Can you not let me give you a present without getting your knickers in a twist about it? It's just my small way of saying thank you. For being a good friend . . . and helping out with Delphi . . . for just, well, everything.'

'But—'

'Hey, do me a favour. It's not a big deal. I like buying presents. Don't make me feel awkward and wish I hadn't done it.'

Had Dex ever felt awkward about anything? Molly seriously doubted it was an emotion he'd experienced in his life. Still, she gave in with good grace and took the case from him.

Then lifted open the lid and felt the breath catch in her throat. 'Dex!'

He shrugged, half-smiled. 'If you don't like it, you can change it for something else.'

'Are you kidding? I love it. Oh my God, but this is amazing . . . this is the bracelet I saw in the magazine last week when we were over at the café.' She stared at him in disbelief. 'But I showed it to Frankie, not you. You were taking photos of Delphi over by the window. You didn't even see the magazine . . . oh my God, this is spooky.'

Dex, evidently enjoying her bafflement, lifted the bracelet out of the case and unfastened it, indicating that she was to hold out her arm. In a daze, Molly did so and watched him refasten it round her left wrist. The bracelet was made of rose gold and constructed from flattened links of varying shapes; some were oval, others were round, rectangular and diamond-shaped. The end result was quirky, different and an intriguing mix of modern and antique. She'd spotted it in the magazine, on the arm of a glamorous blonde Olympic swimmer, and had looked to see if there was any mention of where you could buy it. But there hadn't been.

She looked at Dex. 'I don't get this. How did you do it? How did you know?'

He looked pleased. 'I was at the other end of the café with Delphi. I couldn't see what you were looking at but I heard you telling Frankie you'd love one of those. So I went back later and asked her to show me what it was you'd liked so much.'

Impressed, and touched by the thought that had gone into it, Molly said, 'But it didn't say in the magazine where the bracelet had come from. I double-checked.' Not that she could have afforded to buy it for herself anyway.

'I know. I did that telepathic thing,' said Dex. 'You know, where you send a message out to the cosmos . . . astral projection . . . and ask the question. And the answer came back to me. It just magically appeared in my head.'

She gave him a look, raised one eyebrow.

'OK,' said Dex. 'I contacted the swimmer on Twitter, asked her where it came from. She told me the name of the jeweller. Luckily, when I contacted him, he had another one in stock.'

'Well, that's very clever. You didn't have to do that, but I really love it. So . . . thank you.' Molly wanted to kiss him but couldn't bring herself to do it. Because what if she couldn't stop?

'Good. I'm glad you like it.' Dex looked as if he might be waiting for a kiss. When it didn't happen, he said, 'You're going to wear it, then?'

'Of course. I'm never going to take it off!'

'And Vince'll be OK with that, will he? He won't mind you wearing a piece of jewellery given to you by someone else?'

'He won't mind.' An idea popped into Molly's head and she said, 'Ooh, let me go and find something. Back in a sec.'

Upstairs, she rummaged through the top drawer of her bedside table, finally locating what she was searching for among a tangle of necklaces and other random items of jewellery.

Clattering back down the staircase, Molly said cheerfully, 'Look at this, it'll be perfect on the bracelet! I've always wanted an excuse to be able to wear it.' Dropping the charm into Dex's open palm, she watched him study the quirky little rose-gold frog on a shovel. 'Isn't it gorgeous? And they go so well together – it's like they were made for each other.'

Then Dex raised his gaze and she saw the expression in his eyes. Did this mean he didn't like it after all?

'Where did you get this?'

'Well, it was the weirdest thing. I found it. Guess where?'

He shook his head slightly. 'No idea.'

'In my coat pocket! In the pocket,' Molly mimicked putting her hand into an imaginary pocket, 'of my coat. Can you believe that? And I have no idea how it could have got there!'

Dex said, 'I bought it for Laura.'

'What?'

'This charm.' He was turning it over in his hand. 'I bought it for her for Christmas, from an antiques shop in the Burlington Arcade.'

Molly stared at him, dumbfounded.

'And she wore it on a bracelet? I mean, I did see her down here that one time . . . but—'

'She didn't wear it. I was planning to get her something else instead. It was in the pocket of my jacket . . . then it disappeared.' He was frowning, struggling to remember more detail. 'It just wasn't there any more . . .'

Her heart gave a double-thud of realisation.

'It was the night after Laura died,' Molly exclaimed. 'When you came into the café after my evening class had left. I made you a coffee, remember? Then I brought you back here and you ended up falling asleep on the sofa.' Terrified that he might think she'd stolen it, she blurted out, 'I didn't take it out of your pocket, though, I promise!'

Dex broke into a smile. 'I know that. Don't worry, I wasn't about to accuse you of theft. And I was pretty much in a state of shock that night. I can't honestly remember a great deal about it. Except that it was hammering down with rain.'

'OK, hang on. Let me just go through it.' Molly closed her eyes in order to concentrate; with her artist's eye for detail she was pretty good at recreating scenes in her mind. The weather had been horrendous that evening, the rain torrential. Dex had been wet and shivering, which was why she'd insisted he take his jacket off in the café. And she'd hung it next to the radiator, over a chair . . . The same chair over which her own coat had already been draped . . .

She opened her eyes and looked at Dex. 'That night, did you take the charm out of your pocket while I was in the kitchen making you a drink?'

'I don't remember. Could have done. Hang on . . .' the cogs in his mind were visibly clicking into place. 'Yes . . . yes, I did. I did.'

Molly nodded slowly, relieved the mystery was solved. 'Your jacket and my coat were both on the same chair. You took it out of your pocket and put it back in mine. That's how it happened.'

He looked at the charm again. 'And you've kept it ever since.'

'I put notices up in the café to try and find out who'd lost it. And in the Swan and the village shop. But nobody ever came forward. Well, you've got it back now. That's brilliant, I'm so glad.'

'Hey, I don't want it back.' Dex held the charm out to her. 'What would I do with a frog on a shovel? Wear it as an earring? Come on, take it. It's yours now.' Placing it into her hand and folding her fingers closed, he said, 'I think it's great that it found you.'

They stood there for a long moment, facing each other, his warm hand enclosing hers. Molly concentrated on keeping her breathing under control; Dex couldn't begin to imagine the effect he was having on her adrenalin production.

'Dada . . .' Delphi, her eyelids drooping, had clambered on to the sofa and was now ready for a nap. Pointing to the pashmina on the floor, she kicked her legs, shorthand for: pick that thing up and use it to cover me like a blanket while I sleep.

Dex did as he was instructed and Molly experienced an acute sense of loss when he let go of her hand. Honestly, talk about a hopeless case. Get a grip.

'Have a sleep.' Dex ruffled Delphi's hair and dropped a kiss on her forehead.

''eep.' Delphi stroked the edge of the pashmina against her cheek.

'Do you think Amanda will like the painting?' Molly's heart ached as she said it. Who knew, maybe in a year's time Dex might commission another portrait of the three of them together, himself and Amanda with Delphi between them, the perfect happy family.

When she turned to look at Dex, to see why he hadn't replied, he said, 'I'm not seeing Amanda any more.'

What?

The words seemed to crackle in the air between them like electricity. Molly felt the tiny hairs quiver on the back of her neck. Her mouth dry, she said, 'No?'

Dex shook his head. 'No.'

'Why not?'

'She wasn't right.'

Oh, the inappropriate rush of relief. But also, poor Amanda. 'When did this happen?'

'I told her yesterday.'

'And was she . . . upset?'

'A bit. Only at first. She'll be fine.'

'But . . .' Molly glanced over at Delphi, now sound asleep on the sofa; should she tell him? God, Amanda might have put on a brave face in front of him but she had to be devastated.

Dex said drily, 'So you knew about that too.'

Yikes. 'About what?'

'You're rubbish at trying to look innocent. Amanda not being able to have children.' Dex half-smiled and said, 'It's not true, by the way. Turns out everyone in the village knew about it except Amanda.'

Was this how it felt to have an out-of-body experience? In the distance, Molly could hear him explaining how the misunderstanding had come about. The rest of her brain was digesting the fact that the couple were no longer a couple. Just last night she'd had a hideous dream that Dex and Amanda were getting married in the village church and the vicar had kept having to raise his voice so the vows could be heard above the sound of her own anguished sobbing. And now this. The relationship was over. Amanda wasn't infertile. She was also out of the picture.

And I can't feel my feet. Or my knees, come to that . . .

OK, awkward now. Dex had been talking and she'd missed it completely.

'Sorry, what was that?'

'I said, so there won't be any more dinner parties. Not with the four of us, at least.' He shrugged. 'Although if you and Vince wanted to take pity on me and invite me over for fish finger sandwiches I probably wouldn't say no, what with being a desperate singleton and having no shame.'

It was as if someone had wrapped elastic bands around her throat. Molly swallowed with difficulty. 'Um . . . I'm not seeing Vince any more either.'

Dex's expression changed. He grew still. Finally he said, 'You're not?'

'No.' More elastic bands.

'Since when?'

'Since a couple of weeks ago. Before he left for Canada.'

Dex was now slowly shaking his head. 'Why didn't you say so before?'

'I don't know.' Molly felt her cheeks heating up; it would hardly be appropriate to say, because you had Amanda. 'Just seemed easier, I suppose.'

'I wish you'd told me.'

'Why?'

Silence. Her heart rate increased. Dex looked as if he was about to say something important. Then he exhaled and turned away. 'No . . . just . . . you should have said.' He swung round to check on Delphi, then distractedly raked his fingers through his hair and turned his attention back to the portrait on the easel.

Another silence. Protracted, bordering on embarrassing. Molly turned to look at the painting again too, zingily aware that they were now standing side by side, their arms just a couple of inches apart. If she moved hers now, maybe to casually rest her hand on her hip, skin-to-skin contact would be made.

No, stop that, don't even think about it.

'Which bit was the most difficult?' Dex's voice made her jump.

This. This is the most difficult bit, right here, right now.

'To paint? Um . . . well, hands are always hard to get exactly right.' To give her own hands something constructive to do, Molly reached out to indicate which part of the portrait she was referring to. Just in case he had no idea what hands looked like.

'And getting the eyes right. That can't be easy.'

'No.' Molly gazed into the painted eyes on the canvas, dark coffee-brown with even darker rims around each iris, glinting with amusement as they watched her in return. It had been quite a challenge, staring into those eyes for so long.

'Teeth must be hard too,' said Dex.

'They are. That's because they're made of tooth.' OK, that was just stupid. And looking at his painted mouth was getting her too flustered. Molly surveyed the shaded hollow at the base of his throat instead. While she'd been recreating it on the canvas, how desperately she'd longed to reach out, brush the tips of her fingers over the real hollow and feel the warmth of his skin. How she longed to do it now.

'I wish you'd told me about Vince,' he repeated.

Was the air in the room vibrating? It felt as if it was. Trying to breathe normally, Molly said again, 'Why?'

But Dex shook his head. 'Doesn't matter. I just . . . oh God, this is crazy, I can't believe I'm going to say it. The only reason I carried on seeing Amanda was because you were with Vince. And I know how that sounds, but it's the truth. I knew he wasn't right for you and it killed me, seeing you together . . . I was jealous, OK? I can't help the way I feel and I know you aren't interested in me . . . and I definitely know I shouldn't be saying this now because I'm just making everything worse and last time I tried I made such a mess of it and it was all awkward for ages afterwards. So God only knows why I'm doing it again, but I can't carry on not saying it. Because it's true. Oh shit, I'm sorry.' He closed his eyes and half turned away, exhaling in despair. 'I'm such an idiot . . .'

Molly didn't speak. She couldn't speak. She could barely think. Reaching out and pulling him back round, she took his face between her hands and kissed him full on the mouth. Gently at first, then harder as his arms came around her and every nerve ending in her body jangled with joy. Oh God, had anything ever felt so right?

Finally, out of breath and having completely lost track of time, she pulled back and looked at Dex. 'Yes, you are an idiot. You could have told me all that stuff months ago. We could have been doing this months ago . . .'

'But I tried,' Dex reminded her. 'You made it very clear you weren't interested.'

This was true. She had.

'That was then. You're different now. Anyway,' said Molly, 'you were the one who told me about your track record with girls. I didn't want to be just another of your quick flings . . . use once and throw away. OK, maybe months ago wouldn't have worked,' she conceded. 'But weeks.'

Especially the last few. They'd been torture.

'You don't make things easy, do you?' Dex smiled, then leaned forward and kissed her again. 'Maybe we had to wait this long to get it right. God, I never thought I'd get another chance. Just being friends was killing me, it was like torture. But I had to keep telling myself it was better than nothing at all.'

The words were making her tremble. Molly held out her hand and said, 'Look at me, I'm shaking.'

'Because you're scared?' Dex took the hand and closed his fingers around hers. 'I am too. I've never felt like this before. I love you, Molly.' His voice cracked with emotion as he uttered the words. 'And just so you know, I've never said that to anyone before either. Because I've never felt it. Apart from Delphi,' he amended. 'But you . . . being with you . . . it's just completely different. From the first day we met, when you threw that fish into my garden, I knew I liked you. But it's gone on from there . . . grown . . . and now the thought of not having you around is . . . well, I just couldn't bear it. I love you,' he said the words again, almost in wonder. 'And I mean it.'

He really did. Molly felt so happy she could burst. She wasn't going to say it back, not just yet, but she already knew she loved Dex too. Was she taking a massive risk, getting emotionally involved with someone whose history was about as colourful as it was possible to get? Maybe, but it was a risk she was just going to have to take. Because there were no cast-iron guarantees in life anyway, were there? Look at Frankie's husband Joe, officially the man least likely to cause you a moment's worry.

'The rest of the village is going to be disappointed when they get to hear about this.' She wrapped her arms around Dex's neck and breathed in the delicious scent of his skin. Now at last she could touch that hollow at the base of his throat.

'Really? Why?'

'They had you all paired up with Amanda, playing happy families.'

'Oh, I'm sure they won't mind. Anyway, speaking of families.' In her ear, Dex murmured, 'We appear to have timed this rather poorly.'

'Why's that?'

'Well, there's only one thing I'd really like to be doing right now . . .' He nodded at the sofa behind her and Molly, turning to look, saw that Delphi had woken up and was watching them with interest. 'But it seems we're not going to be able to do it just yet.'

'Babadadaca.' Delighted to have attracted their attention, Delphi beamed and opened and closed one tiny hand at them.

'Nature's contraceptive.' Dex's dark eyes glittered playfully as he gave Molly's waist a squeeze.

'Never mind. It's taken us all these months to get this far.' Molly had never felt happier or more alive. Her skin had never felt more hypersensitive. Giddy with love and adrenalin, she said, 'Always good to have something to look forward to.'

Dexter reached down to kiss her again, as Delphi clambered off the sofa and tottered towards them. His lips curving into a smile, he murmured, 'Definitely. And it'll be worth the wait.'

'DADADA,' Delphi bellowed, arms outstretched as she launched herself joyfully at his knees. 'DAAAAAAAAH!'

Chapter 54

The party was being held at the Saucy Swan. Everyone was here. Pausing for a moment to survey the scene, Molly marvelled at the changes that had taken place in their lives over the last year.

None more so than Dex, whose changes had been pretty seismic. They had also, quite possibly, been the making of him. Yesterday he had officially become Delphi's father. The adoption order had been heard in the family court, the final papers had been signed and the order granted. It had been an emotional moment for all involved and even one or two of the social workers had wiped away a tear.

Not today, though. This was September the first, adoption celebration day. Molly's heart gave an involuntary leap of joy as Dex reappeared from outside with Delphi on his hip. Without question, the last couple of months had been the happiest of her life; each day that passed just increased the amount of love she felt for him. The sex had been worth waiting for, but it was about so much more than that; she simply couldn't imagine a life without Dex.

'Look at you, ogling your boyfriend.' Appearing at her side, Frankie gave her a teasing nudge.

'Would you rather I ogled yours?' Molly nodded at Henry, who was talking to Joe and Christina. Frankie wasn't rushing into anything but Henry was fine with that; he was happy to be patient, spend weekends down here in Briarwood and give her all the time she needed. Meanwhile, an unlikely but touching friendship had developed between them and Joe's other family. Amber, thankfully, was back on track now. Her AS level results hadn't been as catastrophic as they'd feared and Shaun was helping her to catch up with the schoolwork she'd fallen behind on. Next week she would be starting back at school for her final year and Shaun was shortly heading off to university, but their brother-sister relationship had been forged and would endure. Best of all, the old Amber was back, cheerful and motivated and once more enjoying life to the full. The episode with Doss and his grubby druggy friends was behind her now, well and truly a thing of the past.

'I love Muriel, by the way.' Frankie smiled as the bright red mobility scooter with the small dog perched in the front basket manoeuvred its way through the throng of guests. 'We were chatting to her earlier. What a character.'

'I know. She's fabulous.' Molly was glad she'd stayed friendly with Muriel; since the end of her ill-fated relationship with Vince, she'd fallen into an easy email correspondence with his glamorous, outgoing grandmother. And when she'd told Muriel about the adoption party, it had seemed only natural to invite her along to help them celebrate.

Frankie pointed and said, 'Ha, look at Addy dancing with Stefan and Hope!'

Together they watched them; Hope was living with Stefan in his caravan now, radiating happiness and enjoying being welcomed into village life. A journalist, getting wind of their romance, had turned up in Briarwood and attempted to make a story out of the unlikely pairing. Having met with polite refusal to co-operate with him from . . . well, everyone, he had been forced to give up and go home again. Those who knew about the relationship were delighted for the pair of them. And Addy adored her grandfather's new lady friend.

'Lois calls her Wicked Stepmother,' said Molly. 'Hope loves it. They're getting on so well together. Actually, Lois is looking amazing, don't you think?'

There was a kind of glow about Lois. Her dark glossy ringlets swung around her shoulders, pinned back on one side by an oversized red silk rose. Her hourglass figure was encased in a scarlet and white flowered frock, cut low to show off a tanned and spectacular cleavage.

'I like that dress she's wearing.' Frankie paused, then said tentatively, 'Remember when Lois took those few days off last week? OK, this might sound stupid, and not that she needs one, but does it look to you as if she's had a boob job?'

'So, tell me to take a running jump if I'm being too personal, but can I ask you a question?'

Lois had just sat down to rest her feet for five minutes. She had no idea who the old lady with the mobility scooter was, other than that she was apparently a friend of Molly's. Swallowing her mouthful of ham and tomato sandwich, she met the woman's bright gaze and said good-naturedly, 'Fire away.'

'Are you pregnant?'

'What?' Almost choking on the just-swallowed sandwich, Lois covered her mouth.

'Whoops, sorry. It's just that I've always wanted to be one of those Miss Marple types, super-observant and noticing the clues everyone else has missed. And I saw the way you were checking those sandwiches just then.' The woman nodded at the array of plates on the table before them. 'You left the ones containing mayonnaise and soft cheese.'

'Maybe I don't like mayonnaise and soft cheese,' said Lois.

'And you're drinking plain orange juice.'

Luckily everyone else was out of earshot. Although it wasn't something she was going to be able to hide for much longer anyway. And the woman had been observant. Lois exhaled and murmured, 'Yes, I'm pregnant. You must be some kind of witch. No one else knows, though, so if you could be discreet I'd be grateful.'

'Bless you, darling, discretion is my middle name. Actually it isn't,' said the old woman, 'it's Anthea.' She stuck out her hand, beautifully manicured and heavy with jewels. 'I'm Muriel, by the way. And congratulations.'

Lois said wryly, 'Thank you.'

'Oh dear. Not planned, then?'

'You could put it like that.'

'And the father?'

'Doesn't know. Will never know.' It was actually a relief to be able to talk about the situation that had been occupying her thoughts for weeks now. Ironically, it was easier to discuss it with a stranger. 'It's OK,' said Lois, 'I'll be fine. We'll cope. I did it before.' She indicated Addy, now dancing energetically with her friends. 'And I know I can do it again. I just don't seem to have the best judgement when it comes to men.'

'That's a shame. What was your daughter's father like?'

'Waste of space. Lazy, selfish and handy with his fists when he'd had a drink. So that put me off trying again for quite a while. I know I look like a good-time girl.' Lois's smile was rueful. 'But the truth is, I very rarely have a good time.'

'How sad,' said Muriel. 'And this latest one? What was he like?'

Ridiculously, Lois felt a lump expand in her throat; the pregnancy hormones were running amok. 'Honestly? He was wonderful. I thought he was perfect, had such high hopes . . . it was only the one night but I really thought it could be the start of something amazing.' She paused to gather herself, then said matter-of-factly, 'Until the next morning when he woke up and couldn't get away fast enough. That's when I realised I'd got it wrong again. He ran away and I haven't seen him since.'

'Oh darling, poor you. Men can be such utter pigs sometimes.'

Hearing Muriel say the words made Lois smile. 'He really wasn't a pig, though. That's the thing; he was genuinely nice. I just seem to scare off the good ones.'

'But you could track him down if you wanted to?'

'Yes, I could.' Imagine asking Molly for Vince's number, oh God. 'But I won't. I do have some pride.'

'Well, if it's any consolation, I think he's mad. And it's his loss.' Muriel leaned over and patted her arm. 'You seem perfectly lovely to me. I wish my dear grandson could meet someone like you.'

Amused, Lois briefly wondered what Muriel's grandson was like. Then, pulling herself together, she said, 'Except I've rather taken myself off the market for the next year or so, haven't I? So you'd have to ask him to wait.'

The party was still going strong at six o'clock when Lois noticed Muriel struggling to put her jacket on and went over to give her a hand.

'Here, let me sort you out. There you go.'

'Thank you, darling. Most kind.' Smoothing down the lapels of the elegant ivory velvet jacket, Muriel said, 'I've had a few gins which doesn't help. Now, you could do me another favour if you like. My grandson's going to be here any minute now to pick me up, but he says he'll wait outside for me. Would you be an absolute angel and carry my bag, so I can concentrate on driving this machine without tipping it over?'

'No problem.' Despite everything, Lois was intrigued to meet the grandson. Taking the oversized patent leather bag, she walked alongside Muriel as she began to steer the mobility scooter towards the door. 'Are you going to say goodbye to anyone before you go?'

Muriel gestured across the room, to where Molly and Dex were chatting with the social workers who'd been part of the fostering and adoption team. 'Don't worry, I won't bother them while they're busy with their friends. I'd rather just slip away then email Molly later. Whoops, watch out, Wilbur! Hold on tight!'

Outside the pub they didn't have long to wait. The car appeared in the distance and made its way sedately around the village green.

Lois blanched when she saw who was behind the wheel of the spotless, rust-free vehicle.

Vince was evidently pretty stunned too.

Oh God, so that was why Muriel's grandson had been so set on waiting in the car.

'Excellent timing, darling. We've had such fun,' Muriel exclaimed. 'Now listen, I have no idea how it happened but you're going to have to be careful getting me off this thing because I'm the teensiest bit squiffy. And you mustn't ask this lovely lady to help you because she mustn't exert herself.' Double-checking that no one else was around to overhear, she stage-whispered, 'She's pregnant, you see.'

Vince looked as if he'd been hooked up to the National Grid. The shock was both visible and palpable. His gaze slipped from Lois's face to her more expansive than usual chest and still-flat stomach.

Well, not completely flat. The rest of Briarwood might not have spotted it yet but there were the faint beginnings of a curve that would become more noticeable in the coming weeks.

Lois felt her cheeks burn at the unexpectedness of the situation. By way of contrast, all the colour had drained from Vince's handsome face.

Finally he mouthed, 'Is it mine?'

Oh well, seeing as he'd asked the question. Feeling a bit faint but standing her ground, Lois mouthed back, 'Yes.'

'Excuse me? What's going on here?' demanded Muriel. 'Why are you two looking at each other like that? What am I missing?'

'Does she know?' Vince's voice was hoarse with shock, his gaze fixed on Lois. 'Did you tell her about . . . ?'

'No,' Lois blurted out defensively. 'I did not.'

'Oh, good grief,' Muriel announced as the penny dropped. 'I might be ninety-three but I'm not completely stupid.' Twisting round on her mobility scooter to properly face her grandson, she said, 'So it was you, my boy, was it? Spent the night with this wonderful girl then couldn't get away fast enough in the morning? Vincent, what's wrong with you? She thought you were the one! Why would you do that to her?'

'Oh, please don't,' Lois begged, mortified. 'It doesn't matter. I just wasn't his type—'

'Well, you jolly well should be! You'd be perfect for each other,' Muriel exclaimed. 'Mark my words, I know these things and I'm always right. Vince needs someone like you.' Grabbing the scooter's accelerator handle, she careered round in a reckless circle and waved airily as she and Wilbur – ears flying – zoomed towards the pub. 'OK, we're heading back inside for another drink. You two can sort yourselves out.'

OK, this was officially horrendous. When Muriel had

disappeared, Lois said, 'It's fine, don't worry. God, your grand-mother's embarrassing.'

'I know. I'm sorry. But . . . you should have told me.' Vince gestured helplessly in the region of her stomach.

'Really? Because you would have been so overcome with joy? Come on, we're both adults. You woke up in my bed and couldn't bear to look at me.'

'But that wasn't any reflection on you,' he blurted out. 'I was ashamed of myself, don't you understand? I'd never done anything like that before in my life. I was in a blind panic, couldn't believe I'd done something so shocking and . . . shameful. It wasn't you at all, I swear.'

Lois shrugged helplessly, not trusting herself to speak.

'And afterwards I couldn't stop thinking about you,' Vince went on. 'I wanted to see you again. But by then it was too late, I told myself there was no way in the world you'd want to see *me* . . .'

Was this true? Did he actually mean it? Back on the defensive, Lois crossed her arms and said, 'It doesn't matter, you don't have to do anything. I'm a coper, I can manage on my own.'

But Vince was eyeing her intently, already shaking his head. 'Are you joking? You're having my child. I don't walk away from my responsibilities.'

The way he was looking at her was making her heart race. The way he said the words was making her think they might actually be true. After a moment Lois said, 'So what are we going to do now?'

'OK, first thing, I need to take my meddling grandmother home.'

Home to Bristol. 'That sounds like walking away from your responsibilities to me. Well, driving away from them,' said Lois.

'And then I'll be back. By eight o'clock, OK?' Vince reached out and took her hand. 'I promise.'

'You do?' This time it came out as a croak.

'I do. Hey, I can feel you shaking. Stop it.'

'I don't think I can.' Even her voice was trembling. 'I'm scared. And I'm *never* scared.'

'Don't be.' There was a warmth in his eyes; he was visibly relaxing now. 'You know something?' said Vince with the slow beginnings of a smile. 'This could turn out to be . . . just what I always wanted.'

Chapter 55

Was it actually possible to feel happier than this?

It was the morning after the adoption party. Having heard the sound of wooden cot bars rattling, Dex had gone into the nursery and lifted Delphi out of her cot. Now, always disgustingly perky first thing, she was sitting up in the centre of his king-sized mattress, surrounded by mounds of snowy duvet.

'Love you, Delph.' He ruffled her fine dark hair and tickled her ears.

'Dadada.' She beamed back at him.

She'd been saying it for weeks. Now, finally, it was true. He was legally, officially her father. Every time he thought about it, Dex wanted to burst with pride.

But really, what a year it had been; both the worst and best of his life. Laura's death had knocked him sideways and everything had changed from that day forward. Who, though, could have predicted the amount of joy that had resulted from it? Gone was the carefree bachelor lifestyle, the high-flying career and the flashy car and apartment that had gone with them. Gone, too, was the endless stream of girls in his bed . . .

Well, nearly. The money wouldn't last forever; in a couple of years he'd have to think about going back to some kind of work. But for now Delphi was his number one priority.

And he was perfectly content with the girls currently in his bed.

'Going to give Molly a kiss, then?' Dex indicated the still-sleeping form beneath the other half of the rumpled white duvet.

Carefully, Delphi lifted a handful of Molly's hair off her face and planted a wet kiss on her uncovered cheek.

'Ah.' Molly opened her eyes and said sleepily, 'That's a lovely way to be woken up.' The charm bracelet on her wrist jangled and glinted in the sunlight as she rolled over on to her back and scooped Delphi into her arms. 'Morning, sweetie pie. You smell gorgeous.'

'Why thank you,' said Dex.

'I was talking to your daughter.' Molly poked her leg out from under the duvet and nudged him with her bare foot. 'If it's compliments you're after, a cup of tea might help.'

She looked so beautiful, lying there with her cheeks flushed with sleep, her eyes bright, her glossy blond hair spread across the piled-up pillows. And Delphi sprawled over her chest. Dex knew without question that Molly was the one for him. He loved every single thing about her. She'd helped to make him into a better person and just being with her made him want to be better still.

Watching her now, Dex experienced that inner surge of joy once more. He hadn't told her this, because there was a limit as to how soppy a normal man could be, but each day he woke up, he loved her more than the day before. And every day, too, he found himself thanking God that some other bloke hadn't come along before him and snapped her up first. Just the thought that he could have missed his chance with her—

'Ahem.' Another playful nudge. 'Still waiting for that cup of tea.'

Upside down on the bedside table, Molly's mobile phone began to ring.

'Probably one of your other boyfriends,' said Dex.

'Brilliant! Can you reach it?' She held out an arm. 'I've got a baby on my chest.'

When Dex picked up the phone and saw the name on the screen, he laughed. 'It is one of your other boyfriends.'

She took Delphi's fingers out of her mouth. 'What? Who?'

'Vince.'

'Seriously? God, I hope nothing's happened.' Concerned, Molly grabbed the phone from him and said, 'Hello? Is Muriel all right?'

Dex watched as she listened to the reply, then visibly relaxed. Molly nodded at him and whispered, 'She's fine.'

Then Vince said something else that made her eyes open wide.

'Hang on. Sorry, the phone slipped . . . can you just say that again?' Her face a picture of disbelief, Molly switched to speakerphone so Dex could hear too.

'. . . OK, I'm here in Briarwood, at the pub. The Swan. With Lois.' Vince sounded as if he were reading from a statement he'd prepared earlier. 'Sorry to be calling so early but I needed to tell you before you heard it from my indiscreet grandmother. And I felt you deserved to know the truth before the rest of the village finds out.' He cleared his throat and carried on. 'That evening you ended our relationship, I ended up spending the night here. And now Lois is pregnant and I'm the father. Obviously this was never meant to happen but we've had a long talk about it and . . . well, we're going to see if we can give things a go. So there you are. That's the situation. I hope that's OK with you.'

Dex looked at Molly. Molly looked back at him in

astonishment. Finally, she exclaimed, 'My God, Vince, of course it's OK! This is . . . amazing. You old devil!'

'I know. Quite out of character for me.' Vince sounded somewhat dazed himself. 'But sometimes these things happen for a reason.'

'And Muriel already knows, does she?'

'Yes, she found out yesterday.'

'Is she thrilled?'

Vince's tone was dry. 'Thrilled is the understatement of the year.'

'In that case,' said Molly, 'we're thrilled too. Congratulations. To both of you.'

Audibly relieved, he said, 'I'll tell Lois. Thank you.'

'Also,' Molly added, 'tell her no wonder her boobs are looking so fantastic.'

'Right.' After a moment's hesitation, Vince said uncertainly, 'I'll pass that message on to her too.'

When the call was ended, Dex took the phone from her and said, 'Now he's going to think you're a complete lesbian.'

'Did you see them, though? They were just magnificent.' Molly mimed the voluptuous outline of Lois's stupendous breasts, then smiled and shook her head. 'Well, well, who'd've thought it? Lois and Vince. That's some news to wake up to, isn't it? The things that go on in this quiet little village.' Her eyes sparkled with mischief as she gazed up at him. 'Still, he's just going to have to get used to us. Same as you did.'

Dex lay down on the bed next to them, while Delphi played with the frog-on-a-shovel charm on Molly's bracelet. 'I'm never going to get used to you. You're in a class of your own. Although, I have just had a thought.'

Molly tilted her head and leaned across for another kiss. 'And that is?'

'If this thing with Vince and Lois works out and he ends up coming to live in Briarwood,' Dex's mouth twitched, 'you'll always have someone on hand to deal with your rust spots.'

Molly raised a playful eyebrow. 'Hmm, I was rather hoping I wasn't going to get rusty, not now I've got you.'

JILL MANSELL

A Walk In The Park

This was her guilty secret . . .

It's eighteen years since Lara Carson vanished into the night, leaving first love Flynn Erskine with lots of questions – and no answers. He's stunned by her return to Bath and can't deny the spark between them. But is there something she isn't telling him?

Lara's childhood best friend, Evie Beresford, is thrilled to welcome her back – especially as she's about to walk down the aisle with her dream man, Joel. But life's never that simple, is it? Things are about to change drastically for everyone involved. And it all starts on the morning of Evie's wedding . . .

Just *Heavenly*. Just *Jill*.

Some of the warm acclaim for Jill Mansell's novels:

'As frothy and moreish as a summer cocktail . . . your beach bag will be empty without it' *Heat*

'A warm and thoughtful read, populated with engaging characters . . . I raced through it' *Daily Mail*

'Smart and grown-up chick lit at its very best' *Good Housekeeping*

978 0 7553 5585 3

headline
review

JILL MANSELL

To The Moon And Back

When Ellie Kendall tragically loses her husband she feels her life is over. But eventually she's ready for a new start – at work, that is. She doesn't need a new man when she has a certain secret visitor to keep her company . . .

Zack McLaren seems to have it all, but the girl he can't stop thinking about won't give him a second glance. If only she'd pay him the same attention she lavishes on his dog.

Moving to North London, Ellie meets neighbour Roo who has a secret of her own. Can the girls sort out their lives? Guilt is a powerful emotion, but a lot can happen in a year in Primrose Hill . . .

Everybody loves Jill Mansell's novels:

'This is a warm, witty and romantic read that you won't be able to put down' *Daily Mail*

'The perfect pick-me-up. Utter indulgence' *News of the World*

'As frothy and moreish as a summer cocktail . . . your beach bag will be empty without it' *Heat*

978 0 7553 5581 5

headline
review

You can buy any of these other bestselling books by
Jill Mansell from your bookshop
or *direct from her publisher.*

FREE P&P AND UK DELIVERY
(Overseas and Ireland £3.50 per book)

A Walk In The Park	£7.99
To The Moon And Back	£8.99
Take A Chance On Me	£8.99
Rumour Has It	£8.99
An Offer You Can't Refuse	£8.99
Thinking Of You	£8.99
Making Your Mind Up	£8.99
The One You Really Want	£8.99
Falling For You	£8.99
Nadia Knows Best	£8.99
Staying At Daisy's	£8.99
Millie's Fling	£8.99
Good At Games	£8.99
Miranda's Big Mistake	£8.99
Head Over Heels	£7.99
Mixed Doubles	£8.99
Perfect Timing	£8.99
Fast Friends	£8.99
Solo	£7.99
Kiss	£8.99
Sheer Mischief	£8.99
Open House	£7.99
Two's Company	£8.99

TO ORDER SIMPLY CALL THIS NUMBER

01235 400 414

or visit our website: www.headline.co.uk

Prices and availability subject to change without notice.